The
Golden
Age
of
Promiscuity

The Golden Age of Promiscuity

Brad Gooch

Alfred A. Knopf   New York   1996

THIS IS A BORZOI BOOK
PUBLISHED BY ALFRED A. KNOPF, INC.

COPYRIGHT © 1996 BY BRAD GOOCH
ALL RIGHTS RESERVED UNDER INTERNATIONAL AND PAN-AMERICAN
COPYRIGHT CONVENTIONS. PUBLISHED IN THE UNITED STATES BY
ALFRED A. KNOPF, INC., NEW YORK, AND SIMULTANEOUSLY
IN CANADA BY RANDOM HOUSE OF CANADA LIMITED, TORONTO.
DISTRIBUTED BY RANDOM HOUSE, INC., NEW YORK.
http://www.randomhouse.com/

OWING TO A LIMITATION OF SPACE, ALL PERMISSIONS TO REPRINT
PREVIOUSLY PUBLISHED MATERIAL MAY BE FOUND ON PAGE 303.

LIBRARY OF CONGRESS CATALOGING-IN-PUBLICATION DATA
GOOCH, BRAD.
THE GOLDEN AGE OF PROMISCUITY / BRAD GOOCH.
P.   CM.
ISBN 0-679-44708-3 (HARDCOVER)
1. GAY MEN—NEW YORK (N.Y.)—SEXUAL BEHAVIOR—FICTION.   I. TITLE.
PS3557.0478G65   1996
813'.54—DC20   95-49318   CIP

MANUFACTURED IN THE UNITED STATES
OF AMERICA
FIRST EDITION

TO THE MEMORY OF:

JOE BRAINARD
HOWARD BROOKNER
CHRISTOPHER COX
TIM DLUGOS
MORTY MANFORD
ROBERT MAPPLETHORPE
J. J. MITCHELL
LUIS SANJURJO
LARRY STANTON

Contents

Acknowledgments

THANKS TO THE FOLLOWING PEOPLE,
WHO HELPED WITH THIS BOOK
IN MANY DIFFERENT WAYS:
ALAN BOYCE, EDWARD BURNS,
SHARON DELANO, RICHARD ELOVICH,
CHARLES GANDEE, SAM GREEN,
JOY HARRIS, REINALDO HERRERA,
ROBERT HILFERTY, GIA KIM, SONNY MEHTA,
DARRYL PINCKNEY, MICHAEL SCALISI,
D. W. SINGLETON, DERRICK SMIT,
COLIN STREETER, JAMES TAKOS,
JERRY TARTAGLIA, SHELLEY WANGER

The
Golden
Age
of
Promiscuity

Columbia

Sean felt a tingle.

It was at the bottom of his spine, in a sac like the bulb holding the silver mercury at the stem of a thermometer. It was in his head. And it was in his penis, a curious flower which had been growing and shriveling for twenty years, as in a series of line drawings by a Victorian botanist.

It was in the phone, too. Sean opened his eyes and reached out. He could barely hear the ringing above the late-afternoon sounds of the traffic. It was as if he were encased in a conch shell from which he could only hear the amplified roar of buses, subways, taxis, and cars along Broadway on this April afternoon. He had painted his sixth-floor dorm room pale pink, tan, and yellow, so the walls seemed like tinted photographs in a family album.

Like the framed ones of his parents during World War II that he kept by his mattress. Their faces were almost light green, their lips tangerine. His father's uniform was brown and green: leaf colors. The outline of the cap traced the outline of his face. He looked handsome. A technical sergeant. And his mother with her legs crossed like Rita Hayworth's, posed on a stone fence in front of the standard brick high school in Turret, Pennsylvania. Her wavy brown hair cascaded down like a healthy horse's tail.

"Ullo?"

It was Arnie calling from John Jay dormitory. He wanted to come over. Sean did feel he owed Arnie something. The first week of spring semester he had gone to the Gay Lounge in the basement of Furnald Hall. The lounge looked like a corner of a Salvation Army store, with weak lamps and battered armchairs. Arnie introduced him to Columbia's gay dean of housing, who helped bump him up from a freshman suite in Carmen, the high-rise, to his single room in Furnald Hall. Since then Sean had done nothing to live up to his gay status. He never admitted to the group, or Arnie, that he hadn't even had sex with a man.

"Mkay," Sean said, agreeing to Arnie's suggestion that he stop by. Then he rolled back onto his pistachio-striped mattress on the floor. Asleep again: Sean's long brown hair was tossed over the pillow, his sideways face sunk into its dirty whiteness, his hazel cat's-eyes shut. The rest of his smooth, long-limbed body was languidly collapsed across the sheets. His lips had unconsciously parted.

• • •

Arnie was at the door. He walked in and sat astride a metal desk chair pulled backwards into his chest in one motion while Sean, who had just put on a pair of Boy Scout shorts, stood with his hand on the door handle.

Arnie was not easy to look at. His body always seemed askew and in motion. One eye wandered; one shoulder always twitched. His shoulder-length hair was a combination of straight and curly. Today, he was wearing denim overalls and a red T-shirt. His Earth shoes peeked out from under the chair like tree roots. One shiny political pin stuck on his suspenders showed a black fist. Another, an inch below, showed a black flag of anarchy on a white background. Arnie was adjusting his wire-rim glasses. His pale face had the flecky markings of a piece of melba toast and ended in a pointed goatee.

Sean eased awkwardly down on the mattress again, feeling like a guest in his own dorm room. Instead of looking at Arnie, he took in the room. The pale-pink-and-cream paint job enlivened by a purple racing stripe. The cracked porcelain sink in the corner. A hot plate on a knee-high refrigerator painted bright orange. A thin white curtain blowing in from the window. One low bookcase, its most prominent book, a thick volume of *The Collected Poems of Frank O'Hara*, published the year before, 1971. Sean loved literature and was planning to be an English major.

Sean was boyish, innocent, fervent, controlled. Having adapted to his time in inhospitable Pennsylvania by finding power in being a young intellectual specializing in leftist political tracts, Timothy Leary's sermons on hallucinogens, and hippie Buddhist mantras, he came off as both superior and shy, and definitely zoned out. Unlike so many others who had sublimated their fears and worries about such basic, sticky high-school issues as popularity and desirability, he had kept intact a fresh curiosity and vulnerability that registered as sympathetic. That his openness was repressed yet so close to the surface made his elusiveness somehow positive and even alluring.

At this moment, though, Arnie seemed much more comfortable than Sean. Now he was at the sink filling a cloudy glass with some lukewarm tap water. "I haven't seen you back at the lounge," he said, fishing.

"You're so political," Sean replied overconfidently.

"It's not that political in the lounge. It's to pick up boys. I mean, meet other gay men. Are you hung up, Sean?"

Sean didn't know the answer.

"Are you a gay man, Sean?"

"Of course," Sean replied, defensively.

"Because I am. I think that gays are going to be part of the vanguard, along with groups like the Black Panthers and SDS."

"I took off the last two years after high school to work with peace groups," Sean revealed. "I'm twenty. It was mostly paperwork."

"I'm twenty-nine. That's how many times I've dropped out, been thrown out, evicted, what have you."

Sean was taken back at Arnie's age. He looked, or at least acted and dressed, Sean's age.

Arnie then stood in the middle of the room and gave a speech as the late-afternoon sun turned the lenses of his spectacles into two golden cymbals.

"I'm almost thirty," Arnie began. "I was at Stonewall on the night of June 27, 1969. They were mourning Judy Garland's death. I was more into the Stones myself. But that afternoon her funeral had been at Frank E. Campbell's funeral home on Madison and Eighty-first. It was a wake. And having it invaded by the police was like the police in some Eastern European country breaking up a political funeral. . . ."

Sean was laughing by now, so Arnie slowed down. "Slide over," he said as he moved next to Sean on the mattress, producing a little bottle which looked as if it were filled with kerosene.

"It's poppers. Ever have any?"

"No," said Sean innocently.

"It'll help you get into me," said Arnie.

"I'm into you just fine," said Sean, trying to push away, like a boy pushing off a dock in a lake to get away from the oppressive talk of adults. "But take me anywhere you want."

"You're deep, Sean."

"You know that's not true."

"Here. Smell this."

Arnie put the bottle up to Sean's nose. Sean took a sniff. The stuff was bitter, astringent, wicked. It raced through a track in his upper body. His nostrils were the starting gates. But when the effects reached his heart it was as if the insides of his chest had been firebombed.

"I gotta lie down," he said involuntarily. Sean was gyrating on the inside while on the outside he was becoming more and more rigid, like a corpse. "I feel cold. I feel sick. This shit is vapid."

"How stoned can you be if you can say 'vapid'?"

Arnie was leaning over Sean. His face was in his face. He was ugly but alive with possibilities. He kissed Sean by putting his tongue way inside his mouth. Sean was being passive, as usual. Why can't I just push him off? he thought. The smell of Arnie was like bad fish and marijuana.

"It's easy. Keep going."

"I feel really sick."

Sean wrestled himself free, hurried over to the sink, and started to heave into its cracked porcelain basin. He realized it was the poppers as he slumped onto the floor. He smiled a soft smile at Arnie, who had taken off all his clothes and was now stretched out totally naked on the mattress, puffing a crinkly joint he'd rolled.

"Want some?"

"I felt I was suffocating. I'm just getting my breath back."

Arnie stood up and put his arms around Sean. "Maybe you need a massage."

Through the window a sunset was beginning to suffuse a tumult of clouds. It was nearing the time of day that always made Sean uneasy, usually brought on by the loneliness of making his own meals on a hot plate. He somewhat welcomed the aggressiveness with which Arnie broke through the space between them, even if the coming-on was obnoxious.

"Come here, Sean. Onto the bed. I'll just massage you. No sex."

Arnie kneaded into his back while Sean remembered many moments and places from his childhood. He was flashing back. There was the cliff at Wyalusing Falls, where a cabin had been built for Marie Antoinette to escape to if she ever got out of France. There were fields of corn along the dirt road to his uncle's house, where the creek rose and carried off an aluminum rowboat. There was the hot sun on the second-floor back porch, where he sat and read while omnisciently eavesdropping on the boys passing a purple peewee football back and forth in a nearby yard. He loved the sun.

Arnie interrupted the revery by confessing, as he massaged Sean's lower back, that he had been a different kind of boy. His parents were liberal Jews. His great-aunts and great-uncles had actually been members of Stalinist cells. They celebrated his every arrest and detention. They encouraged him onto the buses to the peace marches in Washington. He used to seduce dozens of boys in his Long Island high school, especially the varsity athletes, making a reputation for himself as a giver of blow jobs. Weirdly enough, the boys who had felt his lips around them respected him with silence.

In high school Sean kept his own sexuality hidden. Consequently he received little respect. He was safe but shunned. High school was a very spiritual world, where all the kids felt and knew more than they could say. Their lack of talking was balanced by a weird knowing.

Sean was still unraveling. Soon he gave in to the massage from Arnie, though he felt that there was something inauthentic about it. But maybe not. Sean was still on his stomach. Arnie bent Sean's arm back behind his back to make him feel him. Arnie felt clammy to Sean's touch. Then he rolled Sean over, tenderly sat his buttocks on his chest, and let the thing drop into his mouth. Sean loved and hated its bitterness, like a stalk of celery or a leaf of Chinese broccoli. It was growing darker and darker, and he reached for the electric light switch, but Arnie pulled his arm back down as if it were a lever on a slot machine. Eventually Arnie let go the molasses into Sean's mouth. Sean swallowed the stuff, which left him feeling wiser. He looked straight into Arnie's eyes, almost accusing but then smarter than that, just leveling. Arnie looked back humorously. This was no big deal for him. He stood up and began to pull his proletarian uniform back on.

"I loved that," said Sean in a forced voice.

"You did not. But I did."

Sean felt a clutch in his stomach. "I don't know if I ever want to do it again."

"I don't know if I do either. But it's not going to be a regular thing anyway. You think it is. Because straight people think that way and straight people brought us up. I assume your parents were straight."

"I assume. . . . But then there are more important issues in life than gay and straight."

"Yeah," agreed Arnie, shrugging, his hand on the doorknob, "but that's not what I'm talking about. I'll come get you this weekend to take you downtown to show you around."

• • •

A few hours later a more agitated Sean called Arnie up. Arnie had been asleep in his narrow bed in a closet of a room in John Jay Hall, the anonymous dormitory where Lorca had roomed when he was a student at Columbia for a year in the 1930s. Arnie's TV was on. He had gone to sleep by its gray light.

"Arnie," Sean blurted out, "I've decided to be a gay film-maker. That's going to be my star in life. I'm going to hitch my wagon to it."

"But Sean," Arnie tried to say, his voice filled with gravel, "I had the impression you never even had sex with a man before today."

"When I was thirteen my best friend, who was twelve, was my boyfriend for a year. I blew him over a Monopoly board. I put whipped cream and canned pineapple rings on his prick and ate them off like a sundae."

"You didn't tell me that."

"I used to look in the *Village Voice* every week for the ads for dirty movies where they showed a sailor or a biker in grainy stills," he continued. "I felt like my heart was being shot through with an air gun every time I saw one of those little icons. I can practically smell the newsprint. Senior year I saw an inspirational film distributed by Billy Graham called *The Cross and the Switchblade* and fell in love with the hood and came forward because of his greasy image."

"But there's no such thing as a gay filmmaker per se. Unless you mean a pornographer. And there are some great ones of those. I can introduce you to them. And to the stars. When we go downtown. But right now I'm asleep."

"Something like a pornographer," Sean went on obliviously. "But more than that. . . . Art."

"Have you ever gone to a porn theater, Sean? The 55th Street Playhouse?"

"No," he said, embarrassed, his percolating chatter finally quelled by his embarrassment.

"Let's talk about it tomorrow."

Sean was like two people. Half the time he was slow, saturnine, melancholy, passive, indifferent. He held most of his energy in reserve. But every so often he would erupt with ideas and talk and motion.

He had just flipped over. But he had no one left to bother with his ideas. So he dragged a desk chair to the open window, where he sat, nude, smoking a Tareyton, feeling the breezes pass over his body like hands fidgeting over a ouija board. He stared down at stray students crossing Broadway to pick up a late-night coffee or yogurt at the corner deli—Take-Home was its name, advertised by its red neon sign. For Sean, the words "gay" and "filmmaker" were coming together like two wires just touching to make a current.

•   •   •

The next morning Sean had his weekly appointment with his psychiatrist at the university counseling center, housed in a brownstone on West 112th Street.

While he talked, Sean stared from his black swivel chair through a window box of red geraniums at the cars parked on the sunny street outside. His assigned therapist was a middle-aged man in a gray herringbone suit with a mustache and glasses who might well have been a professor. Sean didn't ask. The therapist was cornily second-rate enough to stick to the usual cliches of therapist-client behavior. He asked the questions, Sean gave the answers. Their simple, economical exchange was not qualified.

The only anomaly in the office of bookcases and answering machines was a stuffed black raven perched high on a wooden pole. The bird was perhaps meant to evoke Poe's lines about quothing the Raven "Nevermore," but to Sean it looked like an overdressed socialite with a hatful of black feathers. The bird seemed smart. When Sean wasn't making a blur out of the straightforward window, he swiveled to look up at the thing, with its pair of dark, jewel-like eyes. The bird's menacing darkness seemed a doorway to a more intriguing place.

"And what about your father?" asked the therapist in his somewhere-in-New-England accent.

"My love for him was mostly expressed in fetishes. I liked the way his bare feet looked when he put them up while he was reading the paper. He was second-generation Irish, but agnostic. I liked the boxer shorts he wore while he was shaving and the mirror that reflected his face. There was the sting of his belt on my behind when I was crawling under a dining-room chair to escape his Zeuslike wrath." Sean said "Zeuslike wrath" to get a rise from the doctor, but it didn't work. "But we never hugged or kissed."

"And your mother?"

"In my small town in Pennsylvania in the 1950s she was like a southern belle, a little better than everybody else. She always made me wear clean clothes, like red corduroy pants that were way out of style. She told me secrets about my father and his Catholic family. She was some kind of Protestant. She undressed in front of me. When Dad was out of town I slept in her bed with my dinosaurs. Her vanity table was like an altar."

"Why didn't you act out your sexuality before yesterday afternoon, do you think? Except for the boy with the pineapples you told me about?"

"I don't know. It came up those two extra years after high school I lived at home to work on peace campaigns and draft resistance. I had a girlfriend who lived near a strip-mining area. But when I'd leave her house at night I'd drive looking for hitchhikers to pick up. In the men's room in the public library the graffiti screamed out to me. I didn't just see the scrawls, I heard them. But I didn't budge. It's when the black fire in me began to burn."

"We'll have to talk about the black fire next time."

"I was just being theatrical."

"We'll have to talk about 'theatrical' next time."

Sean sulkily gathered up his blue book bag and slung its one loop over the shoulder of his green army jacket on his way to the makeshift balsa door. Bureaucracy and spirituality don't mix, he was thinking.

"Sean . . ."

He was surprised by this. Perhaps this was the departure from the script he'd been waiting for. So he turned around eagerly.

"It appears that you live first through your mind and then act on your thoughts, rather than the other way around."

Sean felt flustered, happily flustered. The therapist was beginning to get on to something. For a moment.

"Does this have anything to do with being an only child?"

"Mmmmmmm," Sean shrugged, putting off the dumb question. Psychotherapy seemed to be a hit-and-miss exercise.

Sean felt alone again as he pushed through double doors past labeled doorbells into the air outside.

• • •

On Tuesday, April 18, things began to come apart.

Sean ran down the stairs of Furnald to join the crowd he heard gathered below. It was a hot, dry day, and the students were out in force to try to shut down the university for the duration of the American military involvement in Vietnam. "On strike, shut it down," they chanted, stamping across the once green lawns, now brown and patchy from only a few years of such treading. Stereos were turned way up, blasting Rolling Stones songs from windows as if they were political speeches, especially "Street Fighting Man." The weather held for a few days as the dares of escalation were taken up by student leaders. Five buildings were occupied: Pupin Physics Laboratory, Lewisohn, Kent, Hamilton, Mathematics. Long red banners hung from their higher accesses like party streamers. Speakers delivered messages from the sundial. No one had much patience.

Lots of organizations brought out their banners, as strong and beautiful to Sean as medieval jousting flags or the posters of the Parisian artists of the Gaité. There were the Columbia Anti-Imperialist Movement; the Dien Bien Phu Family; the Young Lords; the Asian-American Political Alliance; the Workers League of Young Socialists; Students for a Democratic Society.

"One side's right, one side's wrong. We're on the side of the Viet Cong."

"Ho-Ho-Ho Chi Minh. NLF is gonna win."

"Join us. Join us."

Sean was swept along with the rest of the student body. He belonged to a band of dour pranksters who disrupted a bland-looking biology class to insist the professor address issues of defoliation in Vietnam, about which the stunned lecturer apparently knew little. He was near Hamilton Hall when its doors were tied shut with ropes, an action responded to angrily by the Majority Coalition of conservative students, who wanted in. And later he helped shout "Sieg heil! Sieg heil!" as the police burst through the doors of Hamilton. They began making arrests left and right.

By Friday it had all quieted down. The singing of birds could be heard as students were silently splayed every which way on the steps of Low Memorial Library, the administration headquarters. Sean had always seen its dome as a bald head. That day he came out of Furnald in a heightened mood. Something was different in the way he was dressed. He had on a T-shirt and shorts cut so they exposed his buns and legs. He felt a cross between L'il Abner and Daisy Mae. The effect though was partly haphazard, not yet contrived. It was a child's sort of calculation. He had dressed according to the tingle he was feeling again.

Arnie showed up on the steps of Low just minutes after Sean had stretched himself out to observe everyone walking by. They looked to him as if they were undulating with the heat, like peasants artily filmed in the intense heat of the rice paddies of Nam. (A Jean-Luc Godard documentary on Vietnam had been screened the week before in Ferris Booth Hall.)

"You wanna smoke a joint?" Arnie asked, sitting down, with no extra words. Sean made out Arnie's bony body, exposed by his black T-shirt with dog tags hanging down and by his British military shorts.

"Arnie, I wanna go downtown this weekend."

"I'll pick you up tonight if you want."

"I want."

Their talking was interrupted by some people who came along, some of them seeming to be there just to meet Sean. Or at least so he thought. The pot was making him even more self-absorbed than usual.

Over the next hour different friends of Arnie's, usually in the vanguard of the Gay Lounge movement, came up to him or Sean. Most fascinating was Morty Manford, who made his way haltingly up the steps, as friendly as he always was at Furnald, where they were on the same floor. As Morty came closer, Sean saw bruises, dark flowers in uneven rows that had risen to the surface of Morty's normally pale skin. He had been hurt when he had seized the stage to protest defamation of gays in the media at the Inner Circle Dinner and Lampoon Show for City Hall reporters in the ballroom of the New York Hilton.

"Did they figure out who it was?" Arnie asked, his voice the equivalent of sleeves being rolled up.

"It was the president of the Uniformed Firefighters Association. He threw me down an escalator. Hi, Sean."

"Hi, Morty."

"We're taking it to court. I was severely kicked and beaten."

"You sure were, you dear thing."

"It's all grist for my poli-sci paper, 'The Nonviolent Zap as a Political Device.' "

At this Arnie embraced Morty in a hug as sweet, sinuous, complicated as a rose. He was kissing him on his darkened eyes, on all the bruises, like something from a Passion ritual in an ancient church in Mexico. To Sean the gays on campus seemed to be part of some intense subtext, and he felt a bit overwhelmed. He sensed more sorrow, and more separation, than he could handle. So he stood up. The grass was wearing off enough now for him to move.

"I'm gonna go listen to some Coltrane," he said, to the puzzlement of Arnie and Morty. Neither of them made much of a fuss about his leaving.

"See you later tonight?" he asked Arnie.

"Hope," was all Arnie said.

•   •   •

Arnie never did call. So Sean stayed in his room drinking red wine from a Mateus bottle while tipping back in his chair looking out the window and listening to echoing shouts from the street. The Coltrane he was listening to was *A Love Supreme,* played on WKCR, the campus radio station, its deejay ignoring the politics of the moment for a whole sound undivided by partisanship. Eventually Sean passed out on his mattress.

The next morning he woke up feeling determined, and set about eating a breakfast of cereal and milk he had laid on the floor on pages of *The New York Times*. Over the *Times* he spread the *Daily News*. He was searching for an ad for a dirty-movie house. If Arnie wasn't going to show him the way, he would find it himself.

The ad for a movie house in the West Fifties didn't tell the names of the features. But he could tell the nature of the place from its trademark picture of a young man whose head was cricked back as if he were being eaten from down below, as if the viewer were seeing the top of a tree whose lower leaves were being fed on by lots of unseen animals, as if ant bears were inhaling parts of him with their vacuum snouts or licking him with their elongated tongues. The young man's hair was fiercely dim. Sean heard, rather than saw, the badly reproduced photo—it sounded like snare drums and a blues trumpet—as he had once heard the graffiti in the library men's room. So he took the train down to the 59th Street stop.

He was glad today was Saturday. The entrance to the movie theater was hardly furtive, but the street was relatively quiet. That first day, when he stepped into its tacky lobby with its plastic overhead lamps emulating Sputniks or Saturns, gay porn movies were a genre as obscure and mysteriously alluring to him as Indian movies, which similarly had their own star system operating independently of Hollywood. A poster he studied on the side of the lobby after he paid a woman who actually looked Indian showed a guy in a uniform with a swastika armband leading around another, more disheveled, nude boy on a leash. Sean moved quickly to a winding tower of stairs leading to a balcony and stopped until he could make out where he was, letting his eyes adjust to the strong contrasts of light and dark, feeling as if he were in a garage with a flashlight aimed directly at his face.

Sean had not yet fully entered the adult world of guilt and sorrow, so he did not really consider the other customers human. They were merely dark silhouettes, or cutouts. He knew the others were close, because he could hear their breathing. Sometimes he felt them move up to him. A hand might brush like a soft wind against the rear of his jeans. Or he might hear one of them saying something to him: "You wanna go downstairs to the lounge?" "You wanna smoke a joint?" Sean responded to that one. "Sure."

He followed a young guy vaguely similar to himself down a few steps of the balcony. The theater was graced by a wrought-iron balcony with fine tracery work. He watched men in the orchestra below seemingly propelled solely by their shoulders moving through and around aisles and rows and movie seats and climbing over each other. The place smelled like old hay in a zoo. Sean's druggy brother was thin. He fixed on his thin wrists passing him the J. Its tip glowed as bronze as a penny. He sucked in the perfume. The guy's hair was curly blond. "You wanna go in the men's room and I'll examine your ass?" he was saying softly in a parody of medical jargon as the narrative on-screen lurched forward as jumpily as a silent film. Then he started telling Sean how his father had been a preacher, a Baptist healer, an Oral Roberts. How his father had the longest dong and he had inherited it. He was inviting Sean to parties at his apartment in the Village, orgies. The joint was growing smaller as Sean's comprehension of the movie was growing larger. He rudely and clumsily escaped the sexual internist and moved to a far aisle seat, where he became absorbed in the movie.

A Nazi officer in an ill-fitting uniform looked like the thin, knotty young man Sean had just left: same wrists of bone. The badly cast commandant had Magic-Markered a swastika on the rouged behind of a boy who was crawling behind him on a leash. His few lines were delivered in a high-pitched, highly fake German accent. The movie set consisted of a cage, an antique English mahogany desk, a riding crop lying unattended on the cold concrete floor. Background lounge music supplied most of the content of the performance. Everything was said nastily: "Vut, do you mean to disobey me, you svine?" Interspersed were repetitions of penis in ass, penis in ass. The cauliflower of someone's something was caked in white Crisco. It was the repetition of the imagery that put Sean in a meditative state. He was so happy. He felt a pleasant disconnection he sometimes experienced just before falling asleep, his soul feeling as if it were being torn along a line of perforation from his body.

Intermission meant more discomfort. A No Smoking warning filled the screen for five minutes. With it went a taped announcement warning against smoking, pickpockets, loitering. The auditorium was infiltrated by a hazy light. Sean looked about guardedly. He lit a cigarette to try to calm himself. Each face he looked into was like a close-up of a fleshy root. He was overreacting. Zoom in on eyes so red they could have been a demon's. Zoom in on fly open in gray trousers, size 38 waist. Zoom in on a middle-aged choirboy's pink puffiness. Spineless, Sean thought. Then he turned back as the theater went dark.

The next movie was a *Rear Window*. Each night an accountant came home from work to his apartment furnished solely with a spider plant and a camera on tripod with a telephoto lens. He'd undo his tie. Train his camera on a huge apartment building across the street. Scan its windows until he found two boys going at it. Every night he found different combinations of these boys jittering in apartments as sparsely furnished as his own: a waterbed here, a potted spider plant there. Once a woman lowered herself down on one young man as if she were a chip investing herself onto a gambling table as a dare. Each segment opened and closed thirties-style with a circle widening or shrinking, like a stylized iris of a human eye.

Sean was fascinated. He was more than fascinated, less than calm. When the film ended, he knew enough to escape before the lights came up. He made his way back down the winding tower of stairs onto the orange shag carpet of the lobby. The drug friend with the coat-hanger wrists was leaving along a parallel line. As they neared the glaring outside light of the front doors, Sean spoke to him.

"Have a good day" was all Sean said. But he felt as if he had said, "Beneath this mundane city lies another city in which spells are being cast, magic is being practiced, people's heads are spinning. I want to move there."

His drug friend gave him a questioning look. Sean felt his own joyful aloofness came across as goofy, as needlessly coloring outside the lines.

•   •   •

Danny's: a dance bar on Seventh Avenue, a few steps down from the street. Thursday night. Arnie had finally called Sean back. He was following through on his promise to guide him downtown. He had also arranged for his friend Billy Narcissus, an experimental filmmaker, to stop by to help with Sean's new career wish. Arnie liked to make things happen. He was all plot and politics.

Sean nudged Arnie. "Look at that guy. Do you think he means what his shirt says?"

A blond kid, late teens probably, but prematurely ravaged, was dancing in a blue-white football jersey with the number "69" emblazoned on its front.

"Go ask him," Arnie suggested, his goatee covered with beer froth.

Arnie was still treating Sean as if he were a tourist who needed prodding and encouraging. By the end of the night Arnie would never have that feeling again. Indeed, within a few hours he turned from catalyst to protector, discovering that much of Sean's distance from the scene came less from the usual fears of coming out or being discovered than from a certain passivity. He was less shy or scared than he was self-involved, vague, and indifferent.

The boy in the "69" football shirt was reflecting light off his blond hair almost as effectively as the aluminum beer cans lined along the wooden bar adjacent to the small dance floor where he was exhibiting himself. He was dancing to the souped-up theme from a blaxploitation film—*Shaft*—with a big weighty man dressed in a gray workaday suit, white shirt, and thin cranberry-striped tie. He and the man, who appeared to be about thirty years older, made friendly choreography. The boy danced like a corkscrew, revolving ever more intently into his own chosen spot. His partner danced around him, bumping the globe of his stomach against different parts of the boy's body: buttocks, stomach, arms, thighs. He was dancing the Bump. His younger partner obviously felt that no dance with a name was worth dancing. His casual gestures seemed to be saying that all such constructions were out. Helping to keep the beat devilish, a thin young bald man in brown suede bell-bottoms, with a metal belt as imposingly ornamental as Sinbad's, was standing above them on a bench beating a tambourine lightly against his thighs.

The oblivious dancer's white chinos caught, and held, Sean's eye. Especially as they changed color, saturated successively in the oranges, reds, and greens of hyperkinetic gel lights aimed at the floor. The hoodlums who had fascinated Sean in Turret, Pennsylvania, with their prison records, greased hair, and pocketed blades (signifying freedom) always wore white chinos, stretched tight to the consistency of skin, unlike the jocks in his hometown, who wore football shirts and baggy pants. The dancer seemed to be sensitive to the heat of any attention—and as soon as his partner went off, he was standing in front of Sean.

"Have a drink with me and my fat friend," he said evenly.

Sean laughed. "What's your name?"

"Anthony," his voice cracked innocently. Sean already knew that the sound of innocence was merely accidental, not a clue to any inner quality.

"Wanna come, Arnie?"

"I'm calling Billy to check," Arnie said, freeing himself from them with a little shuffle. "Sometimes he gets lost in his own mirror."

"Meaning?"

"You'll see."

Sean went off with Anthony to sit at some square wood tables in the front room. A Saint Christopher medal around Anthony's neck glinted as they sat down. Sean found himself downwind of a strong, bitter cologne, like the Jamaican cologne in a dusky bottle with a crown top his mom gave him for his twelfth birthday.

"I'll have an amaretto on the rocks," Anthony said, treating his friend like a waiter as he sat down with them.

"Seven and Seven?" Anthony asked Sean helpfully when he saw the clueless stare on his face. Sean wasn't used to cocktails.

"My name's John," said the older man warmly. "Do you come here often?"

"John the john," Anthony interjected with a forced hoot.

"Never," Sean answered, ignoring Anthony, assured by the levelness of John's fatherly voice.

"I'm an insurance broker with a successful business in the city, and a large home elsewhere," he went on, his guardedness seeming a bit silly as it was entirely unprompted. "What sign are you?"

"I'm an Aquarius," said Sean confidently, his sign having been enviable in high school. "What sign are you?"

"Aries with Libra rising," the businessman answered.

"I've always thought that was a contradiction," Sean smirked, feeling as if he were being witty. "How could Libra rise? It sounds so balanced."

Soon there was a cross fire of looks. Anthony caught someone standing nearby staring intently at Sean. Following Anthony's alert gaze, Sean locked into the slit eyes of the onlooker, dressed in army fatigues, unshaven, with a slightly demented air. Sean managed to imagine something of Clark Gable about him. Meanwhile John was studying Anthony's face to determine if there was a chance to reinsert his own eyes, and feelings, into the bidding. Words were said. Sweet, loaded drinks came and went. When the equation had finally been settled, after lots of emotional adding and subtracting, Sean found himself sitting across from the Soldier of Fortune while Anthony and John were bumping again, this time to the Rolling Stones' "Brown Sugar."

"Name's Leon."

"What kind of name is that?"

"I served in Nam for six years."

"Oh yeah?"

Sean couldn't disguise his enthusiasm. He was always eager to experience whatever he felt qualified as real life. If someone had a job, any job, he found them immediately fascinating, emissaries from a real world he wanted to live in beyond college, which hadn't held much interest for him in his first year. A record of service in Vietnam gave Leon a halo of black bullets and green camouflage.

"I killed men," Leon began. As he talked, he jerked in erratic jabs, delays, forays, punches. His voice seemed stripped of modulation, perhaps by speed, so there was only a flat forward momentum. Yet for all its relentlessness, the plot never quite unfolded.

"You're such a Ratso Rizzo," said Sean, immediately bringing up one of his favorite movies.

"I was a sergeant in charge of a regiment," Leon was saying. "We had to go through a swamp. . . . A swaying grass bridge snapped. . . . There was a gook coming across it towards me. . . .

It was one of those choices when you're in a corner and it's your life or his. . . . Like they were Sioux or Pawnees. . . . Now I got a job in the Sanitation Department. . . . Guys come in our men's room at the station to proposition the drivers, and they get smashed up real nice, they lick the bowls sometimes for kicks. . . . I was a football player in high school on Staten Island. . . ."

Until now Sean had been listening as if he were a good student in a lecture on a subject he was interested in.

"Feel me," Leon said next as he began to draw Sean's hand down towards his crotch. Sean liked the feeling of being drawn down as if into a whirling pool of water. It didn't matter to him that the ex-soldier was so bony. Plus the Seven and Seven had kicked in.

Then Sean felt the blade. He realized that Leon had drawn a big knife such as Eagle Scouts used to cut away dead wood on camping trips. He let his palm be guided up and down the cold steel, careful not to close in too much so that he could be cut and draw blood. Leon expressed pleasure by stretching out his khaki leg to rub against Sean's jeans. He made Sean feel the tip as if it were a part of his body. They exchanged wry smiles while the knife was under the table.

"Sean!"

The alarmed voice was Arnie's. Sean looked up bravely, trying not to show his embarrassment.

"Billy's here," Arnie said slowly, as if coaxing a potential suicide off the ledge of a high building. "Let's go," he clumsily underlined.

Sean withdrew his hand from the cold metal. As he did he realized that he had walked into a dream while awake. He had discovered he had an ability to walk into dreams. He didn't know if that was good or bad. What happened with Leon was too subtle for him to belittle with a corny "goodbye," so he just screeched his chair away from the table to stand up while Leon rearranged himself, repocketing the knife, pushing back his greased hair.

"What did you think you were doing back there? That guy was trouble. Trouble like ending-up-in-a-ditch-with-your-neck-slit trouble."

"The two wires of love and violence are crossed in me," Sean explained trippingly on one of his forward rolls as they crossed the dance floor. "It was his smile. I was once told by an astrologer that my Venus is in Mars."

Arnie would recount the incident of the knife under the table to all his friends the next day. It would lead to Sean getting a reputation on campus as a wild thing, quiet but wild. And having such a reputation in turn would make him determined to find a way out of being a student.

• • •

"Billy Narcissus, Sean Devlin."

Sean loved what he saw. Arnie's friend was looking as if he had just stepped out of a B-grade movie poster. He was leaning back against the tacky wood paneling with one leg up. His blond hair was cut in a Dutch boy. His face was a dream cowboy's out of one of Andy Warhol's movies: strong bones, pink skin, Aryan complexion. He was wearing a black motorcycle cap and a black T-shirt made from cheap, shiny material. His tight white jeans outlined a bulge so pronounced Sean was sure it must have been made from a sock stuffed down the front. Billy wore round black rubber boots, not American exactly, more of a style that reminded Sean of Malcolm McDowell in *A Clockwork Orange*. (The *Clockwork Orange* look was popular that year among some of the trendier guys at biker bars down by the river—the black hat, the baton, definitely the kicker boots.)

Billy reached out his hand to touch Sean's. "Arnie says you're interested in art films," he said in a soft voice that carried above the thumping music only because of its focused intensity, its difference from all the other sound waves in the bar. Indeed Billy turned out to be all business as he motioned officially for Sean and Arnie to sit with him at a round table on which burned a mosquito candle wrapped in netting.

"Have you seen *Boys in the Sand*?"

"No," Sean answered.

"It's everything you don't want to do. It's a tasteful movie shot through gauze starring Casey Donovan, who's a real pony. You know what I mean? Blond hair, blue eyes, tan skin. I mean, it's an advance over most of the trash they show as gay movies where cum shots are synced to 'Climb Every Mountain' or 'June Is Bustin' Out All Over.' Arnie said you want to be a filmmaker, right? What we can't forget is that the movie grossed six thousand dollars its first hour at the 55th Street Playhouse. The producer's a friend of mine. He said he opened this movie and the next day went out and bought himself a BMW." Sean could hear the New Jersey in Narcissus's less-than-mythological voice. He wondered what his real name was.

"I want to be a filmmaker, but I don't even know how to run a camera, or what kind of film to use, or . . ."

"I'll tell it to you," Billy graciously offered. "Let's get out of here, though. I hate the smoke. I hate the dark corners."

Sean was thinking that everything Billy said, and the way he said it, could be dubbed with Marlene Dietrich's voice and work better.

As they dodged through the dance floor—as chaotic as a billiards table—Sean again saw his friend Anthony, his "69" shirt now shadowed with sweat. He felt a pull, sad and happy, as Anthony made a lewd gesture to him, sticking his right middle finger through a hole made from his left thumb and first finger and then moving it up and down rapidly. It was a hieroglyphic Sean wanted to decipher more closely. As they faced the first breeze at the swing of the front door, he backed off. The front part of the bar was actually shaped like a triangle, and they were now moving into the door at its apex.

"I'm gonna stay awhile," he said quickly to Arnie.

"You're not going down on any more Davy Crockett knives, are you? Or are you cruising for a switchblade now?"

"No—I promise."

Billy reached into a pocket just below his black belt and retrieved one of his cards, which he then passed casually to Sean. "For your Intro to Film class," he mumbled. Etched in black on the white card were his name and number and, to the right, a fancy line drawing of a large standing mirror in which was reflected a sinewy, suggestive torso from which grew a large pistil of a penis.

"Thank you," Sean replied politely as he stuck the card, its whiteness seeming to glow, into the pocket of his blue work shirt.

He then headed straight back to the bar, where he ordered another Seven and Seven. The drink was still fresh when Anthony, to whom Sean had been sending impish, leaning looks, finally extricated himself from the dance floor and from his partner, who followed behind, not looking so pleased to see the returned Sean. There was little talking. It was as if the night had driven itself off a cliff of wordy talking and was now crashed pleasantly in a meadow roaring with the sounds of grazing animals and manic crickets.

"You wanna dance?" Anthony breathed full and loud into Sean's ear so that a chill brushed its course through Sean's chest and down his back.

Sean had never danced with another man before. He had stayed away from the advertised gay dances at Columbia's Earl

Hall. The song was Diana Ross's triumphant "Ain't No Mountain High Enough." He felt a corny relief of a kind he'd never felt from any political action. Soon his relief had little to do with Anthony. The music was like a hymn for a new religion of pyramiding pleasures. It was a fireworks of released mythologies. Sean stomped his feet.

The dance floor was dense. Its highest point was a black cowboy hat on the head of a black man with a red cowboy kerchief tied around his neck. A brown handkerchief doused in amyl nitrite was being passed freely around the dance floor as guys with no shirts held the knotted part up to their nostrils until their hearts began to quiver. There were lots of tambourines by now. The deejay was in his balcony, spinning records in a garnet light. "Mary! Mary!" went up the inexplicable shouts. "Mary! Mary!" Sean joined in. Then Anthony touched him on the shoulder and his thoughts returned to earth.

On the sidelines Anthony and the older man conferred. Their speech was lost in the muffle of the beat.

"Come with us to the Triangle Hotel," drawled Anthony fully into Sean's quizzical face. "He said you can. But you have to sleep on the floor. In the morning he leaves and you can crawl in bed with me."

Sean, a bit confused, agreed. He didn't quite get the picture. They staggered out of the bar. Sean sat uneasily on one of the jump seats of a big yellow Checker cab while Anthony and his admirer made out in the fuller couch of the backseat. Sean watched the streets roll by through the hand-held camera of his blurred vision.

The Triangle Hotel on Fourteenth Street and Tenth Avenue was a labyrinth. It was mostly a safe place for johns to bring prostitutes or hustlers of all denominations. All its hallways eventually converged. The inside of the elevator was painted metallic pink.

The room they were given was a parallelogram. Sean stretched out immediately on its scratchy wall-to-wall carpet, his nose in the rug's fibers, using a Gideon Bible for a pillow, and as an unsatisfactory blanket, Anthony's secondhand bowling jacket. The other two made noises in the bed next to and above him.

In the bright yellow light of the next morning Sean finally woke up. The businessman was gone. Sean was planning to simply slip out the door, but Anthony was brushing his arm over him like a cat's tail from his superior spot on the mattress above.

"Come to bed," he whispered throatily.

So Sean did for a few moments. He tasted Anthony's tongue. He admired the flax of his hair on the gray pillow case for a while as they held each other under the translucent yellow sheets. Sean could feel the hardness of their penises as they rubbed up against each other's bellies. It was a sweet and time-stopping sensation. But then the disorientation became too much for him. He had not said seven words to Anthony all night.

"I'm gonna pee," he lied romantically in his ear, scheming his getaway while licking Anthony's neck for one last taste of Jamaican cologne.

• • •

It was noon. Sean couldn't believe how hot and harsh the sun was. It was a scalding shower. He made his way down Fourteenth Street, past the meat warehouses. The sidewalks were filled with bloody carcasses hanging off big metal hooks, wrapped in cellophane, being loaded onto trucks. He had to dodge their huge bodies as they dangled like hanged men. A loose, swinging hook almost stabbed him in the skull until a truck driver intervened, his forearm tattooed with a faded blue cobra.

Sean cut over to Hudson and eventually to Christopher Street. He didn't have any destination, but knew he didn't want to ride the IRT back to Columbia. He already felt finished with college. The Nam vet's blade had somehow cut a safety rope. He now felt free to drop his body into some quicksand. His education in revolt had been good—and sufficient—basic training.

Through the rising waves of heat from the sidewalk Sean made out Billy Narcissus leaning against a wall next to the Theatre De Lys. He was so surprised by the coincidence, and by Billy's blasé treatment of life as if it were art, that he abruptly backed himself against the metal fence along the entrance to the dirty bookstore across the street to happily stare.

Billy's look was the same as last night: black biker's cap, black shiny T, black boots. The startling change was that he was now dressed in a pair of see-through stiff plastic shorts, revealing his large penis leaning lazily across a bushy patch of dark hairs. The exhibitionism was particularly stimulating. Not seeing Sean, or pretending not to, Billy paced up and down in front of the theater and then reclaimed his original spot. He had a lost-boy quality to him. His indifference seemed precious, posed, but also inevitable, a kind of poetry. Sean would soon find that Billy had been so fatally charmed by seeing Cocteau's movies, especially *Orpheus* with a dreamish Jean Marais, that he naively needed to live out their mood of absorbed, intellectual self-indulgence. The impulse for his showing off his penis was actually conceptual, or partly so.

Sean crossed the street towards him in a diagonal line.

"Billy . . . Sean."

"Oh," Billy said, not embarrassed, as if having just been woken up and immediately resuming his more savvy, businesslike personality. "Just getting home?"

"Just not getting home."

"Come to my place and I'll deliver on that lesson I promised last night."

For the first few steps Billy was ahead of Sean, who looked steadily through the transparent shorts at the exposed behind. Sean considered its smoothness with the gravity of an explorer appraising a new continent. Then he quickly caught up. Billy raised his arm in the air. A Checker cab skidded up alongside the curb next to them.

"Where do you live?" Sean asked, almost amazed that such a creature would have an address.

"West Fifties," Narcissus vaguely instructed the driver.

The ride was a crap game. The rolling dice were the various buildings, street signs, numbers, letters thrown in their faces from both sides. Neither looked at the other. They were saving themselves. Rather, both looked out their respective windows. It all added up to lots of risk and confusion. Manhattan then was a city for gamblers in time and place. They were there: $3.00.

Billy lived in a tenement building near Eighth Avenue. His elevator was a metal crate hoisted and lowered all day long by splitting cables. Billy simply posed against the elevator's sidewall, leg up.

"Do you ever come to life?" Sean asked boldly.

"I'm most alive when I'm most dead," Billy answered softly. Sean was fascinated.

The apartment was three rooms. The first room was a living room, mostly unfurnished except for a big full couch covered in a white sheet. Its windows on Eighth Avenue served as twin stereo speakers broadcasting an atonal composition of traffic noise. Billy led Sean straight through the white drawing room, so empty of amenities, so full of the anxiety of street noise, into the room to the right.

"This is my movie room," Billy explained. "It's like a temple to myself. You'll see what I mean."

This second room was as black as the first room had been white, but equally teeny. On one table was a Bell & Howell arc lamp projector, its big wheel a modern waterwheel manufacturing a grist of images. Sean immediately lay down with his back fitted into the bolster cushion along one black wall's floorboard. As Billy pulled down a white home-movie screen, its texture iridescent silk, Sean scanned stacked shelves holding hundreds of reels of film and a dozen different cameras. Along another black corkboard wall was positioned a flat table, its horizontal reel spools like eyes. Sean was amazed to be lounging among all this technology, as much as in an old silent-era movie studio crammed into one modular bedroom in a two-bedroom crash pad. Posters for Billy's two features were taped to the walls: *Black Reflections* showing Narcissus posed against a brick wall, and *King Boy* showing him posed against a throne in the same black T-shirt and white jeans as in the first poster.

"Let me show you one of my movies," said Billy as he dimmed the lights to black, then stood with his arms crossed throughout the hour-long movie while Sean lay as if on a beach, letting the images roll over him in silver waves, trickles, dashes. "It's about art," Billy said as an oblique introduction, then didn't speak again.

The movie was mostly filmed on Christopher Street at the Silver Dollar, a dirty diner towards the Hudson River. A farm boy has a romantic interlude with Billy, whom he has just picked up. They drink black coffee. The reflections in the plate-glass windows are oil slicks of pastel pinks and greens. With no explanation, the boy is struck blind. His last visual memory is Billy Narcissus. He becomes Billy's devoted lover. He taps his way down Christopher Street in the afternoon. He comes home to Billy, feeling his body ever so slowly in search of the picture he carries in his head. The film closes with the miracle of the restoration of sight to the boy when Billy rubs coffee into his eyes like Christ spitting on mud and rubbing it into the eyes of the blind man to heal him. Then the movie sputters apart in a bunch of erratic strobes. All the credits are Billy Narcissus's name: producer, director, writer, actor. If he could have filmed himself he would have.

As Billy rewound the tape on the projector, Sean spewed his excitement in pieces of thoughts.

"It's like a Greek tragedy," he said. "But it's like a gay Greek tragedy. You're a god in it. And you're the audience for yourself as a god. So you're the god and the human. So it's not Greek anymore. Or Christian. It's beyond."

"I really am in love with myself," said Billy evenly, packaging the reel in a tin. "But I've found the technological metaphor for it. I'm an auteur filmmaker. I'm the star and the director and the producer and the writer. I'm Sternberg and Marlene Dietrich rolled into one. That's my contribution, my statement."

"Wow," replied Sean. "I'm the opposite. My favorite quote is from Pasternak: 'My soul—my self in others.' "

At that comment a hush seemed to fall over the room. Billy had seen something. It wasn't like him to connect. And Sean wasn't feeling particularly exhilarated or "on."

"Talking about myself makes me numb," Sean went on, not sure what he was saying.

"Enough," Billy shot back. "I want to show you about cameras, and projection, and editing. Because you could be a classic. I'm an independent. Like a footnote. The real stars are always footnotes. But you could be the real thing. Which means mainstream. Which means your movie could make six thousand dollars in the first hour."

"I don't know if I believe what you're saying," said Sean. "But I want to learn the stuff."

So the lesson began. "This is a Bolex—it's the camera Andy used for his films." Billy handed Sean a camera which looked like a conglomeration of jewels. There were a few lenses, levers on the side. The camera possessed a tallness. Its covering was black leather. "You can carry it easily. It takes sixteen-millimeter film. You can change the three lenses for close-ups or far away." Billy went on to show him a Super 8 camera. "It's the wave coming," he said. "You can make films in eight millimeter and blow them up to sixteen." The gray operating table on the side was a Steenbeck editing machine. Sean was worried at how perfunctory filmmaking seemed to be. He saw where one frame was sawed from the next, then spliced with tape onto another frame. A clip-on light glowed down on the pieces of celluloid. Strips hung like laundry on wires over a shopping cart on wheels.

"I want to lie down," Billy said, unconvincingly, as he led the way out, his boots slow castanets on a bare wood floor.

The third room was a room of mirrors. "It never ends," said Sean as they entered the final room, equal in size to the others, windowless, but filled with amber artificial light from dozens of light bulbs controlled by a single dimmer next to Billy's mattress on a box spring. The ceiling was all mirrored. The walls were covered with cheap mirrors well Windexed. As prominent as a sculpture was the room's triptych dressing screen of hinged mirrors.

Billy stripped off his silken polyester black T-shirt while leveraging himself on the raised mattress. His upper body was a smooth landscape of solids and fluids, his skin as pale as a Victorian woman's. Sean felt he was in the boudoir of a courtesan. Incense burned down in a corner like an unwanted cigarette, tossed. Billy exposed his penis to Sean as if it were a silent microphone of flesh on which he could sing. Sean did, reeling from all the various reflections of Billy rising up around him. As he went on, he looked up occasionally. Billy was always busying himself with tuning the light dimmers so that he would look perfect in the dressing mirrors, the triptych, or so that his bicep would intrude purposefully in the contextless air.

Sean strangely enjoyed the feeling of being so unnecessary and yet so indispensable. "You're the real thing," he kept saying thoughtfully. But Billy was already far gone into his fix.

"He was like a southern heroine on heroin," Sean would later describe the afternoon to Arnie.

●   ●   ●

Sean was dozing again in his new place downtown on Perry Street in the Village. It was summer. He had moved out of the dorm but didn't yet know that he would never return. He would practically just forget to return in September. So much began to happen.

The room in which he was asleep, at the top of five flights, was furnished solely with his big mattress. Its stucco walls were slanted in, but not by design. The air in the room was hot and still. In the kitchen, a green metal table with a pink rose design inlaid on its top had been left by the last tenants. The two windows in the bedroom revealed a blue sky through the grid of a rusty fire escape.

In Sean's head images were turning, as usual. The only change after moving downtown the week before was that now his fidgeting had increased, his anxiety, his feeling of searching after something all the time. The more he felt plunged into life, the more he felt on a surface of images, as if the world were an accumulation of specks on the convex of an eyeball. The lightheadedness—of downtown, and of filmmaking—was beginning.

The actual pictures he was seeing inside his head at that moment, though, were lazy memories. Sheridan Square was his new subway stop. To get home he would walk up Christopher Street, which in that year, and in the few years following, felt like a strip of privilege, of suburban young men, mostly white, well fed and well clothed, who were here without ever seeming to need a job. (When Sean needed money, he worked parties for the Columbia bartending agency at the apartments of alumni.) They leaned against cars. In the summer their work shirts faded soft and blue, as did their jeans. Many wore two-hundred-dollar Tony Lama boots. Or construction boots from the army-navy store. Every other guy was leaning into something—an iron fence, a jeep, a plate-glass store window—and every other guy was smoking a joint. Sean often thought of the word "hazy" as he walked home. Flashing onto Bleecker, Charles, Tenth, or Greenwich, he noticed portable color TV sets winking. Even his parents didn't have a portable color TV set. He had become unexpectedly involved in the revamp of the bohemian and working-class-Italian neighborhood of Greenwich Village—a casual, friendly invasion.

In his apartment a different set of images was playing. A toy-like Kodak Instamatic projector cast a diffuse light on a pull-up screen balanced on crisp metal legs. Silent images were softened to a bruise by late-afternoon light admitted through the two windows.

A young woman with black hair, a face of strength as well as of exotic beauty, was sitting on a stage in a lotus position, seemingly masturbating herself through the fly of her black jeans, her hand subtly stroking while she never stopped talking, moving her lippy mouth, and never stopped sending Morse code with her expressive arching, pointing, reaching, and shrinking eyebrows. Her middle finger was lost in the zipper of her jeans, which looked black velvet because of poor production values. Cheapness and luxury often occur as palm and forehand of the same sensibility.

When Sean came to, the face was losing separation from the screen. Sean had taken those pictures earlier in the week with his new Beaulieu 4008-ZM Super 8, borrowed from a friend who went to NYU Film School. He was re-creating Billy Narcissus's setup in his own virgin space. The cartridge-loading camera was resting in a corner on a taupe linoleum floor.

Sean was waiting until next Sunday afternoon, when he could return to take more footage.

The Firehouse, GAA, and Zaps

The Firehouse opened up to Sean like a revolutionary manifesto. When he walked in, he remembered the feeling of beginning to read *The Possessed*—revolution for him being mostly just a genre of good literature. With his camera carried in a big, black, boxy over-the-shoulder case replacing his blue bookbag of the past semester, he dug his fists into his jeans' pockets.

The headquarters for GAA—Gay Activists Alliance—was located in an engine house abandoned by the fire department years before on Wooster Street in SoHo. In nearby industrial buildings artists had been continuously moving into unpioneered loft spaces with no heat, broken floors, grade-school windows. Most of their weekends were spent fixing bad plumbing or blow-torching ceilings or installing bathtubs. Through the dusty windows the artists looked to Sean like steelworkers, often with long ponytails, in overalls made of what appeared to be sturdy drawing paper. That day he happened to be appropriately dressed in a pair

THE FIREHOUSE, GAA, AND ZAPS

of white painter's pants and brown L.L. Bean boots bought at the army-navy store on the corner of Christopher and Bleecker. As he ducked into the dappled coolness of the Firehouse, he felt the same rushed temperature change, and mood change, he had felt dipping into Episcopal churches in Turret as a boy. He wasn't Episcopalian. He had passed through those arched doors to hide. And to stare at the cartoons in the stained-glass windows. The pleasure he used to take from their hieratic, faraway, exaggerated stories— stories more about feelings and ideas than about plot—he was beginning to take these days from pornography.

The walls of the first floor of the Firehouse were lined with white tiles. It was here that the political activists held their Saturday-night dances. Sean glanced at a mural along one wall. A small card taped to the side advertised its artist, "John Button." His mural had the immediate charm of newspapers blowing down a street. It jumbled together big black-and-white photographs of Walt Whitman, Gertrude Stein, Huey Newton, Allen Ginsberg, Vito Russo. Slashed across the map of heads were banners of words: "Gay Power," "Gay Pride," "An Army of Lovers Cannot Lose."

"It's a family portrait," informed a brash voice.

Sean flinched as he looked around to see a familiar young man with long hair and mustache and beard, a lambda sign pinned on one strap of his overalls. He felt as if he had been interrupted by a caretaker in an old house turned into a museum.

Then he recognized that the revolutionary curator was simply Arnie, looking a bit more radical than a few months earlier. Sean would find during the coming months and years that Arnie would often show up unexpectedly, slightly made over to best catch the light of the moment.

"Is Annie Boyle speaking today?" Sean asked, peeling himself off somewhat, not making too much of the coincidence because he was so intent on his appointment.

"Not just a woman, but a woman's woman, Sean?" Arnie teased, only half-jokingly. "She's upstairs. I'll show you. But you should really come to the dances and go to the third floor, where we show videotapes of our zaps. We can't just dance our way to liberation." Sean noticed that Arnie liked to say "we" more than "I."

"You remember Morty Manford?" Arnie asked, as he led them up a narrow, loosely fitted, spiral metal staircase. "He was just arrested in a zap of a fund-raiser for Mayor Lindsay at Radio City Music Hall. He chained himself to that railing that swirls up into the sky like something out of *Anna Karenina.* . . . This is your stop."

Arnie kissed Sean, as usual, on the lips, then continued up the helix with a backwards look that seemed almost reproachful, as if Sean should be continuing with him to study the videotapes he'd already seen once of zaps—gay activists, including Arnie, being led handcuffed down the steps of City Hall, or a lost-looking bank manager in a brown suit with wide lapels being shouted at in a marbleized lobby by a semicircle of activists. "Are you proud of yourself for denying loans to homosexuals?" screamed a leader's twisted face about the official policy of his bank. "Answer the homosexual," came mocking voices from off camera.

On the second floor, past a coffee machine, worn couches, and unstable chairs, in front of the doors to the unisex bathrooms, Annie Boyle was standing, addressing about a dozen women. She was talking as if she were singing, moving forwards and backwards, keeping some sort of chanted rhythm with her words. In a man's white shirt again, black jeans, her hair down and serious, she did not seem to have stopped since the last time, a week before, when Sean had happened on to her speaking to another roomful of women. He'd asked if he could come back and she'd said yes. Intensity was the foundation of all she said and did. Sean liked that intensity.

Annie liked it too. She told them she was from Wayne, New Jersey, an Italian-American bedroom community on a isolated mountain forty-five minutes from New York. She had grown up in love with rock 'n' roll; she had seen Van Morrison once at a concert in Madison, New Jersey, and took rides into the city whenever possible to go to the Fillmore East. A picture of Rimbaud on the cover of a New Directions book had made her decide to become a poet. She was now twenty-three, three years older than Sean, working as a graphics designer for a local TV news show; she had spent the week before creating caricatures of the Democratic candidates McGovern and Eagleton. The job made her feel as if she were inhaling fine particles of styrofoam. So she gave these talks for women on "Self-Love and Masturbation" to be able to breathe again: "to feel the mud between my unpainted toenails," she would say. Surrounding her on easels were pictures she had taken with her Leica camera of clitoral glands, inner lips, hoods, and shafts. Women would volunteer for these intimate portraits after her talks. She was indicating them with a pointer without even making the obvious jokes about such a school-marmish procedure.

"They look like flowers, but not even the same flowers," Annie was saying. "Here's a rose. Here's a hydrangea. Or you could say they were portraits, faces in a portrait gallery."

By now Sean had caught her in the tilting frame of his Super 8. Always distracted, he was finding a way through the camera lens to focus his life. The teeny parallelogram was like the magnifying lens he once found in his schoolyard through which he forced the sun to make a piece of paper burn.

"I had two long romances, like marriages, with two men. They were the kings of deers to me, their antlers a tracery of neurological paths set in crooked bone," Annie continued in her relentlessly poetic way, using simple speaking as a kind of performing. "But I would always hit up against a resistance. We would fight. It was because I needed to masturbate and I was afraid to admit it. So both romances broke up."

Sean felt excited, actually. He felt aroused by—what? He was questioning himself. He felt aroused by freedom. But freedom and identity were canceling each other out. He felt the comedy of having been on the trail of what he thought was his own gay liberation only to become more interested in this unusual woman than in any man he'd met so far.

"The only men I go with now are ones who can delve into mutual masturbation, both of us conducting our own orchestras simultaneously in a kind of stereophonic symphony," she said, her voice breaking into a rainbow of inflections. "There is a paradise through the gates of our clitoris. I'm going to follow a solitary, loving trail within. My heroes are Whitman, Emerson, Thoreau. I am the woman Whitman, the woman Thoreau. Get it? My love is personal. But self-love allows love for flowers, other women, gay men, to grow."

Sean felt there was lots of heart in what she was saying. Revolving in a magnetic field of wacky-seeming theories was an entire Venusian planet of heart.

One woman made a disapproving grunt. A debate started up. Sean's film ran down. Soon the afternoon talk was threadless, finished.

He walked up to her. Annie recognized him from the week before.

"What are you going to do with me? With my Veronica's veil of a face?"

"Let you be yourself in movies about daily life, like Andy Warhol did."

"Did you ever read Rimbaud's *Season in Hell*?"

"No."

That's how their friendship began. That afternoon, they walked all over the cobbled streets of SoHo. The setting sun cast a copper or Technicolor red light on the buildings, like the colors of old mining towns. Sean walked forward on his feet as if there were an air pump hidden in his heels giving him too much leverage. Annie walked slowly, almost thoughtfully. When they talked about it later, the walk seemed to have had a romantic feel, the romance of friendship mostly, of a beginning.

"Where are you living?"

"The Chelsea Hotel."

"Wow. To me, as a would-be filmmaker, that's like a prod in my butt."

"Have you ever been prodded in your butt?"

Their laughs at Annie's direct question were like lassoes, growing wider and wider.

"What sign are you?"

"Pisces. What are you?"

"Aquarius."

"So, have you ever been prodded in your butt?"

"Not yet. Are you straight or gay?"

"You just heard my talk. Lesbianism doesn't work for me. Neither does straight feminism. I definitely like frontier men. But I believe that sex is a torch inside that illuminates a self that can stand on her own."

Annie hadn't even been looking at Sean, just listening as they both walked in the same directionless direction. She suddenly began to stare at him. Sean's hair was long and wavy that day; it seemed to be trying to touch his shoulders. She said what she liked best was his oblivion, as if his thoughts were more grown-up than his body, his presentation of himself.

"But you should be more cutting in the way you dress," she added. "You'd be happier."

Her afterthought caught Sean's face in a quick brushfire of
moving feelings.

"Why don't you dress in leather?"

"Like in a biker film?"

"Like where you're from. But the dark side of it, the bad side
that maybe you lived through more in your head than in your feet.
I'm dressed all tomboy, theatrical and fierce. You look suburban to
me in your white painter's pants, roughed out for a camping trip."

"Hah. What about what's under the pants? What's the difference?"

"A girlfriend of mine named Camille O'Grady wrote a song,
'Your mind is a dress, change it.' Sometimes if you change your
clothes it's a trial identity, stretching you. Like if you have a different kind of sex with a different kind of person. It's a discovery of a
new piece of land in the vaster continent of your own identity."

"Where do you get your Delphic-oracle voice? So seriously
targeted?"

Annie shrugged.

• • •

She was right. Later that week, Sean didn't put on leather, but he
pulled on slate-colored bell-bottom jeans with sandals, a white T-
shirt, and love beads. Over them he drew a suede fringed jacket.
He felt as if he had just become part of someone else's photograph.
The feeling was relief. Then he walked the streets.

He saw a single sneaker, patched, graying, on a stone porch on
Washington Street: an abandoned Adidas. His tactic was to walk
the hatchwork of streets looking for excitement. He imagined that
in the sneaker, absorbing the light of a lamppost, and of the full
moon, too, there would be a phone number. That the phone number would lead him like a clue on a treasure hunt to someone else
who was obviously as absorbed in searching for signs and mysti-

cal significances as he was. He reached his hand into the spongy vessel, but there was no scrap of paper there. He felt momentarily pushed back in time, all suffocating and strange, full of the smells of childhood and of dirty socks and sneakers, of the creepy over-wrought sounds of owls and doors creaking, of physique magazines and Boris Karloff movies. These were some of his private talismans.

He picked up the sneaker and walked with it over his hand, as if it were a puppet, to his developing-room of a studio apartment. He spent the rest of the night filming as breezes carried party noises through the big blank windows. Sean set the sneaker on a shoebox that he covered in blue velvet. On the blue velvet he pasted big, childish gold stars. On the lush, faux-elegant stage the sneaker became a diva of an object, a piece of sinuous sculpture made of malleable material. He used a curtain of red velvet as the backdrop, lighting long purple and black candles around the weird altar. It became a creepy ritual. Sean was having so much fun. He knelt in front of the creche to film. For hours.

The next afternoon he brought home a cheap stereo, a reel-to-reel tape recorder, a police lock that was a black pole set in a groove in the floor that leaned into the frail door at a forty-five-degree angle. On the brown stereo with smudged plastic cover and two little hatboxlike speakers he played the one album he'd bought, in a classical record store in a basement on Eighth Street: Olivier Messiaen's *L'Ascension,* just released that year. Its organ sounds were haunting as he recorded them from the album onto the tape, his soundtrack.

A week later he moved in a Steenbeck editing machine, just like Billy Narcissus's. Now both windows were nailed shut, so the air blowing from a floor fan was the only relief from suffocation. He had begun to worry about robberies after moving in all the equipment, the equipment he had finagled by registering at NYU

Film School for the summer, using a loan from his parents. Sean didn't go to classes but was able to lease cheaply with his student ID: in his mug shot his hair fell in tresses. He played the Steenbeck as if it were a piano, or a spaceship's operating panel. Its cold metal gleam soothed him. He was splicing images, then soundtracks. Strips of sepia-looking film hung over a nearby basket. He was working directly with the print, not a copy. Splicing the images was like sewing. Sometimes he was sewing sound to sight. He said to himself, flatteringly, that he was tailoring clothes for the naked mind.

The finished movie he watched—lying slick with sweat on his mattress, happy to be working in the hours nobody counted—was lush and odd. Annie's face intercut in different combinations with the curtained sneaker. Both images were religious. Annie became a Madonna, the sneaker a makeshift chalice. The music was organ. All the colors were suffocating sepia or crimson, like the upholstery in a great-aunt's home. Where was his aesthetic coming from? Sean wasn't quite sure.

•   •   •

"I'm worried that I'm a cold fish," Sean said to Annie as she opened the door to room 410 in the Chelsea Hotel, though not explaining his confession any further.

"It's big in here," he continued as he walked in, shouldering his black bag. "It's not a house. I like it. It's not a domestic space."

Through the door, Sean had heard Annie playing guitar, borrowing riffs and slides from Eric Andersen's "Thirsty Boots," probably as she sat by a far window on a pile of chartreuse pillows. Sean wondered if her cultivation of privacy and self-love was contrived, or loony. But he suspected that it wasn't.

"I don't need a domestic space, but I do need friendship, tight-ness," she admitted.

"You're not talking like you do in front of audiences, exactly."

The room was big, white. Almost no furniture cluttered the expanse except a 1780s English four-poster bed (left by the last tenant) pushed in front of one of the two far windows. There was another room, a bedroom, off to the side. A step-up bathroom. And a kitchen looking largely unused. Everything else in the vast main room seemed to have a purpose: guitar, mike, typewriter on gray stand, stereo, tape recorder, adjustable drawing table. Down-town Manhattan below Twenty-third Street was a twinkle through the windows facing south from the back of the hotel. Its landscape was spackle, its shimmer slowed down in Sean's vision by his mind moving as slowly as a car making a careful turn to maneuver down a hairpin curve of a mountain road in Colorado. He had taken a Quaalude an hour earlier.

"I want to make movies that can never be sold," Sean finally blurted out, "so that in a hundred years everyone will want to see them."

"Why are we talking like this?" Annie answered. "Let's sit on my meditation pillows."

She indicated with her eyebrows where she meant.

Sitting across from her on the floral pillows, Sean became fully aware of her amazing aura, which would help propel her into a special sort of celebrity as singer, poet, personality, whichever she chose to display. They talked about how personality should be cel-ebrated above all the other arts. They agreed that performance art was the highest art, especially talk and gesture, which are so unchartable.

Annie was no cabaret act. Sean knew that night that her fasci-nation was rather in her allowing herself to grow angelic. It was a quality he felt he didn't have. He never challenged himself. He was entirely weak. His strength was in all his growing fascinations, fetishes, compulsive obsessions.

Then Sean pulled his arms around her. This grab was uncharacteristic. He was really just trying to take his own breath away. It worked. Annie saw him as gentle.

"I don't want to do anything silly," she said.

"Then let's do something strenuous, like let me film you some more, closer up, caught."

Annie's was the face of a Gypsy: dark skin, cracked lips revealing fragile teeth, black eyebrows, interpretive dark brown eyes.

"Take off your clothes," said Sean as he clicked a cartridge into his silver camera. "Then grab on to the radiator."

Amazingly, to him, Annie did. He hadn't realized he had such authority. Without clothes her body was as much a skein of skin and bones as a deer's, as a stretched kite. Indeed she looked more like a unicorn than like a deer, because of the lucent gray-whiteness of her skin, and of course because of the mystery of her daring looks.

Sean set up his tape recorder next to her as she held on to the horizontal pipes of a radiator running along one wall, squatting with her butt on the acid-orange rug of the Chelsea Hotel—one of its disturbing, cheap carpets woven from a nightmare of garish threads.

"Just talk to me, tell me what I need to know about you to know you really well," said Sean in a voice as subdued as what it was saying was exaggerated and aggressive. "Let's be efficient."

The black in Annie's eyes became coal-like at that moment. Sean was giving her the challenges she needed, and which she usually gave to other people. Conversely, she brought out a hunter in him he recognized but rarely experienced. Usually he was a wounded prey, stuck with a spray of arrows, yelping. Tonight, the psychological weather was different, but not too different to scare him off.

"I always liked hanging around with the boys when I was a little girl," Annie was saying, her back curved around. "I was a tomboy. We lived in a normal house with a porch. My father worked in a brewery. My mother went to confession with a black veil over her face. The first boy I made it with was Terry Maloney. He lived in a garage converted into a house with his single mother. We lay in the backseat of his car and he pulled into me so hard I felt as if I could smell for the first time. He was killed in an auto accident on the road to Edward's Lake. Then there was Mitch, whose head was shaved after he went to prison for robbing a barber. Walter was the first boy in my class to have pubic hairs. He showed them to me. I gave him what he wanted. I was a class slut and loved it. My tits were sticking out strong and straight then. I loved it when boys spat on the sidewalk. I spat too. So the more of a tomboy according to society's labels I was, the more of a woman I became, physically."

By now Annie was sitting on the floor playing with herself. "If you get my little mirror from the bathroom, I'll show it to you."

Sean came back from the glaring bathroom with a round hand mirror. He started filming again. Annie held the mirror down below. The reflection was tinted in silver. "It's like a split lip," she said as she exposed herself.

She crawled over to her bed, drew from underneath the hanging white satin coverlet stacks of glossy magazines in colors as garish as lipsticks from Woolworth's. She held them up to his camera one after another, showing the different shapes of the lips. Sometimes one side was larger than the more shrinking other. No symmetry.

"I love that you have men's porn magazines."

"What are *called* men's. I find them educational—to look at other women's bodies, to find how mine compares. It's like bodily self-awareness."

"This is getting me excited," Sean admitted. "But I don't want to be beholden to the wrong god, like a cat god instead of a snake god or whatever."

"What you do with me can only create bigger ripples in what you do with others. Like sexual karma."

Sean left his camera on its side, a discarded toy. (Eventually it shut off like a tired eye.) He turned off the light of the standing gooseneck lamp. "Turn that back on," she said. He pulled on its old-fashioned chain. She got up off the floor and they climbed onto the bed together next to floating purple clouds in the night sky. "I feel like I'm a witch, flying, when I'm in this bed," Annie said. After he unscrambled himself from his clothes, Annie pushed his hand down on himself, and put her own hand down on herself. He knew enough about her—just from the talk at the Firehouse—to keep moving in her direction. "You didn't finish telling me about yourself when you were a girl," he said hopefully.

"Then it was 1967, graduation year. I listened to *Sgt. Pepper* and changed focus to guys with spiritual forces, long hair. I fell in love with a boy who went to Brandeis. We smoked grass until he fell on me in a field and I felt it so much I could cry, not being funny. . . ."

Annie told Sean she was drifting off into thoughts made of senses, not of sights: smelling hay, feeling something rough like the wool of a shepherd's cape, hearing heavy breathing, smelling garlic and onion, tasting toast held by a sweaty hand.

Sean was seeing pictures, the sense he emphasized above all others, that and sounds, not just sounds but spoken words, dialogue. He was always seeing pictures, and hearing voices, like Joan of Arc, trivial conversations between strangers in a Laundromat playing over in his head with no understandable connection to anything in his life. He was at summer camp, Sky Lake, near Buffalo, New York, age fifteen. The champion of their cabin was telling him to carry his sneakers to a girl down by the river, it was a coed camp, they looked through knotholes at girls, and Sean proudly refused but really wanted to deliver the cruddy sneakers, and then the champion asked him as a kind of truce later in the week if he wanted to try his costly after-shave lotion and Sean unscrewed its cap, then spilled the rusty smelly thick liquid over his hands carelessly, losing the connection with his new big brother . . . losing the connection as if it were a faulty TV set's with a bad antenna . . . the same cologne smell which had drawn him to Anthony in the "69" shirt at Danny's a few months back.

When they finished they lay in the quiet. This time Annie turned off the light.

"I don't feel spent, I feel awake," Sean said softly.

"Maybe you should go out now and share it with the world. We'll never ever have a pull on each other, okay? We can have it with others, Sean. But let what holds *us* together be no holding, just to see? . . . And maybe to make it even more pricey you could move in here. We'll make it like the Factory."

"You're big on comparisons."

Sean felt entirely awake. He put his clothes on tenderly because he was putting them on himself. That's how carried away he felt.

"I'm going to take your advice and go share something somewhere somehow. And you do yours. . . . And, oh, I want to move in, too."

•　　•　　•

Sean left Annie, and his camera, behind. But he didn't get far. He walked haltingly through a green hallway lit as eerily as a billiards hall. Rode a small elevator from the fourth floor feeling all the time as if his brain were trying to scale the walls of the inside of his head. Then exited around a corner into the impossibly detailed, psychedelic lobby of the Chelsea, its walls cluttered with paintings exchanged for rent by Andy Warhol, Larry Rivers, and other painters whose brightest pastel works were especially favored by the owner of the hotel.

Exiting at the same moment from the elevator on the other side of the check-in—its Plexiglas shield reminding Sean of package stores in Pennsylvania—were three men in gray suits and hats wheeling a steel medical cart, transporting a body, evidently dead, zipped inside a black body bag.

"Checking out?" asked the bald manager behind the counter, playing the thin air for laughs.

Sean did laugh, following the death cart with his eyes as it made a bumpy exit through the front glass doors. Pausing to let the cortege roll ahead of him, he stared briefly around.

In the lobby sat a woman who breathed heavily, as heavily as a vacuum cleaner. She rested on a neo-Gothic wooden bench padded in bright red vinyl while clutching to her congested chest the leash of an auburn dog whose tongue stretched down to the carpet with thirst.

"Lady . . . Lady," she kept calling to the lowly dog, but never followed the name with a sentence.

Stretched out underneath a glass coffee table lay a middle-aged man in a black plastic outfit (more of the *Clockwork Orange* fad), blood running from the corner of his head and splattered on the glass tabletop. Fidgeting next to him was a very thin man, seemingly his lover or friend, blind, dressed in a shirt decorated with a design of flowers, tapping his walking stick frantically against the table, waiting for the help that must have been called for. Soon cops with walkie-talkies, guns, and nightsticks wedged into the lobby to help take the man to his room while his friend trailed behind.

In through the calm that now prevailed in the lobby walked Jonathan. He was tall, over six foot four, with neck-length brown hair like Neil Young's or a Renaissance angel's, uneven teeth, wearing hip-hugger jeans and a plunging white T-shirt which showed off sprung wires of brown chest hair. He had on cheap brown round-toed boots and lots of bad gold chains; his thick-knuckled fingers were bejeweled with rings. What caught Sean's attention was the vibration of expression he could almost hear when he looked at Jonathan. It was as clear to his ears as a song you hear once on the radio and immediately know will be a hit. Sean looked closer, but looking closer didn't reveal much more: clifflike forehead, copper-brown animal's eyes, eyes that were clearer, brighter, more innocent, more intelligent than he expected when he first noticed the boy's trashy outfit. Jonathan did not waste gestures, or time. Like Anthony at Danny's, he had heat sensors to pick up any interest or attention. Walking by on his way to the elevator, he blasted Sean with a direct look. Sean kept looking, though he remained aware of the mordant wit of the attendant behind the Plexiglas screen of the check-in desk and wondered what he might be making of all this. He sensed immediately that Jonathan was even more capable of risk and impropriety than he was.

Standing in front of the elevator door, Jonathan asked him a question with his hands. First he pointed up, then made a referee's fumble motion to erase that motion, then pointed towards the front door. Sean understood that he was asking if he wanted to go to his room or outside. He cricked his neck to motion towards the door. Jonathan loped in front of him.

The wind on West Twenty-third Street was a combination of natural wind and the stirring of air from passing cars. Only the H

and the O were working on the neon HOTEL sign lit several stories high on the front of the dark brick twelve-story Victorian
Gothic stage set of a building. A bronze plaque, like a plaque in a
cemetery, dully commemorated three writers said to have lived
there. Sean thought it was a sign you'd be more likely to see in
Paris rather than New York. A sound in Sean's head said "Andy
Warhol" because Warhol had filmed *Chelsea Girls* there in the last
decade.

"You want a coffee?" Jonathan asked, having set off already in
the direction of a crumpled, overlit coffee shop on the corner of
Twenty-third and Eighth.

Along the way, through a crowd of faces as overexcited, it
seemed to Sean, as revelers in gothic tales, the two traded facts
and information. Sean was surprised that Jonathan was only eigh-
teen.

They continued their conversation at the waxed counter of the
coffee shop, over which Sean slid his hands continuously. Two
walls of the shop were big, dirty windowpanes, lit by fluorescent
lights as bright as those which lit the chickens on rotisseries in
take-out delicatessens—Sean's dinner most nights in the West Village. From the outside everyone inside looked like bums, at best
like painters in the 1930s or -40s Horn and Hardart's where they
supposedly drank bitter coffee from white cups. From the inside,
the pressure of the intense lighting and the eyes passing by on the
sidewalk bore subtly down. "I feel like we're in a painting Hopper
threw in the trash," Sean said to Jonathan, who didn't bother to
react, not having caught the reference.

"I'll have a caramel donut with a glaze top."

"So what was Flushing like?"

"Don't remember. I left when I graduated in May. I go back
and see my family. We're Italians. Like *The Godfather*."

"That's intense. I just saw it last week."

"I don't mind bullshittin' with you, man. You're foxy enough. I don't feel there's any cash reward, if you know what I mean. But there's something else. Like you're my friend. Like you would do things for me no one else would."

Sean felt warmed by that comment, opportunistic as it seemed on the surface. He loved that Jonathan was willing to let their friendship start in the middle of the action, as if nothing mattered but immediacy. It could be a kind of trust. He was flattered, too. Not by Jonathan's attention, since he didn't particularly pay attention to Sean. He only paid attention to himself. But he allowed Sean to be there. Sean found narcissists relaxing. That's what Billy Narcissus had meant that day, when he had recognized Sean as a voyeur type. Sean was beginning to realize Narcissus was an odd filmmaker. Because he had to make himself the subject, he came alive in artificial light. Sean preferred to find those who came alive in artificial light so that he could turn on the switch for them.

Sean felt hands pulling his insides from within as if they were pulling the ropes of a stage curtain. He was attracted to so many parts of Jonathan. Sean was definitely a romantic, perhaps from his Celtic lineage. He watched Jonathan's hands as they gripped the cup of coffee and mangled the garish glazed donut. He concentrated on the clarity of his eyes: no blur, no distortion. Jonathan's long legs banged against the Formica sides of the counter. They were in constant motion as they wrapped around the revolving stool.

"You have a case of the jitters."

"You ever read any existentialism?" was Jonathan's answer. "I read it senior year, all of it. You could say there's no difference between a human being and the hood of that car out there. It's all just stuff."

"Well, I'm not sure that's the gist."

"I'm a hustler, for guys and girls. I advertise in the *Advocate* under 'Models/Masseurs.' Is 'models' a funny name for it or what? And in *Screw*. I get off on it. But that's not what I'm saying. What I'm saying is that I think I have the extra gene. You know how criminals have this extra gene so they can't stop themselves? I can't stop myself from impersonating the greats, like Jimmy Cagney with a gun sticking out of his pocket."

"You like movies?" said Sean, catching at a loose string in Jonathan's unraveling fabric of words and colorful, irrational notions. "Me too. You wanna go to movies during the afternoon sometime? At the Thalia, on Ninety-fifth and Broadway? Or the Olympia, farther up?"

"Yeah. You're young for me. No money. But you understand me, and that's gonna do more."

Sean did actually love something about Jonathan. The sheer length of his body, his Italian features, and certainly the weird energy of his mind, with its disconnected exuberance. All this was sexual to him. He fell for the comment about understanding. That was the hustle. Or maybe, he would think, mulling this over later, maybe it *was* understanding. But he was barely three years older than Jonathan.

There were clumsinesses, tender insecurities, too. Jonathan's awkward soft spots were impossible for him to conceal no matter how hard he talked. That's why Sean had wanted to film Annie, and now Jonathan. He could definitely tell that he liked someone when he wanted to film them. Or that's how he described this instinct to himself: "liked."

That night they went back to the Chelsea Hotel. Jonathan was staying in a cramped single room at one end of a hall. Not at all like Annie's empty expanse on the fourth floor. He was on the third. There was simply a mattress on springs. A sink wedged into one corner. A window onto Twenty-third Street, with its all-night jam session of garbage trucks, taxi horns, shouts.

At one end of the room an appliance carton was set on its end like a pillar. Jonathan sat on it dressed in nothing but his BVDs, wielding two drummer's sticks he pounded against the cardboard, his legs dangling, his long feet tapping, while a sleek radio emitting a phosphorescent light from the floor played a program of avant-garde jazz on WBAI. Most of Jonathan's jamming consisted of talking.

Sean lay on the mattress. "I'm going to film you," he kept saying, almost as if trying to excuse his being there. He never tried to lick or touch Jonathan. Instead he lay there assaulted mostly by Jonathan's voice. And by his drumming.

"You erase everything false in me," Sean murmured to Jonathan when he finally crashed next to him on the mattress at dawn, causing Sean to knock his bottle of beer onto the floor.

• • •

Sean carefully observed flecks of snow falling through two long windows. He was tilted back that night in an old-fashioned wooden barber's chair in the middle of his and Annie's room. They had found this curiosity at an outdoor flea market on Sixth Avenue. Months had passed. The temperature had dropped. Sean's shirt was off, his nipples red against the paleness of his skin, his natural olive tone having turned much lighter in the cold months.

"I can't believe you're gonna do this," said Jonathan, animatedly training Sean's Bolex on him. "Why don't you just go the fuck straight to a cross and get yourself crucified? I'll crucify you myself—hah! Should I shoot your nipple or your face?"

Sean thought about the question seriously. "Get both in. Crop at my belt." His belt was a simple brown leather strap with metal buckle.

Annie was passing down the center of the room in a dress of gauze wrapped around her like a caterpillar's chrysalis. "Just remember that Eros is a different kind of god than Jehovah and that the meaning of this is to find joy in these jolts of unusual energy. I think it will be fun. I want to chant while it's happening."

"Be sure to chant into the tape recorder" was Sean's only reply.

"Some nights when Jonathan's visiting us I feel like we're a postnuclear family," Annie went on.

From out of the bathroom came Jim, a tall, thin, reserved, and self-possessed man in his early thirties wearing wire rims, the blues of his shirt and jeans as washed out as a blue sky, his brown hair thinning. He seemed like one of the intellectuals of New York past, the intellectuals who twisted their wire spectacles' frames in their fingers—dangerously close to snapping—while they argued.

"Scalpel, doctor?" Jonathan joked. Jim smiled with only half his mouth, uncomfortably. He didn't share Sean's interest in boys from the boroughs. Jim was holding silver tools that looked like surgical instruments—needle, scissors, tweezers. On a round marble side table rested a silver bowl in which ice was melting. Annie walked around turning light switches on, then directed a photographer's light covered with a white umbrella—like the umbrellas from *Death in Venice,* which she and Sean had just seen recently— onto his chest and face.

"Okay, okay," Jonathan said grudgingly, responding to a searing squint from Sean. He started the camera whirring.

Jim placed a cold nugget of ice on Sean's nipple. Sean had met him at a bar called the Stud at the corner of Perry and Greenwich. In the lantern light of the bar they had discussed piercing, a subject of which Sean knew nothing. Somewhere out of his fascination with anything scandalous or outré or exhibitionistic and out of his childhood identification with American Indians, whom he rightly or wrongly associated with piercing, came a talk of several hours.

Jim was a medical intern at St. Luke's Hospital, so he seemed to have precise balance in his hands, a carpenter's level in his eyes. "This won't hurt," he said softly.

"Shhhhh," Sean responded.

First Sean felt a numbing, like the numbing he felt when he went under anesthesia for appendicitis, like the cold of the iced lemonade the nurses brought. Then he became as simple as one of the snowflakes falling outside the window. He felt beyond the camera, Jonathan, Annie, the surgeon with his rings for Sean's nipple. His ideas were a ladder kicked away by this sensation which could later, on looking back, be called pain. He felt good. He felt as if he had been nailed into his body. He tasted the salt on his tongue. Felt the wet tears in his eyes. Felt bigger than anyone else in the room.

How had he become split into pieces? He was tracing all this in his mind as if it were a big map. It was a mistake not to have gone down to the cellar when he was thirteen with Jimmy, the newspaper boy. It was a mistake not to have walked home from the library with a youthful offender. It was a mistake not to have drunk beers by the river with the football team. He had this drive for freedom that was as obvious as a penalty flag. Sean was self-righteous. He felt that these moments of unacted-on desires when he was a teenager were splinterings. They explained why he was setting out on a path of acting out. Rather than actually thinking, he was feeling his way down a dank, mossy hallway.

Then he came to. As if from an operation. He looked down at his nipple and saw a silver ring dangling. He already knew he would remove that silly ring soon, let the hole heal.

The first face he saw was Jonathan's, peeking around the camera. His face looked like a bulldog's, or like a leather catcher's mitt with twinkling eyes inset. Sean liked him there. But also knew he couldn't depend on him. So his eyes panicked, looking for Annie.

When he finally located her hovering over the tape recorder he felt he could rest.

She slid a wet ring, like a piece of grass, onto his finger.

"It's made from lightning bugs," she said. "That's why it's glowing. I just made it while you were . . . uh . . . under. I bought them at a white-magic store. I filmed the lightning bugs—from Alabama, she said they were—before, when they were alive, twinkling in their bell jar. So it's on the footage Jonathan shot. You can use it."

All soft there.

• • •

Sean began to visit bathhouses during that fiercely wintry February of 1973. His favorite was the Everard Baths on West Twenty-eighth Street, built in the nineteenth century by an Irish beer industrialist. Its once posh neighborhood was now a non-neighborhood of import-exporters, trucks loading and unloading, and at night, shadows as long as monsters' teeth. The place seemed to Sean like a hammam, a Turkish bath, though he had never been to any Turkish baths, or to any Russian baths either. Registering on him was the exoticism of its fake Roman front, a marble mausoleum with a curved half-moon window looming and lots of curlicues everywhere.

The place was exotically run-down. In the evenings or on weekends out-of-town customers (from Buffalo, Tulsa, San Francisco) waited in its adjacent bleary coffee shop to rent a room. Those more in-the-know stood in a small hallway to the right of the check-in cage for a chance to bribe the traffic director, terminally sullen, with an extra two or three dollars. He'd grumble "Room" to a colleague of his—who looked like a retired cop—in a white apron as smudged as a pizza man's, and they'd pay their ten dollars as the ex-cop pushed through the window of the cage

a thick white towel on which rested a key on a loop, like the keys
Sean used to attach with a safety pin to his swimsuit when he was
on the diving team at his local YMCA. The same gray cat was
always sleeping beneath a fan on a desk in the manager's office.
The smell in this sensorium was a mixture of steam, feet, sweat,
paprika, acrid cleaning fluid. Sean would find his half-locker (he
couldn't afford a room), stuff in his civilian clothes, wrap the
towel around his waist, slip the key onto his ankle like a charm,
and begin to walk the halls, not bothering with rubber thongs.
Older men wore thongs. Younger men eschewed them. They
walked up and down the flights of stairs between three floors.
The fourth was temporarily closed after a nasty fire. (A few years
later the whole place would burn down on a May morning, nine
killed, seven others hospitalized, bodies hanging naked from the
second-story ledge, falling to the sidewalk, running through
black smoke in all directions in towels and shorts as the first fire
truck finally pulled up.)

There were other baths. Eventually Sean tried them all. At the
Continental Baths, Barry Manilow and Bette Midler had performed, and the operatic soprano Eleanor Steber was promised to
give what was billed as a "black towel" concert later in the year. He
disliked that bathhouse's smell of floor wax and Windex. Later he
tried the Saint Mark's Baths with its chrome snack bar where
yogurt and apple juice were served, its chic industrial deco black
tile showers and its steam rooms with shipboard portholes. The
baths in Midtown were less frilled. There was Man's Country in
the Village, with a Tinkertoy model of an Everlast truck on the
third floor along with a fake prison cell made of rubber bars, a
close cousin to the jungle gyms in children's playgrounds. He'd
heard rumors of a baths in Harlem but never went.

The absence of sheen in the Everard made it his favorite, comfortably reminding him of the tawdrinesses of Pennsylvania or

Middle America, far from the European pleasantries of the Village. In the main dormitory men with bellies like mounds of ice cream lay under towels diminished to mere hankies by the large volumes they tried to cover. Hasidim with scraggly beards and hawklike hands loitered on the edges of cots seemingly left over from the Civil War era. The old men's skins were dried, thin onion skins, almost translucent. Sean wistfully believed that all younger guys shared a cosmic consciousness and a wry sense of humor.

Mostly the Everard was a place of secrets and confessions. Sean cruised its rows of small rooms, as constricting as Jonathan's in the Chelsea. He shuttled from one cubicle to another. When he was a kid, hiding in his bedroom on the second floor running his movie projector or making albums of Brownie camera shots, his uncle Jack, a retired coal miner, joked, "Sean could be happy in prison." The Everard was a labyrinth of hallways of small cells. Men sat in them, completed their rites and rituals, then started to talk: about their jobs, their boyfriends, their wives, their infidelities, their peccadillos. Once someone confessed a murder to him. Through the walls Sean could hear a belt slamming against flesh, the smacks replaced a half-hour later by murmuring and low talk and humming. Always the sound of doors slamming, like screen doors in summer. These were lay confessionals. Even if he'd had the money, Sean wouldn't have taken a room. He liked being in someone else's room, being a visitor rather than a host.

The baths were Sean's secret. He didn't tell Annie, with whom he was more forthcoming with feelings than information, or Jonathan, with whom he was more forthcoming with information than feelings. He kept all these memories in a separate room in his mind, lit by a bare light bulb.

The rooms in the Everard were subdivided by sauna-style stained-wood walls that didn't reach all the way to the ceiling, as if designed to allow an aural wind of smacks and moans and murmured confidences to blow from room to room. Sticking out from the walls were single captain's beds with two lower drawers where paraphernalia could be stored: amyl nitrite vials, gym shorts, lube.

"Will someone please fuck me?" screamed out a man lying facedown, his sweat-soaked skin as slick as a porpoise's. The door was open and his thin behind was trembling in the shadows. Someone whispered to Sean that the implorer was a famous composer. No one suspected such secrets would ever travel any further.

"In the old days it was more circumspect," said one back-porch sort of man, his skin pockmarked by gin spots, a trim body, yellow hair, old enough to be remembering the 1950s, as they sat together by a round hot tub in which some men floated like sea horses, their heads bobbing out of the rising steam, their manes wet. "There were security guards then," he was saying with ancient-mariner intensity. "Once one of them turned us out of the saunas, calling us 'animals, you animals! You have to go to your rooms!' He was a policeman hired to see there was no queer stuff going on. It was all just hypocrisy." On the poolside TV *All in the Family* was broadcasting noisily, its familiar laugh track reverberating off the tiles and the acoustic panels of the peeling walls.

Sean met a writer of adventure novels, a bearded James Bond man's man—his beard a young forest of pines compared to the Hasidim's gray tumbleweed. He told Sean he'd divorced his wife. He invited him to become his typist to type his latest novel filled with thighs, tits, purring engines of speedboats, private prop jets, Fu Manchu mustaches, race cars, motorcycles. Sean visited one evening. When the author was out buying Kentucky Fried Chicken he switched the radio station from Top Ten to avant-garde WBAI. It was a show of will annoying to his tanned, increasingly imperious host on his return. A chicken feather stuck out from one piece of fried skin. Their moods turned downward like a frown. Their planned trip to Acapulco—and Sean's job—were canceled. These brief encounters were breezy, moody, totally non-committal, easily collapsible.

A chef tied Sean one night so that one leg was attached to the doorknob of the ajar door, then left him there while he strutted the hallways dressed only in a black leather vest and gray-white jockstrap, the strap's material as stretchy as bandages. Sean felt as if he were an element in a Rube Goldberg cartoon. In his mouth was stuffed a mound of string. No one actually entered the cubicle, but they stopped to look, then walked on casually. Sean liked to watch everyone in their half-clothes: here a battered green GI cap, there a gray work shirt with the sleeves cut off. The roamers were like knights, nude, except for the heraldic devices of their Yankee caps or dog tags, placing captives in distress, endangering them, saving them, placing themselves in distress. What little boys, Sean thought. The shock was how innocent it all seemed from that tied-up vantage. And how relaxed he felt tied in rope as thin as the draws for venetian blinds.

A singer from the opera reduced all his solos to the word "pig." "You pig," he said to Sean as he drew his head down in a wrestling lock. "Are you a pig? Make a sound like a pig. That's a good pig." It was simply the word "pig" that seemed to enliven him, helped him develop penetration in his otherwise soft oval brown eyes.

Sean once saw the swineherd in a production of *Parsifal* at the opera and fancifully imagined that his songs were all grunts and squeals, different German words for "pig." Sean's snickering attitude annoyed and confused his companions in their expensive orchestra seats that Good Friday.

"It's fun, but it's angry" was Sean's contribution to the talk with the man by the fuming hot tub. "Tying up, smacking, wrestling. What are we all angry about?"

"I guess fist fucking is the ultimate of that way of thinking," the man said, laughing, happy to be making an observation.

Sean didn't know exactly what "fist fucking" was. But the term seemed self-explanatory, so he didn't ask.

A Cuban named Roberto—whom Sean met in the shower, where mildew made sponge of the tiles—rewarded him with a gig taking photographs for a hair-coloring catalog. He was a vice-president of Clairol. Since the job paid for the editing of Sean's first movie, he then invited Roberto to attend the NYU Film School screening. He noticed Roberto leaving the screening room after a few minutes, his well-cut suit casting a shadow like a raven's on the teeny screen.

•   •   •

Sean's date for his screening was Annie. He had a sense that together they made a striking image. They read as cleanly as a photograph. He was shrewd, and odd, and enough of a natural filmmaker to see them from the outside, as strangers would see them. He was a voyeur of his own life. He also trusted Annie more than anyone else, and felt a warm familiarity with her strange antics.

With them was Jonathan. He walked behind, attracting lots of attention in his fatigues from those favoring the military look. In a minute he was sitting next to a stranger, showing him his gun, actually a cheap lighter. When Jonathan pulled the trigger a flame shot up, or would have if he hadn't let the fuel run out. His quick friend ended up lighting Jonathan's cigarettes for him all night with matches.

"I'm the star of this movie, right, Sean?" Jonathan joked from the row behind, slapping his hands on Sean's shoulder blades.

"Of any movie," Sean complied without turning around.

The title of the movie, advertised on a cardboard sign propped on an easel in the lobby: *Sean Has His Nipple Pierced.*

When he did turn around, he looked through the audience, the kind where a few people filled one row while another row would be entirely empty. About fifty attended. Sean didn't feel excited or nervous about showing the movie. But he was quite taken that he knew only half the people there. He didn't care that friends were going to see his movie. That was just friendly, home-movies stuff, like his dad showing movies of their trip to the Washington Monument to stifled neighbors. Strangers made art. He wanted a way to advertise his secret desires. These movies were his version of a phone number left in an abandoned sneaker on a Village front porch. They were risks. Without strangers, he felt no risk, no danger.

Annie was charged, too. Partly because she was introducing the movie; mostly, like Sean, because the theater of black plastic contour chairs was filled with strangers, male strangers, gay strangers. Her vertical wish to be an independent woman, her campaign for self-love, had tied her recently in a knot about what to do about men. She found she could seduce certain gay men simply by her independence. They were seduced by independence, not need. As if the standard roles of women were the turn-off rather than anything biological. Sean had been the key opening this secret door to her. But she had discovered that his own tilt was more fully towards men. He wasn't phallic with her. But there were phallic gay men who allowed her the experiences that made her happy with herself in her current phase. Actually, Sean had recently moved out of their bed of mutual masturbation, positioning his old mattress in the extra bedroom. And Annie had started giving talks to women at the Firehouse on "Loving Gay Men's Bodies." Some old fans turned against her. Some new ones signed on.

Just before the houselights went down and a spotlight made a circle onstage like a spinning nickel of light, Arnie popped into a seat in the row in front of Sean, turning about to catch beamed light in his face.

"Saw it in the *Voice.*"

"You have a good-omen feeling about you tonight," Sean said evenly through his teeth.

"I have someone for you to meet," Arnie whispered back in a clutch of breath before turning around to see Annie already standing onstage in nothing but blue denim overalls and shoes made of black straps of cloth.

"I am the female Walt Whitman," she began, as she often did. "And Sean Devlin, whose movie you'll see tonight, is filmmaker as muse. His images tell it like it is to us in a world that has few leaves of grass worth chewing, few bulrushes worth peeking through at young men bathing in the nude. His movies are all about longing. They are like poems. You know . . . the way that poems can be Roman candles launched into the sky at night to try to attract attention so that the poet hopefully won't be alone much longer, or the way a refrain of *ki-ki-ri-ki*'s is sung by a songbird hoping for the returning echo of *ki-ri, ki-ri*. You'll see what I mean."

After returning to her seat, she and Sean slid their hands into each other's like high-schoolers on a date. Sean felt good among the uneven number of three friends. There was protection without too much demand. As the images began to flutter he was distracted, acting out in his heart the feeling of a big preview. Or, more precisely, imagining Andy Warhol at the early screenings of his first intentionally boring movies at Cinematheque near Gramercy Park ten years earlier. Sean had read how Jonas Mekas tied Warhol to his chair during the second screening of *Sleep* to make him sit through it, returning halfway only to find the rope unraveled in the empty chair. Was that opening like this? he wondered, cozying up in his soul to Warhol's coolness.

The movie was a corsage of dirty yellow and red images: Jonathan on the red phone, Annie praying, a sneaker with Olivier Messiaen's music playing through it, jerky Chelsea Hotel hallways, Sean's exploding red tit, lightning bugs illuminating a bell jar, Puerto Ricans dressed as pirates in a rowboat with a billowing sail made from a bedsheet navigating the Central Park pond waylaying a rowboat of young women to carry them off into the woods to drink and party. *Fin*.

Clap, clap, clap.

Arnie was about to draw Sean, as if by the chin, to meet whomever he had planted in the audience. But instead a man came up who immediately drew Sean's attention away and kept it.

"I liked your work. It's not totally original, but it's in a brave tradition."

Startled by the precise notion, Sean tried to understand the man, who was somewhat indecipherable. Not because he was aloof. He wasn't. He communicated openness, warmness, availability. He was indecipherable because he conformed to no set genre. His hair was gray-white, his skin as smooth as a teenager's. His hands were those of a statue's, his blue eyes those of an astronaut. He wore blue jeans with a T-shirt and an expensive black jacket and black shoes as soft as dogs' ears. His voice was filled with an American twang—open vowels, an inability to find closure at the end of sentences, shifting music. Yet what he was saying sounded as old as Western Europe in its precise connoisseurship. Although he was actually fifty, as Sean would eventually find out, he looked thirty.

"I'd like to talk to you more," said Edgar Savage, pulling out a little spiral notebook, writing down a number with a silver pen on a page he ripped out and handed to Sean.

"I'd like to talk to you too."

Sean accepted the paper in an entranced way. It was an enchanted falling-in-love feeling, not uncommon for him, but this time sweetened by a sense of opportunity.

Meanwhile Annie had been engaged by Arnie as a replacement for Sean. He introduced her to Rupert Jones. Like Edgar Savage, Jones was contradictory. Tall, dashing. A few years earlier, when he came down from Harvard, he had been compared to James Dean. Tonight he was dressed in a black woolen suit, an English suit. But he had bumps to his character Annie sensed and would come to discover soon enough. His job: design curator at MoMA.

Together they were two tall black candlesticks.

"Rupert, will you take me out with you?" she blurted.

"Are you willing to wear a disguise?"

"Look at me and answer for yourself."

On the staircase outside the fire doors, Jonathan was finishing smoking a joint, dumping its gray ashes into a miniature red fire bucket, allowing a breeze from a cracked window to brush over his exposed body. Sean watched a bit jealously as Jonathan took pleasure from Arnie, who was wiping his tongue over his extensive torso—his nipples, his upper arms, his hairy stomach. Like a swallowing wave, Arnie, the back of whose curly head looked like froth, finally sucked away the entire bottom half of Jonathan's spent body by grabbing with his mouth onto his identity, his rudder, and pulling it, too, down into a warm lake of disorientation and abstraction.

"Ooahhgrrrr," Jonathan mooed.

On the Penthouse Terrace of One Fifth Avenue

Did you know that in 1973 vodka outsold whiskey for the first time in history?" someone said who'd just read the previous year's statistics in a magazine.

It was late Sunday afternoon. The balcony of Edgar Savage's penthouse apartment at One Fifth Avenue was filled with friends drinking Bloody Marys or white wine, smoking joints, topping each other's voices, looking out at slate-blue clouds, bruises on a pink sky, while a wild fall wind blew apart everyone's hair, usually long or curly. Slick puddles from last night's rain were still gathered here and there on the flagstones.

The bald man who was knowledgeable about vodka sales was dressed in a suit so white—its waist-length jacket resembled a Spanish bullfighter's jacket—he looked to Sean like a daguerrotype, especially as the sky behind him was giving off the dull brightness of scoured stainless-steel pans.

"No," Sean answered. "I was thinking that 'overcast' is the weather word for what photography calls 'overexposed.' "

"No, no, no," interjected Dorothy Dean, a short black woman with a severe haircut and wire rims, whose voice was as castigating, misanthropic, and weird as W. C. Fields's. " 'Overexposed' is a model who's been on the cover of *Vogue* twice. 'Overcast' is Marlon Brando in *The Countess from Hong Kong.*"

"Dorothy is a fact checker at *The New Yorker,* if you didn't already guess from her precision," interjected Edgar, leaning back against the iron rails, a long, thin wineglass shaped like an orchid bulb in his hand, looking taller than Sean remembered from the screening.

"Just call me Cassandra," she added.

Edgar had actually been talking to a long-black-haired young man in a poor boy's cap, blue lipstick, and a smart black leather sports coat. His family had been portrayed the year before in a cinéma-vérité documentary on public television. He announced himself a homosexual during one of its segments, then moved from California to New York to the Chelsea Hotel to pursue Andy Warhol and a career in a rock band. Now his mother and he were both close friends of Edgar's. She was sitting on a low ledge in her blue denim dress, covering her mouth with one hand, in hysterics, feigning embarrassment over whatever her nineteen-year-old son had just said.

"Homosexuality certainly isn't anything I would choose for a child of mine," she had told a TV interviewer a few months earlier.

"My problem is that I have the soul of a white faggot trapped in the body of a black woman," Dorothy Dean went on, spooling her words through her mouth as if she were leaving teeth marks on them. "And a short black woman at that!"

Sean was still learning the ways of this repartee. He had seen *La Dolce Vita* at a drive-in in the backseat of his parents' Ford Galaxie. Its closing scene of an all-night party of beautiful-looking people that ended at dawn on a beach near Rome was his first subliminal lesson. Just pull a string in your head and let it spin as if it were a top, he thought. At the same time he felt that this was a game for an older crowd. He would always be only half there. His other half wished to be lying on Jonathan's abused mattress listening to him talk dirty in his fakest guttural voice on the smudged tan phone.

Annie bent down intently in front of a minimalist composer whose recent cyclical symphony she had attended in a loft in SoHo where everyone sat on the floor on soothing Indian rugs. "I loved the music because it seemed to drive me out of my mind with its repetitiveness, but then I realized I was actually going *into* my mind, deep into my mind," she complimented him.

The red flannel shirt the composer was wearing resembled the throw rugs in the loft. His wife was standing behind Annie in a dress that looked like a lace nightgown, her shoes white open-toed strap-arounds. She was the director of an experimental theater company. Her long, straight hair made her look like a Victorian schoolgirl.

"What are you working on?" she asked Annie, her opposite in black jeans, a big knitted Indian bag over her shoulder.

"I'm doing a script for Sean about Patty Hearst. I want to play her. I want to turn the demands of the Symbionese Liberation Army into a song—you know, two million dollars' worth of food to people with welfare cards, social security pension cards, food stamps, medical cards, parole or probation papers, jail or bail release slips. It's a beautiful list. A laundry list of society's dirty underwear."

"I prefer Brooks Brothers boxer shorts myself," interjected Dorothy.

"Dorothy, you know what they used to call foreskins in the fifties?" asked a translator from the Russian who was married to a stage and TV actress. "Lace curtains," he answered his own question.

"You know what they called blacks?" asked R. J. Thorpe, his big teeth revealed in a smile shaped like a rectangle, so that the effect was that of a zipper being opened. His skin had remained as smooth and blond as his hair, so that though he now was in his thirties, he never seemed to age.

"Suedes," Dean snapped, glad to be able to take a figurative pair of scissors to R.J.'s tongue. "Talking to R.J. is like reading the front page of the newspaper," Dean then announced generally. "It's all the information that's unfit to print."

"Going home with sailors was 'eating seafood.' "

"Licking toes was 'shrimping.' "

When Rupert Jones arrived on the terrace, it was as if a black cashmere scarf had been wrapped around the neck of the gathering. He looked smart, dressed this time in a black leather jacket, jeans, chaps, Wellington boots. His hair, shorter than anyone else's, was Brylcreemed into sprouts of spikes. Annie and he both made extended hand signals that were like whisper warnings. They were telling each other to hold on until they could get together. "He *really* looked like James Dean when he was younger," someone was already inevitably insisting about Rupert.

"I brought a copy of Auden's blow-job poem for you, R.J.," Rupert said, in a voice reminiscent of a television cowboy, of Cheyenne, handing over two typewritten pages, stapled and creased longways down the middle. He had drawn them out of an inner pocket.

Rupert's inflections were not lost on Dorothy Dean.

"When I knew you at Harvard, you talked with so many affectations you sounded as if you were Evelyn Waugh on forty-five revolutions per minute," she said accusingly. "Now you've invented this low growl. Why the change?"

"Did I ever tell you about the first time I met Auden?" stalled R.J., trying to interrupt Dean's wounding. "It was at a party on the roof of his apartment on St. Mark's Place. He was so sloppy he let his tie fall into his vodka cocktail. When he noticed, he simply threw it back over his shoulder."

"He used to wear his house slippers on the street."

"He was the sloppiest poet in the world, even filthy. Dirty teacups in saucers rested for days on those big volumes of the *OED*. There were crumbs everywhere. Insufficiently cooked tripe was his favorite dish."

"His boyfriend would be entrapped by undercover cops and he would have to go to the police station to bail him out. That's why he finally had to flee America—to save the cost of bribing the sex police, for whom his boyfriend was such a patsy."

"Remember the story about his tripping on mescaline? Auden went out at eight in the morning, saw the postman, came home, wrote poems. He said it was an entirely ordinary day. He hadn't noticed anything extraordinary. Then he realized that the postman never walked down the street at eight in the morning. So he concluded he must have been hallucinating."

"But all is washed clean in the blood of certain lines of poetry. He did write, after all, 'Lay your sleeping head, my love / Human on my faithless arm.' 'Lullaby' is to swoon from, or over."

R.J., Rupert, and Dorothy had all known each other at Harvard in the 1960s. "Then I discovered the party," Dean would always add after that fact was sprung. They used to hang out at the Casablanca, a club downstairs from an art-movie house in Harvard Square. Now they were moving as uniformly as a ouija board marker to a corner pointed northwest. It became their promontory as the light grew weaker, the air cooler.

"I've been translating Rimbaud's poem about being seven," R.J. offered.

"If they can't read French, screw them," said Dean, triggered.

Two women, lesbians, had been at Radcliffe at the same time the others were at Harvard. They were knit into their own discussion along one wall. One wore long silk bell-bottoms, so pronounced in their lower fluting they made her look like a dressy mermaid. The other, solider woman wore wool pants woven in a Scottish plaid design. The two were talking with the minimalist composer's wife. The subject: Peter Pears's debut in Benjamin Britten's *Death in Venice* recently at the Met.

Sean felt as if he were a big ear, left rocking lopsidedly on the floor like a child's toy, adding little, absorbing much. He was an eavesdropper in all these groups, a true participant in none. This was his novitiate in a lot of brightness he didn't yet understand. He wanted at moments to leap forward with his own words, but he was naturally wise enough to know that his were so different from those being spoken that they would fall everywhere like dull copper pennies. Better to keep them hidden in his pockets for a while.

When purple evening finally phased in more fully, the group moved in clumps back to the suite's main room, where a bartender was standing behind a table draped with a white cloth. He reminded Sean of his own bartender gigs at Columbia a mere two years earlier. A few globally famous people joined the babbling crowd. David Bowie, in town on his *Diamond Dogs* tour. A print of a yellow star on a blue background done on rice paper by Bowie hung on Edgar's wall. "I didn't know he was an artist." "Lots of those English rockers came out of art school. Didn't John Lennon?" "That's Lotte Lenya," Annie filled in Sean on the red-haired woman sitting on the floor next to a lacquered black grand piano. Sean, though, was still busy worshiping Bowie.

Edgar's main room was all art and furniture. Wooden missionary couches. White wicker chairs. A fifties curvilinear hassock covered in a fabric of Sputnik patterns. Saffron-and-clay-red Indian rugs with computer printout designs. Tallest in the room was a ten-foot-high totem sculpture with painted faces and a feathered headdress at its top made with rubber tubes and metro tickets. Sean recognized a few photographs on the walls, by Christopher Makos, William Wegman, Gordon Matta-Clark, and Robert Mapplethorpe. The Mapplethorpe showed Edgar in his Brooks Brothers khakis talking on a white phone, its wire tugging like a leash from the beyond of the not-shown. The light cutting on a diagonal through the photograph, as well as the texture of the platinum print, captured the aura of things seen on cocaine, of which there was now plenty being cut, spooned, passed, or sniffed through a straw. In the picture it was as if Edgar, squinting, were a saint and the phone his symbol.

Edgar liked conceptual art. Some of the photographs on the wall were simply documents of art happenings. The photographed house split nearly in two—like a tree trunk by an axe—had been cut by the artist with a saw recently in Englewood, New Jersey, its left side lowered to emphasize the cut. One white wall in his main room was covered with words and lines in solid black bookish print concerning "context" and "sign," "presence" and "absence." These messages pleasantly skimmed past Sean's understanding. A black wire sculpture as unruly as an Afro fidgeted in one corner of the room. A tall chair, made of bamboo sticks, seemed a lifeguard's chair on the shore of a Polynesian afterlife. Another artist favored by Edgar took photographs of video images: one showing a saxophonist's hand was really, Edgar told Sean, "about the many shades of gray." A favorite work of Sean's used three neon light sources in red, yellow, and blue, reminding him of a pinball machine.

By now Annie and Rupert were idling with Sean in the corner with the frazzled sculpture. Rupert was inviting Annie out after the party to a few gay bars. She was only too happy to go. "I can tell your fortune with the tarot deck someday if you'd like," she offered in return.

"How about some morning after we wake up in bed?" Rupert answered, the coils in his voice warmed by adventure.

"What do you like?"

"I like to dress in a worker's uniform and drive a truck, picking up hitchhikers or meeting other truckers at roadside rests. What do you like?"

"Well, I was deeply into mutual masturbation for a while, and still am. But I'm beginning to long for a fuller ride again, but with gay men. I find straight men almost to a man to be adrift in space capsules of Cartesian mentality."

"I think I follow you."

"You seem to have lost your human coloring more than Sean—you're more ashen. But he shares your mixture of the highest aesthetic discernment with a love of street life."

"Come on, let's go soon. Didn't Sean ever take you out?"

"No," she said without judgment, while Sean, having been listening to himself talked about in the third person, could only think to shrug.

Wandering off, he was surprised by the thinness of the music. The bartender was handling the records as well. They were mostly the popular hits of the moment. But as Sean grew more stoned, pieces of lyrics stuck in his head like broken bits of beer bottles. "Clouds in my coffee, clouds in my coffee" became part of a beautiful symbolist poem to him. Then a musician of the minimalist school stood up with an alto clarinet. His black baggy clothes, long blond hair, loose stance gave him an orphic quality. He drew everyone up into his instrument, producing sounds somewhere between siren screams and relaxed sighs.

When the mesmerizer had finished his calming performance, Edgar moved everyone out the door. He put a hand on Sean's shoulder to invite him to stay rather than propel him to leave. Annie and Rupert both extended their hands to Sean in rushed goodbye signals, but without touching his. They hurried through the black slice of door, which felt to the exiters as if it were narrowing every minute.

Edgar and Sean sat down and began to talk. For both of them it was as if a window had been cracked.

• • •

Edgar drove a yellow sporty convertible. Acid-lemon yellow. He and Sean continued their talk in the car with the top down. Edgar was shifting with a loose arm. Sean was hunched down and back, like an astronaut, in a tan vinyl bucket seat. The radio was tuned to opera. It was a rebroadcast of a bit of *Otello* from the Met with Kiri Te Kanawa singing. Edgar turned the volume up so high Sean felt compelled to look at the sky through the colored confusion of Sixth Avenue heading uptown past Radio City Music Hall. The sky seemed to him to be made of bluish-black hand fans being pushed aside to reveal small cracks of light, the stars.

"The sky's very deco tonight," he said, trying to register the delicate impression in words. "Like the roof of the Music Hall."

"I think I know what you mean without the benefit of actually looking up," Edgar replied, making a U-turn to head back downtown.

"Where to?"

"Dunno. Maybe Crisco Disco. Although Flamingo's having a special party tonight, I heard."

Sean reached back for his Super 8, which he produced and began using in the same movement. He trained the attachable eye of his lens on Edgar driving.

"Do you want to make home movies or do you want to make myths?"

"I want to make home myths."

Edgar seemed glad to find Sean an even match for him, or potentially an even match.

"I've never been to Flamingo," Sean said. "Until you get there tell me your life story. I'll never ask you to do it again."

"You mean that's the form? Like sonnets with their road map of rhymes?"

"Did you go to Harvard with the others? They'd bring up sonnets, I'm sure."

"I went to Yale," Edgar began. "From Palm Beach, Florida, where my father was a realtor. I was close to my big sister, bigger by one year. When I was a child I showed a flair for ballroom dancing. My sister and I won a contest. I collected rocks, shells, stamps. My father died and left me money, which I used to go to college. Then I worked at the Chase Manhattan Bank for too long. I began collecting again. It started with Eileen Gray furniture. But the preposterousness of conceptual art caught me. I sold my furniture and my silver. You saw what I like. I like photographs. You're a filmmaker who's somehow like a photographer. You seem mad for control, and of course for the giving up of control. It's working so far."

"Why did you bring it back to me already?"

"Because I'm larger than you—in magnitude, I mean. But you could catch up. I hope so." He said that with a pat on Sean's upper leg that caused him to pull back quickly with the camera.

By now they were closing in on Houston Street. Lights were skimming all visible surfaces like dragonflies on black silky water.

"Here's Flamingo."

"It looks like a day job."

They parked at the corner of Broadway and Houston, eye-level with a first-floor bank under a looming white industrial clock. Walked up a flight of steps to an unsettled lobby where a man in a suit sat at a desk. He greeted Edgar with a flash of a smile and a peaceful handshake that highlighted the glinty rings he wore on every finger. With his mystical gold necklaces and gray-white hair and snipped beard, he seemed a modern satyr.

"To get a membership, for forty-five dollars, you have to come up and meet him at noon on a Thursday," Edgar told Sean. "No matter who you are. The day I enlisted there was a line of guys down the street. He interviews you, asking leading questions like 'What sign are you?' "

Sean reacted with an unimpressed murmur.

"There are so many people I want you to meet. Not here. This is irresponsible fun. But uptown ladies and curators who could help you."

"I don't like to lick the asses of rich people."

"Let them think they're licking yours."

By now they were in the full main room. Different lights the color of fruit juices were playing along all the shiny walls. Big white peacock feathers rose out of Oriental urns. Black vinyl couches were fitted together at right angles. On a chrome counter along one entire wall were laid out different fruits: bananas, apples, pineapples. Sean paid attention for a while to a song that repeated a French phrase.

"There's something deco about this place too, like your sky and like Radio City Music Hall," Edgar said.

"Yeah," said Sean, his camera closed in its case at his side. "I don't feel so alive here, though. It's too . . . uh . . . white. Like heaven or something. I miss hell."

"That's funny. Let's go."

On the way through a quadrille of guys dancing with lots of high circus-horse leaps and twirls, Sean felt a flushness he liked. He checked out the tropical grove of everyone's clothes: T-shirts with martini shakers or Rolls-Royces etched on them, fuchsia shirts, cream-colored canvas bell-bottoms swaying over brown Frye boots, silver necklaces with geometrically shaped medallions. Van McCoy's "The Hustle" was playing, its rhythms slack and irresistible, as they soon shuttled out a door shuttered like a verandah's. Another bar was set up out front, though all the drinks in the club were nonalcoholic: waters, tall grapefruit juices. The bar was situated next to a jewelry concession of dangling macho silver charms: hammer, fist, construction helmet.

On the way down the stairs to the waiting car Edgar gave Sean a quick history.

"Discotheques really come from France. It was part of a technological revolution. Records could be spun and played through speakers rather than having to hire live bands. I suppose there are lots of garages across America which have the distinction of being our first discotheques. But in Paris right now it's Le Sept. That's where I'd like to be tonight. That's where I first danced to this year's American dance music."

"I suppose," Sean said, donning an unimpressed hipness that fit a bit too tightly, slamming his car door shut behind him, playing idly from the passenger's seat with the dormant gearshift. "But I didn't once want to get my camera out while I was there. So for me it's a dead end."

"Admittedly these are just postcards we're looking at. But at least they're new postcards."

·   ·   ·

As Edgar drove down Broadway towards the darker, quieter, colder part of the island, he picked up his history where he had left off. It was cold enough that Sean could see his own breath sucked to the back of the car as it zipped forward. He imagined his breath was steam from the stacks of a transatlantic luxury steamship. Then he lit a cigarette and manufactured a different kind of steam.

"In New York the first discotheque I remember was Arthur's," Edgar continued. "It was started by Richard Burton's wife after *Camelot* was a smash—Sybil? It had mushroom seats. I guess before that was the Peppermint Lounge. I remember Paul Harvey on the radio in Florida telling us about Jackie Kennedy's dancing the twist there. The Beatles went once. Now it's the gays who've got all the desirable sweat boxes, like the Loft and Sanctuary, or overly perfumed jewelry boxes like that place we were just in, or John Addison's Le Jardin, uptown in the basement of a Times Square hotel. He dresses his busboys in white satin basketball shorts. It's brilliant!"

Sean was thinking how funny it was when real people talked as if they were magazine journalists, entranced by history as it was happening. Information was a kind of small talk for them. It was a key in which Edgar often liked to perform.

Soon their car drifted to a stop downtown in front of the World Trade Center towers.

"They're beautiful, like two stereo speakers," Sean said as they walked between the towers. "Or like two cigarette lighters."

"I think silver is the color of this era," Edgar insisted. "And gray. I like conceptual art because it's all gray, silver, white. The colors of print face, or photographs. The colors of the mind thinking. Meditative. Spacey. Trippy. Keen."

"Keen?" Sean asked quizzically.

He was enjoying the directness of learning from Edgar. He was learning history not written in books. Crucial, local, oral history. Stories he would need to know if he wanted to film his own stories successfully. He remembered from college how Parzival had traveled into the forest to meet the hermit who taught him a lesson or two. The lesson was to be brave enough to ask the question that was on your mind. At least that's how Sean remembered the lesson.

They were now in the plaza between the towers, a kind of saucer like the sloping circular piazzas in some Italian cities Sean had visited where children sent their wooden toy cars riding along curving rims. Philippe Petit, the French acrobat, had recently walked along a wire stretched thirteen hundred feet above the ground between those two towers.

Sean looked up. The silver towers seemed to be leaning in and up, as if the full white moon had been popped into the sky by the pressure of their squeeze. They became to Sean two hands bent towards each other in prayer with a white egg balanced on the tips of their fingers.

Sean started to run, his momentum almost out of character. By running he made a spiral design on the circular plaza as he closed further and further towards a center. "A woman, nude, wrapped only in cellophane, played a cello there," Edgar was shouting down at him, laughing. Sean dropped his camera bag and kept screwing himself further and further into the self-consciously architectural space. Edgar surrounded him by walking the perimeter, smoking.

When Sean reached the center he dropped in a lump on the ground. He heaved as he lay there. The air was pummeling its way into his lungs to fill him up again.

Edgar ran to him through the mercurial light.

•   •   •

Annie swore to Sean—when he and Edgar stopped in at the Ramrod after their World Trade towers pilgrimage—that she couldn't have cared less that she was the only woman there. She actually liked the audacity of her visit, her specialness. So did Rupert, she claimed, who had brought her. She was lending him an association of heterosexuality which was sexy to many of the men jammed into this bar redolent of tar, log cabins, motorcycle shops, leather, hair grease, beer vats, barbershops, skunk oil, knives, belts, buckles, raccoon tails, auto mechanics.

The maleness of the place would come to seem quaint in a few years. But that night it seemed to Sean—almost melodically giddy by now with so much newness—a creative reaction to the "nelliness" of the bars of the previous decades, or of *The Boys in the Band,* which had depressed him when all its characters turned out to be female divas of the weeping-all-alone-by-the-telephone sort, either forwardly or in disguise. In their place these men were holding up new cartoonish male icons: Hell's Angels, football players, mustachioed film actors. On the walls were lots of clues, tonalities whose choice was as political as aesthetic: American flags; license plates; hubcaps; posters for other rugged bars in other cities, especially leather bars in German cities; pennants from recently invented motorcycle associations; tin cans.

Arnie walked over to them for a few minutes. He carried on a conversation about Sean almost as if he weren't there, as if the low roar were a reliable insulation. "How do you read Sean these days?" he asked predictably, still somehow always on the scent.

"He's with his new patron," Annie answered with a hint of annoyance.

"Edgar Savage has a good eye. He could help him."

R.J., smiling, put his arm around Arnie to waltz him to the bar to buy him a beer. Rupert had found a friend in a man whose blue Esso shirt he admired. Sean eavesdropped on them talking about petrol. In the parentheses left by these wanderings, Annie began to talk to a starkly horrific character next to her. He was a sort of creepy gargoyle in modern leather clothes. His hair was long, black, straight, but shocked as if teased with electricity. His leather jacket was bulky American, his blue jeans rolled up like a hoodlum's. He was quite short as well. But his piercing eyes really did seem black, and his voice was clipped in an affected, educated, classic way. That was a combination to which Annie seemed to be drawn in her men. A real Esso attendant wouldn't have interested her as much as he would have Rupert.

"You know when I think civility ended?" Annie was saying to him. "When Ratso Rizzo slammed his hand down on the car in *Midnight Cowboy* and said, 'I'm walkin' here, I'm walkin' here.' That was a death knell of a kind."

It was an observation Sean appreciated much more than Turk, her new friend. Sean wanted to tell her that the line had actually been improvised on the spot by Dustin Hoffman during filming. But he told Edgar instead as they oscillated on the side of the emerald pool table.

"I'm not into civility," Turk said as if his voice were prerecorded. "I'm aligned with the darker forces under the earth."

"Hah!" Annie laughed.

When Turk talked briefly to Arnie, he kept it up. "Your brain's flying too much up in the air," Sean heard him saying. "I want you to ground yourself. Bring your brain down to the wood floor where the scuff of my boots is."

"That's all right," said Arnie, excusing himself. He had a sense of humor about such characters that Annie and Sean didn't. There were lots of quasi-criminals about in the bars.

"I love Turk's hair," Annie was saying to R.J. "It has the stiffness of a broom."

"I heard he might be the axe murderer responsible for all those deaths," R.J. answered. "They ran the victims' pictures in the *Voice*. Did you see them? They're universally ugly. So the theory is the killer must be extremely good-looking to have entrapped them. They think that for once in their life they're getting the golden apple and instead it's a knife between the ribs."

"I think he's too obviously scary to be a killer. I like him."

Annie enfolded her hand in Turk's.

"Where are you from?" Rupert asked formally.

"I'm from Alabama," Turk answered vaguely.

"I want to talk to you," Sean interrupted almost jealously as he quickly guided Annie out the plank of a door onto the pavement. "There've been drive-by shootings," he explained, pointing to the blasts in the plate-glass windows fronting the bar. They turned right at the first block to a small street lit by quaint yellow lights, a bit of the heritage of the Village of the last century.

Suddenly Rupert appeared. Sean felt again as if he were back in high school when he had been the ghost, the enabler, the elbow that led the parties to the action, the nurse, the friar, the messenger. Rupert backed Annie into a stucco wall while Sean's shadow kept flowing over them. Annie was grabbing him and feeling his insistent pressure on her. Rupert moved his hand behind so that he was rubbing her behind as if he were polishing an apple with a napkin. When the shining was completed he undid the zipper of her jeans and started to feel his way through the different switches of her playful zone. "That's where I *think*," she said in a whisper as she bit on his ear. "Let's go to R.J.'s or somewhere," he answered.

Rupert maneuvered everyone next to R.J.'s embattled Volkswagen left over from the sixties, its dirty orange exterior pock-marked with the remains of pastel flower decals. Scraped off the fenders were stickers with political messages, even a peace sign.

"I just went on unemployment," R.J. was telling Rupert as everyone tried to climb into his mechanical pumpkin. "I quit on my thirtieth birthday."

"Since you're a Leo, that must have been in August," Rupert answered.

"I hear they're gonna zap *New York* magazine for being shitty to gays," Arnie was informing Sean by way of goodbye.

Annie, suddenly spooked, turned to Rupert to avoid Turk, who was predatorily looking over at her.

"I hate it when it rains," Turk complained in a loud, raspy voice, though no rain was actually falling.

•   •   •

Instead of going off in R.J.'s car, Sean had gone back to the Chelsea. When he heard the elevator doors slide shut behind him and felt the light on him, his legs became heavy. He swayed a bit. He continued to walk towards the door of his and Annie's apartment, but the impulse wasn't there to turn the key.

He thought that R.J. had been planning to drop Annie when they drove off. It later turned out they had gone to R.J.'s apartment on Ninth Street off Second Avenue. If he had known that Annie's apartment was completely empty, filled only with eerie moonlight shining through its big windows, he might have gone in.

Tonight for the first time Annie seemed just a roommate to him, and he didn't feel like walking quietly past her, or sitting down to talk about what he had done or what she had done. It was the beginning of a long, strange separating that would stretch over the next few months, a result more of Sean's growing need for an adventure of self, as well as the growing adventure of men with men, than of any animosity, anything between them. Sean had been saying recently—spouting, actually, to friends his own age, not to the fancier, more intimidating ones at One Fifth Avenue—that people were not only themselves but also symbols to each other of needs and pushes and bends. Once he believed that solipsistic riddle—and solipsism was unfortunately or fortunately quite suited to him—he could act. This nasty acting made him more scared and more excited than anything else.

So he turned around, made his way down stairs lined by a metal railwork with sunflowers smudged into the pattern. He stood at Jonathan's door and banged.

"You want some speed?" Jonathan asked as a kind of greeting as he opened the door.

"Sure," Sean answered.

Jonathan didn't bother to turn on the light. The glow of the long HOTEL sign outside the window kept the space filled with a yellow brightness in which they could make out the tan masks of each other's faces.

"You want me to order you around?" Jonathan asked, stretched out in no clothes on his mattress.

"I want you to order me around while you're filming me," Sean answered, swallowing the pill with water from a hazy hotel glass. "But we have to put the lights on, then."

"Fuck," said Jonathan as he rose and sketchily flicked the switch.

Sean handed him the camera. He had been restless at Flamingo because none of the guys seemed to have had a hold on his imagination the way Jonathan did. He wouldn't have cast them in his world. He had also been generally restless lately. His pulse hadn't been quickening when he was filming various friends who stopped by. He felt he wasn't showing enough of himself, wasn't risking enough. So having Jonathan film him letting out a few of his demons seemed a new kick.

"Take off your clothes," Jonathan ordered professionally, his hustling consisting of lots of such ordering around with both men and women. "Love is just power with its pants on," he once told Sean.

Sean stripped in front of his camera, though he accomplished the moves shyly, leaving a shadow of cloth around his feet, as if he were a statue with a wrapped base. "Show me," Jonathan said. Sean turned around like a model. "Show me you love me."

Sean dropped to his knees in front of Jonathan. Now the stars were lined up the way he wanted. Jonathan's penis began to stiffen, not straight up, but off to the side, indirectly. He licked the sides of Jonathan's feet, holding them as if they were made of bark, then licked up his legs as the hairs grew sharper against his tongue, all over Jonathan's balls and penis, which he used as a guide pointing him up to the chest. "Show me your face." Sean knew that his face would be distorted as in a convex mirror when filmed so close. "I'm gonna plow you and film you at the same time. It's a trick I'm gonna do." "Do it," Sean said, in an intonation that was a little too falsely starletlike, he decided later, when he listened to the footage.

"I heard the man is always the one who's on top, and I'm always on top," Jonathan explained to no one.

Then he swiveled Sean over on his belly, feeling his pierced nipple from behind. "Where's your ring?" he demanded with true anger.

"I took it off."

"You gotta put it on tonight. I'm gonna do it again. Where's the stuff? In your medicine cabinet?"

"What's first?" Sean asked inexplicably, out of it from the increasing speed of the speed.

"You're first," Jonathan answered just as inexplicably. But they seemed to understand each other perfectly, as if they had simultaneously been taken up in a cloud of unknowing. "No, I changed my mind. *It's* first."

Jonathan took Sean's keys, raided the apartment on the fifth floor, found ring and needle in the mirrored medicine cabinet, returned through the mist of the hallway lighting. "I'll heat it with my cigarette lighter," he said as he walked in, grabbing his fake revolver of a lighter. "You'll have to film this."

The camera, held by Sean's jagging hand, produced images swooning into each other. The film later showed Jonathan's hands working unevenly to repierce the hole, daub the black blood with a handkerchief of shirt, then insert the dull ring. As the ring was being inserted, the image suddenly became magically steady, clean, and clear, as if taken by a camera mounted on a tripod.

Lying there, Sean felt and saw inwardly: lilac tree on a front lawn; white circuit-breaking flash; steam from a kettle; chili ladled into a Ball jar; stuffy garage; car tire punctured by pavement spikes in a bank parking lot; worm-hole tunnel from the movie *Freud*; steam from a nearby radiator.

Finished, Jonathan retrieved the camera. Sean felt as if he had been operated on. The Dexedrine had greatly cut the pain. "I want you to leave it on from now on," Jonathan said. "Yes, I promise," Sean said, feeling good from the commitment of saying so and meaning it. He felt more lyrical than ever. "Am I a masochist?" he wondered aloud. He didn't want to be a masochist, mostly because the word was odd, final, clinical.

Jonathan was in him. Sean was on his belly. Jonathan was filming the top of his torso with one hand, pushing Sean's head over the side of the bed with the other. The one discomfort balanced out the other, like an equation.

"Dawn's breaking on the bald floor" were the only words Sean squeaked, flying, about an hour later.

•　•　•

By the time Annie walked in the next morning, Sean, shirtless, was busily editing film at the Steenbeck in his bedroom.

He swiveled around in his chair when she entered the room, which was taken up entirely with editing equipment, his mattress leaning against a wall, waiting for its occasional use.

"What's that ring doing there? You're bleeding!"

Something about the scene brought out a tender, nursing side belied by her tough-girl image. She walked over to Sean to pass her fingers through his sticky hair, and her simple gesture immediately drew him back to her.

"You have to keep daubing the blood for a few days," he said as he applied a cotton ball to the intentional wound. "I'm going to keep it in this time."

Annie looked into the screen of the machine, where she saw, frozen, the black-white graphic image of Sean sitting in the barber's chair.

"So I have these two piercings—they're like companion pieces," he was explaining with happy eyes. "I need to find a hinge to put in the middle and the movie will be done. It'll be a triptych. It'll last about twelve minutes, depending on what middle piece I choose.

"What happened to you last night?" he added.

"Let's have some tea," said Annie, evasively.

Annie used special cups—round, white, French bowl-sized coffee cups. The two of them stretched out together on the garish orange rug, their legs rubbing. Annie snuggled into Sean's hurt chest as they rolled over on their backs, looking towards the windows through which the smoky daylight filtered. It was very quiet at the back of the hotel. There were none of the street noises that defined Jonathan's room. The feeling was almost of being in the country.

"This is nice," Annie remarked simply.

"Yeah."

"When I was a kid my grandmother used to sing me a song about 'baby bunting gone a-hunting,' " he mused. "My uncle was a hunter, and there would be a whole deer carcass on the kitchen table while she sang. So I always felt there was something intimate about violence."

"What happened to her?"

"Cancer. She lay in a white bed moved into the living room. Once she asked me to get her Kleenex when she was coughing up blood. I couldn't find the Kleenex box. I broke down in a trauma, helpless."

When Sean felt affectionate he often returned to childhood memories.

"Funny that with guys, whom I'm supposedly so attracted to, I just feel anxious excitement. But with you I feel warm."

"I activate your heart chakra."

"I had an idea."

"What?"

"I had an idea that I could take you to the Club Baths on First Avenue. You could go in disguise. It would be like an adventure date."

"Ooooh," Annie responded, aroused as well.

After an afternoon of naps, together and separately, in the bed and on the floor, they roused themselves in the early evening for the adventure. Crowding in front of the stark mirror in the tiled bathroom, Annie worked out her disguise with Sean eagerly helping. They were Halloweenish a few days early. Their mood: childish.

Annie cut her fingernails straight across, combed her hair back, and tied the strands into a ponytail. Sean painted spirit gum under her nose, then stuck on a mustache made of real hairs he'd purchased at a fancy costume shop uptown. In 1974 there were lots of elaborate costume shops everywhere. Other than the mustache, her transition was quickly accomplished. Although she had plenty of unisexual clothes, she chose a couple of things from

Sean's closet she wouldn't normally wear. She liked the feeling of being someone else. "I'm starting to feel like Charlie Chaplin," she joked. She did wear her usual jeans, boots, and work shirt. New were the brown bomber's jacket with a brown fur collar and a blue stocking cap.

"I never thought of you as short, but as a man you're short. How tall are you?"

"Five-four."

To practice they went to dinner at Duff's, a restaurant on Christopher Street. Different friends of Sean's were looking over funnily from nearby wooden booths in the gaslit spot specializing in mildly sophisticated Americanese food—lobster, pasta in clam sauce, white wine. They didn't recognize Annie. Sean was acting diffidently.

The poet James Schuyler, looking portly, his face full and pink, was having dinner with the collage artist Joe Brainard, much thinner than the poet, his hair thick and wavy as a collie's. "Joe's a nail having dinner with a thumbtack," Annie murmured of their acquaintances through her unstable mustache.

A woman with barn-red hair, her body all curves, her manner at once elegant, intelligent, and come-on-ish in a middle-aged way, was having dinner in the booth next to Schuyler's with a gentlemanly critic and English professor at Rutgers. Each other's standard date at the New York City Ballet, they usually talked about their mutual adoration for past performances of Suzanne Farrell's: *Slaughter on Tenth Avenue, Diamonds, A Midsummer Night's Dream.*

That Annie eluded Joe and Jimmy without being discovered indicated her success at their deception. She and Sean were less likely to come across a cluster of art-world friends at the Club Baths, their destination. The baths were anonymous—especially the Club, which didn't have the dark erotic pull for Sean of the

Everard. There were fewer artists, leather kings, poets, or even axe murderers. The Club Baths were bourgeois.

"I remember a Robin Hood episode where Maid Marian disguised herself as one of Robin's merry band," Annie was saying as the Checker cab chugged across Bleecker Street in heavy traffic. "She was tucked into a green hood. I loved Maid Marian."

"I loved Prince John and the Sheriff of Nottingham, the villains," Sean added.

"Predictably."

Eventually they arrived at First Avenue between First and Second Streets. It was Buddy Night: two lockers for five dollars. About thirty men were lined up in front of a booth which resembled the ticket counter of a movie house. Everyone had to sign a name and address, a useless formality as most of them signed aliases. Sean wrote down, "Ken Anger, 191 Hollywood St., Babylon, New York"; Annie, "Art Rimbaud, 69 Rue des Pédés, Paris, France." Then a buzzer made its twitching noise and a door was opened off to the side as an attendant handed them towels, robes, rubber thongs, and directed them with a flourish of his wrist down the stairs to a small locker room.

"Friendlier than the Everard," Sean said in an aside to Annie as they walked down the steps. "I miss all the gruffness."

"I'm telling you, gay lib might wind up being a snore."

The narrow room was lined with rows of white double lockers. Seven men were crowded in, trying to stuff their clothes into the lockers. They were like boys in a YMCA anxious to reach the pool area to dive or swim laps. Annie first took off her boots, feeling her feet were safe to expose. When she removed her jeans, she was wearing a shiny black codpiece that drew quick looks from several of her neighbors. She felt panicked as she saw their eyes shift up from her codpiece to her eyes, then back down again. Feeling her fumbling, Sean walked over.

"Does your arm still hurt? Let me help you get that off." He helped her with her work shirt, under which she had fastened a flattener, a sort of girdle, around her breasts; then he quickly wrapped one of the terry-cloth mini-robes around her. It came to the middle of her thighs. He wrapped one about himself, too, so that she would be less conspicuous. Only a few old-timers in the place were so wrapped.

Holding hands because of the denseness of the crowd, they passed by a shallow pool made of mosaic tiles decorated with Minoan scenes and by showers whose water sprays reminded Sean of nickels falling. Tan wicker patio chairs were casually placed among extremely healthy potted ferns. In a brightly lit TV room Annie speeded her pace because the looks under the lights made her fear discovery. She felt, though, in passing, that the TV room was a safe, easy zone. The men stuffed in easy chairs were laughing at the souped-up bodies on *Hawaii Five-O*. One wall was covered with arty pictures of nude or seminude men of the sort shown in *After Dark* magazine. "Hunks," they were called. Wall-to-wall beige tufted carpeting, brass candlestick lamps, fake brick walls, and a fireplace with a Duraflame artificial log gave the room the atmosphere of a middle-class den in Ohio.

From there they passed into one of the labyrinths popular in many of these bathhouses. The curving hallways spun people around so that they became mildly disoriented. This space-efficient maze was darkly blue, covered in thick carpet. Every few turns a small ultraviolet light would illuminate a badly proportioned figure painted on the curving wall—usually mermen, in keeping with the Minoan mythology. Some men's fake teeth turned black at these passes when hit by the light, causing them to curl their lips together or to avoid the lights altogether. A clump of toweled shufflers gathered, giving each other hand jobs or blow jobs. Nothing too complicated.

Beyond, there was a dark orgy room. Annie loved its cathedral-like silence. "It's a cave where men huddle to avoid the loneliness of the night," she whispered to Sean. Although there were nearly a hundred men milling, no one was speaking. Their sounds were limited to sighs, moans, shufflings. A big bed the size of four king-sized beds occupied the center of the room. On it a black man was pushing rudely into the behind of a white man with whom he was simultaneously grappling, causing them to lose their balance over and over. "They should be in *National Geographic*," Sean whispered back to Annie. A third was holding the balls of the black aggressor in a grip to pressure his mood. Two others were lying in a yin-yang design, a "69." Two more were rolling along the edge of the mattress. It was a dream of a bed out of a children's book in which sizes were miraculously transformed, a Wynken-Blynken-and-Nod vessel. Annie had to stop every two steps to disentangle herself from touchers reaching for her genitals. She actually felt a few erect penises swinging by on their way elsewhere. She felt she was inside a metronome of flesh. Sean seemed much less hassled. The man with the globular belly didn't embrace him from behind as he did Annie. "I'm tired," she whined to the man, unraveling herself, only to be embraced again soon. It was like a bad jungle movie in which vines kept wrapping themselves around lost adventurers.

Next, they climbed the steps from the orgy room to the cubicles above. These two floors of corridors were fiercer. "They're like perverse dollhouses," Annie said of the rows of rooms. "Or Francis Bacon's grislier paintings," Sean answered. "Weren't those his paintings they used under the credits in *Last Tango in Paris*?" she asked. *Last Tango* was their favorite movie, the first they had seen together.

Annie began to appraise the rooms to Sean artistically as conceptual art. She noticed repeating objects: K-Y tubes, spent towels, hookah pipes. She saw the men as sculptural: on their stomachs with a tube of lubricant next to them, waiting passively, or lying on their backs making themselves bigger, advertising their wares like the whores Sean had seen in Amsterdam, sitting in the picture windows of their living rooms as living advertisements for themselves. "Which lobster would you like?" Sean kidded her. Soon her empathy began to expand and she saw only loneliness and desperation. It was as if a painting turned to wet swirling oils in front of her, losing its dry image. She was moved out of any sense of where she was when she noticed a burly character, big and hairy, a construction-worker type, waving her in. She stepped into his cell. He began to kiss her right away and she felt herself swooning from his yellow beard, close in fullness to a Santa Claus beard. "I really like you, but I've had it for tonight," she managed to say, easing away.

"Let's go," Sean said, sensing that the joke had snapped.

They sat for a few minutes in the steam room, where Annie's mustache comically drooped and her bathrobe weighed more and more on her shoulders as it soaked up humidity. There they watched a young man with flipped hair who looked like Prince Valiant being serviced while he continually scouted over his shoulder for a better prospect at every sound of the aluminum door opening and closing.

They talked about it a bit as they exited onto the street, and then never again.

"I thought it would be more fun," Annie admitted.

"Yeah, it's more of a flesh thing here."

"It's romanticism in a mechanical setting. I liked the thought. But the actual faces and bodies are grounding. Compulsion is the catnip. If you don't eat any, all that's left is frustration, hope, loneliness, insecurity. You know?"

"It's more fun in places where people keep their clothes on," Sean promised. "We'll go to one sometime."

"Men have more ways to mask love than women."

• • •

On New Year's Day 1975, Sean rode the subways. He loved descending to the metal trains with their green metal walls, sprayed graffiti, anonymity. Especially on New Year's Day. Sean was always looking for inspiration. He was always renewing himself. Partly because he was absorbed with his reflection in the mirror of his own predicament. Partly because he needed new materials to work with.

Sean was very visual. He was always fascinated by walls, lights, shadows, colors. Arriving at the Eighth Avenue subway station at Fifty-ninth Street and Columbus Circle, he noticed the glaze of the white tile walls, felt the solid columns painted in a dark blue almost purple. The stillness of the underground station at noon appealed to him. The light of its bare bulbs had an evanescence. Sean had recently read de Chirico's one novel, a surrealistic work titled *Hebdomeros*. He was thinking of its terrain. He felt truly happy when he found a correspondence in the outside world to the terrain in his head—square white tiles and purple pillars to geometric piazzas and a clock in a clock tower stopped as if time were a noise that had simply ceased.

When the train arrived, Sean wandered on board. A few stray passengers sat in their own spots, no one in twos or threes. Men with big coats, wool ties tied broadly, hair growing below the brims of their hats. No women right then. Someone had left a *New York Times*. Sean picked it up, and reading the news, he felt that his own epoch was disappointing. The Vietnam War was over, so that the paper felt confident to print final numbers of casualties. Total deaths on both sides: 1,300,000. Sean was relieved that his draft number had been 324, too high to matter one way or the other. Besides, he had grown up in the safe zone of the northeastern American middle class. His father was an accountant in a public utilities firm. Inflation up 14.1 percent. Unemployment, 9.1 percent. New York City was in danger of bankruptcy, with plans for bailout including a proposal for union pension funds to buy bonds from Felix Rohatyn's Municipal Assistance Corporation. Sean was brought down by the news. The outside view, the view of the papers, was depressing. He preferred to read what was in front of his own eyes.

•   •   •

Across from him sat a short, teenage black boy. They were all riding an R train heading downtown. The boy's darkly gnarled hair was cut short, and he was wearing a cheap jacket made of red padding, black cotton pants, and plush black sneakers. In his hands he was holding a red hardbound book, obviously a library book. Sean was trying to catch the title but couldn't as the gold thread of its stitched title was faded.

From a small town where racial lines were drawn between Poles and Italians, or WASPs and Jews—lines that all but meshed invisibly in New York City—Sean had initially been warmed by what he felt was the exoticism of Puerto Ricans and blacks in the city. He felt it was Puerto Ricans who made Broadway glow. Puerto Ricans and Cubans. Up at Columbia, the fruits from the Spanish markets dressed up the sidewalks, and Sean often drank papaya, guava, and banana shakes from a Cuban joint on the corner of 104th. Their subtlety impressed him as so superior to the Carvel shakes—black and white—he had grown up on.

Down in Riverside Park during the spring nights of the demonstrations he had walked to the Soldiers and Sailors Monument at Ninety-fifth Street, where the air was pungent with the perfume of the gingko trees. The local Spanish boys from the neighborhood would appear there, like flowers that only blossomed at night. Like orchids, Sean remembered thinking. His favorites would zip by on their thin bicycles, usually red, usually battered. They would sit their butts on the tops of the old green benches in the shade made by the ragged edges of lamppost light. Or these pirates of the night would connive to go down even farther, through a dark tunnel onto the decrepit esplanades next to the Hudson River, while large brown rats with bright eyes made their own paths, similar to those of the skulking humans. Sean loved best the big flat boats—garbage barges—which silently floated by like ships of death when everyone was asleep in the safer faculty houses along the curve of Riverside Drive. They were urban versions of the carriages of death of Celtic folklore. Sometimes a group would be holding a victim at knifepoint, their voices rising in an exciting grumble. Sometimes a group would be talking like women or exchanging Qiana shirts with rose patterns they found desirable. But mostly there was just the quiet shuffling of bikes, and conversations on the edges of dumb incoherency.

Sean remembered best the night he had met a boy from Colombia dressed all in black—black gym trunks, black baseball cap, black sleeveless T-shirt. The blackness had excited him. Especially as it set off the boy's plumelike eyebrows, the kind that grew together over an aquiline nose. The boy took him home to his family's apartment on West 103rd Street between Broadway and West End Avenue. The family was away. That May Sean and Arnie had slipped off to the Queens County Art and Cultural Center— the old New York State pavilion from the 1964 World's Fair in Flushing—to see an exhibition of Joseph Cornell's constructions. It was one of the funny memories that was a bond for later. The trip had been Sean's idea. He loved Cornell's elegant boxes with their mysterious ingredients: bird cutouts, playing cards, cups, balls, sand, and strips of solar-system maps. Being in the Spanish apartment on West 103rd Street had seemed to Sean like being in one of those boxes. His heart jumped. The living room was all red,

red on red: blood-red shag rugs, wine-red walls, a Valentine's-red velvet couch, ruby-red glass ashtrays in amoebic shapes, crimson pincushions, pink chotchkes. He later forgot what they did there, but he never forgot the look of that apartment.

After he left the jewel box he had walked down the broad boulevard of 103rd Street back to Riverside Drive, strolling this time, taking the air as if he were a gentleman from the last century. His leisurely stroll was interrupted as he felt himself being shot at by a passing car filled with men and women, dressed exotically in a blur of plumes and sharkskin as if they were on their way to the Cotton Club. A thin tube had peeped through a side window. Sean felt the whisk of a bullet graze his forehead. Then the car disappeared in an exhaust of loud music. He just kept walking, stunned as much by the casualness of his survival as by his near death: his skull could have been smashed into bits of broken plaster. New York City possessed a colorful violence, always.

One night Sean was held up by three Spanish juveniles in the dark of the park. He only had about two dollars in his wasted wallet. The skimpy sum made them angry. Sean was soon flat on the gravel, his cheek against the soil, being kicked by thin sneakers. During a lull in the abuse, he realized they didn't know what to do next. One started talking about having a gun. He felt that they were embarrassed by their own amateurish awkwardness and indecision. To stay was to push their vulnerability. So he decided to run, all the while imagining he was feeling a bullet in his back. It was as if he were continually running through the same repeated sequence of trees, like in the educational black-and-white movie version of *Occurrence at Owl Creek Bridge* shown so often in his high school. Then he was back in the dorm. Then he was pulling on himself, jerking fast, dreaming of his tormentors.

•   •   •

The popular theory about drugs then was that grass led to acid which led to heroin. Heroin was becoming as popular as soul music, jazz, ragtime, and mood rings. Sean hadn't noticed such a sequence in drugs in his own life, but he had a similar theory of sexual experience with different races, of its escalation and meaning. His first taste of other races had been the Spanish boys in Riverside Park. Inured to olive complexions, he was then able to imagine the taste of black skin. He began to smell a recognizable cologne—tart, strong—on certain black men passing by. He eyed the scorpion necklaces hanging from some of their necks, and the size of their basketball sneakers. More and more he liked the look of very dark skin, skin which brought out the pink or cherry coloring of tongues and the insides of mouths. Sean found himself staring through the wire fences around basketball courts in the park as if through a forbidding grid. One night he finally brought home to Furnald Hall someone from the park who played, he claimed, with a professional basketball team. Sean lay back, running his fingers through the underbrush of the looming athlete's hair, letting the long, six-foot-five body try to find room for itself on his floor mattress. His onetime visitor went home to his wife while it was still dark.

Sean stopped flashing back as the IND train stopped at Broadway-Lafayette, one of the largest and most complicated of subway stations. As the young man with the red book descended, Sean followed. The smell of ammonia was strong in the station. So was the atmosphere of sleaziness, reminding Sean of all the worst homosexual landscapes: bus-station men's rooms, dangerous parks, the backs of parked trucks. They were spots where dead bodies were always being uncovered like clues in a board game.

The boy, whose eyes curved like almonds, was giving him sidelong looks. Brown almond eyes. Sean caught up.

"What are you reading?"

"*Catcher in the Rye.*"

Sean was surprised to find such a sign of sophistication. He was also disappointed to have his hoodlum stereotype blown apart so easily. But he felt safer heading into a scary men's room with someone who knew who Holden Caulfield was.

Its green metal door was ajar, creaking as they pushed in, chains jangling. No one inside today. Universal smell of cleanser mixed with an even stronger smell of urine and ashes. A central light bulb exposed all the imperfections of the gray-and-green linoleum flooring, pockmarked and broken like the surface of the moon. A single toilet stall at the far end had no door. The boy walked over. Sean followed. Soon they both pulled their pants down. They were swept up by a completely irrational choreography: did everything. Sean felt his throat stripped of its soft, protective mucus. He felt his behind similarly strip-mined. He did the same to his friend. When he was inside him he felt as if he were in a vise. The two of them were glad to get away without any interruptions from the police.

As they left together, Sean pretended to himself that he and his smaller friend were Adam and Eve kicked out of the Garden of Eden. Not because the cubicle had been such a Paradise. But he felt desultory, let down somehow.

But when he looked over at the red novel carried so securely in his young, laconic friend's palm, he felt elated again.

"Come with me, I'll film you," he said.

•   •   •

Edgar received the midnight phone call in bed with all the lights turned off. The ringing kept on, so that he finally turned over and picked up, simultaneously flicking on the switch of a metal pole of a reading light. He had been sleeping in his soft cotton Brooks

Brothers striped pajamas. To Edgar, these were secure swaddling clothes.

"I think I have a problem," Sean was saying through the mechanism. "I have a burning when I pee. I have a clicking feeling in my asshole. I'm so tired I can barely scramble an egg."

Edgar's bedroom was starkly vacant. Minimal. Its only ornament, a pyramid of glass by a woman artist humming chartreusely in the corner of the room, humming from its geometry rather than from any sound. Edgar fixed his look on its several linear illusions while he gave advice.

"It sounds as if you have a case of the clap. I'll give you a number for Dr. Bennett in the West Seventies. He's the world's expert in all this."

The next afternoon Sean weakly stepped down the two steps to Dr. Bennett's office. When he rang the bell, its two pale green doors snapped open like parts of a mechanized version of a French château.

The mood of Dr. Bennett's office, hidden away on the Upper West Side, reminded Sean of the Flamingo discotheque. Here, too, the singularly male tones, the blazing orchids and the distant trendy music, "Can't Get Enough of Your Love, Babe," broadcast through overhead speakers as softly as Muzak Mozart, seemed designed to accommodate some unnamed but obviously shared lifestyle. As this wasn't Sean's taste, he didn't feel the delight.

"You look like you could use your own Accu-Jac Two," joked the doctor's receptionist, a young man with a tan brush of a mustache, his flannel shirt a rich mix of Indian-war-paint reds, firwood greens, eyeliner blues, the cuticles of his fingers each showing perfectly pale white quarter-moons. "Unlike Accu-Jac One, this one will fornicate you *and* masturbate you, and has a speed control, depth-control suction, and stroke-length control. Price, five hundred and fifty dollars. . . . My name's Tim."

Was he doing a routine? Did he somehow mean this? Sean noticed thankfully that Tim exuded a ruddy healthiness.

"Who recommended you?" Tim asked more levelly as a shinily bald lab assistant in a white medical smock walked by, running his finger examiningly along the tops of gray metal filing cabinets, somehow subtly communicating humor in his pace rather than in his expression.

"Edgar Savage."

"Oh," replied the receptionist, taking notes.

"A regular customer?"

"No. But he sends us many clients. He's a social friend of Dr. Bennett's."

Sean found a seat in the waiting room located through an arch to the right. Two other men were sitting on soft couches covered in plum, peach, and beige fabrics, the smell of freshly cut yellow mums faintly mixing in the air with that of an acrid new coat of cream paint. One of the men waiting looked like he came out of a Brooks Brothers ad. Sean recognized the style from Edgar. The other was in jeans smeared with tar, and he had a pink owlish face sprouting whiskers. The mood throughout the office seemed upbeat. This general practitioner obviously had an optimistic, devoted following. Sean wondered why, and soon found out.

Waiting for his turn to meet Dr. Bennett, he looked through the pile of magazines on a squat teakwood table, all of them gay-themed, replacing the usual doctor's office selection of *National Geographic* or *Family Circle* with *Mandate* ("Magazine of Entertainment and Eros"), *After Dark, In Touch, Blueboy* ("The National Magazine About Men"). A cover story in the *Advocate* prophesied that the new year, 1975, would be "the Year of the Disco." Also out was the premiere issue of *Drummer,* the first gay S&M "slick," forty pages long, with an article on prison life and biker clubs as well as an excerpt from the novella *My Brother, My Slave.* Its cover was a line drawing of a big brother holding up his T-shirt to reveal garish, misshapen muscles. The only regular publication on display was *Time,* its excuse for inclusion a cover story on Air Force sergeant Leonard Matlovich's legal maneuver to be reinstated in the military. The headline: " 'I AM A HOMOSEXUAL': The Gay Drive for Acceptance."

A sci-fi feeling of being on another planet, an entirely gay planet, drew Sean back in a puff of memory to the 55th Street Playhouse, where he had seen a Jack Wrangler movie a week before. He forgot the title. In the movie, Wrangler, in tight jeans the shade of a powdery Alabama sky, was driving home through San Francisco. When Wrangler tuned in to his car radio, a station was broadcasting a gay announcer delivering only gay news. When he arrived home, the telephone repairman, the super, and the electrician were all different gay stereotypes. Predictably, Wrangler wound up in a sexual knot with each one. The movie impressed Sean mostly by its evocation of a science-fiction world in which everyone was gay.

Sean was comparing the more far-out and cartoonish characters in gay porn—cowboys, marines, truckers—with the more ordinary bosses and secretaries portrayed in the straight flesh films he'd snuck into in Times Square, when suddenly he was interrupted by the doctor.

"Mr. Devlin?"

The doctor had the same chesnut complexion as his receptionist. Sean felt an attraction as he followed him into his soap-opera set of an office, where he was soon slumped in an Edwardian desk chair upholstered in green leather that the doctor had gestured towards with his strong, weathered hand. Sean liked the glowing sheen of the doctor's head, the intelligence in his eyes. There was something fatherly about doctors. Having a young, desirable doctor gave fresh wind to old sails. I think I could find something to like about any man, he thought to himself at that moment. It turned out the doctor was a Columbia College grad, and so they had a few moments of hurrah, though Sean had to admit that he had dropped out too soon to have many warm memories.

"I was a philosophy major," Dr. Bennett revealed, braggingly pointing to one of the many degrees encased in glass on a background of tasteful pink-and-cream-striped wallpaper.

"I was lapsed," Sean admitted.

Dr. Bennett had decided to become a general practitioner with a cushy practice, enlisting mostly homosexual men with innocent cases of clap or crabs, though more resistant strains of gonorrhea were showing up, too, usually blamed on soldiers back from Vietnam.

The office's furniture owed its appearance to sleight of hand. Its huge green velvet drapes, like those pictured in nineteenth-century still-life paintings, weren't really covering windows. Most of the books on the low shelf had obviously been bought at a flea market: unreadable titles, long-lost mystery novels from the 1920s. A marbleized fireplace with brass stokers was fake.

"Let's take a look at you," Dr. Bennett suggested, segueing smoothly into the next, inevitable phase.

He accompanied Sean only as far as the hallway, where the fluorescent lighting marking the rest of the rooms began. There he passed him off to Barney, a goofily friendly man, the one in the smock who had been testing for dust earlier. As Sean returned for a series of tests and checkups over the next few weeks, he began to think of Barney as Dr. Bennett's sidekick, relating to Bennett as if he were his superior on a talk show. He made his boss look good. He completed the dirty work, leaving the doctor to sing the songs, songs usually of Latinate pharmaceuticals.

"Barney will test you out," said Dr. Bennett with a slow wink.

It all happened as fast as a streak of flashlight against a wall in a blackened room. Sean was stretched flat on his stomach on an examining table, his nose pressed into a teeny radio speaker playing an oversized symphony. Barney's gloved middle finger went up his quivering rectum. Sean held on to it as forcefully as a baby holds on to an adult's thumb. Next a proboscope with a light on its tip peered up there. A tonsil stick was inserted in the cleft of his penis to collect paste. Thermometer. Blood-pressure gripping. Overhead-spotlight staring. Knee banged. Throat scraped. Eyes dilated with drops. Slowly Sean felt a crying feeling, then a panicking, left alone in the room as the door shut. The clear music seemed menacing or sterilizing. He had done something very bad. He was in a police lineup. He did not know what was happening. He had never felt so weak, so yellow, so compromised. He felt he had been handed a lovely gift at birth, only to let it rot.

The eventual entrance of Dr. Bennett with a hand held out was like all those murals of Christ, Sean thought, casting back to the apses of Greek Orthodox churches he had visited during his summer in Europe. They pictured the haloed god pulling scarred, black-faced damned souls out of hell with one strong arm.

"Errrgh" was all Sean said.

"I'm afraid you have three ailments," the doctor immediately reported. "Venereal warts in your anus, which we will need to remove with special surgery; a case of gonorrhea in your penis, treatable by antibiotics; and amoebas treated by Flagyl, which might make you feeble for a few days."

"What?" Sean asked quietly while feeling a roar in him, a trembling wave of nearly black unconsciousness. He had lost something, been gypped of something.

"These are quite normal responses, lifestyle responses," the doctor answered from a distance, as if drawing on his academic studies of Druids or dervishes. "I'll write up your prescription and tell you something helpful when you zip up."

When Sean joined him in his office he was making a line drawing of a prescription on his pad.

"What's helpful?" Sean asked.

"If you go the baths to find recreational sex, it might be helpful to take two antibiotic pills first, so that any bacteria to which you might be exposed will be killed before taking hold."

Sean's understanding was at first blank. The pills were poison without death. He was mentally photographing Dr. Bennett's face carefully, feeling that here was some sort of bargain. Then he gladly accepted the sophisticated solution: a finer, easier response than his earlier heavy cake-and-ale of provincial guilt and bad feelings.

"Write it down," Sean insisted.

The doctor's writing made a scratching sound.

●　●　●

Sean spent the next few weeks limp. Annie would bring him his favorite chicken-and-rice soup from the Chinese take-out. Then she would leave to rehearse at CBGB's, or the Other End, where she was lining up gigs.

"Flagyl is made with little bits of arsenic," Arnie clued him in over the phone.

Sean believed it. Going to the bathroom was like crawling through a field of yellow that was drawing him always backwards to a listless sleep. There was no standing up. He was a scarecrow. When Dr. Bennett and Barney removed the venereal warts, they entered his anus with burning equipment. It seemed a medieval Inquisition of the insides of his body. He found it difficult to separate the physical from a moral shadow.

The first weekend he felt refreshed he went to the Everard Baths. There among the human intertwinings in the orgy room stood a monumental Dr. Bennett, nude with poppers in both his nostrils, dominating a relief in which three other men were all over his body, like the marble snakes of the statue of Laocoön Sean had seen in the Vatican Museum, though in the original the dynamic was of resistance on the part of the main figure rather than indulgence. All those about him were similarly hooked up to vials, bottles, soaked handkerchiefs. Tubes might as well have been looped out of his nostrils into their anuses and out of their anuses through each other's mouths. It was truly a testament to the doctor's belief in his preventive tablets that Sean had taken for the first time that night. He snorted at the private joke.

Punks, Sex Garage

I t's an omen," Annie said, standing on the Bowery in a winter's wind. She was talking about a bird, a blackbird, always a rare sighting on the streets of New York. This one was balanced on a high wire stretching down from the nearby Amato Opera Company to CBGB's, where Annie was playing that night. The cab they left behind appeared orange in the dark of the night.

"A good omen or bad?"

"Good."

Sean was looking in a jumble over at Annie in her black leather outfit modeled on fifties biker chicks' as well as on what the gay guys were wearing in the clubs she loved over by the river. He felt a first flash of how much she depended on omens, signs, portents. Hers was a religion of coincidences. It wasn't enough that someone called; Annie had to have just been thinking about him a few minutes before. All around their apartment at the Chelsea she burned incense sticks, laid out tarot cards. Next to her bed she kept a golden *I Ching* with a beautiful narrow red silk page marker that Sean liked to slide between his fingers while they plotted and giggled on her bed.

"Where did your mystical views come from? It's not like New Jersey is exactly Tibet." They were standing in the middle of the gray sidewalk in front of the small swinging doors leading into the club.

"I think my mother has Gypsy blood in her. Can't you see it?"

Sean could make out a fascinating occult physiognomy if he looked: especially her nose, crooked as the nose of the Indian chief on old nickels with feathers exploding behind the promontory of his head. Her black hair, cut as if chipped from bark, took on a fierce otherness. She wanted to evoke different outlaws—gays, Indians, Gypsies—to express her feeling that the top of her head was a geyser. At least that's how Sean romantically formulated her insistent attitude. Or perhaps it was the joint they'd smoked in the car that was thinking in him, all golden as it smokily collapsed when he said the word "blessed" unprovoked, out loud, causing Annie to giggle.

He found time while he was looking for evidence of her Gypsy blood to notice how she was presenting herself for this important concert: black leather vest, white blouse opened in a billowing V, black jeans, belt slung down around the shirt, which was tumbling over her pants. Mostly she was a silver-and-turquoise jewelry totem, covered with lots of hearts, crosses, leather bands, wisps of feathers pinned to her vest, medallions. She was a fantasy welling up out of the sixties but transposed, Sean decided. Hers was hippiness fiercely redirected. He could analyze her messages more clearly than he could analyze his own. He often used her as his pointer, taking his cues from her. Where she looked for omens in the world, he looked for omens in her. His was a similarly juvenile irresponsibility, differently expressed.

"That's where Lauren Hutton lives."

Edgar, ever the historian, was interrupting almost in mid-sentence and mid-stride as he walked up while pointing across the street to a vanilla-beige cake's-icing of a building. The building seemed to be delighting in itself with its many stories (six) and its tracery of fire escapes. And so was Edgar delighting in himself that night. The wind messing with his silver hair, his brown leather jacket zipped to its limit, he was pleased with their simultaneous arrivals, its timing a signal to Annie as well, who was noticeably more loving to him than usual as she wrapped her arms around his waist and Sean joined them in a three-way circle warm in its geometry.

"Shall we?" Edgar asked, relying on some cue from past doorways. The doors, numbered 315, swinging on their hinges, were subdivided into smoky rectangular panes, smaller versions of the bigger panes in the front walls to both sides, creating the impression of a college rathskeller gone to seed.

Inside, the long hall of a club was tight, crowded, painted black like so many spray-painted bathrooms or glo-painted apartments in the neighborhood. A typed list was being checked at a table by the door. Confusing coat-and-cigarettes booth to the side. All the stools along the bar on one side taken; a wall phone ringing in everyone's ears. A long alley of tables on the other side, all facing the stage. Orange and red neon beer signs hung from the black ceiling like heraldry: Löwenbräu, Miller, Piels. The stage was far back beyond the pool table, a distant destination, an eye watching the place fall into pieces as it filled up. Next to the stage were two flights of stairs leading down to a bathroom where pasty-white kids, some of them squeezing mimeographed books of poems under their arms, shot up together or singly. Near the single toilet in its corner they could feel up each other's bodies, pee, snort, float trial balloons of propositions.

The club had been getting a stripe of publicity for the new bands being billed: the Ramones, Blondie, Television, Talking Heads, the Shirts. Some of these were being labeled "glitter backlash" in print for their minimalist, tight reconstructions of garage bands pre-Beatles, the era when the members were still kids collecting transistor radios and 45s, so there was nostalgia in their blacker, whiter, block-style presentations, the giggling insider stuff of early movements. Amos Poe was filming for his movie *Night Lunch,* with its Scotch-taped-together look. A couple years later the word "punk" would be used, certainly for the Ramones, if not for the Talking Heads or Television, usually named "art bands."

At first glance, Sean was surprised to notice the dress: so much black leather. It was fifties-hoodlum black leather, Elvis leather. He had become so holed up in the gay clubs to the west that he hadn't realized the same look was being devised here as at the Ramrod or the Eagle's Nest. The two movements were two wires touched together to fashion a similar mood: snarling, reactive, liberating, and artful. But there was also lots of geeky elementary-school wear, purposely unglittering: white button-down shirts, black sweaters, tan chinos, Buster Brown shoes.

Annie went off into a crowd of chalky faces.

"It's like a magic act if you go with someone to their own performance," Sean was shouting at Edgar. "She's here. She disappears. And then she reappears in another realm, far away. Like the magician who puts a black hanky over a dove in a cage downstage that instantly reappears on a twig midair."

A moving into chairs, tables, pumpkin-colored banquettes in the cave of the back was creating a frequency like a tuning fork's. People seemed to know they were about to hear something very interesting. Until now Annie had performed her works at the St. Mark's Poetry Project as one of the new young poets who were borrowing from performance and rock 'n' roll, moving away from the flat, sophisticated, lockjawed, and ironic delivery of the first- and second-generation New York school poets who had headlined the place for ten years. John Giorno and Anne Waldman were Annie's peers in adding beat, hip, pelvis, drum, and guitars to their poems. But she pulled the lever the fastest and strongest. She was the most out there, finding a strong place from which to emote—her earlier work with women's masturbation at the Firehouse having primed her.

There was even a photo of her in *Mandate*. When Annie spread open the issue for Sean on his editing table, he spent a half-hour looking at it. Next to her picture they had typed her up as a "best bet," talked of her performances at St. Mark's and the Other End, reported an incipient deal with Arista Records. But he soon became more interested in the rest of the magazine, in the pressing of flesh between art and sex. Lots of pages were given to Al Pacino's new film, *Dog Day Afternoon*. There were gelatin photos of Baryshnikov, who had defected from the Soviet Union the year before.

Most intriguing to Sean was the monthly *Mandate* man. These weren't porn stars, but regular guys. That month's—February 1975—was Frederick, a friend of a friend of Sean's. There he was with his Greek-statue jawline, Greek-statue curly hair, feline eyes, in a double-breasted "gangster-banker" suit in his stretched living room; and in the next picture, nude, long penis hanging down, nipples onyx marbles on a rolling surface of plaster skin. Sean loved how silly Frederick looked. He wondered if he could do it. No. He realized he was fascinated by anyone who would pose. And then there were photos of men smiling up from the floor of a baths' orgy room. Again, not models: regular citizens with day jobs, proud to affirm a sunny feeling with their goofy eyes and puffed lips and unexceptional bodies.

Annie came on like the bird she had just pointed to: black, exotic, seemingly capable of just vanishing. Her two support band members, on keyboard and drums, looked like American Indians, their hair so long, their irises reflecting the blue of a distant gelled light so that neither of them seemed of this world. But they added a hemispheric global whirl of sound to her otherwise urban, and urbane, performance. Annie was thinking Rimbaud, Baudelaire. They were thinking Thunder God, Peyote Cyclone. The mesh worked, muting the tougher, current, almost journalistically seismic lyrics of her chanted songs. One was "Words to Be Broadcast Over Eagle's Nest Sound System." Most didn't catch the references. But they caught an unusual cleft. "AM radio bondage songs / out of touch / brought back hard / in the nose / in the legs," she sang. "The dynamite sounds / jukebox / still in my head / my head / knocked against that wall / wet / smelling one guy after another." She closed with a song written by her friend Camille O'Grady—they went to high school together, were working New York in a similar fashion. The ballad was called "Toilet Kiss." "Toilet kiss / Porcelain piss" were the lyrics Annie repeated over and over. It was as if the dark blue light had enveloped her onstage, the sort that flares in Hindu art behind goddesses with the legs of centipedes.

Sean's breathing stopped short when he noticed Bob Dylan leaning against a wall on the side where the noise emptied out: the club was an uneven saucer acoustically. Many other audience members as well took in Dylan's hair, eyes, presence intermittently while Annie expressed her confidence onstage. With studied humility, Dylan jockeyed to talk to Annie backstage after her ceremony of a performance. Sean noted all this history satisfactorily. Then he split for the bar.

"It's Jonathan," Sean said as he pitched among all the shoulders to get to the bar.

"I sniff trouble," Edgar laughed, following behind him like a shrewd driver maneuvering behind an ambulance to get through traffic.

Jonathan, who had moved from the Chelsea a month ago, was leaning, slightly transformed, against the bar, tooling a green beer bottle in his big palm. Sean felt the same vertical thrill he had felt the first time he had seen him in the lobby a couple of winters ago. But now Jonathan's hair was cascading down his back, rock-'n'-roll style. He was wearing a motorcycle jacket a size too small for him with the word "Deutschland" stitched confusingly across the back. With him was a petite blond young woman dressed similarly, drinking from a similar emerald bottle.

"Buddy, this is Stacey. This is my buddy Sean I was telling you about. The freak?"

"Yeah . . . yeah!" she said, obviously having heard a few stories that agreed with her as she looked with renewed interest Sean's way.

Edgar was happy to order everyone beers from the bar. He felt his mission would protect him. Stacey careened Sean off to a tight corner to talk privately.

"Jonathan said you're into film," said Stacey, seizing at Sean's attentiveness. "Are you? 'Cause we are. I want someone to film him, butt naked, with his hair that falls all the way down to his crack. It's blond, you know. And it should be in a film. I like him to prance around in the nude while I admire his every feature."

Sean divined something of hippie paisleys and girlish polka dots about Stacey.

"Are your parents German?" he asked when he noticed the surprising light blue in her unfocused eyes.

In the dusk of another corner to which Sean then had been led, Jonathan pressed home the same points. "I told Stacey all about you and we've been talking about this night."

"What about it?"

"How you're a filmmaker. How you adore me. And she does great things to me with her hands. But really she digs keeping her clothes on and me havin' my clothes off while I get into different positions. Another guy joins us sometimes. Once me and the other guy went to this birthday party of this teenage chick and we both just sat on the couch together cranking off while they made wishes on us. Get it? We were like the candles."

"I think I'm supposed to do something with Edgar later, or Annie."

"Edgar can come. One of the positions Stacey diagrammed for me has the back of someone's head watching me, no face or nothing, dressed, but watching."

" 'Diagrammed'? This is pretty far gone."

"You said it."

"But is she diagramming movie shots?" Sean asked professionally.

"Mostly Polaroids. You got a Polaroid camera? We like to watch me develop from yellow to real-life colors."

Sean was happily amazed at what he was hearing. Jonathan never lost his ability to talk seemingly from upstage right in Sean's own head. He satisfied Sean's apparently bottomless need for the casually bizarre.

"You're like coming across a deer in the forest," Sean said.

"No comprende, caballero."

The next parts of the puzzle were put together quickly, as when a jigsaw piece, or crossword, allows time to speed up and solutions to fall haphazardly into place.

Annie told Sean she was going on to Phebe's, a couple blocks up the Bowery, with Bob Dylan; it was where the Ridiculous Theatrical Company actors hung out after performances. They would have gone to Max's on Union Square, but it had recently closed.

Sean had read a eulogy for the place in the *Voice* that week. Annie's black lipstick left a smear on his neck. It turned out Edgar didn't want to be the back of the head in Stacey's staged shots of Jonathan. But he had a Polaroid camera he said he wanted to give to Sean. So they all stopped by his penthouse, then went on to the apartment on Perry Street near Hudson—two blocks west of Sean's first Village apartment—where Jonathan and Stacey were living in picturesque chaos.

The apartment resembled a sitcom set from the fifties, a decade when sunken spaces were particularly mesmerizing, as apparently were bear rugs and tiger skins, judging from the popular magazines. All were follies of design in a straightforward era. The sunken spaces had the advantage of being like navels.

In Jonathan and Stacey's the kitchen was a tiny balcony entered by way of a peepholed door accessorized with door chains, police locks, latches. The flap of kitchen was sliced off rather quickly by a New Orleans–style wrought-iron balustrade that curved down into a scroll lining a drop of three steps into the main room, the only other room except for a black-tiled bathroom. The apartment's walls, like the building's stucco exterior, were painted a green Stacey described as "puke." Its big plus was a horizontal window running the length of the apartment, on the sill of which she was growing pots of geraniums, little umber circles.

"Let's make the diagrams come alive," Stacey sang. "Diagrams" was obviously one of the cooing words at the intimate nexus of their love and voyeuristic extravagance. It was the extravagance Sean felt drawn to.

"Are we going to fly tonight?" he asked hopefully.

"First let's take mushrooms," Jonathan advised, digging into the freezer for a plastic bag containing chips of the ancient mysteries of the Aztecs.

The mushrooms were at once bitter and tasteless. Sean swallowed them while experimenting with the Polaroid, delighting with yips and whoops as pictures came whirring out the side like paper towels off a roll. He wanted to take the pictures Stacey wanted him to take in her diagrams. And sometimes he did. But as the peyote began to saturate the lining of his stomach and move out from there, his heat, and heatedness, rose. When he closed his eyelids, patterns of minimal exactitude, of dots and lines and angles, impressed themselves on him as if on a screen or a slide. Was that where his secret emotional weight really lay? he wondered. In experiences such as he was having at that moment he missed having Edgar nearby to discuss matters. Then his eyes were pried open by Stacey. Or so he felt.

"Let's go. He's in the tub. He's in the shower. It's like a jungle in there. Hurry."

To Sean's ears Stacey was squealing.

The pictures weren't so far from the standard cheesy shots taped to truckers' cabins rumbling all over America—though with a guy featured instead of a girl. Stacey wanted Jonathan dripping wet. She liked angles from behind, with his hair a waterfall cascading. She manipulated her hand around him like a snake around a scepter for a few regal shots. He stretched to show his own renditions of ecstasy. And of course she behaved as if his erection was a call to messianic somethinghood. It was at least safer, Sean thought, than drinking at the West Beach bar on Christopher Street, where a killer had been picking up different men, taking them home, slicing them into meat pies.

The Polaroids piled up like playing cards. They were often just black-gray-white atmospheres when the camera misfired. Or they were garish shots of losers in a forbidden circus. But Sean imbued them as he took them with all of his pictorial intelligence. He saw Goya in the cloud of a pillow. Or El Greco in the marble of

Jonathan's skinny butt. Or Warhol in his own peeping. They had their fantasies. He had his.

"Look at Sean," Jonathan was bellowing to Stacey, who was so amazed by the drug that her back was up against the wall. "His eyes are oozing out of his head. He's so into me. His forehead is a flashbulb."

"His eyes are tadpole jelly," she joined in.

Sean believed them. He felt a little bad about it, too. He didn't know what he was doing in this room. Jonathan and Stacey were together. He was apart. I'm having a bad trip, he thought to himself.

He stopped taking pictures.

•   •   •

Jonathan and Stacey had finally washed down enough Valium to fall asleep on their double mattress on the floor.

Sean, still awake, having declined the pills, felt the light of early morning as a wash of prickles on his skin. It was as if the sun's rays were the tongue of a family dog waking him to go for a walk. All stumbles, he left Jonathan and Stacey's front door ajar, nimbly maneuvering his way up the stairs of the building onto its roof. There, next to a jungle hut of a water tower, he sat at dawn, vibrating from the last peals of the mushrooms.

It was chilly, so he held himself together, a pea coat borrowed from Jonathan's closet cloaked over his own black leather. He stared across the street to a pink building. Pink! He was amazed at a pink building in Manhattan. Then he noticed a light blue one next to it. Gray! Apricot! The floral buildings, invisible to him until then, reminded him of Lisbon, where he had once docked briefly. In Lisbon he had been looking for exotic, pastel colors. He found them in tiles and oversized bougainvillea. But he had managed until that morning to overlook the tropical beauty mismatched in his own northern city by its winds, slow cold months, snow. He watched as dozens of morning birds, veering off course, cast shadows on the buildings. Starling shadows scudding on a pink West Village wall!

Sean was taking his retinal pleasures. Those were usually his ladder out. But this morning he was held down. It was the bad trip's bad feeling. He wanted to stand up to it as if it were a big black grizzly bear, not just the black scissoring shadows of birds on walls.

So he gathered himself to call Sister Mariah Maria.

●   ●   ●

Three days later Sean walked across the close of the Cathedral of Saint John the Divine towards a faux-medieval gray stone tower attached to an office building, where Sister Mariah Maria had set up her offices. A nun in a liberal order that allowed her to practice psychotherapy and live in her own apartment, she was one of those in line waiting for the Episcopal Church to begin to ordain women priests. Sean felt as if she were an aunt of Annie's as she was also a woman staking out a wilderness trail. And so he felt comfortable.

Or as comfortable as he could ever feel with therapists. He tended to go to them for a few sessions, serendipitously, as he had gone to his college shrink. And he usually went to ones in the Morningside Heights neighborhood, a neighborhood he associated with his one weak year in college. Getting off the subway at 110th Street and Broadway, he felt diminished.

Sister Mariah Maria had been highly recommended to Sean by Canon Michael Nelson Swarth. Sean had met that grand old wizard while a student. During the days of the small Columbia riots of 1972 he had taken to going to morning prayer with a thin friend, as elegant in his intelligence as Oscar Wilde, who was a friend of Swarth's. Indeed the friend, Neil, a volunteer as altar boy at those 7:15 masses, used to quote Oscar Wilde at least once every time they met. "As the master used to opine," he would say, using a voice well out of his age league to refer to Wilde, " 'Every saint has a past and every sinner a future.' "

Sean enjoyed these morning services. The hour made him feel as if he were padded in cotton, as did the mumbling of everyone reciting the lines of psalms in singsong. Central Casting couldn't have supplied a more solidly eye-catching figure than Canon Michael Nelson Swarth, a priest in his sixties who dressed in Russian gold robes, his white beard a statement of separation and eccentricity, yet attuned in its ecclesiastical references to a place and therefore not too aggrandizing, his eyes alert, his voice paying attention to caesuras lost to most since the seventeenth century, his dog's-head walking stick varnished oak. A Jamaican woman at Mass felt she had been cured of cancer by Canon Swarth and so came every morning as her assumed part of the bargain. An ex–merchant marine was sexton. Stone angels unfurled banners on which Latin tags undulated. Sean made out stories in the Tiffany windows that he had first thrilled to as a boy. It was like taking a comforting bath.

Canon Swarth inevitably invited Sean up to his apartment. Located in the diocesan house of the cathedral, the apartment, "Chapel Perilous," as Neil insisted on nicknaming it, was not dissimilar from the chapel. Its windows, though, were covered by bronzed mirrors. "I hate nature," Swarth explained of his crotchety lack of a wish to look out on the trees and squirrels. A glittering case held the tiny communion cup of the czarevitch who had been shot during the Russian Revolution as well as the young martyr's photo in a locket. Fabergé eggs lined shelves. A chandelier created auburn shadows in pewter mugs. Three Irish setters disrupted all conversation as they tumbled over their stainless-steel bowls full of food. Canon Swarth had gained his attentive respect when Sean once tried to bow out, secretly having plans to visit the Continental Baths. "We can feed you better than you'll be fed where you're going," Swarth warned, his eyes flashing like scimitars. The Slavophile canon taught him a Russian mantra to be timed to his breathing. Sean practiced the mantra running along the beach at Fire Island that summer but soon dropped the meditation as merely a finely embroidered toy from a distant but powerless pashadom. He was similarly not entranced by his few lunches at the canon's, where young men similar to Neil in the tailoring of their gifted minds drank sherry, talked high and low, but seemed too anemic for Sean. (Best was when he had brought along Annie, who held her own against Swarth in a Glenfiddich scotch drinking contest.) Yet Sean would always elect Swarth for advice such as choosing a therapist. He followed up, calling Sister Mariah Maria, who knew him from occasional appearances in the past three years at cathedral parties.

The sister was pleasing in a schoolteacher way. Her thinning red hair was cut in acceptable wisps. She preferred gray or tartan dresses. Her attitude was not at all judging or fragile. She seemed more cracker barrel than pulpit. She loaded Sean with biscuits of common sense and sent him on his way. Or she merely listened, the more ordinary psychiatric tactic. Sean lay on his back on a gray couch in the tower room shaped like a mummy's box.

"I wonder where it comes from that I enjoy watching so much. I like three-ways because they give me an out. And yet all I think about are these scenarios. It's like I'm burning up with sex and am equally sexless."

"What's your earliest memory of a three-way?" Sister Mariah Maria asked in a North Carolina curlicue.

"My mom and dad and I. I used to hump up and down on the backseat when we went on long trips while they sat up front like royalty."

"You're slipping into fantasy again," Sister Mariah Maria warned in a voice too measured for Sean's taste.

"Well, it's more like free association," he disagreed.

"Tell me the most exciting things you saw when you were a child."

"My mother taking down her girdle in front of me. Whew!"

"What else?"

"Ask me about the most exciting things I didn't see but was told about and so imagined."

"Okay. Consider yourself asked."

"Terry told me he'd show me his pubic hair the next time we were in the boys' room in fifth grade. He didn't but I imagined it. Dad told me about sitting out most of his high-school football games on the bench. I pictured him on that bench. I heard that Duane, a slick hood, made Jerry, a pimply guy who did his homework every day, get down and lick his penny loafers in geography class in front of all the girls. Jerry was good at German. I heard that Walter smoked in the lav. I imagined his billowing smoke going into *my* lungs. I ached for cigarette smoke in my lungs."

"Your eyes seem to be untaken roads. They seem to be accesses for your mind, or your imagination, but not your body."

"Oh," Sean answered, disappointed in himself, as well as in the sameness of the message from all shrinks.

The session ended after forty-five minutes. He said he'd call for another in his series of appointments. But he knew he wouldn't. Sister Mariah Maria affirmed an interpretation of his life that was targeted, even accurate. But he knew somehow that accuracy was not what he needed that season, though perhaps in another, matured season he would.

Sean didn't really want to mature yet. He didn't really want satisfaction yet.

Satisfaction is counterproductive, he thought smugly as he wound his way down around the variously shaped steps of the tower.

•   •   •

"It's filled with lingam."

Donna Blaktikh, a trustee of the Museum of Modern Art, thin, tanned, wrapped in different severities of black, decorated in different base metals, was describing a banner of Shiva fluttering from her upper balcony into the main room, where her Sunday-afternoon cocktail party already sounded like an atonal choral work with lots of electronic simulations of "tink" and "tank" sounds.

"We got it on our last trip to India," she said of the fluttering painting, an icon that appealed to Sean because of its sexy, golden prettiness.

"Is there any relation, do you think, between 'Shiva' and 'shiv,' the Gypsy word for knife?" Edgar asked loosely.

A glass sheet shaped like a bird's wing took up an entire wall of the Upper East Side apartment. Outside was a cold concrete garden with minimalist sculptures by artists who had taken the notion of the stick figure into a zone where prehistoric and futuristic met. That's where Donna's husband, the other half of the "we" who went on the Indian trip, was letting snowflakes fall into his plastic cup of gin. He was a vision, like some character in a drawing-room play. He was as fat as his stone companions were thin.

Sean eyed the waiter in the short white jacket behind the bar, serving drinks at the rate of two a minute to a crowd of not more than twenty-five who had the thirst of more like a hundred for liquor. He remembered himself in those same squeaky shoes. He liked the way the young man's hair fell in bangs. He realized that he still felt as if he were one of the bartenders. Would he ever cross over into feeling like a guest? Do all guests really feel like waiters?

"Edgar, I think that some kind of programming in me has been strangely wired," he blurted.

"Tell me more," Edgar said, responding to one of those rare moments when an interesting comment is also revealing, not merely an inventive scrambling of old words in new patterns.

Like Edgar's penthouse parties, the Blaktikhs' parties attracted the most identifiable profiles of the moment. But Edgar's parties had more of a "gone," druggy afterimage than theirs, more of an air of partying down. At the Blaktikhs' was a woman who painted Proustian watercolors and lived in Paris, where she held a vernissage biannually to sell her visual fairy tales of a fancy life supposedly lived in the last century. She was the heiress to a fortune made by her father, who designed the Bloomingdale's escalator. She was talking to Brice Marden, whose paintings were showing in a mid-career retrospective at the Guggenheim. The concert singer and recitalist Jessye Norman was twirling around dancing with a big man who collected art and had an electric company. Their laughter was like a cyclone. A prominent collector of photographs and photogravures, once a Secret Service officer in the White House of John F. Kennedy, was standing next to his young blond architectural-photographer boyfriend. Up and down the stairs ran a rakish blond dealer for Ileana Sonnabend. He was insisting on playing a mellifluous pop ballad, "A House Is Not a Home," then telling everyone how it was based on a line from an essay by Schopenhauer or Hegel. He changed the name of the philosopher twice while talking to a hippie with a long ponytail who was accompanying a woman who said she was collecting Bridget Reilly op-art eye-burners for her house on Martha's Vineyard.

"Let's take a seaplane next summer for lunch to Marissa's house on Martha's Vineyard," the C.E.O. of the electric company was saying to his partner the opera diva as they clicked their heels up like preposterous marionettes on light ropes.

Sean felt too much like a bartender to just walk up to Robert Wilson, who was tall, with round owl's glasses, dressed in a black cashmere turtleneck and blue jeans, his big hands and long fingers like tree roots that take their time spreading over the ground before finally digging in. Sean had just seen his play *A Letter for Queen Victoria* that week, at a regular Broadway theater in Midtown. He loved its dreamlike quality and the painterly look of its surfaces made of hypnagogic images. It reminded him of Magritte. It made him feel like a comb had been passed through the insides of his head.

"*A Letter for Queen Victoria* was finger-painting therapy for mental types," he said to Edgar, getting the hang of it.

Sean was dressed the most "downtown" of anyone there, in jeans and leather. It was the outfit Annie had suggested. He liked its message of daring, its feel of comfort and casualness. He was glad to sink into a sleek, soft couch next to Edgar.

"I guess it's not Russell Wright dinnerware you want to discuss," Edgar guessed.

"Hah! No. It's my voyeuristic habit."

"You mean your night with Jonathan and Stacey?"

"That started it. That and the mushrooms. I wonder whether I'm ever going to look up and find a window and through it see any stars. You know what I mean?" Sean was getting carried away with a poetic sense of his own destiny. It came on him suddenly sometimes, felt good, but never led anywhere.

"I think I follow."

"Let's talk."

"You keep saying that."

"But talk is like sex, at least for me. And looking is like . . . Oh, who cares?"

"Yes," agreed Edgar, happy to turn off the grand boulevard of such discourse about Sean's self onto a more practical side street. "I think you should try to get your film into the New York Film Festival in the fall. It's the best place to be right now. One of the administrators is here."

Edgar went up to the woman, who worked closely with the director of the New York Film Festival. She had a short, bouncy haircut, like secretaries in sitcoms from the era of Sean's childhood that were still playing in reruns on Saturday mornings. Her manner was all about assisting, nurturing, organizing. He could tell she was going to help him. Sometimes he felt that people were doors. He could feel them shutting in his face—most of them. But occasionally one would open and a golden warm light would seep through.

"The air gets thin at the top," she was warning as she went on about the ins and outs of having a film accepted.

"New York City is full of these proverbs about work and career—they're like sophisticated lines for fortune cookies," Sean said later to Edgar when he was recounting her comment. But that afternoon he just murmured an assent to indicate to her simply that they were both now on the same team, his team.

●   ●   ●

Edgar had a mentor's notion one afternoon soon afterwards to take Sean to a press party for Fred Halsted, whose new movie, *Sextool,* was set to open at Lincoln Art—a theater on Fifty-seventh Street. Every time he passed that theater he felt fondly, as fondly as he felt walking once or twice a year on holiday visits through the shadow of a certain chestnut tree on Church Street in his hometown, beneath whose rough, dark-green leaves he had first participated in a circle jerk.

The party was a far-out mess. It was held in a hotel in the West Fifties in an beige suite crammed with gay journalists, the ones from the tabloids anxious to capture a few brightly throated shockers from Halsted, the ones from the mainstream papers keeping a certain distance, not certain whether their employers would back the notion that this was indeed a crossover film, or that it would gross its promised five million dollars.

Halsted's earlier films *L.A. Plays Itself* and *Sex Garage* had been shown in a special series at the Museum of Modern Art, and Edgar felt Sean, whose movie seemed close to approval for the film festival, should meet his peer. (*Sex Garage* ended with a young man making love to his shining Triumph motorcycle.) Edgar liked breaking taboos and was radical in his sense of what Sean could get away with. While Sean's taste tended toward the pornographic, he was always anxious to shoot through a scrim of art and religion.

As Sean took in Halsted leaning into one of the off-white windowsills, talking loudly, even irately, to a surround of journalists who were holding little glasses of alcohol mixed with tonic, he felt angry, interested, competitive, aroused. He did not feel at all casual. "The movie isn't even the best part," Halsted was bragging. "It was just a warmup for me and Joey. After we did nine takes we would go on balling all night after the film crew left." He was referring to his lover, playing opposite him in the film.

"Why isn't the film full-length?"

"I didn't pad it. I said what I had to say and stopped."

The voice that came out like puffs of a cannonball didn't match the look of the man in repose. Sean stopped listening to the staccato of his aggressive message to watch the director during the moments when he was gathering his thoughts or retreating.

Halsted seemed more retiring than either his films or his pose implied. He was dressed like a serious graduate student in baggy blue corduroys and a sweatshirt, sipping a Tab. He was short enough—about five-eight—so that his feet, when he sat down on the sill, did not reach the rug. His light brown hair was shoulder-length, his blue-gray eyes filled with a sound Sean wanted to hear more of. But the other voice kept interrupting.

" 'I'm the meanest man in the world.' That's what I always told my dear friend Divine. I take her to dinner every time she comes to L.A. But a few weeks ago she took me to see *Female Trouble*. I said, 'That's a good movie for high-school girls.' She said, 'Fred, now you've gone too far!' "

Those nearby laughed without much conviction.

"Joey, get me a Tab," Halsted yelled as a glint of amber like a UFO traveled through his eyes. Then he threw the empty can at Joey so it hit him on the side of his head.

"Tender" was the word that came to mind as Sean looked at the target. Joey was a slighter, younger, slimmer, smaller, prettier man than Halsted. Blond-haired, with brown eyes as placid as a doe's, Joey wore tight white jeans and seemed to take some deep pleasure from the mean dialogue Halsted was starting up, at least in front of the press. Theirs was a romance as wild and weird as Cupid and Psyche's, Sean decided. He wanted to film the story of Halsted and Joey as just that, with a scene where Joey would polish Halsted's boots so they were as shiny as dark mirrors.

Or Joey attached to a typewriter in an elaborate mechanism. Sean imagined him bound to a chair by a rope around his chest like a lassoed calf. A bandit's red bandanna would be drawn through his teeth and tied around the back of his head. Naked pink skin contrasted with the black leather of a businessman's chair. Joey's elbows would be attached behind the chair, his wrists connected by handcuffs, his ankles shackled, his head slowly shaved by an unseen hand. The only movement possible for him would be typing. Two vials of amyl nitrite would be stuffed up his nose and his eyes would be as red as a devil's.

Sean was startled by the rapid force with which these new images were beginning to spill through his mind.

"I call them my 'sweet dreams,'" Wolf interrupted, having squeezed himself somehow into a synapse between Sean and his thoughts. Wolf worked at the Strand Bookstore and made money on the side drawing erotic sketches for specific patrons. Recently he'd published a book titled *Epaulettes* Sean had admired in a dirty-book store. He felt the fin de siècle decadence of Wolf's imagery was inspired by Beardsley. But in place of impish, elongated androgynes were unshaved brutes whose black sunglasses mirrored the silhouettes of Harleys. These antiheroes looked and acted as if they were penises turned into big, bald, two-dimensional men, allegories of different sexual moods. Torn jockstraps were stretched over the faces of boys with their tongues sticking out. Lots of urinals gleamed among a crosshatching of detritus, the ashes of leftover fetishes.

"Aren't all pen-and-ink artists Manicheans?" he asked Wolf seriously.

"I don't know," Wolf answered crossly. He had started to talk about his drawings of the Puerto Rican hustlers on his street. They were his "sweet dreams." But since he'd been bumped off course by Sean's intellectual question, he shifted into a short autobiography, as general in its cartoon of a sinner's profile as a medieval saint's-life in the depiction of its opposite.

"My foster parents got tired of me so I came to New York City," he began. "I went to design school, had a lot of lovers, drank, and nearly died a few times. I ride a Triumph and am into pornography."

"I'm into pornography, too," said Sean, amazed—unusually amazed, given the context of the party. "I think it's a kind of folk art, a reservoir for gay men to mine."

"Are you into Nazis too?"

"Hadn't thought about that."

"I think Nazis were the truly modern men. Their look, their masculine code, mythological and primitive, without the gentle personal details we have no time for. Faces, for example. Who needs them? Americans are the perfect successors to the Nazis. Much of America is a result of the immigration of Germans into the heartlands. But we don't do it nearly as well or with as much style."

Sean didn't back away through the door to the bedroom because he was shocked or overcome. He heard Wolf speak with flat interest, finding neither a soul mate nor a foil. But Sean felt his rap was quite predictable. Less so than the drawings, which touched his heart with their inky darkness, their outsider's evocation of a child peeping through a cellar window at a perverse encounter. It was the same difference Sean felt between Halsted the interviewee and Halsted the filmmaker.

Set up in the bedroom were two projectors screening different scenes from *Sextool*. One was just beginning: Halsted charging out of a tunnel, breaking a bottle against a metal gate, threatening the receding camera with its jagged claws. The second screen was farther along: he was making Joey hold his blue boxing bag for him so that the blows slammed, padded, into Joey's body, then giving his Ganymede his bloody fist to lick its wound dry, then pissing on him down on his knees licking a mirror, his helplessly calm face an image shattered when Halsted slammed into the mirror with his uncontrollable black boot.

When Sean returned to the main room, the afternoon light was soft and even. He chatted some with Halsted between his professional exclamations.

"Do you really think our stuff can cross over?"

"Yeah. My cinema's not fluffy-sweater faggot porn. It's art. My films are usually screened to straight audiences. Lincoln Art is a straight film house."

"Well . . . sort of," Sean gently challenged.

"In Europe they love my movies. It's the fags who get nervous. In L.A. they were writing that there wasn't any sex. I care about a mood, an atmosphere, a spirituality. Edgar was saying your film might be accepted into the film festival."

"Not yet."

"There's a French film called *Exhibition* that's definitely been taken. It's a documentary about a porn actress, Claudine Beccarie. Fassbinder's new movie is out in New York, *Ali—Fear Eats the Soul*. See it. See anything by him. He had a movie come out in Germany last year all about gay life, that was praised as much there as *Love Story* here. The wall is coming down."

"You mean in Des Moines they'll be lining up to buy tickets to see *Sextool*? Or *Sean Gets His Nipple Pierced*?"

"You'll see."

Sean was enjoying the bright cheer of Halsted's comments. But soon the director had maneuvered his persona back into a major display of Sturm und Drang.

"But isn't it true that nothing happens in your movies? That they're primarily head trips?" a reporter holding a small tape recorder had the misjudgment, or judgment, to ask.

Suddenly Halsted went off. "What's 'nothing'? When I broke the beer bottle in the first scene, I could have used a prop. I had thirty stitches in my hand at the end of the day. Take this!"

Halsted thrust his hand deep into an aluminum bucket filled with glass beer bottles. He started smashing them against a lamp's pole, against the edge of a coffee table, against a window, which shattered sympathetically. He took two glasses from guests and threw them towards a wall. A few reporters in the room began to panic.

"Help me out of here," Sean heard one of them say.

"And what about our lovemaking? Whose head is that in? Joey and I were married last month. We're going to Sweden to legalize the proceedings in June."

By now Joey had come around. Halsted swung at him with a fist that made a cracking sound as it whammed somewhere near his pretty eyes, turning one quickly into a darker crater. Joey remained entirely solicitous.

"Calm him down, Joey, calm him down," a manager of Halsted's was saying as if this were an ordinary occurrence in the zoo of their lives together.

Halsted swung his entire body onto Joey's, bringing them both down onto the floor. The more violent Halsted became, the more stroking and petting and cuddly Joey was. It was an exercise in yin and yang that Sean was finding fascinating.

But Edgar tapped him to leave. "Soon it'll just be us and them," he warned.

As they strolled through the wide-open door with its French-vanilla panels and fake gold Louis Quatorze handles, Sean looked back at Halsted and Joey, now in near-nakedness, clothes ripped, Halsted holding high a tube of K-Y.

"He thinks he's Neptune with his trident," whispered Sean to Edgar finally, making him turn around. Sean was always mythologizing things.

"Seems more like a hissy fit to me," Edgar slapped back.

The elevator whirred almost immediately to their floor. Sean and Edgar were alone in their descent. Most of the other guests had left after the first gusts of violence. The afternoon had been strong enough to stimulate Sean to lots of immediate thoughts.

"Why did you bring me?"

"Seems obvious to me. I think you're working some of the same terrain as these artists."

"Hmmmmm. And Billy Narcissus too. But the difference is that they're all exhibitionists. Like clowns. Send in the clowns. I'm not such a freak. I'm just doing recordings and—"

"I'm not saying to turn into one of these directors who are finally porn actors or will be so defined when the confetti settles."

"So what do you think? . . . Sometimes someone can say something."

"I don't have any oracles. You'll turn further into something else when you undo the cocoon."

"I see," Sean said as they reached the ground floor.

●   ●   ●

A quiet night at home. Annie was out of town but she had left her music out. The latest addition to her paraphernalia was a computerized board she'd been making trippy music on. She'd been telling Sean about her experiments, talking about a German band called Tangerine Dream. Sean talked back at her about concerts he'd been attending at the Idea Warehouse in SoHo: the audience mostly sat in meditative trances on the floor. There was no general label used except "spacey" for this music made from advanced computer technology.

That September night Sean found himself worked into a corner, dressed in soft pajamas, smoking a J, listening to a water-wheel of tapes left behind by Annie of music made mostly with electronic keyboard and taped sound effects. After smoking for a while he broke open a bottle of Black Label scotch, stretched out, felt good.

He waited a long time. Finally the phone rang. "Hi. It's Satan. I met you at the Ramrod last week, remember?" "I remember. C'mon over. My roommate's in Nashville."

Sean felt scared, but knew he was only scaring himself—like a kid inventing snakes at the bottom of his bed ready to invade his feet. He stared into the bathroom mirror as he tied a black piece of rawhide around his neck. It was so bright in there. His heart was thumping happily. He'd met a gamesman he liked. A hunter of hunger like himself. He dressed in lots of industrialized black, as if he were going to CBGB's rather than Keller's or the Eagle. The ring on the beige phone signaled a visitor from downstairs.

When Sean opened the door he was quite satisfied. His visitor was as humorless as he was. He didn't know why, but he liked his few encounters to be serious. No light moments. He stood aside to let him in.

"Hi, Satan," he said. Well, there was a bit of humor in that greeting. By now the music sounded like a magnification of a per-colating coffee machine. "The music won't stop," Sean promised throatily as he went about dousing lights, covering chairs in ghostly white sheets. Then he turned around again to look into a faceless sort of face filled so far with lots of silence.

"You want to worship Satan tonight?" his friend asked, with an intelligent clip to his talking that appealed to Sean.

"Yeah." He knew his own formality was lacking.

The Satan of a friend was bald-headed, though in his twenties also. His black leather jacket was zipped to his neck and remained so. His black jeans were splattered with white paint. His boots were round, black, childlike in their simplicity. The frame of his body was large. He wore black glasses with heavy black frames. The effect was of a computer nerd, appropriate to the music. But a computer nerd whose program had gone berserk. He had the lined face of a geek but the smoothly impersonal body of a robot.

"Get down on your knees," the diffident robot ordered as he manipulated the box on top of the television to pick up Channel C, the public-access cable channel.

"Take this," he was saying in a monotone, handing him a black pill he claimed was speed. While waiting for the effects to expand, Sean lay on the rug, comforted by the heavy weight of a boot on his cantilevered cranium. Why am I so impersonal? Sean was worrying. Guilty feelings were usually part of his more adventurous escapades.

Satan tuned into *Mr. Fixit,* a cable show starring a young Yugoslavian photographer, Anton Perik. Sean could see a sideways stripe of the segment from his vantage on the ugly carpet. On the show Taylor Mead, whom Sean had admired playing Viva's giggling "nurse" in Andy Warhol's *Lonesome Cowboys,* was telling a TV repairman about a home remedy for hemorrhoids: a well-oiled light bulb screwed up his ass.

Satan lowered the volume so the soft busywork of an organ made a trampoline of suspended sound on which their acrobatics could be carried out. Sean felt the black pill open up inside his lungs expressively. Then he began to feel as if he were flying. The flying was accompanied by pain administered by his blank friend. He felt a strap across his back that of course reminded him of the time his father had strapped him with a belt for an insignificant, and forgotten, infraction while he scrunched beneath a curved dining-room chair upholstered in dark-green Belgian cloth. He used to admire the upholstery's soft tan deer holding themselves as proudly as antelopes. As a kid, he saw the chair as a monument to hidden shame and tears. He had jutted his jaw forward then, and he jutted his jaw forward now.

The strapping stopped. A cold shower began. Icy water from a tap overhead in the bathtub was a test. He couldn't remember what it was a test of. But he always liked to pass tests, so he set himself to pass this one. The next and last test was standing in a big, open, curtainless back window, naked, playing with his thing as if it were a clarinet. This was a solo recital for those in the buildings behind who counted on the Chelsea for such departures. He had played the clarinet as a boy, running up and down Mozartian scales in a frenzy of breathless, mediocre achievement. He was again allowing himself to be diminished, to be put in a shrinking box, to be watched. Why, he asked himself. "Unfinished business" were the words that came into his head as directly as a telegram.

"I'm staying at the Y across the street," Satan said acoustically as he cast off into the doorway.

Sean was entirely confused by now. He was just as confused when he found his wallet lying open. All the green bills were gone. So were some bank cards. Obviously he'd been robbed. But was it part of a scenario? Did Satan need money? Did he tell him where he was staying so he would stalk him? Was it a kind of appointment for a rendezvous?

Sean walked past the TV, stopping to push the volume fuller. It was now *Midnight Blue*. They were giving a quick trip through some of their recent acts: a pubic haircut; a topless tropical-fish store; Ricky Farkle, the four-hundred-pound stripper (56-44-59—"You sound like the Verrazano Bridge," said the host); an orgy for seven hundred at a Catskills resort; double-jointed Dr. Infinity, who could take himself in his own mouth; Tuppy Owens, the young woman at a film party who confessed to liking public sex, then went down on the cameraman, causing the picture to shake.

When Sean looked into the bathroom mirror this time, untying the rope from around his neck, he looked the way he looked earlier. He was expecting all sorts of receding images, faces from his past, personas of the present. Instead he was face-to-face with the undramatic marble of his own skin, the lineless look of his eyes, the vampirelike tips of his ears. He felt nothing special. For Sean an absence of revelations about himself was definitely special.

"I'm not feeling a thing," he announced to Annie when he finally got her on the phone in Nashville. "It's like I'm cold-blooded!"

"It might just be new feelings rather than the absence of any feelings. It might be perspective rather than self-absorption. Maybe you're growing up. I'd go with it. . . . And of course it might be the drugs."

"Oh . . . okay."

•   •   •

Sean's film was finally accepted for the Thirteenth Annual New York Film Festival. The big movies that year were from Europe: Louis Malle's *Black Moon*, Marguerite Duras's *India Song*, Miklós Jancsó's *Elektreia*, Werner Herzog's *Every Man for Himself and God Against All*. Orson Welles was an American steeping in the luxurious steam of making European-style movies. His *F for Fake* was fashioned from documentary footage showing the famous art forger Elmyr de Hory living on the island of Ibiza. Halsted was right: another askew documentary was *Exhibition*.

The opening night of the festival took place in Avery Fisher Hall on September 29. The rest of the films, including Sean's *Triptych*, were screened at Alice Tully Hall. Sean went to opening night with Edgar. As a director of one of the films, he felt a bit important riding up the escalator. But ever since what he called his "emotionless experience" with Satan, he never had any startling shivers of transformation or any comment at any event. Some moments he just felt calmer than others.

The movie that night was Visconti's *Conversation Piece*. Most attending were dressed in tuxedos or black dresses that glittered. They arrived already a bit anesthetized from dinner at nearby neighborhood restaurants—Aunt Fish, the Ginger Man, O'Neal's—where they had sized each other up in advance. Afterwards at a reception on cold marble decks they held cigarettes, drank test tubes of champagne, dished the film. During the actual screening, in which the audience was turned into one swath of restless black velvet, there had been titters, boos, shushes, and only a mild smattering of embarrassed applause at the end. Sean felt let down because the film was made in English and starred Burt Lancaster. He kept silent through the whole long test of sitting still.

At his own screening he was more involved, but not excessively so. It was as if his spine had been straightened after his night with Satan. He rode in a limousine hired by Edgar. Crammed in were Annie, R.J., Rupert. They were all given tickets to sit behind Sean in a side loge above the audience. The film went on at seven-thirty, which was not a prime time. His film, as its title implied, rolled simultaneously in three separate strips. The cost of editing this way had been steep. Edgar contributed. Two strips of the piercings of Sean's tit—the more Apollonian supervised by Annie, the more Dionysian by Jonathan—flanked a center strip. In the center was a long interview conducted with the black boy he had met in the subway on New Year's Day. The sound was garbled and clotted. Sean had filmed in the toilet cubicle in the Broadway-Lafayette subway station, the kid sitting on the john. It was a simulation. He bribed his subject to return to the site of their New Year's Day encounter that had led to his own case of the clap. Sean remembered that when he walked out of the station the first time. He wished he had filmed the battering wetness forcing him down. It was nature's version of the mood he was trying to set in his movie, only better.

His revisions and indecisions were interrupted by clapping. A spotlight rolled around from the ceiling to catch Sean sitting in the balcony. He stood up. He didn't bow. An usher tapped him on the shoulder. He made his way down a confusion of stairs through the backs of halls. Backstage at Alice Tully reminded him of the Gaiety dance theater on West Forty-sixth near Broadway, where you could pay thirty dollars to go into the wings with one of the performers. There, lined up in different which-ways, would be dancers with their admirers. He could recite their names like the Barnum-and-Bailey-style announcer before their appearances: Vance, Oliver, Paul, Roy, Keith, Juan. The offstage choreography seemed more creative to Sean than the cheap rip-offs of old Broadway stripper routines, unwitting homages to *Gypsy,* taking place on the runway out front. In the wings of the Gaiety he had met tall, listless, sinewy Sky, a dancer from Brooklyn who barely shuffled onstage. Between shows Sky liked to loiter superciliously around the lounge—where the guests were served Hawaiian Punch laced with Alexis vodka—while performing studiedly oblivious pull-ups from a doorjamb. When Sean took a Polaroid of him one night, Sky had the image laminated in plastic to keep stuck in his bright yellow silk boxing trunks.

Sean's memory of those yellow trunks was interrupted by the dull shock of walking onstage to be bathed again in a spotlight from above. He didn't smile: not appropriate for the movie.

He knew he was now on the other side of the projector light he had first felt boring down into the screen at the porn theater when he was in college. Now it was in his eyes. Of course he summoned up the live ghosts of the go-go boys, who were more used to accepting applause, working the moment, than he ever could be. In his mind, too, were the hustlers at the Haymarket on Eighth Avenue in the Forties, who knew just how to position themselves in the rose light from the jukebox so that it caught the brims of their tan cowboy hats or the denim edge of their hips. Or the women-by-choice at the Gilded Grape, who walked grandly past the pale pallor of men in suits along the bar, predicting perhaps some seismic social shift: the worship of men in dresses as fabulous as ostrich feathers. The twinge in Sean was nothing so simple as happiness at attention. He did know more than that. He knew that by walking into that curtain of starry whiteness he had become a character in his own life, and so was reduced for himself just as he became expanded for others. He knew it. It was a finger snap of a realization too quick for words.

"You wanna get out of here?" Annie adroitly asked him when he made it to the plastic-cups party in the lobby. She was dressed in a Charlie Chaplin Edwardian dilapidated suit with a mocking red carnation in its lapel that might as well have squirted water.

"Why do they call it limelight? It's as white as the Milky Way," Sean joked. "Yeah, of course I wanna get out of here."

Annie was the only person he could side with, because she knew at least as much as he did about the phantasms they were becoming privileged enough to confront.

Edgar was involved in quibbling, a hobby of his. So Annie, Sean, R.J., and Rupert left. No one noticed.

•   •   •

The rest happened like a news report: quick, linear, horrifying.

Sean had never seen an apartment that gave such mixed signals as R.J.'s, a railroad apartment on the fifth floor of a walk-up tenement on East Ninth Street. Its front room was a salon of limited-edition books, joints, fifties physique magazines, paintings by Larry Rivers, Jasper Johns, John Button, Joan Mitchell, scattered pink pages from the *Advocate,* glasses half-filled with bullshots (vodka and consommé), and Navajo pillows lumped on the floor. Sean was beginning to find R.J. the liveliest person he'd ever met. He could see why Annie and Rupert spent so much time with him. They were joined there by Turk, with the wiry hair of a janitor's broom. R.J. was playing *Switched-On Bach* on a crappy brown stereo.

"Haven't we gone beyond the Moog synthesizer?" Annie teased. "I liked your movie," R.J. was saying to Sean in his way of talking continuously without enunciating, so that his mumbling of the long, lyric, Irish flow of his words became its own performance on the edge of lost meaning, lost purpose. "I liked it, but I thought it had too much distance, too much bullshit. You don't need to hide. You don't need to do a fan dance." While he delivered this opinion his face changed into different people's faces. His big white teeth filled the room like a Cheshire cat's.

That year he was in his mid-thirties but looked literally golden, in his early twenties: a value pronounced in the gay subculture but widespread. He was blond. His skin was tan, flecked. His eyes were light blue. He wore torn jeans, a white polo shirt, and beaten brown boots. It was words that he loved. He was logorrheic. Words and wormholes. He moved about a round dining table filled with a clutter of pieces of paper and volumes of poetry, drawing names out of the air like some metaphysical gossip columnist.

"I was in the Hamptons at Jerry Robbins's doing a crossword puzzle one Sunday," he was saying apropos of nothing. "The clue was 'world-famous choreographer.' The answer was 'Massine.' But Jerry got stuck because he insisted on trying to fit the name 'Robbins' into the squares." Then R.J. laughed and laughed, as if he were erupting from all the excesses of the world's funny vanity.

"Pissing it away" was the phrase many used when talking about R.J. The son of an admiral, he'd gone to Harvard on a painting scholarship. He'd enlisted in the Navy, worked as a reporter for the *Washington Post*. He had talents as a poet, a painter, a journalist. But he also had a weakness for life and a disdain for careerism and products that put him out of the easy reach of validation. He burned brightest when most ephemeral: talking, breaking down, talking, licking, talking, dancing to "The Hustle" and "Fly, Robin, Fly" at the Ninth Circle. Dorothy Dean, whom Sean met at Edgar's terrace party, was R.J.'s match in disdain. If the era was at its height in the risks of performance art, then those two surpassed in their lackadaisically limp refusal to frame themselves.

Even Chris Burden—the body artist who in a gallery performance had himself shot in the arm by a friend with a .22, and who lay on the floor nude while an aide hammered a star-shaped stud into his sternum, until he finally sat himself in a chair, had all his hair cut off, and dressed himself in an FBI uniform.

Sean surveyed R.J.'s round table. A book of Auden's was open to the poem "Lullaby." Scattered about were scraps of paper with first names and phone numbers written out. The pink pages of the *Advocate* with its list of call boys—was spread wide open, with some entries circled in blue. Sean read one that wittily ripped off a Lichtenstein painting (many of R.J.'s enthusiasms had such hidden surprises): "DO NOT CALL BRAD: He is not for everyone. A hunky 22-yr-old athletic bodybuilder, who possesses intelligence, a sense of humor and the ability to understand what versatility and masculinity really mean." R.J. often spent the afternoons— after finally waking up around three—calling the ads.

"Do you know Lyle, the Indian boy?" he asked Sean of his latest infatuation. "He dances barefoot on the bar of the Anvil."

"No, let's go," Sean pushed restlessly.

"Once I answered an ad from two guys in Massachusetts," R.J. went on, his voice a bit hoarser. "They wanted a human dog for the weekend. When we ate in a restaurant I had to kneel down under the table."

"What is love?" Sean always remembered asking at that moment.

"There was a Navy lieutenant I loved. He kept me shackled in a footlocker at nights. When I went to live in France, he insisted on flying over to find me because he missed me. That blew the whole thing. A twisted mind is harder to find than a good man."

Sean felt a touch chilled by that comment, and in its closeness in sentiment to his own feelings. He pictured an awkward meeting on a tarmac. Then he stumbled into the living room to nudge

Annie and Rupert to leave for the Anvil. "To watch Lyle dance," he promised.

"I could watch Lyle dance a Hula-Hoop on the grave of a nun," Turk said with his usual strange turn of phrase.

"He's too young for me," Rupert decided.

"I'll dance with him" said Annie.

"I feel sick," Rupert complained, convincingly.

"I'll help you," Sean responded quickly, anxious for a mission to distract him, and anxious to get closer to Rupert, who had always been either R.J.'s or Annie's friend.

"Help me onto the fire escape," Rupert said, obviously keen on him too.

So they both fit through a narrow window to emerge onto a metal fire escape: the usual braces over an East Village tenement. Across the way domestic contortions of various couples were lit up for all to see. Rupert began to heave over the side. His spume was violent, green, awful. Sean held on to Rupert's thigh, giving strength by showing his own frailty. A lovely full moon glimmered in a light drizzle. Sean bravely kissed Rupert full in the mouth, tasting the vomit without any censoring of the sensation. That was as full as any act could ever be for them. It was now as if they were blood brothers, as if they had mingled the blood of their thumbs. Even though they never really got to know each other, their hearts were in each other's pockets whenever they saw each other from that night on.

"Let's go," said R.J. jealously, his voice growing raspier.

So they all went to the Anvil, a new club downstairs from the Triangle Hotel, where Sean had spent the night just three years earlier—it seemed so much longer to him—with the boy in the "69" T-shirt. Its atmosphere was circuslike. Bars looped in and out of the mostly male crowd. Nets hung down. Native American Lyle was dancing over the tops of the bars in his bare feet, a lei tied around his ankle, a loincloth over his crotch, a shell necklace shaking as he nimbly avoided shotglasses. Onstage in a growing cloud of lavender smoke, performers were suspending heavy beer mugs from chains clamped onto their nipples or foreskins, sitting on rubber dildos, taking a fist or half a foot halfway up their rears to expansive soundtracks of orchestral music. (Soon it was Deodato's disco version of *Also Sprach Zarathustra.*)

A man and his wife in the audience fit the loose caricature of being "bridge-and-tunnel" or "from New Jersey" because of their loud mouthing-off, their out-of-town thirst for making fools of themselves. They were certainly the only husband and wife in sight. Indeed, she was the only woman there that night. They hands-on-hipped their way onto stage as an understood dare to everyone, and themselves, their arms greased in Crisco, and fist-fucked a performer apiece.

Sean escaped by wandering into the back, where tiny screens were set up overhead on which dirty movies were being continuously projected. He watched Toby Ross's *Cruisin' 57,* a takeoff on *American Graffiti,* with lots of authentic hamburger-stop fifties music, the guys all dressed in argyle sweaters and chino pants.

"Let's leave." Annie was tugging on him. "Let's walk through the piers. It's a night to hit the streets. Besides, Turk is occupied with some married Swede from New Jersey."

So they exited the tumbling bar. As they cut their way through the blackness of West Street towards the warm glow of the Village farther below, they could catch a glimpse of the World Trade Center towers through tangerine-colored steam. Soon enough, rising before them like a black castle, was Pier 48. Bats were flying their ultrasonic paths inside, but it seemed as if there should be flocks of them bursting out of the black holes of the grotesque shambles of rotting wood, an emblem of the last century's shipping energies gone to ruin. Instead of "Abandon All Hope Ye Who Enter Here" or "Arbeit Macht Frei" the sign over the entrance read: "Property of the City of New York. No Trespassing. Violators Will Be Prosecuted." Sean and Annie allowed themselves, along with about fifteen hundred others that night, to be swallowed in its blackness, their eyes soon enough adjusting to the slivers of light, the various mirages in which moonlight was disguising itself.

"This reminds me of our night at the Club Baths," Annie said in a whisper, the whisper of children entering a house they've decided is haunted.

The pier had more levels, balconies, and walkways than a Broadway theater. Silhouettes appeared everywhere. It was a land of shadows, seemingly all shadows, no bodies. Annie and Sean walked up a flight of swaying wooden stairs that led to a landing leading nowhere. Sean stopped them in time by putting out his arm.

"There've been injuries," Sean explained. "A hairdresser I know fell from a ramp and broke his kneecap. A kid I went to college with fell from up there, twenty-five feet up, fractured his leg, broke his wrist." He was pointing to a ceiling, its solid material so broken and corroded that it simulated a crystalline dome. Missing planks of walls allowed stripes of eerie moonlight to slice the space. Gaps in floorboards let in sounds of black waters that slapped under all the smoking of grass, sniffing of poppers, slugging of beer. Fireflies of joints were being lit here and there.

"Look," Annie interrupted, pointing like a general over a plain at a series of small skirmishes of fires being set on the main floor by obviously playful, or smashed, arsonists. The ripped flames were then sucked up towards the roof, carrying stray papers along with them. (The next March the entire folly would be obliterated by fire.)

"It's a pillar of fire," Sean affirmed.

The topography reminded Sean of Chutes 'n' Ladders, a board game he'd played as a kid. He and Annie kept tromping up unsteady flights of stairs, then down ramps connected by elbows of wood to other stairways they had to walkingly slide down as steeply as ski slopes. In one claustrophobic chamber at a great height Sean grew mesmerized for a while. He stared silently, bemused: a figure whose head was encased in a hood, a collar around his neck, leather pants, brown dress gloves, black tall boots, his chest and arms bare, aiming his garter snake of a penis towards the mouth of a bearded man on his knees, in denim jacket and boots, his legs spread. The bearded kneeler was drinking a fine line of pee that traced an arc funneled into his waiting mouth.

"Staring is bolder than doing," R.J. joked, leaning, arms folded, against a nearby knotty board. "Rupert got sick and went home. Do you want to see Turk and his trick? They're in there."

Sean and Annie did walk into the next cubicle, where Turk was fiercely tying the hands of the Swedish young man behind his back, threatening to throw away the wedding ring he'd slipped off the scared-looking youth's finger. Sean rolled his eyes in a disturbed gesture as Annie and he both abandoned the revealing pantomime.

On the way home they stopped at the newly opened Empire Diner on Tenth Avenue. R.J. was with them. It was a thirties diner revamped to maintain the original chrome and steel with Broadway lettering. A hired piano player was busy at an upright along one wall. The long black counter, as slick as a skater's finale, was lined by swivel stools. Steel tables with tubular legs were crowded with chili, vodka, and arugula. The deco sensibility infusing the newer discos had found a twenty-four-hour restaurant. Before they even sat at the tables, in the dark sheen of which they could see their own simplified faces, R.J. had taken off to talk to the cook. Five minutes later he was back, saying he had a job as a "sous-chef" in the kitchen, starting immediately. The head cook was a gardener for the composer Aaron Copland, so the story was going. He was also a dealer in speed and cocaine. The silver diner, which was swept all night long by reflections of cabs and idling cars, was the best spot downtown to score such drugs. The next time R.J. appeared, he was talking so fast his teeth were grinding. Annie and Sean couldn't catch his drift.

They finally fell asleep towards morning in Annie's wide bed. But their tenderness was disturbed in the early hours by a phone call from R.J.

"Listen," Annie said to Sean in a rolling-over maneuver in which she tried to leave the bed and dress herself in one continuous motion. "Listen, R.J. found Turk stabbed to death in his apartment. Let's go."

Sean felt a rawness intruding, the rawness of unfolding events.

•   •   •

Sean and Annie walked into Turk's room in London Terrace, a mass of apartments in a cliffside of a building that ran along an entire block up the street from the Chelsea Hotel. When they arrived, R.J. was committed to a bottle of whiskey he'd found on a counter in the closet-sized kitchen. He was drinking the liquid rust in a huge snifter. R.J. was beyond acknowledging Annie and Sean other than by motioning with his head towards the bed dominating the alcove of the studio apartment.

There, tied by his hands and legs to the four posts of his queen-sized bed, was the naked body of Turk, his hair as freaked as ever. Most riveting was the huge kitchen knife sticking out of his bare chest. The knife created a sundial effect on his pale, gray body. The shadow of the huge blade, left half-exposed, and its black rubbery handle, now lay across the very spots where his blood had congealed into rubies and garnets. Sean hung back. Annie dared advance to the bed. The cold skin changed shades even as she stood there: pink to gray to white. She saw Turk become marble. And then she began to cry, but there was no one who could comfort her.

"I'm leaving," she said angrily to Sean as she walked out, rattling the door behind her.

Sean and R.J. investigated each other's expressions with helpless bemusement as they waited for the men with the black zipper bags to wheel Turk away on a silver cart.

• • •

Sean knew what was going on when he walked in that afternoon. Annie's clothes and pose and gestures told him everything in a glance. She was like a skillful politician able to reveal all in a picture, sitting on a few liquor cartons bound in brown duct tape, dressed entirely in white, a simple white dress.

"Where are the white gloves and mantilla?" Sean joked.

"I'm going to San Francisco."

"Why? What happened?"

"Turk's death bummed me out."

"You'll have to testify at the trial."

"I don't see how that Swede could have done it. I would have thought it was the other way around."

"Two bartenders have been killed from the West Beach bar at the end of Christopher. Someone else was killed on the pier. Someone else at the Leather Flats at 165 Christopher. He was last seen at West Beach on those nights. Besides, two weeks ago Ernie, who worked with R.J. at Grolier's, stabbed his lover to death outside the Anvil because they were quarreling. Now he's back to normal, facing life in prison."

"I think it would be best to find a mellow, shady hole in San Francisco, take lots of acid, hide, return."

"Like you, I find it hard to put all this gruesomeness together with our real feelings and sense of adventure."

"I think it's a witch's brew we're drinking. And I think it's just starting to take hold. We're members of the peaceable kingdom. But what about those who aren't who start drinking from a steaming cauldron?"

"You know I love it when you talk like that."

"What else do you know? You're full of gossip today. Like R.J."

"You're like family to me. My only family here."

"I feel that way about you too, Sean. But what makes someone family?"

"When you can be with them without hot and cold flashes. When you call them from the police station, the hospital, or when you're locked out."

"That's funny but true. People you feel the least about are the people you feel the most about."

When Sean looked at Annie sitting in the window, he reviewed at once all the wonderful details of their three years of knowing each other.

"I feel as if I've been punched in the stomach and tongue-kissed at the same time," he said.

"I love you, too."

The Mineshaft

One hazy moonless night in October 1976, Sean walked through a door at 835 Washington Street in the meatpacking district.

Out walking across the cobblestones of the alleys just south of Fourteenth Street, on his way to the Spike or the Eagle, he spotted a shadow in a cap making his way through an unmarked door. Following on a hunch, the same sort of hunch that had led him to the sneaker on the street a few years earlier, he walked into a preview opening of the Mineshaft. In later years many said they were there that night, or on one of those first nights, as ten years after the Stonewall riots hundreds swore they'd crowded into that neighborhood bar controlled by at most a dozen drag queens.

What Sean saw wasn't the Mineshaft Mineshaft, not what the place would become in a few weeks. He was in the downstairs room that would later be called the Den, or simply Bar #3, until recently the corner "Butcher Restaurant and Destroyer Den," where truckers and men in bloody aprons drank beer that came splashing down from bronze taps. The door he nudged through wasn't the single black door opening onto a steep staircase of what R.J.—when he became obsessed with the place, treating it as a shrine—told him he had counted to be seventeen wooden steps leading up to the checkpoint. The main door would be pointed towards by a white arrow painted on an otherwise resolutely black outside wall. This time, though, Sean simply pushed his way through a gray metal service door.

He immediately loved something about this dimensionless, dark first-floor room with sawhorses for furniture, a single red light bulb screwed in the ceiling, and a low bar made of cartons of cans of Budweiser beer. The bartender slotting tapes in a small tape deck reminded Sean of a pirate with his fiercely misleading eyes, goatee, slack uniform patched from denim and leather. He was like the pirate who filled one of Sean's earliest full fantasies in the cover illustration for the Salvation Army magazine *War Cry* one Christmas: a pirate in blue breeches who pushed the sole of his boot towards the viewer in a hypermasculine posture Sean would later recognize in Tom of Finland drawings. (Sean saw Tom of Finland's work for the first time a year later at Stompers, a boot store on West Fourth Street started by a composer who won a Prix de Rome but became so entranced by the quickly accelerating vertigo of the Mineshaft life that he gave up what his friends called his "straight" life. When Sean saw his neatly arranged exhibition of Tom of Finland's drawings of cops in ballooning britches and of curvaceous ballplayers he thought "gay Vargas.")

All the bartender in the den that night was missing to qualify as a pirate was a cawing parrot on his shoulder. He had the eye patch. The music he spun was trance music he and his replacements favored for the next several years—music that included Philip Glass, Steve Reich, and many of the other mini-malists Sean and Annie had listened to at the Chelsea, music that was labeled "sleaze" by "disco" adherents. By dawn there would always be full electronic Vangelis chords mixed with Mahler while attendants stuffed black hankies and paper towels into— or taped pieces of cardboard over—cracks in the wood and cement that were admitting offensive rays of morning's early light. Big pieces of plywood painted black were nailed over the faultiest sections.

At first only seven or eight customers were scuffing around that night. Sean later figured the owner decided to make everyone climb up to a main floor after the opening so that their nights would eventually push them to climb down again, to descend into what was actually a ground floor but would feel like a deep well of spirals. He knew one or two of the other customers yet seemed to recognize all of them. They became at once characters in the plot line of the Mineshaft, which for Sean by the end of that fall was a novel he couldn't put down, a novel he wanted to stay up all night reading: a boy he had seen at the Y in his white apron of a towel would appear, or a man with a handlebar mustache he'd noticed behind a desk at a travel agency, or one of the stony pillars of leather men he saw night after night until seeing adjusted into curiosity and curiosity into desire. (Many of them wore frozen expressions, like Lot's wife, as if they were looking back in stern shock at their first intimations of their own wishes.)

In a few weeks Sean came across the face of a Spanish Counter Reformation saint. He never knew his name or talked with him. The saint—"Our Man of the Urinals," Sean called him to a few bar wits—would turn immediately right into the bathroom off the main room, Bar #1, upstairs, bend to arrange his cowboy boots in the corner, fold his jeans in a square and balance them on top of the boots, his snakeskin wallet stuck in the boots, then his T-shirt and underwear in smaller squares, like a ziggurat of fabrics, until he was totally naked, his stomach in rolls like a scroll. He would kneel on the black-white tile floor between a urinal and a toilet so that the order from right to left, facing in, was: urinal, urinal, man, toilet. He fit a white plastic filter into his mouth as if it were a retainer, or a set of false teeth, so that he became an imitation of a urinal.

"He's beyond Chris Burden," Sean said to a friend the first night he saw the performance, a reliable tableau in the grotto of the first-floor loo.

One Sunday afternoon after Rupert became a bartender and security guard, and after an evening spent with the Counter Reformation fetishist, Rupert led him in dressed in a fuzzy gray union suit and handed him chrome polisher, bleach, and a toothbrush, telling him to clean that bathroom so that it gleamed like a Vermeer painting. (Rupert's art sense blared through loudly every so often.) As incentives—or missives of attention—he rolled cans of beer across the floor from the bar he was tending. The sound of metal rolling on tile was pretty in an industrial way, like sewing machines whirring or factory whistles blowing. In a few hours the washer was a smudge, an error, a sort of dust storm of a presence. The gleam of the plumbing set him off against a crazy pattern— crazy because so exaggeratedly uniform—of tiles.

But that incident came later. After the Mineshaft had been open a few months. After the regulars had identified themselves to each other enough to sink deeply into the weird thought processes of the club so they could begin to improvise.

• • •

The shadow Sean knew most blatantly that first night had turned out to be Arnie. It was Arnie's biker's cap—so small it was perched precariously on his head—he had followed in earlier. Sean's life in

New York had only the most tenuous, fragile continuity. Increasingly he was making sense of things by collage, or montage.

"I'd laugh if it wasn't so somber here," Sean almost whispered to him.

He was referring to Arnie's outfit: black biker's cap, tight white T-shirt (thirty-five dollars from Fiorucci's on East Fifty-seventh Street), blue jeans with unstitched seams exposing his behind. Sean wondered how Arnie had navigated the door-to-street-to-taxi phase of his evening.

"Nobody's here."

"What you doing?"

"I want to talk to you."

"You sound interested tonight."

"Yeah. I'm on fire."

"You're kidding. Nobody's here. We're in some abandoned bar. What's going to happen here?"

"Something good, I feel."

"The suspense is killing me."

"You weren't really into me in college."

"You mean like *that*? . . . No."

The talk in the bar was made of lines that didn't quite connect.

"That guy over there's a Columbia student . . . a graduate student in philosophy."

Sean looked over. The shadows were dappling on a dark pond. Out of them the philosophy student moved quickly, seeing he was being discussed. He knew Arnie, introduced himself with his left hand. In his right he was holding a green hardbound copy of James Joyce's *Ulysses*. Sean was surprised by the display of literature as well as by Jeffrey's (as his name turned out to be) appearance. He didn't fit the general look of urban cowboy, urban biker, urban hoodlum. His thinning brown hair—frazzled as if just passed over by a wand of electricity—was pulled back in a ponytail, a scruffy version of a Talmudic beard beginning to grow, his horse's face made odder by eyes that whisked back and forth quickly as if sweeping a space out in front of them. His clothes, larger than his frame, projected an uncalculated slump. They looked as if they belonged to a bigger schoolboy from another era: button-down short-sleeved white shirt, green slacks, tied shoes. Sean bent towards him to hear his soft voice, clipped with a trace of a Middle Eastern accent. He immediately liked Jeffrey, and continued to see him there over the years even though he was so far outside what soon became posted as the place's dress code. But in the club Sean never actually observed the uniformity ascribed to it by people's gossip or even by its own dress code.

"You're famous up at Columbia," Jeffrey was saying in the soft singsong of an admirer. Sean couldn't tell if he was his personal admirer, or merely an admirer *type* who treated everyone with the same worshipfulness.

Sean didn't answer, though, because he was thinking back to when he last saw "the Reader"—Sean's nickname for an anonymous patron of the Everard Baths. The Reader would lie in his cubicle, a bright light illuminating his captain's bed, reading a dust-coverless hardcover book, sometimes red with gold lettering, the thick size of a commercial novel, his bookmark always a green leather Tyrolian affair with leather tassles hanging down. Sometimes he would bring his own clip-on lamp from home, creating an even more devastating shock of electric light for those passing by. He was using advertising. Sean never found out whether the ploy worked or not. His towel was wrapped around the Reader like a skirt about to pop. He had a body Sean saw as a muscular walrus's, a walrus reading through gray lenses with steel frames.

Was Jeffrey doing the same with his book? Sean's attention landed again in the short field of recognizability the three of them had cleared for themselves in the bar, now up to about ten customers.

"I'd give it all up just to cook and clean for a cop in a trailer park in New Jersey," Jeffrey exaggerated, proving to Sean that he was an admirer *type*.

"The Firehouse burned down from arson."

"For a firehouse to burn down is some kind of joke. No?"

"Pier 48 burned down in March."

"There are more fires in New York than there were in Cambodia last year."

"You want to look around?"

"No wonder they're calling this place the Mineshaft."

"The farther out the space, the farther away people can get in their heads."

"Sean, you crack me up."

• • •

When Sean left, a perfume of cigarettes, cigars, sweat, pee, and grass left with him. He told the cab driver to drive across Bleecker to Great Jones Street. Cabs were so cheap that season that a pair hiring a cab could pay less than if they bought two subway tokens.

Sean moved out of the Chelsea Hotel when Annie left town the year before, but he still didn't feel comfortable without her. He always hoped she'd move back from San Francisco. With an "in the meantime" attitude he'd rented a third-floor loft on Great Jones Street. Taking a poor-me tack, he'd quote Carole King's melancholy line about "why doesn't anybody live in the same place anymore?" But Annie's departure at that moment was right. They both knew it. They had been halfway houses for each other. And as much as the tug remained, the meaning surrounding the tug had grown weaker. They had been gradually setting each other free in a gesture of quiet, sustained respect. Their love had always been an impossibility.

Having only just enough money to live on from Edgar, from some showings of his film, and from a thirty-five-hundred-dollar New York State CAPS grant, Sean thought about taking a job working on TV documentaries. But, after a few years, he felt too immersed in the culture of living downtown. ("I try never to go above Fourteenth Street" was a saying of R.J.'s that he'd follow with a laugh full of joy.) Sean's clothes grew dirtier with each year: black T-shirt darkened by a swath of motor oil, a cut-off denim jacket, a necklace with a silver pentagram dangling around his neck, jeans as stained as a pinto's coat.

When he walked into his loft that night, he felt that this was a safe port. He could go to a bar like the one he was just at or he could walk the splintered bare floor in his loft still feeling safe. He had been smoking a lot of grass lately, so he was sometimes paranoid, unwilling to go to bright, stiff, wide-open parties. But only sometimes.

• • •

Sean did have a young black man, nineteen, living with him. Paul had been working as an attendant at the Twenty-third Street YMCA. "Well, it says on the sign over the door of the Y, 'When you enter, be a friend or find a friend,' " Sean used to joke.

The two had actually met, though, at the Gaiety, where Paul was a dancer, making much of a kind of jungle-fever choreography. He loved the simplicity of seeing Paul dance to "Fame" by David Bowie, and as he was deciding that he wanted to know him, he realized he wanted him to move in.

In the backstage area where Sean paid his thirty dollars there was no particular abundance of old over young as he expected.

Stage-door romance has its own inverted chivalric rules and explanations.

"Do you want to live with me?" Sean whispered into Paul's ear.

"That's all you want?"

"I'm stoned on my ass."

Paul was leaning his back against a sooty redbrick wall. Pulleys hung in tangles. Other dancers in their red silk boxers, cotton T-shirts, white Adidas running sneakers with green stripes were either entertaining customers by allowing them to wipe their tongues like wet washrags along their sweated bodies or were smoking and joking with each other. The lot of them reminded Sean of street urchins in Dickens. The rasp in the voice was a universal, perhaps.

But Paul was almost different. He was certainly the biggest: around six-one, hair cut short, muscular for those lanky days. Sean found out his story quickly. Even though he played at street sense, he was a New York kid from a family with some wealth and power. His father was a professor at John Jay College. His mother a painter who showed at a gallery on West Fifty-seventh Street. He had been a problem boy. His problem was that he beat up homosexuals in the Ramble in Central Park with friends. So his parents sent him to expensive private schools that masked their part-psychiatric, part-penal intentions. His family was prominent at the Cathedral of Saint John the Divine. On Christmas Eve he would have to sit with his parents, his brother, and his sister in the dark wooden pews flanked by carved angels set up in the altar area as VIP seating for the midnight service. Paul knew Canon Swarth, too. The canon had flunked him out of the cathedral's boys' school.

"I feel like there's this coyote in me leaping up and up and up. I don't ever really relax. Even though I'm lazy."

Sean rested with those words. Paul talked oddly. Sean felt he could talk to him, listen to him, be around him in all moods because his words were in an orbit of their own. Sean didn't want to be crowded by anyone's words, at least not words freighted with thoughts that didn't give him thrills. He had been feeling uncompromisingly strange lately. He heard in Paul's comment a mannish voice coming through the adolescent drawl. This other voice was weirdly cynical and beyond things already. That intrigued Sean. Paul did love to talk. When he didn't brood, he talked. Even when he seduced, he talked.

"I want to be so beautiful you'll want to mummify me," Paul actually said to Sean with a breathtaking fanciness. Then he invented a wide smile so that he suddenly became full of messages of healthy, brotherly love. The oscillations kept Sean engaged. So did the wrapping: yellow kerchief tied around neck, bare chest, black jeans cut as briefly as bikinis with the white lining of pockets peeking underneath in which both his hands were stuck, brown construction worker's boots. These were workingmen's pieces cleverly cut up, shifted. Paul had a strong sense of his own glamour.

"Stay, watch me—we'll leave together."

Sean liked the demand in Paul's insistences. He had come to appreciate young men, adolescents even, who felt as if they were older brothers, or fathers. He thought fondly back to the boy carrying *Catcher in the Rye* who had given him a gift of the clap in the subway bathroom at Broadway and Lafayette. He was liking the contrasts in his partners: black, white; older, younger; rich, poor; tall, short; thin, big. He was feeling almost loose that year; nothing was too serious.

"Life is a series of illusions culminating in oblivion," as Jeffrey had mumbled to him one night at the Mineshaft.

Sean waited through the specially added weekend midnight show for Paul to finish. He was slumped in one of the theater chairs screwed into the floor in the middle of a row towards the back, not in any of the exposed ringside seats along the edge of the runway where dancers occasionally swung parts of their bodies— a thigh, an arm, a crotch—towards the scrunched faces below, who looked as if they were basking in the light of their flesh. Sean liked the small-town accoutrements of this old burlesque house: red velour curtains, plush padded chairs, a searching spotlight unsure of itself. In his hometown a playhouse with such dollhouse proportions had been humbly named the Little Theatre.

"It's Burning Anthony from the Boys of Paradise Strip-O-Rama," barked a carnival-like announcer through his megaphone from high up in the projection booth to cue the first dancer, a tousled, brown-headed, wiry boy who swiveled in black leather hip-hugger pants thin as plastic, the top of his chestnut torso naked, his lips painted vermilion, lip-syncing to the Stones' "Brown Sugar." He had borrowed his look a bit from Mick Jagger's in *Performance.* The format was once down the aisle clothed, once stripped. "The Wild and Unpredictable Jim," the announcer dubbed the next contestant, who danced an off Irish jig in a black leather baseball cap and vest, shyly avoiding the length of the runway. Tony made up a gymnastic dance to a *Chorus Line* number including toe-touching, sprints, jogging, diving, stretching. (As Michael Bennett's deconstruction of a standard Broadway musical had just won lots of Tony awards that month, the choice was trendy and popular.) Under Rico's black shorts he was wearing red tiger-skin underwear. Ricky, "Cupid's Poison Arrow," as the excited-sounding announcer described him, lingered over his G-string. Gino performed a flamenco in jeans and keys and cleated boots (which he removed while twirling around on one leg). Sky tossed his T-shirt into a waiting face, then dropped to the stage for twenty push-ups to the "Theme from *S.W.A.T.*" As prominent as the dancers was the audience member they nicknamed "the Seal," who sat in the same seat each weekend night, front and center, clapping his hands while yelling "Arf, arf, arf," spilling from his chair in a suit spoiled by all his nights of working so hard at praise.

"I keep a big black book in which I've recorded all their performances," he said in his surprisingly satiny speaking voice to Sean later that evening in the lounge. "Next to each name I have my own personal rating of each performance from one to ten on a given night."

Sean was waiting in the lounge because Paul hadn't shown up on the runway, or backstage. Finally he appeared as the houselights were brought up, revealing shabby melon-colored walls that looked more like corrugated cardboard than the ridges of sequined material they had seemed before when shadows were violet. Paul had become entangled in the wings with a client who offered to pay him more than his night's fee as a dancer, so Paul had taken the man up on the deal and missed his performance.

Sean did feel as if his heart had been momentarily crushed. But the owner of the club, who it turned out doubled as the announcer, expressed more than enough anger for both of them, raising his voice in degrees, his mustached, apopleptic face a balloon letting out air in short screeches. Sean almost felt sorry for the owner who was having such trouble breathing, the uncontrollable straining of his big belly barely held back by the buttons of a dingy white shirt. "You'll never work again!" he shouted.

"We'll talk tomorrow," Paul said calmly, putting a hand superiorly on the man's shoulder as if allowing his obvious wisdom to flow into the owner's lesser container.

Sean wondered if the tactic would work. To judge from the calm reclaimed by the owner's face when Paul laid his hand on him, the answer was probably yes.

Sean took the few minutes they used walking down the turning stairs of the theater in a bright glare to put his own ego cleverly forward.

"I was reading a letter from an abused wife today in 'Dear Abby,' " he said. "Abby wrote her back a little parable about a girl walking down a road who came across a snake who charmed her into picking him up. He bit her. When she wondered why he had double-crossed her, the snake answered, 'You knew what I was when you picked me up.' "

Paul always loved that little story Sean had told him so smartly. After that, he would disarm Sean periodically by simulating rattlesnake sounds, using his tongue, teeth, and mouth as if they were castanets.

"You knew what I was when you picked me up," Paul repeated as they laughed their way through the different lights of Times Square to hail a cab.

● ● ●

Their first night in bed was their only night that resembled a romantic night in bed with a lover. Paul found his way through Sean's body as if it were a dark apartment he was burglarizing. Sean was alerted through all his senses to the presence of the rummaging stranger. He smelled an oily frankincense on Paul's skin. He held on to his body as if it were a buoy, both their tongues swabbing each other in different places at different times. It was as if they were ignoring one another in their mutual search for satisfaction. Yet all the while they were becoming closer by sharing a similar destination, like travelers who become friends by chance on a train. Paul finally broke into him so hard that

Sean screamed from the short-circuiting. He felt as if he were wetting himself or making a mess in his pants. Next he was shivering. Paul caused the shivering and he was the warm blanket on top of him, pressing him down. Sean was the sort who if put in a straightjacket would become calm from the pressure and constriction. So Paul on top of him, a much heavier weight, was a calming burden, allowing him to float downstream on a big river of sleep.

• • •

Tonight, three months later, walking into the loft after the preopening of the Mineshaft, Sean sensed that Paul was asleep in the front room.

He drank hot tea—a slice of lemon tossing in its dark blue ceramic molded cup, a gift of Canon Swarth's from a community of nuns with a kiln in Vermont—while he sat at the low coffee table reading a conversation with Elton John in *Interview*. He smoked some marijuana—the "Acapulco Gold" his different pot dealers were always promising him.

Paul was sleeping under a camper's blanket on the floor of the front room, his covered body lit by moonlight divided by windowpanes. The windows in the front room were enormous, like those in Sean's elementary school. He remembered in the eighth grade a literature teacher devoting an entire semester to reading *David Copperfield,* each student standing by his desk as he or she read a paragraph, while a listless boy with a window stick changed the angle of the windows and the position of the dark orange shades to suit changing sunlight, temperature, and the rapid moods of his commander. This teacher was a middle-aged woman with gray hair pulled back around her thick peasant's head, who dressed a bit like a secular nun, in black dresses with white lace frills at her neck and her wrists.

Sean didn't want to wake Paul up. Otherwise the front room was empty. He was feeling that he would need to start working soon. He squinted to see cinematic ghosts filling up the room, characters caught in the tintype of the reflections of his windows. He would need to get his Super 8 rolling again. Or even buy a new sixteen-millimeter camera.

"It's like building tunnels and bridges to help navigate a river," Sean had explained about moviemaking to a few prisoners at Bellevue Prison Medical Center, where he taught three times that year for the hours of "community service" he needed to collect his film grant.

"What are you doing here?" Paul asked in the morning when he found Sean's head tucked into his own rigid, flat stomach covered by a stubble of black wiry hairs.

"I fell asleep," Sean managed to say, his face smudged and creased from having spent the last few hours on the floor under his dad's old scratchy army blanket.

"Where did you go?"

"A club that felt really black."

"You mean Keller's?"

"No. Black *atmosphere*."

•   •   •

Most afternoons Sean would sit at the low coffee table, smoking a few cigarettes, carelessly reading through papers and magazines. He was trying to do business on the phone, but he was so unsure of himself that he became awkward and somewhat alien in those talks. His voice didn't even sound like his own.

"The phone is like a conch shell," he said to Paul as he was passing by.

"That phone's a dildo," Paul said back with so much enthusiasm.

Paul never paid much attention to Sean's phone work. Rather he was simply happy to be left alone back among all his piled wood. Like his mother, Paul was a painter. He continually threatened to go to Pratt but never did. Into the backroom he dragged big unused pieces of wood, which he smeared with childish apricot-or-pumpkin-colored brushstrokes squeezed from tubes of expensive Dutch paints he'd bought.

Within three months he had simply become "company." Sean liked company.

"I just want to make enough money to hire people to be emotional stand-ins," he said to R.J. as a joke on himself.

• • •

None of Sean's friends ever showed up at the club before one in the morning. The familiars at the club increasingly became Sean's emotional stand-ins, to an extent he had certainly not intended.

He usually went first to a dinner with Edgar. Often they went to One Fifth Avenue, an entirely white restaurant on the first floor of Edgar's apartment building. Imitating a thirties Cunard shipboard, its sharp, silver walls and corners smoothed here and there by art-deco portholes, One Fifth was a more elegant version of the Empire Diner. Sean was consistently dressed down wherever he went, in his scarred leather and oily jeans, prepared for later. He ached when he had to explain himself to anyone, but he found a way.

"Allen Ginsberg and Gregory Corso showed up to have lunch with Edith Sitwell in 1958 at her Sesame Club in London in sandals and turtlenecks," Edgar apologized for him.

"But you don't like beat poetry, do you?" said Olivar, a Brazilian who moved around the world quite a bit.

"Where did you read that about Edith Sitwell? Do you love biographies as much as I do?" asked Elizabeth, an heiress to Irish beer money.

"Are you going to take Elizabeth and me to your club later?" Olivar asked Sean, both teasingly and seriously. They had been through this before.

"I can disguise myself as a man," Elizabeth added playfully.

"No. Up until I go there I'm responsible. After that I don't take any responsibility for anything I do."

"It's Dr. Jekyll and Mr. Hyde," Edgar said in a sharp tone. He hadn't yet been to the club either.

• • •

Sean meant what he said about responsibility ending there, and he said it a lot. That night when he felt the pavement again beneath his feet in his boots, he began to feel good for once. Not that he had ever yet been very unhappy.

Washington Street was cool and windy that November night. When Sean turned its corner the Mineshaft's black metal front door was slamming shut—full and heavy, yet often it was swung wide open like saloon doors in westerns. On it were stenciled the words "Private Club. Members Only." There were more hats than the first night. A huddle of them was maneuvering through the door: cowboy hat like a mountain with a cleft in its top, construction helmet, baseball rover, stocking cap. Sean already felt the fun of thinking irresponsibly. He stretched his back to allow his spine and ribs to flare, his lungs to expand.

Then he waved to, or saluted, actually, Rupert, who was leaning into the window of a squad car of the Sixth Precinct, exchanging information with the cops inside. He was now the Mineshaft's security guard, in his own uniform dangerously imitative of theirs.

The NYPD uniform and badge were the most difficult to wear because of the threat of arrest for impersonation, but Rupert had become the cops' friend and liaison. And flirt, of course. When they pulled out in a streak of red glare, Rupert came back to talk with Sean, keeping an official air of busyness and distraction about him. His studied anxiety went along with the blue serge uniform and classic gold buttons. "A little better than real," he bragged. "That's the way to do uniforms."

"Why you on the street?"

"This is the time of night when the lines get long. I don't want any guys in full leather to have to stand out here with the riffraff."

Rupert was a snob about his uniforms. Sean understood the allure of these stereotypes as boyhood games of power relived, renewed. But not the perfectionism, the fetishism of Rupert. He was like a connoisseur of sex, especially of "outlaw sex," as he put it. The more he talked about high rubber boots, full military kilts, Royal Canadian Mounted Police breeches, sanitation workers' green T's, the thinner the air became.

"How'd you get down here without being caught?"

"For the subway you put a windbreaker over your uniform. When the doors open you step out backwards, look both ways, then step back in, never sit down. Having spit-shined shoes most people assume you're a security guard on the way to work."

Sean didn't challenge Rupert on the discrepancy of pretending to be a security guard en route to a job while imitating a subway cop stepping backwards onto the platform at every stop. He knew that Rupert's mind was powered by a transistor transmitting an off frequency. "Brilliant" was how Sean left the matter of Rupert in his own judgment.

There weren't too many in line ahead of him on the uneven wooden planks of stairs tonight. Just enough—two or three at the

top being checked out by the doorman—for him to zone a bit. He
was half-reading the sign posted:

MINE SHAFT Dress Code
THE DRESS CODE as adapted by the membership
on the first of October 1976
APPROVED ARE CYCLE & WESTERN GEAR, LEVIS,
T-SHIRTS, UNIFORMS, JOCK STRAPS, PLAID &
PLAIN SHIRTS, CUT OFFS, CLUB PATCHES,
OVERLAYS & SWEAT
NO Cologne or Perfume or DESIGNER sweaters.
NO Suits, Ties, Dress Pants or Jackets.
NO RUGBY STYLED shirts or DISCO DRAG
NO COATS in the Playground.

Sean noticed how the different sizes of print, the irrationality of
the typeface scheme, was reminiscent of a letter from prison, a
note from a killer, one that Travis Bickle might have pasted
together in *Taxi Driver.* He had just seen that movie a week before,
envying what he felt was its amber atmosphere. A lot of films
being made then had the same amber tint, Sean noticed, separating them from the lipstick-red tint of Technicolor movies. He
wanted to suffuse one of his own movies in amber. He wanted his
next film to be in color. For him it could be like stepping through
the world-of-Oz partition to be able to consider colors.

Whoever was filling the loose mechanic's overalls in front of
him moved through the checkpoint. It was Sean's turn.

"You got a membership? . . . . That'll be four dollars."

The doorman tucked into a little foyer on the second-floor
landing was full of punctuated energy yet somehow also entirely
placid. He had dark eyes, humorous and ironic, and an even, nasal

voice. Sean had him pegged as an Italian-American from New Jersey—a common derivation in the club. Sitting on a high stool in front of a lit sign-in sheet, like a maître d' at a fancy restaurant, he was the one who enforced the code. "You'll have to check that jacket," he'd say, or ". . . those pants," leaving an occasional shy flower of a boy to walk around in his skivvies, his legs blushing. He knew how to pick them. "What's that perfume—Halston?" he challenged loudly one night.

Another night a hair colorist showed up with three friends at his checkpoint. The doorman hated that his clean blue jeans had an obvious crease down the front of the legs. "If we allowed people like you in, this place would turn into a cocktail lounge."

"What are you talking about?"

"We're sick of your kind."

The contradiction in his moods conveyed the contradictory spirit of the club: cruel, serious, humorous. Tonight the zipper of his loose blue jeans was all the way down. Sometimes he performed sex checks if he saw a smooth face with soft features. A few women had succeeded in sneaking by in disguise—besides those two or three who were officially invited on Thursday nights because of their close friendships with the regulars, or because of their generally kinky lives. Elizabeth heard that Lee Radziwill had been smuggled in; that's why she'd asked Sean to take her in disguise.

To Sean, Larry the doorman was simply a short fellow with long black hair and dirty fingernails, who smelled of cigarettes. He was surprised that others projected so much onto him: a Cherokee Indian, an all-American college kid, a Puerto Rican hustler. The variations suggested drugs, but also the mystery often ascribed to the place, as if it were more than the sleazy dive it so obviously was. The Mineshaft subtly asked for that kind of reinterpretation.

"Anyone fuss with you last night, Larry?" a voice asked from behind Sean.

"Yup," he answered, all business. "You throw them down the stairs from left to right so they break their fall on the banister."

As Sean was signaled into the main room, he felt he'd walked into a pumpkin, black inside but artificially lit by red and yellow glows. It was that amber again, the amber of the movies, but mixed with coal dust. Sean hung a quick, immediate right before adjusting to the low, controlled roar of the crowd. Even their laughs rolled into a single muffled roar.

Inside its crazy quilt of a bathroom—like the black-white tile bathrooms of either the Empire Diner or One Fifth—Sean peed into a gleaming urinal. No open mouths right then. No one passing his palm through his spray. No Bud can left on the rim with a penciled "Fill Me" taped on. No one kneeling down by the toilet looking up as if towards a golden Aztec rain god. When those supplicants were around, Sean felt as if he were again surrounded by the Bowery bums who asked for loose change every morning on his way to the bodega for a carton of milk. (At night they burned bonfires in singed, bronzed ashcans across the street, like centurions guarding someone's empire.) In the quiet, empty bathroom he was able to concentrate enough to make out in the ruby light a folded piece of thick white paper stuck in the plumbing of the toilet. He leaned over, withdrew the square, opened its folds.

The paper was a revelation. On it was a drawing in the mode of Tom of Finland, or Wolf, the illustrator Sean had met at Halsted's harrowing press conference. But this artist was both rawer and more refined. The rawness was in his faces and bodies: the men pictured had faces as ugly as some dogs' and their bodies were as lumpy as laundry bags. They seemed to be drawn from life in the bars where so many of the regulars were close to monsters in their bearing and in their unshaved, brutish faces. Beauty was definitely usurped here by beastliness. The anonymous drawing Sean opened up like an origami was more poorly rendered than Wolf's. Sean was thinking that the drawing seemed to be purposely bad, perhaps so the artist could show his humility towards the power of his scene and his characters. It was close to being a picture of souls, not ideal souls but rather their antitypes: ugly essences purified of any delicacy.

Sean thought for a while without looking too carefully. He often put ideas before things, but this evening he was simply struck by a first impression. When he began to focus, he encountered a fantastic scene of the kind allowed in pornography, a genre close to fairy tales. In a blank landscape of single lines for trees and hills, the most complicated linear concentration given over to a lone Harley parked against an erasure of white sky, a motorcycle cop in a helmet with gun, boots, and bullets was holding up a collapsed biker, slumped, with a full erection, in his arms, while he played with the nipples of his fallen partner's hairy chest. Most of the biker's weight seemed to be shifted onto his shoulder blades. He was apparently drunk or out of it. But Sean immediately recognized in the mood and composition the geometry of Titian's *Deposition from the Cross*. He wasn't even severely stoned yet. His eyes zipped down to the signature on the bottom right: "Jarhead."

Sean swung into the main room. He wanted to meet the artist. He must be here, to have left the drawing folded that evening. The name "Jarhead" was probably a visual clue as well: he'd have a marine look, or at least a military haircut. That was Sean's guess.

Deciding to check his jean jacket, he walked past the music cabin, where the stereo equipment was kept. Then past the wooden bar backed by a speckled mirror, four hanging lights barely illuminating its bartender. A column of cheap plastic cups reminded Sean of the cups in Dr. Bennett's office for collecting urine samples. Two or three bottles of liquor rested awkwardly near them: Smirnoff, Courvoisier. Cans of Bud were submerged partially in a garbage pail packed with ice, spares kept in bins under the bar. Sean never spoke much with that bartender in captivity at a bar given over mostly to skulking.

"Where does a man get a drink of piss around here?" a drunken voice asked. Laughs went up around him as if his wit were actually sharp.

Sean squeezed between the couple of wooden bar stools and a pool table that was never used for billiards, but rather as a flatbed to lean against or lie on. Once at around five-thirty on a Saturday evening / Sunday morning Sean heard a shadow sitting on the pool table with his knees drawn up to his chin complaining in a scratched voice, "No one respects me." His friend slapped him quickly and tartly with a response: "Well, considering you've spent the past five hours letting anyone who wanted piss on you in a bathtub, who would?"

The whole place was jerry-built. When lights flicked on, its wiring was exposed taped to the walls by electrician's tape. No gels were used, just red, peach, or bare white light bulbs. Keypunch operators and graphic designers by day, dressed simply in gray jockstraps or bound in harnesses with loops and straps, were crumpled onto lumber forms: sawhorses, low stockades, fences. Long benches against one wall were backed by stacks of beer cans. The red-and-silver metal cylinders tumbled down occasionally like kids' building blocks.

Sean angled to the near wall where a coat-check attendant used plastic bags to stash clothes more frequently than he used hangers. His station was a shelter, a rustic shrine by the side of a dusty road. A big horse of a man, his shiny baldness making him look like Yul Brynner, had just finished depositing all his clothes until he was left standing in the nude. His flesh was rosy and unappetizing: bloody rosy. Sean stuck his own number check in his back pocket, hoping he didn't lose it as he often did, having to wait to reclaim his coat until the early-morning hour when the place closed. He lost all his favorite pieces of clothes in the Mineshaft.

Circling back to the bar, he passed the shoeshine stand. Late at night he'd often end up hunched next to its metal in a squashed pose, simply feeling gravity. The gleaming stand for resting a boot was shaped triangularly like a piece of pie. But he usually took hours before he reached that nadir. The main room for Sean was first a lounge for standing and talking: tinselly, razzle-dazzle, boisterous. As the preliminaries wore thin he'd descend to the darker rooms, feeling as if he were gradually crouching into the form of a four-legged animal, passing through cycles of devolution.

A tall display case held the trophies of Excelsior, won at different bike runs by the motorcycle club that made the Mineshaft its clubhouse. Sean never made out the particulars of the vertical bronze enhancers of light, which were like replicas of the ancient lighthouse at Alexandria that supposedly used metal sheets to shine the flames of a perpetually burning blaze out to sea.

"R.J., I have to ask you something."

R.J. spent most of his nights at the rustic Bar #1 drinking cognac, his voice becoming raspier and more difficult to understand with every hour, his smile increasing in voltage.

"There's Fassbinder," R.J. said. "I think he's in love with Peter." Peter was a narcissistic hustler obsession of R.J.'s Sean had heard more about than he wanted to know.

Sean looked over to see a fattish man, his face covered in whiskers: a piece of a beard, sideburns, lots of weedy fuzz. Red suspenders were stretched over his flannel shirt. He wore the bulky blue jeans farmers wore, a cigarette inserted in his mouth.

Fassbinder was indeed intensely trying to possess Peter. He obviously liked challenges to test his powers and worth in an open market. A cultish fame was his most formidable asset.

"You want to meet him?"

"Not right now."

Sean hadn't yet seen *Beware of a Holy Whore,* which was show-ing that week at the Film Forum on Vandam Street. That's why Fassbinder was in town, though he supposedly kept finding excuses now that the Anvil and the Mineshaft were open. Those clubs almost seemed, Sean thought, to have been invented by him, with their melodramatic politics, two-dimensional carica-tures, and especially their silence, their tuning down of language. Fassbinder's films with gay characters—*Fox and His Friends, The Bitter Tears of Petra von Kant*—allowed him a wide audience in downtown Manhattan and San Francisco. But for Sean *Jail Bait* was always the closest to the heart of his own projects. He loved the lead: a German boy trying to look like bikers in American B motorcycle movies of the fifties. He loved the ruby-colored juke-box in the bar. He loved the American servicemen lurking. He loved when the boy and his high-school girlfriend shot her father for putting his obdurate bulk between them. He loved the last scene as the girl jumps rope in a reformatory's stone hall: so illicit.

But even with that, Sean didn't want to talk to his hero. He thought it might ruin things. Besides, this was not the moment. Fassbinder was obviously concentrating on his romantic machi-nations. Sean didn't want to bungle the scenario of hearts and traps.

Peter was a close buddy of R.J.'s, so Sean knew his story from R.J.'s voracious telling. How Peter had dropped in from California in the early seventies, a hippie with long blond hair braided down his back. How he'd stand staring up at himself in the band of mir-rors over the bar at the Eagle's Nest that became a frieze of pos-tures whenever the room filled. How he never went home with anyone. Sean had seen him do his routine: mostly now he just glanced up at the mirror occasionally, as if he'd just heard a familiar tune from the past. But as the drugs multiplied he'd sometimes lapse into his narcissistic mode, with R.J. as his devoted audience.

Peter didn't speak or understand German. Fassbinder's English phrases were always shouted, his German spoken more monotonously. But there were fewer of those shouted phrases than Sean, eavesdropping, expected. The courtship between hustler and director was mostly carried on through puffs of cigar smoke, a crotch grabbed, a patch of denim held to the lips. Since Peter's speaking voice was as high and squeaky as a little boy's, he was much more effective silent.

That was the last night Sean saw Fassbinder at the bar. Of course R.J. kept him current on the story, which became as intricate as any of the director's dark movies. Peter took quite a few Concorde trips to Paris paid for by Fassbinder for weekends in hotels. A few years later Fassbinder's lover killed himself. R.J. said Peter was the cause. "Their labyrinthine string turned into a noose," R.J. liked to say, though he often simply made up such tales.

"Do you know who Jarhead is?" Sean asked R.J. He began unfolding the drawing, but R.J. quickly cupped his hands over Sean's fist, indicating he'd already seen the clue about to be produced.

"He's here tonight."

"I want to find him. Tell me just one detail. Any one."

"One of his models is retarded and lives in New Jersey."

"Whoa! How wonderful!" R.J. was pleased to see Sean so impressed.

Sean moved off to the backrooms, allowing his feelings of happy wonder and adventure to develop.

After passing through a hall about five yards long to the left of the awards display case, he felt anxious. He wanted to find Jarhead. He imagined he was moving quickly, but he was actually only stumbling forwards and backwards over the same few square yards. Sometimes he was pushed aside as if by a big wave when a group of temporary bullies muscled him away. But mostly the room was marked by an exaggerated civility, a gentility even. It didn't seem as if acts were happening before his eyes, but rather as if they were happening *in* his eyes. The diffuse rosy light, the smell of rank sweat, the bronze glint of a beer can were triggers that stimulated dreams.

Sean bought another beer from Racey Peters, the bartender at Bar #2. He was a rock-'n'-roll fan with black hair, Satan tattoos, and a syrupy Tennessee accent. After some earlier stimulants, Sean needed beer to keep from feeling too irradiated and insolid.

"Gentlemen, there's a man at the bar who's drunk sixteen piss-loads!" Racey yelled out. "Free beers to anyone who'll unload on him."

When two friends paused in front of the crouched drinker to chat, Racey laid into them as fiercely as the doorman into the hair colorist with the crease in his jeans. "This is not an old ladies' home!"

"We're waiting for Mr. Gaybar," one sang over his shoulder as they moved sideways.

"We have a hot mouth here!" said Racey, this time into the mike of the loudspeaker system. "This man is waiting for your pissloads. He has taken thirty-two pissloads this evening. Free beer to those who piss on him."

Sean planned to make a straight line through the first back-room past the removable wall with its drilled glory holes and into to the second backroom with its darkened stage. But instead he was pulled in front of the scaffolds used for fist fucking.

The setup was a crucifixion: all white electric light gathered in one patch, the scaffolding fixed at high noon. Sean couldn't help thinking of the pillories of the Puritans as he watched a curly-haired young man who seemed to be studious and Puerto Rican splayed within the contraption of shinily crisscrossing belts and straps known as "the Strap," leaving his head tilted upwards from his torso. His jockstrap seemed to be made of bandages; the rest of him was exposed to those crowding around. A balding man whose back was prickly with hair was pushing his arm way up inside to the elbow. (One famous guy had inches tattooed all the way up his arm to mark his prowess.) Sean was surprised at how quietly understated the event was. The stripped young man being explored from within was keeping his silence, yet possessed a five-yard stare.

An ugly brawl turned the quiet circle briefly into a mess of punches, pushes, pulls. One thick-lipped, thick-tongued bulldog of a man, sporting a black eye-patch strung around his head, was forcing his shoulder closer to the action while pulling up to his nostril a stainless-steel screw-top bullet hung on a leather string that held his poppers. Uniformed Rupert stepped in as swiftly and unexpectedly as a comic-book superhero, pulling him away, shoving him towards a wormhole of a tunnel while giving him a lecture on etiquette, on standing back and not forcing on others his "bad breath," as Rupert poetically described the infraction.

"Watch your wallets, gentlemen," manager Wally's voice interrupted over the loudspeaker. "A suspected pickpocket just came in the bar."

When Sean noticed Rupert marching back across the room again, playing with the strobe effect he could produce by flicking the switch on his pocket flashlight, he stepped in his way to detain him, fumbling with the drawing he wordlessly showed.

"That's Jarhead's. He leaves them folded in subway johns all over town."

"Really? Then he's tossing off his works for the greater glory, not for money or fame?"

"Well, it works. You're asking me about him rather than watching the show, aren't you?" Rupert nodded towards the fisting, which had resumed as concentratedly and silently as before, as if it were an anatomy lesson taking place in slow motion. "He's downstairs."

Sean was off. A hatch opened in the center of the floor through which a hinged ladder made a creaking stairway. Feeling too stoned to navigate its steep angle, he decided to descend a set of solider, concrete stairs, holding on to a railing all the way, feeling strangely protected by the harsh blue-gray prison lighting, which made the faces traveling past him on their way upstairs seem all the more entranced. Seeming and seeing were nearly synonymous here.

"Did you see those bats with human faces flying up out of the cellar?" he asked Arnie when he saw him.

But Arnie was too anesthetized by "the tub room" he was inhabiting that night to respond. He was tilted to the wall in a minimal white box of a room with three bathtubs set apart on its concrete floor, which curved downward to a drain. One tub was set back in a tiled alcove. The lighting was soft gray. Again a living theater of degradation was being mounted democratically.

Some rubber-suited bathers came early so they could be certain to occupy the porcelain tubs. A few stayed all night, hour on hour, enjoying the bubbly, bitter yellow water that began to fill the bathtubs as men peed there. Some of the cleverer brought stoppers in their back pockets from home to clog the drains—they could be just as stuffy about their obsessions as opera connoisseurs, and often *were* the same ones who gestured superiorly in the standing-room section at the back of the Met. Beer cans bobbed in the tubs full of liquid. The targets were the mouths of those slumped inside the gray-white tubs: reverse fountains, they swallowed rather than spewed. One night a man tumbled, zonked, from an overflowing tub onto the concrete floor, breaking his head. As an excess of piss filled the bathtubs, dangerous over-flowing scenes were evoked.

"Stop it," Sean told Arnie. "You're too good to get in there."

"What about you? What about us?"

"Don't argue with me."

Sean felt tired all of a sudden. He drew back from where he was, lost his courage. His wandering through the spookhouse had been helped by a suspension of disbelief. But when his confidence broke, so did the spell. Sean needed to find someone, to find Jar-head, not simply to walk and watch, but to let the usual emotions drain out of him as other, weirder emotions filled in.

Soon Sean was on the roof. He didn't remember walking upstairs, through rooms, up more stairs. This was the time of night when he simply landed, as if he had flown there. The transitional moments were erased as instantly as they happened. He felt like a young man who'd flown into a forest at midnight on a broom.

Sean stared up at a moon from the roof as guys threw beer cans down onto the street. Others were kissing dark, unshaved cheeks, murmuring as they did, their leather vests draped casually on pipes, skylights, boxy shapes. Hoots went up as if from owls. On the street below a Herculean-sized, or oaf-sized, fellow with a big tan hat, boots, a mildly rendered state trooper's outfit was blowing a whistle to stop a car from making a U-turn. The car appeared to be filled with Asian tourists. He accomplished all the right gestures: stuck his brim in the window first; stuck his crotch to the window; rested his boot on the bumper. Finally he waved them on, having obviously caused some worry. Applause began on the rooftop and fluttered down to the street. The fraudulent ranger might as well have taken a bow, but didn't. He was too much of a sexual professional for that, too much of a consummate performance artist.

The delight from the rooftop was caused by an impersonation magically delivered. Most of those clapping on the roof preferred acting to the drudgery of real life—taking a police exam or enlisting in the Navy—as a means to possess their boyhood fantasy of men in uniform.

Next Sean found himself in the very last room of the bottom floor. He felt he had floated there like a saint or an angel in a Mexican religious painting until his toes tapped the tiles.

"Surrealism and religion are very close to each other," Sean said to someone he hardly knew.

Sean was always thinking about something. He could forget which floor he was on, which playroom he was visiting. For him the club was an almost surreal escape. Behind the bar serving the ubiquitous cans of Bud stood a bartender with a five-foot-long pet python wrapped around his forearms and chest. His bartender partner was hunched on the bar backwards with his big buttocks hanging into the face of a customer, who took surprising revenge by slapping instead of kissing the proffered behind. Insults were kisses, and kisses insults here. Sean liked the bawdiness of the dark moon of the bartender's ass blaring from the bar like a farting trumpet.

On stage on the far side of the room one exhibitionist's penis was pierced with gold needles, another's wound in barbed wire. A thin milquetoast holding a suitcase as if he were a traveling salesman whose clothes had all been stolen—nightmare material—climbed on stage, opened his valise, began to unpack a line of tan, red, and black rubber dildos, which he arranged in height from the teeniest to the most gargantuan, so the line resembled a hill of medieval towers. He then greased himself with Vaseline and proceeded to sit on each one, ending up sitting on the largest as if it were a giant mushroom and he Alice in Wonderland. There was a smattering of applause for his finale, unusual in the overall sedation of the room. He was replaced by a trio who enacted their own fist fucking without the help of a scaffold or pillory. They wore nothing but chains. The one strung and hoisted—almost an entire arm having disappeared up inside of him—hung limply, his eyes closed, a silly smile on his face.

"I know a big sauna filled with Puerto Rican and Jamaican prostitutes," Sean heard someone say in a German accent.

For a while he was wandering past the room he thought of as the "outhouse," in the back of the main floor. Here men who were enamored of "mud" would allow themselves to steam in the smell of excrement. He walked in to see a full panoramic surround of red-lit hairy buttocks, stained jeans, belts lost like snakes on the stony ground, wall lights covered by smoking T-shirts. One man wore a belt with the word "SHIT" written in studs. The sharp, acrid smell of the stuff rose in the air. The threat, and promise, drove these men into the most cramped quarters in the place, the most forbidden, the asshole of the club. They were climbing again under the back porch. There they exulted in the songs of tongues. The smell was too much for Sean. He didn't actually see what he smelled.

He did take part in the sweaty action sometimes. A young Haitian accountant for Con Edison whose name he could never remember—just his job—liked to drape him over a sawhorse in the back of the Den, where he would strap him with his wide leather belt. Sean felt little. But the punctuation was satisfying, as if he were being written on, as if he were a piece of paper being typed on. The music in that room was a robotic minimalism: spare, psychedelic, circling, pluvial. Sean felt an eagle might well have flown down and perched on the shoulder of an Indian cross-legged with a feather stuck in his braided hair. The music was inspiring him to such trippy San Francisco–style thinking.

Once Sean tangled with "Shortie," small, black, and plump, his head as bald as an onyx. He had some sort of operating share in the Spike and drove a motorcycle on which he perched like a porcelain Buddha on an ornate seahorse to ride to his apartment somewhere in Brooklyn. Sean watched an enemy of his—or suitor, perhaps—throw beer cans down at him from the battlement of the Mineshaft roof, calling "Nigger, nigger." One night he and Sean played a game, what they used to call a "head game" in the bar, where Sean had to repeat various phrases, some taken from the Declaration of Independence, forwards and backwards. Sean enjoyed the futility of the exercise, the perfectly useless concentration.

A physician with red hairs sprouting from his shiny head asked him to drive his fist up him. Sean didn't feel particularly that this was his role. He never wanted to. But he did. Just as his fist was finding his way through the damp cloth of the inside of the man's behind, Sean began to feel faint. He was squeamish about the body. Perhaps this squeamishness was the very discrepancy that made him visit the Mineshaft so often: so physical and yet so punitively drawn. Soon he fell out, allowing his arm to unravel from the inside of the caterpillar.

Penetration and death. That was what was so exciting to so many. To penetrate the dark tunnels was to possess them: pink kidneys, tan skin, celadon-green layers of muscle, black empty spaces. The way out of Hell was through the anus of the Devil, a mouth exhaling bodies like pebbles onto the shores of Purgatory.

Sean was saved from his own droning thoughts by a tap on the shoulder.

"I'm Jarhead. I hear you've been looking for me."

"Wait. . . . Is there anything I haven't done? I wanted to do everything before I met you."

"Let's sit onstage in the Den."

"Yeah."

So they swept along to the Den. On the way Sean checked out the artist whose drawing had been so alluring to him all evening. He didn't want to touch him. Jarhead was ugly in the sloppy way his pictures were. He was short, squat, his own cheeks botchily shaded. But as Sean had predicted to himself, Jarhead's eyes when they turned his way were soft, fascinatingly soft, yet looking in six directions at once. He was dressed in a gray work shirt, blue jeans, black boots: the usual, though even more anonymous than usual perhaps, as if he were one in a lineup of coal miners in a post office mural painted by a WPA artist. (A gay version of one of those social-realist murals had been painted by Sean's friend Richard, an ex–Russian Orthodox monk, on a wall of the Spike that year for the Bicentennial: depicted was a muscular Everyman driving a spike into a railroad track. At a formal, sit-down, all-male dinner given by Rupert at his apartment where everyone was required to wear a uniform, Richard showed up in a full military kilt in a roomful of ordinary police officers and state troopers sipping cocktails.)

Sean liked what he heard of Jarhead's voice—it was tranquil, not tranquilized. His fingers were blunt, with bitten nails, monkeylike with hairs on their knuckles, at least so Sean imagined, unsure in the chiaroscuro light. The voice and eyes seemed responsible for the drawings. The rest was a display of ordinariness.

Sean and Jarhead sat on the floor of the stage—just abandoned by the vaudevillian who transported his dildos in a valise—between an industrial-appliance-sized carton of plastic cups and a tall ladder leading up to a burned light bulb: an addled version of an off-Broadway set.

"I loved your drawing . . . this one."

"My ambition is to redo Tom of Finland from nature."

"I want you to be in my movie."

"As what? Maybe my master won't let me."

"I want your master to be in my movie, too."

"I do my drawings for my master. He tells me what he wants me to draw."

"That's it. That's my movie. It's a gay Scheherazade story. You have to make the drawings to please your master. If not, you're killed. See, instead of telling a story, as in the first Scheherazade, you draw them. Then I dramatize them after a swooning fade. The way they used to do dreams in Hollywood. Or on *I Dream of Jeannie*."

"Whatever happened to a normal life with grandmas and green backyards and turnip pies?"

"Well, if you've got a master you must have asked yourself that question before."

"I followed a voice that was coming from down in the pit of my stomach. I guess you could call it my groin."

"The word 'groin' makes me sick."

They both laughed.

"Scheherazade's good, because I feel as if we're sisters. My friend Annie told me that women in harems in Saudi Arabia have much closer, warmer friendships with each other than women in America. She visited one. You'll have to meet Annie when she gets back. She's a trip and a half."

"It's as weird as shit. Except you film it and I draw it. And I live it more totally than you."

"Should I call you Jarhead?"

"That's my only name. I had it legally changed, like a monk."

Sean thought of Richard again and of the sadness he once saw in his eyes when, standing in full fireman's outfit with rubber boots up to his knees, he'd been looking wistfully in the entrance hallway of his town house at a line of golden Orthodox icons: John the Baptist in a flaming hair shirt; archangel Michael with his protective sword as tall and sturdy as a skyscraper. Sean sensed that Richard was thinking wistfully at that moment of returning to the monastery in Brookline.

"But it's not really Satanism, is it?"

"Naw. Satan is a construct of being a bad boy put onto us from the outside."

Sean heard these last words in a resonating isolation, as if he were hearing them through a conch. He was listening so busily that he wasn't observing Jarhead's transformation into a professor while he talked.

"What are you on?"

"Angel dust. You?"

"MDA."

Their conversation was stopped forcefully by a voice from above like thunder, though not particularly loud. "You'd better be home in ten minutes!"

Sean looked up to see a tall, bony blond man in a cheap plastic rip-off of a black leather jacket, black boots with thin cardboard soles, and severely square metal glasses stride away, his badly cut hair falling down from his costume cap over the back of his neck. Sean immediately understood the tasteful badness of Jarhead's drawing. He located Jarhead's peculiar version of masochism as if with a mental pin, and he understood how far its pure illogic was isolating him. Sean romantically felt Jarhead was the purer artist.

"That's your master, right?"

"Dennis. His friends call him Dennis the Menace."

"He'll be great in the movie."

The mentioning of Dennis called up a sweetness in Jarhead's face Sean hadn't seen there. Sean was happy with the sinister mystery of their love.

"Let's go. We don't have much time."

"Let's go."

Dawn's light was beginning to appear through the cracks in the walls of the Den. When the three of them dragged up the stairs, a full puff of dusty brightness blew in their faces as if just forced out of a feather pillow. The surprise reminded Sean of being caught in the light of a projector while trying to claim a seat in the first row of a movie theater. He felt a panic, almost like an inkling of a sickness. But he allowed himself to sway, and the swaying quelled a feeling of danger as he walked through the second floor past the man splayed on the floor in sheerest underpants, begging to be stomped on, past handcuffed arms frozen in a backwards salute like wings.

Dennis, Jarhead, and Sean waited in what was now a long, winding line for coats, the talk around them made of crushed phrases:

"This place is tired."

"I found the crowd weird tonight."

"You like cops?"

"Yeah."

"Cops like hippies too. But they don't always know how to get started."

"I think the tarot is a portable heretical catechism."

"There's a connection between the tarot and the Albigensian heresy."

"Then I'm right?"

"The soles of my boots are sticky. I'm going to go home and scrub them with Comet."

As they all stepped onto the sidewalk, Sean felt challenged by the violet light. R.J. had been knocking his way down the stairs behind them. Sean put an arm tightly around his waist. "Let's take a cab to your house," he invited himself. "There's nothing more

THE GOLDEN AGE OF PROMISCUITY

beautiful than a cab across town when the first yellow eggs are scrambling in the heat of the morning sky."

"Sean, you're such a poet," R.J. slurred.

"Jarhead's going home with his master," said Sean, weighing down on the word "master" sarcastically, departing from his earlier gingerliness and fascination. He wished Jarhead could come with them, so he was peeved. Drugs magnified and distorted his feelings.

"Let's listen to Mozart," said R.J., having heard a tone that reminded him of himself, looking over at Sean as affectionately as a dog at his boy.

Across the cobbled street, men in bloodied aprons were heaving auburn carcasses of meat, cows hanging from hooks that pierced their necks and slackly opened mouths. Slabs of cow were being transported in slow motion over the sidewalks, wrapped in crinkled clear green plastic, on a flyline of rotting flesh. In the gaps between their bloodied and smelling bodies, the men working the assembly line eyed the pale band of diminished men in tatters of black leather and denim emerging from the hole across the street they knew to be unsavory. Silently, shruggingly, the meat packers expressed their scorn and contempt.

Sean, R.J., Jarhead, Dennis, and Bruno—the bartender who'd been flaring his fat behind on the bar earlier—stared back at them, blankly amazed.

Their amazement was an honest reproach.

Jarhead's Drawings

Sean felt scared and uneasy at the beginning. He had brought his camera. Paul was helping as an assistant. They were setting up in the gray expanse of Dennis's loft.

"What's with these guys?" Paul was asking Sean.

"They're urban aboriginals," Sean answered. Sean had heard the phrase somewhere and was impressed.

"It's terrible to be possessed," he said back to Paul. "And it's the best."

"I thought 'possessed' was like a devil."

"But in the current psychological age 'possessed' is just concentrating on an image that comes from the root of the brain without explanation and without morality."

"Yeah, right," Paul responded sarcastically.

Paul was along for the pay—and for the curiosity of the scenes being enacted. He did feel the possession of which Sean spoke. As a middle-class black who worked as a Gaiety dancer three nights a week, he was definitely a thrill seeker himself.

Dennis's loft, located just down the street from the Eagle's Nest, seemed as big as an airplane hangar. Its grayness was its predominant tone: gray-painted wood floors, gray walls, a tin roof cutting off windows too high to look out. The pieces of furniture were as minimal as those in a contemplative monastery: uncovered gray mattress, a man-sized cell made of black plastic tubes, a dog cage of metal crisscrossings, a faraway bathroom with full urinals formed of thick waves of porcelain, and a tiny medicine-cabinet mirror staring blankly above a sink. Long walls were inset with metal hoops, neck braces, leg clamps: instruments redolent of the Spanish Inquisition. Even the light from the dusty altitude of the windows was gray, pointillist. Sean liked the place because it already constituted a grainy eight-by-ten photograph.

Sean had recently bought his own Arriflex camera for shooting sixteen-millimeter film. He was planning to blow this film he was making up to thirty-five millimeters. His separate sound recorder was a Nagra, its cable tied into the camera. Both camera and recorder were running at twenty-four frames per second so that they were always in sync. Sean didn't care too much about the sound, though. He used a boom mike sometimes that hung down as if in an old Hollywood studio. Occasionally he'd clip a lavaliere mike behind a black T-shirt's collar, or hide a wireless mike in a roach clip tossed casually on the floor. Usually he simply let the images unfold silently, like flowers in time-lapse photography. Porn lent itself, Sean felt, to the silent treatment. He preferred subtitles, or nothing at all.

"Porn is real life cast into the void," he pretentiously told an audience one night at a lecture he was invited to give, his first ever, at Cooper Union. Sean was becoming semifamous.

Jarhead was lying on the bare mattress, its buttons like so many navels. He was dressed in an amalgam of denim, leather, and socks: the sort of unindividuated clothes favored by the entire herd of leather men who had come to fascinate Sean, perhaps mostly because they were sheep in wolves' clothing. He loved their marginality, the hopeless comedy of their tragedy, but he had always felt himself to be a curious flower as well.

Jarhead was drawing with all the finesse he could manage using pencils of different grades and thicknesses. He was sketching a cartoon of a Cuban-looking man with hair as short as a field burned in a flash fire, hairs sprouting wildly across his face, dressed in a soldier-of-fortune uniform decorated with buttons, chains, links, belts, pockets, and medals, his skin a darker shade of pale. In his fist at the end of his crookedly powerful arm he was holding the jaw of a scared-looking, whiter man, with tendrils of long hair, his eyes bulging, his face covered in a beard, his hillbilly body bare. The Cuban soldier of fortune was looking into his face with an expression the equivalent of spitting—mean, leveling in its confrontation of different microcultures. The fantasy seemed to involve some punishment of a professorial face by one of Che Guevara's rebels—the whiter man with his sagging hairy chest could have been a professor of Chaucer at any number of English departments. As in all of Jarhead's drawings, the suffering involved humor, as if it were an inside joke, a reversal of the obvious meant to keep others off the scent.

"Are we living in pain to realize a gain?" Sean asked loudly off-camera.

But Jarhead was too far gone to answer. To draw he had drunk a bottle of vodka, smoked a joint, played with himself, taken a pill, even injected a slick needle into the rubbery amber stretches of his skin. A nurse once told him he had such good veins. The compliment swelled his head with the idea to one day puncture them. These were nonsensical thoughts. But then his strength was in nonsense. His drawings were icons of nonsensicalness. On a low place on the wall, about an inch above the floorboard, he'd tacked a bit of Blake's wisdom printed on a tea bag from a health-food store: "You never know what is enough unless you know what is more than enough." He'd attended Kutztown State College in Pennsylvania.

"If you don't finish that drawing I'll lop off your head with my long curved knife."

Dennis stood in an unlikely pose with a scimitar raised, but dressed in the simplest leather-and-denim wear. Sean felt tickled to have employed this extremely arrogant figure in his completely inflated fantasy and to have seen the conceit work.

"Cut."

•   •   •

Sean's notion had been to take *Invitation* and the other drawings Jarhead had been sketching and turn them into faithful scenarios acted out in the confusion of the moment. Or to walk over to the Mineshaft in the center of a working heat to try to lure, or convince, different men to take part in these real-life dramas. He had been inspired by watching the nonactors in Pasolini's *The Gospel According to Saint Matthew.* Suddenly a farmer with a fantastic beard of sprouting hairs was a prophet. Or the boy from the corner store was an angel holding the scales of righteousness carelessly in his extended arm.

Sean couldn't stick to the plot. He wished he could hold a thought. He felt if he could hold a thought he could be a pure artist, a real artist, like Jarhead. Instead he became transfixed within a few seconds by Dennis with his shocks of blond hair. The closer he looked, the more convinced he became it was dyed. He was of German-American descent, from Idaho. His leather jacket was like the plastic covering of a couch on Long Island. Dennis was exposing his entire chest. He had his jeans pulled down below the sack of his underpants. His glasses were black and reflective. They made filming difficult.

Sean was forgetting where he was again. It was this fitfulness that allowed him to film.

"Turn it on," he said to Paul with no true intent.

Okay. This is going to be a portrait of Dennis. Such were the broad outlines of Sean's thinking. He was incredibly excited by his idea, but he was similarly disappointed by the failure to reach any particular destination. Dennis was glaring at Jarhead. Jarhead was looking inward, paralyzed. Paul was making demands on Sean with his eyes.

"He's not right," Sean announced.

Everyone turned suddenly. It was as if there had been an interruption.

"We have to go to the bar," Sean said.

Sean could barely believe he was taking charge so forcefully. He needed to find the person who could fulfill the outline in his imagination. He was soon striding down the street towards the Eagle. He was aware of the corniness of his situation. This was no longer the release of a few months ago. This was already a sort of hypnotic need.

Sean was fairly convinced that neither his words nor his pictures had any worth. He was in the Eagle, though, looking for an excuse. The excuse he found was standing beneath Richard's Bicentennial mural.

Jarhead followed Sean's eyes to the mural of the flag: red, black, and blue. He smiled.

The almost rakish young man beneath the mural had just swiveled in his sleeveless dark blue denim jacket, exposing a backside on which a pattern of tacks spelled out "Murder, Inc."

beneath the bare outline of a penis embroidered in tacks as well. His dirty-blond hair tumbled down past his shoulders. The rest of him was a dark blur. When their eyes met, Sean picked out the silver-blue of his eyes. That was enough cruising for either of them. So Sean just walked up. The sense of danger advertised by the jacket assured him that he was safe.

"A true murderer would never identify himself like that," Sean said first. "Here's a knife. Tie me up. I trust you."

"Name's Tava," he laughed.

"I want you to be in my movie."

"I'm not Lana Turner and this isn't Schwab's."

"Huh?"

"I make movies, too. I'll show you sometime."

Sean did eventually see Tava's movie. He simply called the number he'd scrawled on a ripped pale-blue Barclay's check with his full name, or at least *a* full name inscribed: "Baron Gustavus A. von Will," and the address "138 Fort Greene Place, Brooklyn, N.Y. 11217." His number was written on the back in black felt-tip pen, all verticals. The presentation was titillating to Sean, with his weakness for all things fantastic. Indeed, the leather bars seemed to him increasingly to be fantastical boy's stuff, in a league with the Wolf Man, the Invisible Man, frogs, snakes, Civil War soldiers, spitting contests, Mighty Mouse cartoons.

The film was animated, part of a class Sean was led to believe Tava had completed at Pratt—though Tava's stories never proved entirely true. A decade later he would wonder why Tava, a sort of one-night stand, should be conjured up in his memories like a genie from a bottle. It was the same with R.J. Their prominence in the hierarchy of his memories was reminiscent of the injustice of the Christian system of heaven: you could walk in late and ascend to the top. Sean had plenty of close, important friends in his life.

Edgar was a good example. But characters like R.J. or Tava were able to elicit pangs and piquant pauses from him later that memories of the others didn't. The movie Tava screened for Sean pictured an animated set of cock and balls. The hilarious cock stiffened and stood with the erect pride of Mr. Peanut. Humorous balls jumped like cheerleaders with muffs. Then Mr. Cock spit involuntarily. End of film.

Tava also showed him a series of sculptures of cocks and balls cut from corrugated metal he had swiped from the old piers.

But the jokes filling the interstices of the silly cartoons and cutouts were missing in Tava that night as he walked Sean down the street outside the Eagle. He was pursuing an overblown idea of his own personal destiny borrowed from the dangerous excesses of German Romantic idealism and egoism, especially the idea of "genius." Sean filled in the chinks with jokes anyway.

•   •   •

Tava had made sidewalk drawings in the pavement of the West Side Highway, a road no longer used but not yet torn down. The antique highway stood over West Street like the skeleton of a dinosaur in the Museum of Natural History. Moonlight exaggerated its rusting so that it appeared pistachio green in patches. Its metalwork was fine. Its disuse allowed its workmanship to show after decades of having been pummeled by vehicles on their way somewhere else.

"Let me show you my etchings," Tava kidded.

He led Sean up a vast entrance to arrive at the actual highway. The gate was a couple of police sawhorses weakly blocking the way. On the way up the incline Sean felt as if he were approaching a wonder of the ancient world. The steepness of the slant was similar to the entrance of the disco favored by Puerto Ricans and blacks, the Paradise Garage, but much more exterior and external and monumental because made of such heavily engineered pieces of stone and connecting curves of concrete. Like the Pyramids, Sean felt, the abandoned overhead highway had probably been built at the expense of lots of lives. He imagined that some of the dead bodies standing in blocks of concrete like ancient statues at the bottom of the Hudson River (an even older highway, also in disuse) had been sacrificed in its construction, shadowed by illegal contracts and payoffs.

As they approached the crest, a kind of horizon line where the ramp ended and a section of highway began (broken off a few blocks beyond so that it led nowhere), Tava was plying Sean with his autobiographical tales.

"My middle name is Adolphus, after Adolf Hitler. Both my parents were killed by the Israelis, so I hate Israel and all Israelis. Their car was blown up by the Israelis when I was only four."

Sean looked over to check whether Tava was letting any irony escape with his anger. He saw only craziness, a giddy craziness. Tava showed lots of white over the blue of his eyes when he spoke: a sign of lying, someone had once told Sean.

Sean noticed over time that Tava was obsessed with the idea of Jews versus Aryans. When Sean became involved the following year with a Jewish boy from Long Island, Tava said to him, "How can you have a Jewish boyfriend? I thought you loved Christ. Christ was blond." Tava made an eight-millimeter movie of himself as Christ on the cross, without a loincloth.

Then he found his own Jewish boyfriend who was half his height and twice as nice. Tava confided to Sean that he used to choke him until he nearly passed out as an overture to their lovemaking. Sean would see them driving around the streets of Greenwich Village in Tava's red pickup truck, a piece of Americana he had acquired, he said, when he had lived on a commune in Vermont.

Soon Tava began to hang around with Arabs. They formed an unusual group at the Ramrod bar, where he used to arrive with them. Many of the cab drivers that year were Arabs, so Sean kept thinking of Tava's new friends as cab drivers. He knew nothing of the difference between Algeria and Morocco, or of the neighborhoods in which immigrants from North Africa and the Middle East had settled in New York City. He did know that until recently Eighth Avenue between Twenty-eighth and Twenty-ninth had been lined with belly-dancing joints with exotic names—Ali Baba, Arabian Nights, Egyptian Gardens, Port Said, Istanbul. The composer Virgil Thomson told him that bit of history when they dined with Edgar at Virgil's favorite French restaurant the next block up.

Tava's story was that he had been a soldier of fortune in Africa and that his friends were adventurers for hire. They didn't really seem to belong in that already strange mix of fake cowboys, old drunks, and young preppy men proud of their crisp flannel shirts. By the time that plot had unfolded, Sean already knew that Tava was harmless. He knew so in the time it took them to climb the ramp that first night to the highway.

As soon as they reached the level road, Tava was pointing out the tattoos he had painted on the pavement: a circle of blue stars outlined in silver, similar in design to the posters for *Jesus Christ Superstar;* a Tibetan necklace of orange skulls; a lit cigarette with a crimson tip; a heart pierced by an arrow. Every hundred steps or so they'd come across another one. Sean felt as if he were in Pompeii dusting through ruins.

"Here's your friend Jarhead invading my turf," Tava laughed.

Jarhead's drawing was sketched in smudged charcoals. Its ugly dark roughness reminded Sean of the crazed portraits of Christ drawn in two-tone blue and black on the sidewalks of Eighth Street by hippie artists begging for dimes and quarters. The blues in Christ's pained forehead were the black purples of the veins of shrimp. But Jarhead's flat icon was a handsome man, his hair swept back like Clark Gable's, in a T-shirt, tight pants, thick ski socks, boots with eyelets like pegs, his thing hanging down like a gun, the dome of a construction hat resting under his shin. The subtlest touches were the big white bedroom pillows on which the demon with eyebrows like attacking hawks was resting his head. The title sketched underneath: *Hard Hat.*

• • •

Tava made lots of noises as they walked down the ramp. His boots had cleats hammered in their heels, reminding Sean of the hoodlums who used to proudly execute a slow-motion tap dance up and down the hallways of his high school every afternoon. When he saw *West Side Story* at a drive-in from the backseat of his parents' car (the same spot from which he'd seen *La Dolce Vita*), he was amazed to find that such a mean and angular dress code and behavior wasn't unique to Turret.

As they reached an old-fashioned lamp the pale green color of the metal roofs of Paris, Tava stopped Sean and kissed him. Sean loved feeling Tava's arms around his back, the aggressive warmth and force filtering through strongly. He had gone so long without anyone near him. He felt as if there were tears in his lungs, congealing musically as part of a fugue of passion.

Then Tava let him go. Sean looked up into a face that had become changed from soft to hard. The constant changes of mood as Tava began to play him like a piano were intriguing to Sean. He wanted to swoon from all the uncorked affection. But he hesitated, because he knew the limits. It was as if you could only row your little boat so far out from shore to a certain middling darkness before turning back. If you went too far, you'd be on the high seas of swooning romance. A whole group's experiences had staked out the harbor's limits, allowing the danger of romance without the warmth. Sean had learned by watching, but watching was a limited kind of learning. Now he just grabbed Tava around his ribcage. He was loving the feeling of being a ballet dancer. Whose choreography to use? Was he was going to let Tava be the prince? Hidden within the standard cartoons of the emerging leather men were hundreds of tiny, subtle cartoons, much more personal and nuanced: of Popeye, or of church acolytes, of Batman and Robin, or of James Bond and his women as inflexible as their bright red fingernails.

Continuing along in a ballet of his own devising, Sean allowed himself to be dragged by Tava's arm hooked along his own right side towards a street a couple blocks beyond the Eagle's Nest. They would occasionally look down and up at each other. Tava was taller, especially in his brown Frye boots. When they turned the corner Sean sensed an insectlike buzz of activity. Four long, huge industrial trucks were lined up like oxen with their backs opening onto a platform. A deal must have been cut to keep the insides of these aluminum hulks available late at night. Tava led the way through a shady corridor between two of them. Sean hadn't noticed the flags of red and black and blue hankies hanging down from the left pocket of the back of his black jeans. They were asymmetrical tails. He knew from *Drummer* magazine what they meant: black, whipping; red, fist fucking; blue, missionary position; left side, active; right side, passive. The civility of the code was as generous as it was clipped and limiting.

"Aren't we going to use words?" Sean joked with Tava. But he saw that Tava's face had turned to stone. They were now in Tava's other world, where jokes were interpreted as coy sashays of fear and avoidance rather than as wit.

Tava pushed Sean into the cave of the truck. The humidity engulfed his face like mosquito netting wrapped too closely, or gauze that prevented him from breathing. There were men everywhere, moaning and grumbling. Tava allowed him to find his way towards the back. He smelled: poppers, perfume, men's behinds, urine, perspiration, leather, marijuana, a general scent that smelled like wet hay. He turned back to see a cutout of Tava cast against the gray screen of the wall. When he could go no farther, hitting the flat metallic back wall, Tava began to move on cue. Soon he was behind him, forcing Sean's face into the corrugation so that he tasted a rusty tang, like the water that flowed out of the faucets at camp.

Tava was forcing his pants down. Sean felt exposed. His flesh was a flag celebrating the exposure he was fully enjoying. Then Tava began to smack him; the noises were so loud in Sean's ears he felt that everyone had tuned in to the breakdown of the fiber of his buttocks in the accelerated motion of Tava's beating hands. Then it was over. The cotton of his own jeans was applied as a salve as Tava raised them over Sean's hurt parts, turning him around. Sean felt pirouetted.

"Do you want more?" Tava asked simply. In the doubleness of his hearing and seeing, Sean agreed.

Tava twirled him around again away from the fireflies of eyes in the dark towards the truck's monochrome metal walls. Soon Sean felt Tava inside him. Pinned to the extremes of the metal frontier, Sean let himself spin fully into the impropriety of swirling tutus, of cover models from romance novels pushing themselves into mattresses of Amazonian foliage with their tan forearms, of jockeys riding deeper and deeper into the forest. And then it was just flesh in flesh. Nothing had ever seemed more personal to him. It was, as the guys were fond of saying then of such maneuvers in the trucks, "no bullshit."

Returning home in Tava's little red pickup truck that evening, Sean allowed the breezes to fan his face. His hand rested on the inside of Tava's leg—his jeans' distressed fabric as soft as the hair of a dog. Tava didn't show him to the door of his loft, but he might as well have. Not since his junior prom, to which he took a girl named Nancy De Something-o, had Sean felt such a light and feathery innocence.

"Be good," Tava said to him absurdly as he jumped down from the red machine.

•   •   •

The flushed, happy feeling didn't last.

Sean felt his loft to be emptier than ever that night as he returned from his date with Tava. Paul was out, as usual, dancing or chasing trouble. The electric light filtering through the front windows was smoky.

So he turned around to walk right back out. His legs felt slow and unwilling, increasingly so as they led him to the cab which took him back to the Mineshaft. They were legs on automatic: always seeming to be walking towards the Mineshaft or towards Jarhead's loft. He knew all the passwords and signs and looks so well by now that he was soon inside, deep inside. He rarely kibitzed in the front room anymore. He just waited until he found a dark spot that felt right. Then he stood there making things happen by waiting for them to happen.

"I want to be in a harem tonight," he said to Jarhead, who sent the signal onwards as if it were an SOS.

"Sean wants a harem tonight," he'd say to different cronies.

"I like that word, 'harem,' " he added to Sean, pleased. "Good word."

By now a lot of the men at the Shaft had shown up in the movie. Showing themselves there became a test, a kind of initiation, like a tattoo of an eagle on a bicep, or a circlet of metal sewn through a nipple. If they were a tribe, they were an improvisatory tribe with no set tests. To Sean's keen pleasure, his dirty little movie was becoming one of their chic tests to pass.

"Can I be in the harem?"

It was Bill talking. He was in his thirties. He'd founded an experimental religious community a few years earlier of both men and women, who rode around in a school bus to monasteries and convents, exerting themselves in a liturgical performance that included Balinese masks, pump organs, a harp, a clarinet, a Mexican prayer wheel, a gong, a saxophone. They dressed as if they were circus performers, in felt capes and tunics with red, blue, green, and yellow dancer's tights. The community came apart the night Bill tried to asphyxiate himself with carbon monoxide fumes in the bus.

Sean had met him through Canon Swarth when Bill was on the mend, his healing turning him towards the far edges of pharmaceuticals, computer music, and the casting of the chests of sinuous boys in plaster. He loved turning their flesh to cement, making idols of them. Now he was living with a German hustler on Bedford Street in a redbrick townhouse that the hustler had received as payment from a client of several years. Bill, who had always loved the serving so valued in Christianity, became his cook, cleaner, therapist, and occasional lover. His soothing intelligence calmed the angry confusion of the classically roaring hustler.

"I'm a bottom," Bill said to Sean.

"I *know* you're a bottom."

During those years nearly everyone was dividing themselves into bottom or top, master or slave, butch or femme. It was an invention of a new world order, which was actually a parody of the old world order.

Bill stood in front of Sean, offering him a joint doused in some new twenty-four-letter chemical. His head was almost bald, his forehead crinkled. But his luscent blue eyes gave him an ageless angel's expression. ("My favorite angel is Gabriel," Bill once told Sean.)

His behind sticking out pertly behind him, Bill was leaning forward in his soft blue denim shirt and blue jeans as if kissing Sean. The gesture was very "Can I, oh please, can I?"

Because of the echoes of the word "harem," lots of so-called bottoms were inviting themselves to Sean's corner that night. "They're all fighting for the bottom," Sean joked to Jarhead when he walked by. Soon they were gathered back at Jarhead's after a din of confused questions and deflected answers. "It's like the inside of a dirigible here," Sean heard someone say.

Sean loved the lights tonight. They were exploding like the white phase of the Bicentennial fireworks. They were klieg lights on a Hollywood set. They were the lights of a prison camp cast on the spidery surprise of an escaping convict's back.

The moving of behinds into place was less graceful than it sounded in Sean's mellifluous instructions. The time was now after four in the morning. The dancers in this impalement scene were staggering, laughing, teetering, crawling, falling-down drunk, and stoned. By the time they had themselves uncovered, the film equipment was overheated, moved from the assigned spots taped on the floor.

"Play music to get us in the mood, Jarhead," Sean instructed.

A worn tape of high-Romantic Russian piano music filled the air like the palms of so many pantomimists in white gloves, both exotic and fidgety. It calmed the effects of the cocaine in many of the dozen participants while somehow also exaggerating, in counterpassages, the drug's nervy cuts and breaks.

Sticking up their behinds were: Bill, R.J., Allen, an NYU Film School student who had put an ad in *Drummer* asking for punks to stomp on him on Second Avenue "in broad daylight." The young man with a limited trust fund who worked for the dealer Ileana Sonnabend and had been at Donna Blaktikh's party. (He had, it turned out, a fascination with groups of young black men he spent hours finding on West Forty-second Street, later insisting to friends, "Once you go black, you can't go back.") A dancer-choreographer who had studied with Merce Cunningham and loved to have an amber vial of amyl nitrite forced up into his nose until he inhaled nothing but nothingness. The vivacious junior seminarian from Washington, D.C., who collected Vuitton luggage, drank whiskey every single night until he put himself under, anesthetized, at the mercy of strangers. The blond aesthete, stiff as cardboard, whom Sean had first met when he was kept by Edgar. (He was now a decorator whose cold passion was for ribbed columns, tables with hard metal edges, blank walls; but under the influence of cocaine he would spread himself across the floor, pinning himself voluntarily, as if he were modeling. He said he felt like a model he'd known who told dark stories of a Baptist preacher who kept him during his teenage years in a cellar of abuse.) A French dancer who always wore greasy black clothes and had a tattoo of a red Edith Piaf rose on one ass cheek and a raven on the other. A blond boy who had starred in one big Broadway drama, but mostly enjoyed shoe-shining sessions that went long into the night with Rupert, and who liked being ridden around any floor as a horse with the bit of a belt between his teeth; only the nailing of his behind to the floor by the force of an anonymous pickup could mollify him, make him nice. A stranger Sean didn't know was undulating on the floor in sheerest underpants, begging for a kicking.

Meandering through the mounds being filmed almost surgically by Sean were Dennis, with a whip that left its lash marks like stitches wherever it chose to curve, and Enrico, with the black belt that sang in the wind like a boxer's bag.

Eventually a few of the bottoms groaned that it was too much, their buttocks scattered everywhere as reminders, oddly, of the innocence of babies, and the angry machines in jeans on top of them embodying the great war of moods fought by men among themselves.

"Great! Great!" Sean kept mumbling to himself.

•   •   •

"Arrrrgh," Sean groaned as he began to wake up the next day, biting onto the mattress, not sure where he was or how he got there, then realizing quickly as he registered the wreckage of the filming from the night before. He felt from the evenness of the light floating through the vast space that it must be about three in the afternoon. The light had settled comfortably by now into all the corners. Sean always noticed light first. He was a filmmaker rather than a painter, he thought, because he saw things in light rather than in color. Black-and-white was fine with him.

"I think the only exciting thing is total obedience," Jarhead was murmuring to him as he sat hunched on a vacant corner of the mattress, drawing a picture of a boxer with a big champion's belt and the words "El Toro" on his guinea T, and a snub-nosed guy kneeling before him nestled into his audacious thighs. Sean checked Jarhead's drawings for quality by looking at their edges. This one was good. In a subliminal crawl space at the top of the drawing were the shapes of boxers in a ring, trapped by light and wires.

"It's a little early in the day, isn't it?" Sean replied, sensing that there were still a few others recovering on scattered mattresses. "Don't you ever give it a rest?"

"Never. Whatever Dennis tells me to do, I do. If he says I can't see my friends, I don't. If I can't call my mom and dad, I don't."

Sean understood, didn't need to ask for an explanation. He had decided that Jarhead was testing himself. He felt that the submitting was a test, just as everyone last night had been testing themselves by taking part in his movie, daring themselves to bare their secrets in a light not only bright but possibly enduring long after they weren't in the mood.

Dennis came by and treated Sean to an exhibition. Sean could see that Dennis's face, made uglier, or more Spanish, or hairier perhaps, was reproduced in all the heroes of the drawings. These were crazy gifts, homages, thank-you notes for his insistence at keeping up the same game Jarhead needed to keep up.

Sean admired the mental power. Again he wished that he could make his entire life, not just his movies, a reflection of such a constructed feeling. But he couldn't quite.

"Take off your clothes."

Jarhead stood in the center of the battlefield of bodies, taking off his few scraps of clothing, having left his pencil idle by his pad. His body was showing the effects of time, gravity, hairiness; there was no attempt at all at a statuesque idealizing of themselves on either side.

"Go get the Ben-Gay."

Jarhead scurried to the bathroom while Dennis strutted around the alleys between the bodies and mattresses, acting furious. He was so convincing in his hyperventilation and jerky movements and irrational talking to himself entirely in curse words that Sean felt he actually was furious. But then he was always furious in just that way. Soon enough Jarhead returned with a green tube of Ben-Gay in his palm.

"Now lie down on the floor and rub some on your nipples."

"Can I do it too?" Sean asked.

"Yeah. You've been playin' it too safe."

"That's why I'm a director."

"You're no director when you've got Ben-Gay on your nipples."

"It's time for his close-up, Mr. DeMille," one of the sacks of bodies coming to yelled out for laughs.

"Shut up."

"*Ta guelle.*" More laughs.

Sean hadn't undressed earlier to go to sleep, but he undressed now, lying flat on the wooden floor, its wood all splinters. For a brief flashing second he saw Tava appear in his head as in a slide show. It seemed so long ago, hardly just last night. As his time became more alive, and more crowded with events, and as it fluctuated constantly due to drugs and the odd hours kept to capture the migrations of these leather men who were his chosen subjects, the hours became years and the years lifetimes.

"Rub the Ben-Gay into your tits."

Sean rubbed the gooey substance on his tender rouge nipples. He felt tiny flames licking at him, but barely. He was warmed by having Jarhead close to him, feeling his hairy legs rub against his own.

"Now rub some on your balls and cock." So they did. The brushfire about Sean's balls was similar to the warm rush towards his nipples that made tiny volcanoes of their caked flesh.

Then came the application to his ass. After a few moments of silent saturation, Sean felt a horrific burning that made him begin to howl on the floor, bleating like a sheep, crying out, barking, snorting. He was being turned into an animal. The Ben-Gay procedure simulated and surpassed the twenty-four-hour trances used by the Balinese in the mountains to undergo transformation into wild beasts. For a few minutes Sean had no control to squelch his own inflamed cries for help.

The turning over the spitfire slowed. Sean looked up towards Dennis, amazed that his face wasn't filled with appreciation for what they'd done. Instead he was continuing his exasperated expressions of demand and disappointment. Sean looked over to see Jarhead intently waiting on the slightest flicker or sparkle from those shallow eyes. He was certainly endowing Dennis with qualities and motives not possibly there, Sean thought. Gathered around Dennis, glowering and unsure of their own consciousness, were the leftover men from the night before.

"You can't draw for a while—forget it," Dennis ranted. He threw Jarhead's tablet of mostly blank pages towards the wall so the pages scattered in the air.

Jarhead didn't visibly react. Sean lay back with a thud, breathing in the eucalyptus-like scent of the Ben-Gay.

• • •

Filming came to a stop for the duration of Jarhead's punishment. It was as if an enforced sadness had settled over the group. During those few slow nights Sean went regularly to the Mineshaft.

When Sean arrived that Saturday night he was so thirsty from the white wine he'd been drinking at a dinner party given by a curator of the Frick at his apartment in the East Seventies that he bravely just asked for a cup of water at the bar.

There had been lots of talk at the party about John Ashbery's recent poem "Self-Portrait in a Convex Mirror." "I have a hard time treating an art review as a poem," one museum curator said. Sean, who loved the poem, tried to swing the conversation back to scat and black men.

When he looked in the cup the bartender handed him, he saw the water turn red as the Nile after Charlton Heston cast down his rod to curse the pharaoh and to bring a blight on the Egyptians. The poisoner in this case was the red light bulb over the bar.

His friend Mick, an art dealer and a cab driver who could be counted on for a free ride home when he parked his cab out front, was not in the mood that night, apparently.

"I feel zero libido tonight," Mick said, lazily looking around the place while pushing his long hippie hair back from his head.

"That's fine with me, that's the best, that's just the way we like it," said R.J., peeking out from Mick's side ebulliently.

"Well, you seem rested," Sean noticed.

"You want to smoke?"

The three of them sat on the useless stage in the room farthest back on the first floor, dragging on a joint so messily constructed it looked like a cloud about to crash.

"This is good stuff."

"Who's that guy?"

Sean had drawn their attention to a pair of legs that kept themselves stiffer and wider apart than the usual legs of those walking about. But as the legs moved into ken, disappointment grew.

"Long Island?"

"New Jersey."

"I love bridge and tunnel."

"Mnnn."

The gray smoke from the joint filled Sean's sails. He was too stoned to remember how to say good-bye. The words eluded him. So he just walked away, down the steps to the cellar. By now the downstairs rooms were jumping. He loved the first room best, which was almost like a set for a severe existentialist drama with its dirty white sink, its toilet, its empty closets into which bodies could be pushed like dirty clothes being stuffed in a hamper. Almost everyone had their shirts off. Shirt stripping had spread like a fad within the last twenty minutes. Rosy light massaged the similarly shaped torsos with the white flags of T-shirts tucked under belts like so many flags of surrender, or for those who stuck them under their belts from the center rear, like animals' tails. Sean picked out one boy whose yellow-striped sweat socks tumbled out of his right rear pocket, effulgently and cryptically.

"Does he like to smell socks?" Sean asked Mick. "Clever."

He began to walk. Past the slamming doors of a row of cubicles. Past the white bathtubs, in which men were sitting, into a dark corridor where hands kept grabbing onto him like vines in an enchanted forest. There he found a stool on which to sit and simply watch. Sometimes someone would notice him and stall, but mostly no one noticed. It was too early for anyone to stop.

Sean moved farther inward to the Den. How many times had he been here? He still felt as if he were discovering something, even on a boring night. Mick was right. This was almost too busy to be a good night.

"All the hot guys are on the Island," Sean heard someone say as he realized that it was already summer again. He seldom went away in the summers, so his sense of the seasons was less etched.

"That's good," the man's friend answered, another voice in the dimness. "That weeds them out. I'm looking for the kind of guy who doesn't go to the Island."

In the Den he met up with two young guys seemingly in their mid-twenties. One had a German or Scandinavian accent, long curly hair, boots, striped baggy shorts. His friend, with a scar across his cheek, was more classically American: short Rock Hudson hair, also in shorts. Sean fell against their wall, as if into the arms of friends.

"Here's your man," the German-Scandinavian said to his companion.

Sean could only look back quizzically.

"You're white, aren't you?" he asked Sean, who nodded. "Protestant?"

That curious interrogation ended, Sean moved into slow-dance position with the friend, whose favorite maneuver was to back Sean into a wall with his own back pushing against Sean's front so that Sean's crotch was pushing forward into him. He'd then draw Sean's hands around to the front of his chest so that he'd be on display, his tits being manipulated. Sean caught sight in the periphery of lots of other visitors trying to involve themselves. His favorite was a black man with the face of Eartha Kitt and the body of a lithesome runner who kept pulling Sean's one arm away to feel *his* pectorals. He was undressed except for hiking boots.

Eventually Sean broke free of the threesome when they formed a sandwich, the German-Scandivanian pushing his back into the American's front, and he pushing his back into Sean's front. But not before the friend had pushed Sean down onto the floor and pounded the front of his head with his thing, which was heavy, leaden, like a water balloon waiting to be squished. Sean was impressed with the density of the flesh being pounded on his face. But he also felt a need to breathe.

"I have to take a breather," he explained to the team, who snubbed him instantly and went into a huddle.

Sean kept walking.

Then he noticed a young man in Nam fatigues, vaguely a bodybuilder, sitting in the chair of the shoeshine stand upstairs. He responded to the idol's marble bulk. They met in a hallway downstairs where they seized each other. The previously aloof idol pushed Sean's mouth into his armpit, where a sulky perfume reigned. Sean made licking love to the pit. His hero stopped him. He pounded on him with his fists in a revving drumbeat, then just walked away. Sean felt embarrassed in front of the semicircle of a crowd that had grown around them. He could almost feel the boos as he followed.

Later, as Sean turned into the narrow lavatory upstairs, the inconstant bodybuilder stopped him. "Sorry about that. But when a crowd grows, it gets to be too much for me and I just have to leave."

"There was certainly a crowd," Sean said, his vocabulary depleted by the lateness of the hour and the prevalence of grass mixed with beer in his body.

"What's your name?"

"Sean. What's yours?"

"Dynamite."

Sean didn't ask him to explain. Actually he didn't have time, as Dynamite had already speedily departed through the open arch of the doorway.

When Sean went to look, Dynamite was standing at the bar in a flurry of excited, laughing, chatting backslapping with an unexceptional young man. Sean wasn't feeling patient, so he kept walking.

"It's light outside!" someone informed him for the sheer joy of passing on this information. They all knew the dare of staying up so late that night turned into day.

"Then it's time for me to go," Sean informed his informant, as if they were intimate friends.

Walking out onto the street, he heard the birds and sensed the pale light of day. Cautious, proud, and worried, he hurried to a line of yellow taxis waiting to rescue him from his predicament.

• • •

Come and Get It, the drawing Sean was filming Jarhead making for his next scene, displayed beautifully mixed messages: a balding man with the broken head of a U.S. senator sat, hairy and nearly naked, in a straight-backed wooden chair, gripping ankle braces in his brute palm. His thing dangled onto the chair, a few pills were scattered in front of the foreskin, and a bottle of Southern Comfort and two beer mugs were stashed behind him. His eyes were as wildly distorted as an all-day sucker. One apish arm pressed down on the chair as if beckoning someone to ingest the outlined pills.

For this scene Sean later dubbed in the Jefferson Airplane song "White Rabbit": "Remember what the dormouse said: / *Feed your head.*"

For Sean, the beauty of the drawing was that it offered two equally provocative choices: the lady or the tiger. You could burrow in his crotch or you could ingest the pills.

With a purposely clumsy hand-held camera—a nostalgic homage to a technologically less proficient decade, the decade of Sean's first inklings—he filmed Jarhead folding the finished drawing and placing it in the crook of the gleaming plumbing of a toilet in a subway john. Inventing these humiliating, or at least extremely revealing, disclosures about himself for Jarhead to enact to be chiseled in film gave Sean a charge. A warm charge, actually. He felt he was collaborating in Dennis's psychodramas, and in Jarhead's. He was both collaborator and traitor. Of course he chose the bathroom at the Broadway and Lafayette subway station, where he had met the black boy a couple New Year's Days ago. He was also in collusion with himself, pretentiously imagining he was doing something in the mood of Bergman's *Persona*. He wasn't. He was making an amalgam of truth here, a caricature of a lie there.

Orgies were a favorite device in those days. Sean had heard of one, so he went along with Jarhead, after the stashing of the drawing, to find the knotted event in the basement of a triangular building on a rusty edge of the West Village. "Oh joy, it's here," Sean said with unusual frilliness to Jarhead when they found the stairs and the black door that opened when pushed forcefully enough. Sean wanted to be included in this enactment himself, like Alfred Hitchcock, he explained, walking teasingly through one of his own scenes. So he had shanghaied Allen, the gaffer who'd put the ad in *Drummer* requesting agony on Second Avenue, to do the filming. The doors of the basement closed at nine o'clock. Those assembled formed a circle. Each stood forward, introduced himself, said what he wanted and needed, then stepped back into a darkness that smelled like an oil slick.

There were about twenty or so participants by the time the doors shut, including Sean, Allen, and Jarhead, who were being looked at skeptically, even with hostility, by the rest of the pack.

Sean was savvy enough to step forward first, his hands gripping the lining of the pockets of his jeans.

"My wish is to be filmed by my buddies here being manhandled and forced to succumb to the wishes of a group of guys intent on my kidnapping and rape."

Sean could feel the relief among the gathered few when he spoke those words. Their worst fear was being voiced—so many of them were bankers or shop owners or professors. But their greatest thrill was voyeurism.

A group of about three succumbed to the power of Sean's wish, though of course he wasn't being entirely straight with them. One gagged him with a white woolen sock across the pores of his tongue. He tasted gall. Another pulled him backwards in a stretch that ended by his being stalled in ropes tied around his wrist. No one could have been safer than Sean, who was having every maneuver filmed. He had managed his peculiar balance of controlling and relinquishing.

One of the three took a seamless swath of cellophane to begin mummifying him, wrapping a shimmering cocoon about him of increasing pressure. They slit at his mouth so his lips could stick through like a fish's, landed, pursing for a drop of water. They laid him across a bar stool so that his head flowed down towards the floor, raising his butt into a promontory, a volcano to be worshiped, and leaving his legs dangling along the back like the feathers of a dehydrated chicken.

Then they made another slit at his behind through his jeans and his underwear. He felt clammy hands. The hands were roving into him from behind. He tried to lurch but he couldn't. He had actually changed his wish. But he couldn't scream anymore, because they had stopped his mouth with flesh. He stumbled into a confusion of selves. He felt the proceedings were tacky, "faggy." His heart was hurt. But he had set this contraption of selves in motion and it hadn't yet run down. So he endured. He knew he could make the entire drudgery look far out, later, in an editing room. He could make himself look daring rather than like a baby unable to control his bowel movements. But right now that's what he was.

When it was time to leave, he didn't know what to say to his captors. So he turned instead to say something, anything, to his crew who, he told himself, were really *his* captives with the cameras and the lights.

"Keep filming me, keep filming me," he kept repeating as they went up more stairs.

"Why do so many documentaries set in New York show people coming upstairs out of clubs in caves and then going downstairs again?" he was asking smartly in the haze of the floodlights.

• • •

Sean's film was becoming more elaborate, more arty, more confused. His most ambitious attempt at a narrative was indeed a complex group of scenes intricately interwoven. He needed to keep his head to gauge the lights, the cues, the voice-overs, the cuts, the takes, the cartridges of film.

Jarhead had sketched a slave auction: a standard enough scene of boys on a rigged wooden stage, their ankles chained in a line, with large men around doing their bidding. Sean had witnessed the event acted out in all its disappointing reality on the stage at the rear of the Mineshaft a few times, with money going to different causes. A lot of the talk was about such an auction in a gay bar in San Francisco being busted by policemen, the gamesters involved having been jailed for violating a nineteenth-century statute forbidding slavery.

"From irony to irons," Sean had whispered to Arnie during one of the overly serious talks about the case in the front room of the Shaft one evening.

He had also recently been to see Pasolini's *Salo* at the Festival on Fifty-seventh and Fifth. The familiarity and resonating abruptness of the movie's images took him by surprise: a boy's jaws being forced open in a scream with a steaming brand applied to one tender tit; a herd of boys showing their curvaceous, naked behinds as they crawled at the tacky shoes of men in ugly boxy suits and their painted women in furs; a serious statue of a boy with a blessed face, nude, holding his arm up in a fisted Nazi salute while his pecker stuck out like a gun; boys in berets leading naked mop-heads on leashes as if they were dogs. The movie landed on a tenderly poised *pointe* for Sean when two of the juvenile soldiers, in green woolen uniforms, guns clanking into each other, danced a slow dance to a whining gramophone. When the lights came up, he turned and saw an audience full of men in leather and Levi's with the same mustached Italianate look of the Fascists in the film. Even Sean felt scared. It was probably the only night that year that he went home to his loft, lit a candle in his room, sat by himself with his knees clutched to his chin. By the next morning he had recovered. All that he remembered was admiration for a plot as complicated as a circus performer's tattoos. The confounding of politics (communist, antifascist) and pornographic desire (for Black Shirt street toughs) made for a perfect blackout.

"It was like our movie," Sean was telling Jarhead. But Jarhead was too busy making a series of drawings crammed with big balloons of dialogue he wanted to hear: "Jeezuz he's a hot li'l fuckah! Drink it, hotstuff! Yeah-h-h-h-h" or "Yeah, Daddy—Yeah" or "I got anudda load or two for you, baby." Lots of the words were smudged over or scratched out, evidence of Jarhead's excitement at having stumbled onto the obvious comic-book strategy. His ear was good. He knew just how to make the wished-for sounds come alive by phonetic stretches.

That night they made the next scene.

•   •   •

The invented setting: the basement of a bar in Philadelphia. (Actually filmed in a corner of Dennis's darkened loft, the scene flashed in words on the screen in silent-movie fashion: "Slave Auction in Philly.") Different Mineshaft extras were performing as slaves on the auction block in cuffs.

Enter (in the actual filming, now) a tall policeman in a dusty brown uniform, his badge identifying him as an officer of naturalization. His beat: illegal aliens. "This guy's tried to enter the country illegally from Russia. He's scared enough to be raffled off as a true slave, truly available."

Closeup on the frightened face of the entrapped one. Sweat on the forehead. In the coal-mine shadows he is linked to the rest. Then the bidding begins. The backs of the bidders forbidding silhouettes surround the lighter flesh of the available few. The policeman, his tall arm obviously higher than anyone else's, is bidding for the illegal alien, who can barely mouth a few English words.

The Russian is sold to his arresting officer for one thousand dollars.

Cut to the basement of the naturalization officer's home. For this scene Sean and his crew traveled on the train to Philadelphia for a day to the home of a friendly accountant, all bald and cheery, who offered his picture-perfect redbrick house on a street named Walnut or Chestnut to their project, extending his usual weekend into at least a few weekdays of adventure. The adventure ended up mostly being a messy tangle of wires draped from his colonial windows, broken knickknacks, and neighbors' suspicions. Sean filmed the front of the tidy nest as an establishing shot, forever implicating the historical landmark in what became an over-exposed innuendo.

In "The Scene" the cop leads the boy down to an ordinary cellar: cold stone floors, a furnace blaring heat, a washer-and-dryer combo, a Doberman barking at a bare light bulb. The only give-away to drama is the cage constructed in a faraway corner. Here the young Russian is locked away with a key on a hoop ring worthy of the Sheriff of Nottingham. Scene follows scene; boots descend clackety steps; the enforcer teaches his purchase to, as he always put it in a Delaware accent, "assume the position." It's Prussia on the Chesapeake. Sean is finally capturing the beauty of a bridge-and-tunnel lifestyle he finds alluring in a countercurrent way. The captive does learn the position. As in a ballet, he moves his silent behind towards the stripes of the bars, and the boss, just back from a day on the beat, takes his pleasure. Slowly and obviously the Russian captive's pleasure becomes evident. Music is played by a paid Lithuanian accordionist accompanying intro-spective scenes of the captive in his cage all day: crying, jerking off, shaving. Somehow Sean uses the lunar restaurant music to set a mood of both melancholy and happy oblivion.

Cut to the usual rape scenes, in which the Russian's hairy behind becomes caked in white from big swipes of Crisco paste, to scenes, spotlit, of the cop signing an amount in hundreds in a big gray checkbook. His devoted serf writes his address in the Soviet Union on an envelope and it is dropped in a mailbox.

"He sends money, my money, home every month. So even though he's MIA, that keeps anyone from getting worried, or coming to look for him."

The cop is seated in his red plush living room, a fire crackling, talking to a pudgy friend in stiff black leather vest, pants, and boots, all a size too small for him. They both bite off the ends of their cigars and spit them into copper spittoons with a loud *ping!* Overdone plush Victorian footstools fill much of the floor space, adding to the claustrophobia of the decor: the actual decor of this accountant from Pennsylvania, who fancied himself Sir Stephen from *The Story of O,* which he used to read before driving up to New York, transposing the genders in his head along the way.

"But I speak Russian," the friend said. "*You* don't speak Russian. I should have him. I'll give you two thousand dollars for him."

"That way I'll make banking money, with interest."

Doubt flickered visibly for a few instants across the tall cop's face. But his swilling of his brandy in its bulbous glass was a sign of an agreement.

Weeping in the cage. Weeping accompanied by penetration. First the tall cop has his way with him, then the new owner, then back again.

"It's so cold to exchange a boy for money that it makes me hot," the tall cop says directly to the camera.

Shots of the boy being led naked, in chains, down the front steps of the Philadelphia town house.

• • •

It was the summer of 1977. Sean had completely lost track of time, friends, parents. Historical events eluded him. Except for the Son of Sam case. He was interested that the Son of Sam had named himself after the dog who instructed him to kill. He carefully read as well all the *New York Times* reports on the CIA's program to develop mind-control techniques. Otherwise his attention was marked at its outer limits by the skylights in Jarhead and Dennis's loft.

Strangely enough, the looser Sean became, the less strictly pornographic his movie was. After the Philadelphia *Story of O* segment, he made his scenario more abstract.

Most helpful in his stretching after phantasmagoria was Bill, the ex-monastic bottom, who turned boys' chests into stone. One of Bill's loves was drugs, perhaps his first love. He had become a Christian monk with his own commune of followers when he took acid in the early seventies inside the unfinished Cathedral of Saint John the Divine. His belief in certain signs had led him to Canon Swarth. Recently he'd been down to Ecuador on a trip to visit shamans in the rain forests who made potions from fungal mucus and roots. He brought a few kilos back.

"You take it and you leave your body for twenty-four hours and travel through the cosmos," Bill was explaining to Sean as he prepared his dose in the loft on a rainy afternoon. "Most people travel the same route, which is the symbol, like a constellation, you see on a lot of the pottery and cloths from those parts of Ecuador and Peru."

"Didn't the beats already take this drug?" Sean asked, worriedly, not wanting to be a pharmaceutical tourist.

"No, that was yage, that was different," Bill reassured him.

"Will you sit with me?"

"After you leave your body, then you return, but in an altered state for about a week, but in your body."

Sean was set to find a way to film his associations, his trip. As soon as he ingested the stuff he started working.

"I always leave my body when I work—this is completely, one-hundred-percent normal for me," he told Bill.

That was the day he dyed the doves. It was a big production. But Bill, Allen, Jarhead, and now even Dennis were harnessed to his mirages. They bought the doves, dipped them in buckets of red, green, yellow, and black, and stored them in bamboo cages.

Of all people, Annie was passing through town. If Sean had been in his normal state of mind, he would have flipped and jabbered and made exultant gestures. But as he was now so deeply enthralled with phantasmagoria, he simply squeezed her tightly and asked her to release the birds from their cages. Annie gladly went along with it all. The colored birds made a mess in the upper reaches of the loft.

Next Sean filmed Annie lying on the mattress talking to him documentary-style. She was nakedly curled on her side, having lost none of her ability to thrill him.

"I love San Francisco," she was saying hoarsely but sweetly. "If you go there you'll see that everything you're doing here—the drugs that open in your head, the films that seem to be showing the unshowable, even the renegade cut of your clothes—Sean, it's all a weak tea. In San Francisco we're tribal. Here you're still European, uptight families in which the little children aren't allowed to speak, are kept from speaking by the tightness of their starched collars."

"The more I don't understand what you're saying, Annie, the more I love you."

He did love her. No one since Annie had been able to move him. So he eventually made her portion of the film all rose-tinted.

"I used to be the most against toy piercings, piercings of the navel, which prick the most but have no erotic daring, no ante. But now I've changed." She was unintentionally ending her segment musing on the limits of ecstasy.

Sean filmed a party of transvestites and fancy disco clowns in white suits with lapels as wide as the flapping ears of an elephant. They all whisked up lines of white cocaine in a white room on a white fluffy couch of feathers against a white door that kept opening and closing as rent boys with long blond bobs, like early Beatles, appeared and disappeared. They always appeared timidly.

They always disappeared into the bathroom, emerging confidently, even imperially. A couple of the black queens exposed their penises to the gathered snickerers, who were soon on their knees or sniffing their behinds. This was a tacky white-trash trailer-park queen's court.

The Sufi whirling dervishes were in town that season. Sean caught them at City Center. He loved that their rolling bodies were not simply rolling for effect but that all together they constituted a map of the solar system, a panoply of blues, purples, moons, yellows, stars. He somehow strong-armed enough of his friends to film a scene in the loft with them whirling over everything—mattresses, bodies, Jesus candles—in robes the colors of the doves earlier. It was very hippie-dippy, but authentically beautiful somehow, too.

Sean ended the movie with the thud of a boot on the floor of an auto mechanic's garage in Clifton, New Jersey, where the scene was filmed. A motorcyclist came speeding single-mindedly down the hill towards the vulnerable garage. His helmet bore the word "Porsche." A grease monkey had already been abusing the young, confused driver of a smashed car. Coinciding with the arrival of the wealthy young motorcyclist, the repairman was placing the victim's head in the bowl of a toilet disconnected from any possible function as it rested like a broken Roman pediment in the mess of gravel in front of the garage. Both of them tested the pliancy of the boy's neck as it was forced into the empty reservoir.

"I want to get that effect they used every three minutes in *Easy Rider!*" Sean was shouting. "You know, where beams of sun cancel each other out, like the confusion of sunlight on a windshield that could lead to an accident, or a hallucination."

Annie started waving to him from a bald hill shaped like a shoulder. The early-evening sun was making her undulations particularly rainbowlike. He was so glad to have her return for this finale: a Daphnis or a Chloe on the hills of Jersey where she began. This perfect symmetry was the sort that mattered to him.

Bill, sitting like a sharpshooter on a fence made of gray concrete blocks, was the lookout.

"Nothing bad happened," Bill said as they packed up the gear just before dark.

That was a phrase used often at the Mineshaft on next meeting after friends had seen someone leaving, "tripping his tits off," the night before with a dubious stranger named, say, "Razor," who was wearing a ski mask. "Nothing bad happened," they'd be reassured.

Mesmerism

*J*arhead's Drawings was a success. The line of ticket buyers at
the chrome-clad Festival movie theater on Fifty-seventh
Street, where Sean has first seen *Salo,* was long enough some
days to make a right angle onto Fifth. Sean and Jarhead briefly
became co-celebrities, a team, like Robert Wilson and Philip Glass
during *Einstein on the Beach.* (Robert Mapplethorpe had taken the
director's and composer's double portrait the year before, all marble hands and eyes and abused shoes and sneakers, making the
two men comments on or afterimages of each other, as if their
wrists were talking to each other's knees.)

Sean and Jarhead were being interviewed on a Thursday night
in October walking around Christopher Street by a reporter from
the *Village Voice* who seemed more interested in locale than in them.

Sean spent some time trying to convince her that he wasn't
working in a celluloid cocoon, that there was a whole East Village
filmmaking force coming out of NYU Film School that he was

akin to. Gay porn was often more of a scrambled code than a key to his movies. He talked about Jim Jarmusch, whom he went to Columbia with, who was working as student assistant to Nick Ray, the revered, tense, and restless director of *Rebel Without a Cause,* who hadn't worked in Hollywood since 1963. He talked about Howard Brookner, also at Columbia with them, who was working on a documentary about William Burroughs. About Amos Poe and his almost homemade CBGB movies, and Eric Mitchell and his scratched East Village home-as-history movies. These were American kids trying to make European movies, following all the European filmmakers of the sixties who had been modeling their films on Hollywood movies of the past. Martin Scorsese was a hero for his *Mean Streets.* But Nancy wasn't really listening.

"Nancy's neat," Jarhead said naively to Sean as they waited on Christopher at ten at night.

"You're just taken by her extremity. She might be cool if you're her girlfriend. But she's looking for a travelogue. She wants us to show her where the whips are, and the slash marks, and the mummified bodies gagged by their own hapless, hopeless desires."

The interview had loosened Sean's tongue. He was enjoying the feeling of his own vowels and consonants. He couldn't stop talking.

Nancy reappeared from the Häagen-Dazs store on Christopher Street off Bleecker, its woody decor simulating an Alpine sauna, a look that complemented the icy slush of the lemon-mousse sherbet in her cardboard cup. Sean had declined her offer of ice cream, hating the lactic lump that would be left in his stomach. Jarhead happily licked around and around his gift of butterscotch ice cream from Nancy.

"Take me to the Mineshaft," Nancy said, purposely mimicking the "Come with me to the Casbah" line.

"It's too early. It's not open," Sean explained too easily, with no follow-up.

"We could talk in David's Potbelly," Jarhead offered as they passed the small restaurant that also worked a dark wood look, though in more of a *Treasure Island* way.

"You just want more ice cream," said Sean. "Nancy brings out the baby in you."

They all laughed as Nancy played at pushing one of her large breasts wrapped in a pink Arrow cotton shirt into Jarhead's mouth.

"Humiliation is humiliation," Jarhead replied.

"We just ran a story about Addison Verrill," Nancy interrupted, reverting to seamier topics as they continued to walk up Christopher. "The film critic for *Variety* who was found hit on the head with a frying pan and stabbed with a ten-inch kitchen knife in his apartment at Two Horatio. My friend Luis discovered him face-up on his bed, nude, when he came by in the morning to work on a horror novel they were writing together, *The Ritual*."

"That's nothing," exaggerated Sean. "Remember Toni Lee? Keypunch operator at the Department of Social Services by day, drag-queen fan dancer by night? Stripping to 'Shangri-La' at the Gilded Grape? The Alley? The Omega? The Bon Soir? Found clad only in sheer underpants, hands and feet bound to bedposts?"

"Or the body found in the back of a truck on West Street?" Jarhead added.

"Or the photographer nude, bound, and strangled in the Chelsea Hotel?"

"The Village stabbings and underwear burnings of four years ago?"

Sean, taken by surprise by the grisly talk, was eased. So he and Jarhead began to pull out more delights for their journalist, like children agreeing to play a corny card game, war or hearts, to entertain a playmate from a different block.

Christopher Street was filled that chilly, peach-tinted October night with young men in Hudson bomber jackets, checkered shirts, brown Frye boots. They continually spilled out of Ty's gripping—almost earnestly—vodka tonics in plastic funnels.

"Vodka tonics are the Manhattans of the moment," said Sean.

"No, vodka tonics are tacky. Manhattans were never tacky," Nancy argued.

Jarhead of course could not say two words on such a topic. His reticence, even inability, supported Sean's hunch that he was the purer artist.

Together they swung Nancy around to a few stops. At Julius a waiter served up hamburgers from behind a skillet while singing "Tits and Ass." At the Spike, where they arrived in a Checker, *The Women* was being screened on a blinker of a screen on thin metal legs. Thursday night was movie night. The sight of bikers in leather giggling about Norma Shearer and Rosalind Russell was disconcerting, life-affirming. Nancy wisely cast the opening of her piece when it ran the following week among the bar's shadows, giggles, dead animal skins, blue gel lights, WPA-style murals of vascular arms and Frankenstein stares and haircuts.

Most of their recorded interview took place at the Maverick on Tenth Street, directly across from the Sixth Precinct police station. The Maverick was definitely a B bar, never making its way later into gay histories, or into too many memories. Sean suggested the Maverick as an inside joke to put Nancy off the scent of the pillories and execution sites she craved. Jarhead went along because his nature was to go along. "He's a better slave than I am," Sean cracked as Nancy wrote down notes.

From the jukebox, which was exposing its machinery like the insides of a wristwatch, screamed "Drop Kick Me Jesus." A Captain Fantastic pinball machine made mad bell sounds. Up a flight of stairs, a backroom was stocked with porno monitors, like those at the Anvil: two boys were doing racy things to each other in a stylish barn.

"I was inspired in my film *Jarhead's Drawings* by Nietzsche," Sean rambled on elaborately, getting too close to the tape recorder set on a wooden table filled with cherry Camparis, tan beers, and light yellow vodka tonics. "He was a wimp who invented a loud-speaker voice everyone listened to. But it was merely the voice he wanted to listen to. It wasn't his voice."

"And you, Jarhead?" Nancy asked lazily.

"My master tells me what to do. He has this voice that just sends me. He put it on a tape recording so when I'm in my cage I just put it over my ears with the plugs so I can hear his voice all night long. That helps calm and focus me."

Sean was savvy enough about publicity by now that he could see those words racing into print. Yet his true thrill was the daring of the words themselves, and their invitation to a more remarkable world.

"Madame Bovary was a fictional character created by Flaubert in the nineteenth century," Sean went on, not making much sense, leaving too many spaces between his thoughts. "She lived dream-ing daily, and trying to re-create in her own life the lives of the women of the romance novels she read as well as the lives of the glitterati of Paris she knew from the gossip columns."

"Yes," Nancy said impassively, professionally tilting her micro-phone back towards Jarhead, who instinctively knew theater and couldn't help blurting his truths.

"I'm lost. Sean has always been the leader. He seems to have some notion of where he's going and why. He's the idea man. I just make drawings to please my master, or to please different straight men and gay men around town who happen to use a urinal where I tack my dirty drawings."

"Jarhead," Nancy asked, almost grabbing onto his shoulder with a desperation that made Sean a little jealous, "what makes you tick?"

"Poor thing," Sean said out loud, referring to Jarhead. But he wanted her to keep listening, he wanted to keep the drinks paid for by the *Village Voice* coming.

"I have a desire to please. I feel that I was born to serve. I feel that my drawings serve the most thirsty, forbidden side of gay men. I don't see beyond that."

"What about call girls?" Nancy countered testily. "You could treat them. You could inculcate their experiences and humiliations. Women are no different than men."

"I can't help who I am," Jarhead answered simply. "I'm neither radical nor square. Those are categories laid on by the outside. I have my masochistic destiny to consider."

Both Nancy and Sean fell silent. Suddenly they were both on the same team.

Crash! A drink fell to the floor.

"A drink always falls on the floor," Sean said.

But the machine had already clicked itself off, as if making a judgment with its jewel of a crimson eye.

•   •   •

As they drove up Eighth Avenue towards Fifty-fourth Street in his yellow sports car, Edgar handed Sean a diamond ring. Sean, as a half-joke, bit the stone to test its carats.

"I love having someone to spoil," said Edgar.

"You've found him," joked Sean, slipping the ring onto his little finger.

The wind blowing through their hair was a leveler. It made them equal. So did the gift. The diamond created a fair playing field: its joy a joke to both, yet as practical as a screwdriver or a wrench in the works of their friendship.

"The last time I was here it was dull," Sean complained.

The last time he'd checked out Studio 54 he'd been forced to stand for a few minutes of scrutiny next to a dark red velvet rope under the silver-and-red marquee of the old CBS recording studio. Steve Rubell lurked in the shadows near his doorman, approving who went in. Hoarse voices shouted "Mark! Mark!" to catch the the doorman's attention. There was a quick release of tension, like a fist easing, as Sean was waved onto the incline of a long entrance hallway mirrored like a funhouse. Some colored tickets were free, some half price, some full price. Clumsy chandeliers hung like those in Long Island diners. A waterfall disguised a plastic rocky surface he was too preoccupied to decipher. He didn't remember anything later except a red pulsing.

"Tonight will be better," Edgar promised. "It's truly democracy in action. It's all the Most Wanted, in both senses, either for their looks and money and fame, or by the police, or all of the above."

"Bow to me," a big blond bouncer joked to them as they approached his clipboard with its typed list of tonight's invited cast.

Happily they were at the rear door on Fifty-third, the "private party" door. Most nights at Studio were private parties. Already Halston had thrown his critical party for Bianca Jagger's birthday when she had been led through the discotheque on a white pony by a giant black man covered in sissified glitter. Her Mandingo seemed more of a Broadway Ubu Roi. At Elizabeth Taylor's birthday party a buttercream cake was wheeled out shaped into a version of her body, off which she sliced one of her own tits. At the Halloween party everyone came dressed as their favorite *Star Wars* character: Darth Vader, Princess Leia, R2-D2.

Sean couldn't remember which way to turn. Donna Summer's "Love to Love You Baby" was pulsating through the crowd. Edgar knew to press into him with the flat of his hand on his shoulder so he would turn towards the party taking place exclusively behind a big black scrim vivisecting the dance floor. For her first parties, one of the club's party organizers, Carmen D'Alessio, a South American with a flashy, sideways style of moving, made A, B, C, D lists. If you had been invited to the actual opening party in April, you were A-listed and felt fine going to all the others. But to have been listed on the B, C, or D lists was a slap.

Sean felt as if he were back in Dr. Bennett's office being plied from all directions by insertions, mind-altering pills. Someone stuck a Quaalude in his cheek and ordered him to swallow. A starved woman dressed in feathers as messy as if they'd been plucked from a monstrous bird was goosing him from behind, sending a frisson of love and excitement up his asshole. A sapphire-dotted cocaine spoon was refracted against the bridge of his nose to music that sounded almost religious: "(Your Love Has Lifted Me) Higher and Higher" by Rita Coolidge, the "Climb Every Mountain" of that time.

At its best Studio caught all the elegance of Sean's kindergarten play *Aunt Drusilla's Garden,* in which he'd played a tulip: bright colors, profiles cut jagged and clean, a permeating violet-gray genie smoke. He particularly liked its cheap impersonation of an opium den blown up American-style to ten times the expected size, or an amusement-park version of the Persian sultan's harem visited by Lady Mary Wortley Montagu in the eighteenth century. He liked the opportunities, too, as if everyone were a door on a game show. It you talked to the right person, looked the right way, you could pick up your car or appliance later.

The modeling agent Zoli, a Scandinavian gentleman, was scouting models that night, though he usually did better later at Cowboys, the more claptrap hustler bar on East Fifty-third, a block over from Rounds. Victor Hugo, Halston's boyfriend, was wearing "punk pants" with a normal zipper fly but outfitted with a hole, like a trapdoor, for his penis to hang down, which it did. He was wearing, too, one of Halston's sequined bandannas. Halston, as always, was tucked into a black cashmere turtleneck and a black Nehru jacket. Sean always confused Halston's name with Halsted's.

Tonight a mountain of recognizable eyes, ears, and chins was moving towards him. It was the October 11, 1977, party for Elton John. Most nights the bar was open, free, paid for by a host. The bartenders in their Adidas sneakers and shorty-short gym trunks were hardly capable of collecting dollars and transforming them into cents. They were better left free to twirl forward, naked to the waist, looking as if they were strapped to roller skates even though they weren't, twirling and twirling with their phosphorescent drinks: a favorite was 150-proof rum mixed with grapefruit juice. They made three hundred to four hundred dollars a night on tips alone. Aspiring actors, models, somethings, they were fine animals, like greyhounds or Arabian horses, though none ever went on to much, the promises never quite sticking.

Tinkerbelle was there, the wispy blond model type who wrote movie reviews for Andy Warhol's *Interview*. So was Bob Colacello, always boyish and starstruck in his owlish glasses. Sean had recently read Steve Rubell on Studio's border policies in Colacello's "Out" column: "We want everyone to be fun and good-looking." Colacello reported in his column, too, Diana Vreeland telling him the place was as decadent as the Roman Empire as they both stood on a banquette watching a trumped-up pageant.

Sean for a while did turn his marbleized, increasingly gray skin sweaty and tan by mimicking what he didn't realize was mostly an updated mambo on the dance floor, where so many husbands and supposedly straight men were daring themselves by dancing for the first time in public with other men. But that night on the Studio dance floor for a few rounds, even though still dressed in his telltale black leather jacket, black jeans, and pointy boots—the only one so dressed, as blue jeans and T-shirts were the usual men's statement there—he was finding himself exulting in the music, and in the mix of men and women, and in the new loud body language. This was the beginning of bodies, and gyms, Big Gym having just opened on Greenwich between Barrow and Morton, advertising for the first time an athletic operation with health juice bars, table tennis, cable TV with large screen, three steam rooms, three saunas. (Sean went a few times, but all those mirages turned out to be under construction, and the constructing never seemed to get beyond a lumber room of wood tools interspersed with a few benches and leaning mirrors and chrome weights rolling on the floor.)

Studio's dance floor reflected one back to oneself, as couples turned into groups, and Sean hopped rather than danced himself into different combinations. The final dare was simply to dance alone. An entire *Star Wars* machinery was re-created observatory-style in the ceiling. Even though the men were dressed down, like tidier construction workers, the women tended to dress for the paparazzi outside: Grace Jones in a fur coat, Liza Minnelli bandaged in cashmere capes. Big were forties-style black broad-shouldered and slim-hipped silhouettes, called "the Joan Crawford look" before, renamed "the Joe Namath look" then. Bright pinks, reds, purples on lips, fingers, and toes. It was as if Truman Capote's famous costume ball in the 1960s had created an appetite for the same jag nightly—he was of course there, in oversized sunglasses, oversized hat, and whimsical scarf.

"Don't Leave Me This Way" by Thelma Houston sounded like a Greek tragedy. Leo Sayer's "You Make Me Feel Like Dancing" was an angel's song, so high and so strained. Those dancing were mouthing his wishes with their bodies as they became entranced.

It was like a spell. The Bee Gees were feel-good monks chanting "How Deep Is Your Love." Abba's "Dancing Queen," a constellation in the sky. Lots of stars were evoked that night: "You Don't Have to Be a Star (to Be in My Show)"; the "*Star Wars* Theme"; Barbra Streisand's "Evergreen," the love theme from *A Star Is Born*.

Sean and Edgar went up to the deejay booth, a slick black boat projecting over the heads of those dancing underneath as if they were themselves jumbles of notes. The booth was a prow of glamour packed with celebrities. Warhol was admitted, of course. The danger was always that Victor Hugo would roll his unreliable arm around and rip off Warhol's toupee. Michael Jackson stood in the gloaming of nine-thousand-watt amplifier banks made in Germany, two floating Teac 1400 turntables hovering in custom cabinets of mahogany. A revolving record bin was deejay Richie Kaczor's lazy Susan—singles, albums, twelve-inchers, numbered and stored—his own head made into an astronaut's by Koss headphones fitted with custom-tailored ear cushions. Michael Jackson in his high voice was asking Warhol about art. David Hockney was aloft, too. Suddenly photographers were admitted by Rubell in a planned ambush, training their precise instruments with only a two- or three-minute reprieve mostly on Warhol and Elton John.

"Can I kiss you?" Warhol asked John, who was wearing a big hat to conceal his new hair transplant. As he didn't answer, Warhol didn't kiss.

"Andy can go anywhere he wants," Rubell was slurring to no one and about nothing pressing.

Yet it was Rubell, stoned on dangerously invasive amounts of 'ludes, Sean couldn't stop watching. Most of the inner crowd crammed into the deejay booth were drawn to Rubell. Rubell was both wolfish and puppy-doggish: wolfish in his sharp business strikes—he knew all about pulling publicity, stashing overhead, circulating drugs—and yet puppy-doggish in his unembarrassed worship of celebrated faces.

"You never drive in a limo," he told Sean as they stood there. "You let your clients take the limos. You go in a town car."

"Good advice," Sean stiffly tried to answer.

The unlikeliness of Rubell's shortness, his penny loafers, his greedy, needy little-boy excessiveness touched off in Sean a feeling of the danger of such extreme availability. A boy from Brooklyn, Rubell was as disgusting in his climbing as he was charming. One tic: he was always pushing forward Ian Schrager, his tall, dark, handsome partner, as inscrutable and cardboard in those years as a prince in a ballet whose only job was to hoist the ballerina. (Schrager was nicknamed "Greta" because he was press-shy, a foil for Rubell's press excessiveness.) Few found in him the pathos of need and performance Rubell exuded. Yet Rubell's enthusiasm for him, his heightened breathing when Schrager was available to be pushed forward, only added to Rubell's own appeal as a promoter and showman who had created at 54 the spectacle of a silver cardboard man-in-the-moon that dropped from the ceiling as a giant silver coke spoon drifted across the floor, trailing a snow of confetti across the dancers below, only to be inserted finally up the moon's nose, lit with red light bulbs; and flower arrangements, heavy on birds of paradise, that sprayed themselves above chrome bartops or on spotlit pedestals; and black plastic walls that offered back versions of darkened, stoned faces. The place always made Sean think of Maria Callas, though Sean had never heard of the elegant opera diva actually being there before her recent death. (On that September night Ondine and other friends of Warhol's Factory had gathered to play her records and mourn her death, they said to each other, "the death of the sixties.") Sean was convinced, and tickled, that the secret that made Studio go syncopatedly, irresistibly around

THE GOLDEN AGE OF PROMISCUITY

was a complex affair of heart and power between a gay man and a straight man.

"People make it out better than it is," Rubell was saying to Sean. "There are many dull nights."

The drone of a head forced to tune in to its own weak frequency desperately: that's how the dead stone on top of Sean's neck felt as he guided himself down the stairs from the deejay booth, away from Edgar for a bit. He was in search of his own mystical place. The pain was obvious. The distractions were as piquant as the cloud of women's perfume so heavy earlier, gradually filled in through the night by tarter whiffs of amyl nitrite.

"There are more sensations in this room than in Bloomingdale's," said Edgar, catching up, then leaving him alone.

Again Sean found himself in an arcade of human playing cards. Almost all face cards, all fronts and no backs, except for an occasional pretty butt. Eric Goode, who had scouted locations for *Saturday Night Fever,* just released, and who later started Area after having spent so many impressionable nights at Studio, was wearing his pj's. Rollerena, a middle-aged gentleman rumored to be a Wall Street broker by day, roller-skated in dressed in a taffeta gown, waving a starry fairy-godmother wand. Disco Sally, a seventy-year-old grandmother, was dancing to KC & the Sunshine Band's "I'm Your Boogie Man." Fran Lebowitz remained as constant as a transgender odalisque leaning across a banquette dressed in a man's suit and punctuating the rosy air with her thin white cigarette. Every so often there was a slowdown when a head of state such as the architect Philip Johnson walked in. There'd be a hush. Then Warhol would rush over, take his picture, the balloon of a mood would wheeze away, and life was allowed to go on. A rich woman with an accent but without a country was worrying because she'd lost a large pearl from her emerald-and-pearl Van Cleef wedding ring on the dance floor. Rubell was trying to somehow get her over her shock. (Proof of Studio's intimate civility: cleanup recovered the pearl at the end of the night, and the next day she received a call asking where it might be returned.)

The big room didn't spin, but if you were smashed, it wobbled and then began to move on tracks, like a Cyclone ride. Sean was smashed. Sitting on a banquette with Edgar, he felt trampled by flowers, suede jeans, Tony Lama boots, falling shouts, sideways glances, girls' behinds, Calvin Klein, big belts with fierce buckles. Sean tried to sober himself by concentrating on the bellies and arms and thighs dancing over a drawbridge from the deejay booth across to the steam pipes on the other side.

"I can't think what to say," Edgar said.

"I'd love to put all these people in a movie. They're as colorful as hippies and more famous. Like Andy does. But I'm afraid I wouldn't be taken seriously. I'm supposed to be hardcore, for now. But I'm sure I could get them to perform for my camera just like Jarhead and his monkeys."

"You're right."

Sean couldn't help overhearing the edgy squeak of a nearby voice addressing its circle. "Did you hear what he did the other night with a number he picked up at the Haymarket? He told him to try on everything in the closet. Then he just lay there playing with himself while the hustler tried on all these clothes he'd designed *himself*."

At that Sean made his way unsteadily upstairs to the balcony. A few sons of political dynasties were shooting up heroin into their lined arms. (They left two years later when Xenon opened— a more modelly disco, nicknamed "Xerox" because of its swiping of the Studio format.) But Sean didn't care anymore. Too much Studio and he always felt like going home to take a shower to wash off the newsprint. As much as he fed on the rapid whir, his was a complex push-pull response. Until he began to scout the balcony to score more drugs, that is. Then he was engaged again. Coke was easy. But Quaaludes, selling for five or ten dollars each, were harder to find. He did manage a pill from a young lady with the smell of jasmine rising from between her tits. He kicked back into an old movie seat, as genuinely aged and slightly ratty as Louis Quinze armchairs, and stared into the Cinerama below, where battlefield smoke enveloped the young men who increasingly took over the floor late, undressing themselves in public for a lift. A net of gray balloons was swaying far above them, in Sean's line of sight, as if ready to drop its load. He was pleased to be so close to the hand-painted gilt of the baroque ceiling done—all chubby angels and scimitars—in the faux-Moorish style of so many American Masonic temples.

The balcony was filled with ongoing blow jobs. Sean knew this was a scene everyone would be too discreet to put in print. So it was a perfect place to unwind from his obsessions, nearly as good as the basement of the Mineshaft. But this was also a more pastoral scene. Girls were being offered up to men clad in cheap jeans and worse boots. Boys' things were rising and falling in time-lapse photography. Sean loved looking down at all the activity on the dance floor below, as he had first looked down from the balcony of the porn theater when he was in college.

He was soon, for a few hours perhaps, or minutes, lost in a dream remembering his Viewmaster reels at age ten: Peter Pan alighting in glistening leaf-green slippers in Wendy's bedroom while a big sheepdog looked on; the infant Christ spotlit by a star of David twinkling like a zircon in a purple sky; Heidi sleeping in her bed of golden straw while Grandpa faithfully scoured the fields below for some sign of help.

I'm part of the demimonde, I'm part of the night, Sean thought, coming to, as if someone had asked him to work his life up into an aria.

Sean couldn't remember how the idea of hypnosis first entered his head. But he knew that the idea, or at first simply the word, began to form in the same way as a movie image. Like the sneaker on the street that had inspired his first film, the word "hypnosis" was working deviously.

All had begun that fall when *Jarhead's Drawings* hit the art houses. And the *Village Voice* interview appeared, with his big picture taken by Thomas Victor, a cheerful, nervous photographer who specialized mostly in authors. The easiest explanation for his interest in self-immolation was that as his own personality began to take on more solidity in the world, a counterforce began to assert itself as well, tempting him into completely erasing himself. A more difficult explanation for him was that he was simply freaked out by all the attention, the moderate celebrity.

"Why me?" he asked his unpainted wall on Great Jones Street.

So he put an ad in the personals section of the *Advocate* and leased a mailbox at the post office at Eleventh Street and Fourth, the one with a bay of official windows set in the curve of its tan brick exterior mimicking the rows of rental mailboxes inside. Even though Paul was shuffling through the apartment with his paintbrushes and bouquets of crumpled newspapers while he was writing the ad, Sean didn't consult him. He felt this was a secret, even something he couldn't talk about yet. Of course his life had been one crossing of the border of the unspeakable after another. So he wasn't entirely worried.

The ad read: "Slave robot in New York City into hypnosis, mind control, total surrender, personality extinction, sensory deprivation, boot camp. If interested, write Zero." There followed a box number of many digits. Obviously his use of an exaggerated, cartoon-strip name, "Zero," owed a lot to Jarhead. Sean, too, wanted absolute purity, a life modeled on high fantasy rather than some checkerboard, compartmentalized making-do. Or so he told himself anyway.

Sean had completely stopped working by now. It was November, then it was December. The city was cold and he was seriously stoned, or drunk on copper-colored Jameson whiskey, from the moment he woke up in the late mornings. Even Paul was more industrious and regular in his habits than Sean was. Sean was definitely on a bender. He didn't call back his agent at ICM when he invited him to a lunch at the Russian Tea Room. The recalcitrance that had given him the will to quit Columbia was now widening its shadow. Every few days he'd check his rented mailbox for a reply. He received several replies from madmen, their scrawls as identifiable as ransom notes written in blood. And there was the junk mail: order slips for Bullet, a butyl nitrite; order slips for its competitor, Locker Room, "Aroma of Man—Room Odorizer"; ditto for Rush, "Purity, Power, Potency."

He would poke through the gray and white envelopes every few days, like a Bowery bum rustling through an ash heap of cinders. Then one morning a reply came typewritten on a machine with oversized letters, all hoops and circles and howls. "Shave yourself," the short note instructed. "All-night sessions involving caging, butt plugs, mental hazing, hypothalamic torture, exercises of sphincteral squeezing, dog training, available. Master Chris is 42, 6'1", 170 pounds, mustache. Does not suffer fools lightly. Call collared on the ground butt-naked only." A phone number followed that Sean realized was in Washington, D.C.

When he called, the voice on the other end put him through an efficient, rehearsed customizing of his mind to advance specifications of his own. Master Chris soon had him on the floor on all fours, eyes closed, belt wrapped around his neck, heavy metal cock ring around the balls like those holding napkins and silverware at a fancy dinner, a butt plug that he imagined worked on the principle of a butterfly corkscrew as he oiled its way up into himself. He had accumulated these enhancers gradually by shopping at a leather store where Camille O'Grady worked part-time in the upstairs sweatshop, sewing together leather skins or riveting rubber firemen's outfits with alloyed studs. "Toys," the leather men called them, a word Sean found too euphemistic.

"I feel nothing but love," Sean was somehow saying into the phone nudged between his shoulder and ear. He had been licking a powder of a brown sugar of hashish before their conversation began.

"I want you to count backwards from one hundred skipping every three."

"One hundred, ninety-seven, ninety-four, ninety-one, eighty-eight . . ."

"I want you to squeeze your asshole, *squeeeeze,* picture it in your mind every time you squeeeeze, like a third eye in your worthless forehead."

In the background of his telephone master's voice through the tiny pinholes in the receiver Sean could hear the tick-tock of an old grandfather clock. Every fifteen minutes a calliope of bell ringing would erupt, an embarrassing throwback to nineteenth-century snobbism. Is he wearing a smoker? Sean wondered in a cringe. Then thousands of miles of dead space rolled back again to reclaim the silence. In his compromising doggie position he remembered in a non sequitur Paul McCartney saying how rock 'n' roll became in the sixties a dare of "decibel creep." But when his Washington, D.C., Master Chris asked him what was on his mind he simply answered, "That I'm a zero, a zero minus, sir, less than zero, a miserable zero-minus piece of shit."

"Good boy," said Chris, who had taught him those lines. Sean hadn't improvised.

"When you go to sleep I want you to curl up on a throw rug on the floor. You won't need a pillow. When you close your eyes I want you to picture zeros, zeros with minuses after them, because that's you. You're subhuman. You're not good enough to be a dog. My dogs are obedient, loyal—when they see their master their eyes exult. They are eager to sacrifice for their master. But your need to serve will grow in you like a black cloud, slowly, slowly. Like a moth being drawn to the flame, you'll be unable to resist. You need to be controlled. You need to be told what to feel, what to think, what to wear, every move to make. You need every mocidum of your thought processes edited by me."

Sean knew that when Chris said "mocidum" he meant "modicum." He wondered if all masters relied on the stiff awkwardnesses of Latinate vocabulary, the stuff of legal briefs.

Then the seductive droning began again. "You probably don't even know how to lick your master's boots. Not just the tops, but the soles. I am so far beyond you, solar systems beyond in the power of my mind, that you can't even begin to comprehend. Hear those dogs barking out there? They're your brothers. But they're far beyond you. You're less than a mosquito. A mosquito at least I think about, because a mosquito can bite me. But you can't do anything to affect me. Your entire purpose in life is to strive to become my insubstantial shadow. Squeeeeze. Squeeeeze. Do you have any questions, boy?"

"What kind of dogs do you have?"

"Dobermans."

And so it went, on and on. At many moments Sean felt he was being held hostage by all the worst sides of his own parents. He had allowed them back in, begged them back in. But at occasional seconds a click would profoundly settle his spinal cord, a click of happiness, like an electric light being flipped either on or off. Chris made him happy by taking away all choice, all responsibility, returning him to the crib. Oh, thank you, Master Chris. You have shown me the path back to the Castle of Eternal Regress!

Sean wanted to speak. But the junior hypnosis session had so compromised him that he couldn't remember the fortune-cookie-style message he was attempting to deliver. So he swallowed his tongue. All he knew was that life in his loft on Great Jones Street was nothing like what he had lived in Turret. He wondered if the strangeness was the leftover margin of feeling after passing from child to adult. Maybe he was just nuts.

"I don't know what I want," Sean said.

"I appreciate the honesty, boy. Come to Washington. But first send me your picture in a dog collar so I can see the neediness in the ovals of the eyes, a hurt-puppy-dog look."

Sure, Sean thought. He flipped as a jokey exercise in thinking through all the photos of himself in newspapers and magazines of the last year. No dog collars, though, he goofed silently. But he did want to go to Washington. He did want to walk like a zombie off the train with no bags. He did want to reside in a cage that could be unlocked only from the outside, a cage with only a mat on its floor. He did want to feel the edges of experience, where winds of forgetfulness blew purple and white, intransigently. But these were private sentences he could tell Chris if he could get up the courage to take Amtrak to Washington.

"I'll talk to you on Wednesday night at nine. Until then you're to eat one meal a day out of a bowl on the floor. You're to lap up one bowl of water. You're to shave your balls. Sleep on a rug on the floor curled up picturing zero minuses. Don't ever wear under-wear. One hour a night insert your butt plug. Whenever you're at home wear your cock ring and your dog collar with the spikes."

"Who could you ever be, Master Chris?"

"I'm an insurance underwriter."

"Oh."

"The need to serve will take over your life. But you must open up to me your mind and your body, like a clam being pried open for my delectation."

"I'll be there."

Although Sean promised to sleep on a rug on the floor, complying with Chris's wish that he find ways to keep reminding his very bones and muscles that he wasn't a full human, he didn't. He figured he could lie to Chris later. Sean's ritual during those weeks was less bold and haunting, more childlike and innocent. On those nights when Sean would stay in—more and more as the winter months became filled with big drifts of snow—he liked to fall asleep while being read to by Paul, before Paul slipped out to the Gaiety to become a chorus boy, a male cancan dancer. "You're the great late-twentieth-century courtesan, I'm convinced," Sean liked to kid him.

On that first night, after his talk with Chris, Paul complied with Sean's wish. Later, if Paul wasn't around, Sean would make do by reading the new novel about vampires everyone was discussing. All the bloodlettings put him to sleep, made him feel weak. He would read one of its savage tooth-slashing scenes punctuated by red pools of drained power and fall off quickly, drained himself. But he preferred the controlled grumble of Paul's voice, the contrast of his peacockish hip street-Negro mien with his senatorial, newscaster's voice. Paul preferred to read aloud from stories with black characters. Sean liked that too.

The first night he did a guttural breaststroke through Herman Melville's "Benito Cereno," the red cloth book's spine breaking from having been left lying flattened next to Sean's mattress so many nights.

" 'Presently, while standing with his host, looking forward upon the decks below, he was struck by one of those instances of insubordination previously alluded to,' " Paul was saying in a voice hollow and resonant that discovered the meaning of the words just as it was pronouncing them. " 'Three black boys, with two Spanish boys, were sitting together on the hatches, scraping a rude wooden platter, in which some scanty mess had recently been cooked. Suddenly, one of the black boys, enraged at a word dropped by one of his white companions, seized the knife, and, though called to forbear by one of the oakum-pickers, struck the lad over the head, inflicting a gash from which blood flowed. In amazement, Captain Delano inquired what this meant. To which the pale Don Benito dully muttered that it was merely the sport of the lad. . . .' "

Sean was sound asleep by the time Paul reached the end of the paragraph. Mostly he was rolling around in his subconscious the words that had passed between him and Chris. He was spooked. Was he really hypnotized now? Under Chris's spell in some corny but true Bela Lugosi / Vincent Price fashion? What if he traveled to Washington, D.C., and Chris did cage him with heavy chains dragging and there was no way out and his parents never heard from him again and his career slid into a curious, unsavory foot-note in books about kinky independent filmmakers? What was at stake? Did Chris know the difference between reality and fantasy? He kept saying, "This isn't a game, fuckface, this is real." So what if Chris did have hypnotic powers and would lure him down into his dungeon? "Have you dreamed about this?" Chris asked him earlier. "No." "Well, you won't have really given yourself over until you've dreamed about it."

As if to satisfy the command, that night Sean had a dream. "Do you really want to go that way?" someone asked him. He clearly saw the cage with its black poles. Sometimes the squat prison looked light, humorous, restful, like the orgone box lit midnight blue that Wilhelm Reich had designed and that Sean had seen in a visit to "the Bunker," William Burroughs's old apartment down the street from him on Bowery. But at other moments in the dream, the blue light would be killed, leaving instead grainy overhead newspaper lighting, the atmosphere of true crime, of mug shots, of documentary photographs of murder sites.

Sean had never woken up in a sweat before. But that morning he did feel his forehead sprayed with pinpricks of wet anguish. Paul was long gone. A few squat purple candles were burning down into bruises. Sean caught sight of a searing stripe of daylight from a window on the far side of the living room. For the first time he wished he'd built windows into his harem of a bedroom instead of relying on muffling curtains and the tricks of architectural disguise. "Do you really want to go that way?" he heard as the question repeated in his head, chillingly, again. But he did hear the voice. Chris's.

"Yeah, right," Sean grunted out loud, puffing himself up, rousing a mug of shaving cream for his balls from the medicine cabinet.

Soon enough his fitful, peevish feeling of rebellion blew over, leaving him free to begin undertaking the checklist of tiny assignments Chris had indicated over the telephone. In the mornings he would pour brown shredded-wheat cereal into a white porcelain bowl, and orange juice into a matching bowl, carrying them on a red metal tray decorated in colonial kitsch—roosters and hens and barn houses—into the main sitting room, where he rested them on the floor. Then he'd lie on the ground snuffling the cereal with his face and tongue, trying to suck up the grainy part, always leaving a stain of white milk on his snout. He had to angle his head sideways to catch the unwieldy squares of cereal. If he looked up, he would catch his reflection in the black marble of a nineteenth-century bust of Mephistopheles. His own face would be broken up into streaks and particles by the busier patterns of the statue's pointed beard. Sean trusted that Paul, who either wasn't home or had just recently slipped into his sleeping bag in the front room, wouldn't find him curled into such a vulnerable question mark of a position.

Sean was pleased with the shaving assignment. He stood in his metal shower stall with its pipes functionally exposed, a mirror hanging from a string, as was a beige brick of soap-on-a-rope, a concept he never quite understood but which he enjoyed when it came his way as a gift. Used to seeing his face in the mirror, he blinked a bit to see his soft balls reflected there as he grabbed them and began to shave the light covering of hairs. He was carried away quickly, going beyond duty to include the ravine between them and his asshole, and the next day the nether beard and mustache surrounding. The only catch to the shaving—and the clean whistle of peppermint shaving cream on his previously unshaved ass—was the eruption over the next few days of tiny hairs, like mattress springs going *zing!* in a cartoon, as they reasserted their urge to bristle and grow. The no-underwear prescription added to the sensation, so walking in his jeans he'd feel a faint shock, almost subliminal, every time the denim would brush in the wrong way against his newly exposed mown crotch. These were reminders. Indeed, all was designed for recalling, recollecting, like the hair shirts and prayer bells of monks. The whole language was monkish, too: "obedience," "sacrifice," "discipline."

Who needs it? Sean thought often enough when he'd catch his reflection in a car parked on Broadway, and he could practically hear the friction of his seedy thoughts against his more dashing appearance as displayed in a dirty back window in need of a wash. (The only moments Sean wanted a car: when he longed to ride through a car wash alone, the big brushes sudsing the car's body, the huge rubber razor straps slapping over his windshield.)

The phone call with Master Chris that Wednesday night was trying. Sean felt he was in a tennis match in which his place was to figure out how to miss all the serves, to fail in more and more elaborate ways, making Chris look better and better. But of course, it's harder to lose than to win. Chris knew how to keep a relentless pace, a breathless restlessness with no stops, no margins for complaining or protesting, no reverberations of "Hey, wait." Sean admired his swift gamesmanship. But then he'd worry briefly, blackly, that for Chris this was no game, just as he'd said. Wasn't it? Was it? And then the ball would come swirling back down the center of the court.

Chris had been teaching Sean these responses, again like a monk in a cloister, though based on pop songs rather than psalms and hymns.

"Fly, robin, fly."

"Right up to the sky."

"Good boy. I want to control your bowel movements. When you go to the bathroom, you must sit on the cold, bare rim, not on the seat."

"Yes, sir."

These plays and replays were always a test for Sean, whose sense of his own dignity was so tall, yet whose need for immolation had become so strong recently.

"Have you been sleeping on the floor, boy?" Chris inquired.

Sean made a sound, an elision of a grunt and a bark on which they'd agreed: one sound for yes, two for no. That is, he lied.

"Did you send me the picture I asked for?"

Now Chris had him cornered. Sean felt like a queen on a chessboard, unprotected by pawns, with no bishops properly positioned for a diagonal preemptive strike, and a turret-headed rook staring gunshot at her from across the board, ready to make his final, deadly move, destroying her and checkmating her husband, the slow-moving king. Sean felt forced to make two abstract, unconvincing growls. The checkmate was that he didn't feel he could rightly explain that he was a semifamous filmmaker whose picture was public knowledge. The checkmate was that to argue so was to lose his necessary veil of inferiority, of Zero-ness, his very name.

To his surprise, and involuntary great interest, Chris, whoever he was, lost it. Sean heard his voice balloon in size on the other end. He felt the earth of their connection shaking. Chris was yelling! He was calling him names! He was threatening to hang up! And then, as if a giant pair of metaphysical scissors had cut the throat of the screaming autocrat, he grew manipulatively (or sincerely?) quiet and concentrated again. He began to interrogate Sean about intentions, about means and ends, in a fashion that touched on his deepest issues, and yet was always strangely attenuated by the phone wire so thinly joining them, the absurdity.

"Do you feel the need to serve, Sean?"

"I do feel joy in serving, sir. I don't know why, but it makes me warm, electrified. Why's that?"

"And how do you feel about giving over all those decisions, all that walking on two legs, dressing like a human, pretending? Isn't it a charade?"

"I feel I could fly, or I could cry. Just to hand it all over. Just to fly from responsibility. And that if taking over could please someone else, then it's like a solution so perfect, as perfect as a triangle or a circle or a square."

"You're beautiful, boy. You're halfway home. But my problem with you is that I get the sense that you've got a full life. You talk about having a loft, about friends. Are you ready to give all that up?"

Sean hesitated. A hill of doubts was growing in his throat that he was trying to climb over, but he kept sliding back. Maybe he was too healthy, too sane, too powerful for Chris's little games.

"I don't know," he said.

That short response started Chris off again. Not angrily this round. No, he was thoughtful, controlled, clear. His even tone was worse, worse because even more mesmerizing in its orbital swipes at truthfulness. What was he? He was a disembodied voice.

"I think, Sean, that you want to compartmentalize your life. That you want to go on having a full life. Without having to check with your master for permission. You want to have all your friends follow your frisky yips and yaps."

"I would like to have it all, sir."

"Well, that's quite a balancing act, boy. But I don't want to work with anyone who wants to put me in a box, a compartment. I want it all. . . . You don't want to be alone for the rest of your life, do you, boy?"

Chris had saved the megatonnage for last.

"No, sir."

"Well, I wish you the best of luck, boy. You're on your own now."

The phone went dead.

Sean felt encircled by black, like the perfect circle in the center of the Japanese flag. It was the perfect circularity he had described to Chris. Sean felt sad. Chris had played his (their?) themes so flawlessly, without any mistakes—Sean would have caught them—that he began to convince himself that maybe Chris was the sounding board for Sean himself.

So he decided to try again. One night he went to Times Square to a games arcade, slipped into a photo booth, swung the heavy gray curtain across the door, slumped down in his black leather jacket, jammed a few quarters into a silver slot. As the flash was preparing to pop in his face, mirrored in a cheap tinny mirror, he drew out a spiked dog collar and attached it discreetly around his neck, staring down the four flashes. Then he repocketed the cheap collar quickly in his black leather jacket, remembering an old school sonnet by Sir Thomas Wyatt about an unavailable lady the poet compared to Caesar's deer, who wore ID necklaces about their soft brown necks, "Noli me tangere, for Caesar's I am." I belong to Chris, he thought foolishly, not yet knowing what he meant. Then he paced, waiting for exhibits A, B, C, and D to drop in front of him. They fell like four connected heads from a guillotine. He had stayed close so none of the lovey couples, mostly speaking Spanish, mostly young and pimply Romeos and Juliets, would grab them by mistake and break into cackles. He didn't want to be a buffoon of an anecdote in someone else's romantic evening. Waving his strip, still wet from the chemical preserving gloss, in the wind of Times Square, he hailed a cab.

Sean slammed himself into the Dependable Taxi Service cab with its heraldic strip of black-and-white checks. The driver in his green Nam jacket jerkily pulled into the traffic of Times Square, forcing down the lever that allowed the number 65 to pop up. A green rain began to fall on the prostitutes in their hot pants, the boys in white guinea T's, the junkies filing in and out of Nedick's. Rain was turning the dirty sidewalks rose. Sean told the driver to go uptown, then down, then west, then east, his imaginary destination changing every few blocks so that he wound up going in a circle. He was just letting a river of neon words pass through him. HESS. COCA-COLA. HOTEL. BAR. BAR. Cine 42 was advertising *Bucktown.* HOTEL TAFT. METRO-POLE CAFE. WOOLWORTH: every one of its letters, spelled down the side of a building, was given its own light box. Gray steam rose in a hiss from potholes. Police gates were drawn over windows. Hunched slouches drank egg creams at counters. A roll of porn movies at the DOLL. GLOBE HOTEL. Cherry-red BOND'S. Blue lights. Green rain splashing. *The Mafia Wants Blood* was showing in some blaze of white light. PARKING. Cars like stars. CHILD'S. DON'T WALK. MARDI GRAS. A cozy bar. A shoeshine stand. BLARNEY STONE. CHARLES BRONSON. *Mr. Majestyk* was showing, too.

Sean aced his wish. He compliantly, apologetically sent the photos to Master Chris, who called back quickly with an invitation full of caveats and precise directions and phone numbers and addresses and times. By now Sean's life had been emptied of people, and enticements. He hadn't spoken to Edgar, or Jarhead, in weeks. Paul had flown off to Berlin with a john. When he left, Sean didn't even entrust an address or phone number to anyone, though he did scribble numbers, as evidence, by the black rotary phone just in case, the most farfetched case. Then he boarded the train for Washington, D.C.

Sean hadn't been out of the city for months. He could almost feel its hyperbole and pressure contracting into a gaseous dot behind him. He even glanced through newspapers, for the first time in forever, picking up bits about the Shah of Iran visiting Washington, Anwar al-Sadat visiting Jerusalem, Menachem Begin visiting Cairo. This was a season, the winter of early 1978, when so many from around the world were flying in for long weekends. "You travel to the Philippines and every hairdresser is interested in news about Studio 54," Bob Colacello told him there one night. The Mineshaft, ditto, especially among the frogs in Paris, who only went to Manhattan or the Pines on holiday. But that's just why Sean was thrilled to be crossing a border again. Besides, he was thinking with his dick.

The train pulled into the stately station in Washington with level stealth. Like the invisible worm burrowing into Blake's sick rose, Sean thought, this trip seeming to bring up in him every lyric poem he ever knew. A cab took him to a specific street Sean had written down after looping its way around the Dupont traffic circle. He made his way up a banister that glided along curving steps of cracked wood. He knocked at a wood door divided into long wood panels. No building in New York would have been so unguarded. No buzzer. No bell. The door opened.

Sean studied Master Chris's clothes to distraction: the dark blue button-down police shirt, the pale jeans, the black shiny policeman's shoes, the college ring with its clunky garnet stone surrounded by golden busywork, the silver watch held by a chain that clamped around his wrist with its brown hairs. When Sean finally managed to look up, he saw a handsome (in a department-store-catalog way) man with graying brown hair, a brush of a mustache, eyes magnified by steel rims. He immediately sensed that Chris's masculinity was more hyper, and squarer, than his own. Stepping out of his mind was always a disappointment. But in this case not overly.

"Once you come in this door, boy, you're mine."

Sean found if he looked down towards the pomegranate-colored Persian rug on the dark wood floor he could concentrate, be more willing. This was a way to return to the domain of the telephone, where voices and thoughts were all that were real.

"Sit yourself down on that red chair, boy. This will be our first, and last, talk as humans." Chris paused between his phrases for effect. Sean sat. Unfortunately he was overly conscious of Sean the filmmaker, Sean the boy from Turret, Sean with the memory for Renaissance love poems. They all sat there with him, perched on the back and arms of the upholstered red chair, like a chair in a dad's den. Sean felt he was in Ward Cleaver's den. He was thinking of bolting.

Then Chris handed him a tumbler of Irish whiskey on the rocks. Then he handed him a joint. Some fun began. Sean was growing mesmerized by the way Chris played his long fingers with their round nails along the seams of his jeans and the stitching along his zipper. His fingers reminded Sean of something, someone, somewhere, at a moment of heat. Chris began to hypnotize him. He had him count backwards again. Then he had him down on the floor at his shoes, licking them according to the ticks of the grandfather clock. Oh yes, Sean realized in a quick fissure, the clock! The dogs were barking again outside the door. He almost felt sentimental, as if he were home. What was in that joint? Chris was leading him on a leash attached to a collar around his neck. He was no longer dressed. His clothes were stashed next to a pile of *Life* magazines under a heavy oak table. He was being led into Chris's bedroom. Sean was now quite happy. He had arrived. He'd shaken off those other Seans, left them in the smoking den.

No, this wasn't Chris's bedroom. It was a totally insulated room with padding on the walls, straw on the floor, a cage in the middle, medieval-looking pokers and peelers and back scratchers hanging ominously on the walls from bronze hooks. It's what they called "playrooms" in New York. With rents so low, three hundred or five hundred dollars, lots of Sean's friends, more especially Edgar's friends from uptown, would pay rent on a small apartment on the lower East Side just for weekends to stage dramas such as these. Edgar told him they'd been called "bump rooms" in the fifties.

As important as words had been in their courtship, they were equally unimportant now. Chris and Sean barely spoke again. The Latinate strength of Chris's words was now concentrated in his hands and forearms. He swung Sean's body around as if it were a side of one of the cows on Washington Street. Quickly Sean was chained into an entire jewelry kit of silver nets. Around his head was placed a version of a football helmet made entirely of straps held together in different patterns by snaps regulated to size and to the whim of the mummifier. Sean's head danced with pictures of mummies, straightjackets, Haitian zombies. The deregulation of daily life and thought Chris had managed before by hypnosis was now more effectively handled by clinks, and locks, and lassos. The relief, at first, was similar.

There were some verbal clues, too. In the middle of the night, when the lights had been darkened and Sean tried to sense almost extrasensorily the dimensions of his cage, Chris would appear as a tall shadow in the line of light cast by the opened dungeon door. He would hunch down on his creaking knees to speak into the cage bedtime stories with an agenda. "Kidnapping is good," he murmured. "My friends are all masculine. One's a cop. One's an MP. One's a senator's aide. One's a foreman." Sean wondered briefly how "senator's aide" fit in. Must be something special about him besides his job description. "We kidnap, we take advantage. You won't know who's who. What's up. Which side is which. We take them in cars. We break into houses. We abandon them in public parks for the guards to discover." Then he was gone, leaving several ideas tucked inside Sean's half-open head.

Food was the part of the setup that began to excite Sean the most. He saw Chris purposely sprinkling an indigo-blue powder into his bowl of water in front of him, then onto the brown chunks of his food. All the eating out of bowls below his antique Mephistophelean bust had been a preparation for these meals. Sean began to lose count. He knew he was being drugged. He loved the numbness proceeding so carefully through his fingers and toes. His heart was muffled in a cloud. He felt things up his behind, rubbery fingers examining. Once a bitter pee rained down on him. He had little control over himself, but those recriminations from his own body were minor irritations. He longed mostly to know what time it was. By now his mouth was bound, his tongue tacked to the roof of his mouth. He was certain it had been days, just by rhythms almost unheard. He was relearning time the way an animal does in the field. But there light is so important. Worms know time, too. He was burrowing into a hole as subtle as the flecks passing almost unseen, like static, over the eyes of someone whose sight is beginning to fade ever so slightly, and of a frequency of high squeals only heard in spots of resounding quiet.

Eventually they came for him. He assumed them to be the senator's aide and the cop and the others. They handled him as if he were a baby, lifting him, blindfolding him against the searing light. There was a staircase. Doors opened and shut. The laughing klinks of a dinner party going on. On TV, the eleven o'clock news. A cold blast from a window. More and more stairs. Down to more doors. The rocking of the car, the closeness of being folded, he was sure, in a trunk that smelled strongly of petrol and fertilizer. A big metal rake rattled precariously close behind his own back and skull. This was a ride as if on a hobbyhorse careening out of control to which he'd been carelessly strapped.

A needle had definitely been slipped into his skin somewhere along the way. Its liquid was hot, traceable by temperature as it passed slowly through his blood vessels. At moments he felt he was all jaw. Finally he did not know where he was. He'd been removed. They were in a park. It was the middle of the night. An owl was hooting. Snow lightly covered the ground. A distant gunshot. He felt a river nearby. He was lying on the ground. Faces were coming into his. He was blissfully nothing to them, or to himself.

And then came the problem. Someone had carelessly (purposely?) moved a bit of the cloth around so that it was filling his nostrils. His mouth was already stopped up. He knew he was suffocating. All along he'd felt he'd been moving back up the birth canal, as when a film is shown backwards in fast motion: people walking quickly backwards up the steps of the monument; doors revolving backwards in the wrong direction, throwing their travelers out onto the devolving street. He'd been dropping all his qualities along the way, hastily sometimes, carefully sometimes, but all. Moving back to the extinction that came before accumulation. But now the pleasant giving up was being forced to come to a different conclusion. A mind within his mind took over. He did something. He was sure. But he didn't know what.

While he was doing whatever he was doing a river of pictures rushed through him. Supposedly at death a life is reviewed in snapshots of memories. Perhaps because he was going in the wrong direction, back into death through birth, the pictures weren't exactly memories, but possibilities, pure pictures of feelings experienced before or after: an outhouse by a stream, a trailer park filled with white-trash kids flipping knives, a dandelion next to a can opener, a baby boy Sean loved just before he was christened, a folding chair at the funeral of a bachelor uncle who died so young his service was held on a mother's second floor, all sorts of cars and washing machines and appliances at "The Parade of Progress," where an ambassador from Tunisia gave stamps from his country. Stamps the colors of a life in a desert.

What Sean probably did was yell, but yell from the well of his stomach rather than from chest or throat. Or maybe he threw up. He never remembered.

The next morning he woke in the thin snow. He looked tenderly up at the young park ranger in a brown uniform and mountainous hat who was looking down at him, pulling his face apart with big black gloves. Sean imagined the ranger was looking tenderly, too.

"You want some jerky?" the ranger asked, chewing on a raw, red strip of beef as if it were gum as he leaned over.

"Hi," Sean answered. "Hi."

U-Turn

Months went by. After Sean's near-death experience, he lightened up. Eventually the weather lightened with him. Paul had moved to Atlanta with another go-go boy. The Steenbeck in Sean's front room glowed bronze, the color of an old cannon, during late-spring dusks. He'd stopped making movies for a while to give himself a break from the pantings that had swirled him down into so much trouble.

One balmy night, though, after catching a performance by Meredith Monk of her *Plateau 1* at the Saint Mark's Poetry Project, Sean went across town to the Ninth Circle, a knotty-pine-walled bar in the West Village started as a steakhouse in the sixties, now a gay bar, its booths having been yanked. One regular was famous for having actually been present at Stonewall—his badge of honor—and for panhandling as a high-school kid on the streets, but when he ambitiously suggested painting exhibitions and poetry readings at the bar, a big loud "Aarghhh" went up around him.

Sean came in on sneakered feet, rather than his usual motor-cycle boots, after walking down a street lined with perfumed light-green trees. In fact, tonight for a change he'd slid into a faded yellow T-shirt, blue jeans, and Adidas sneakers with green stripes.

The Ninth Circle was a rec room of disheveled types, like the "lost boys" in Wendy's treehouse in *Peter Pan.* There were lots of college students, young poets and painters. All the hellish echoes in its name were dissipated by their expectant faces. Crammed up and down the bar, they wasted quarters on a faded jukebox that played middle-range hits—"The Closer I Get to You" by Roberta Flack and Donny Hathaway, the Bee Gees's "Stayin' Alive" from *Saturday Night Fever,* Barry Manilow's "Can't Smile Without You." Scotch-taped overhead were favorite posters of the moment: Mark Spitz in a dark blue swimsuit, his teeth making a thin white line under a bristle of a mustache, a necklace of Olympic gold medals hung ceremoniously over auburn nipples; Mick Jagger, thin and perverse and "unisexual" (a word made popular by the hair salons) in *Performance;* Arnold Schwarzenegger, a budding blos-som of gray, platinum, and silver muscles in *Pumping Iron.* Saw-dust swept the wood floors. A bartender with a wedding ring remained available in cheerful jeans that embraced his wide hips and full behind. Beneath another row of posters, the most elabo-rate of all for *Jesus Christ Superstar,* boys still in the first phase of their moons would toast anything, many ordering shots for the first time in their lives.

The poet Tim Dlugos in round plasticene glasses gave a Catholic ex-seminarian's spin to all his comments, then quickly burst into a cyclone of giggles that rose into the exhaust system of the low ceiling. Tim often talked to Richard Elovich, a young writer who had already assisted Allen Ginsberg and Jasper Johns. Richard's love interest at the moment was James Grauerholz, an Aryan from Kansas who was assisting William Burroughs, employing punk hardness as his business technique. In James's big, knuckly hands, an attaché case became an instrument case, or a bomb. He spoke the word "William" as if it were a title: "der Führer" or "il Duce." Sweet Larry Stanton, his hair the color of yellow hay, his high cheekbones combined with slits of blue eyes, making him at once wise and wise-ass, took home as many rattled blow-throughs aged fifteen or sixteen as possible to make icons of them in his vulcanized Pompeii portraits. His best were called "Untitled." Mark Lancaster, an English painter in his thirties who was assisting Jasper Johns, was always on his way from a cocktail party whose details he flaunted, and trashed, as he involved himself in the glee of the next gin. His drinking of gin seemed the only English thing about him. With Mark would be Kevin Sessums, a teenager, perky, not camouflaged in the usual teenage sulkiness, his lips as fluted and cherry-crushed as Mick's in *Performance* or Marilyn's in *Niagara*. Joe Brainard stuttered, tried to buy friends drinks in his usual getup of cowboy boots and a white shirt unbuttoned to the navel, with a few spare hairs curled like Popeye's. Someone once told him he had a sexy chest and he'd shown it off ever since. His hair was as wavy and Scotch-terrier-like as Sean's dad's. Joe took lots of speed that year to make his mad collages even more intricate: an extra crushed carnation made from soda napkins here, a Lucy cartoon there.

Luckily, Richard Elovich introduced Sean that night to Willie Nichols.

"Hi."

"Hi."

Sean didn't think much about it at first. He sized up Willie's spot at a table with other Burroughs acolytes. They all wore black. They all fancied themselves businessmen-artists. Theirs was a new hipness that went along with punk, not in Sean's and Annie's fifties leather style, but more in the style of the band Devo. "We are not men, we are Devo," its four members, in suits and thin ties, chanted as if they were computer chips. Sean recognized at the table two of Burroughs's knaves, one with red hair, one with black; both looked as if they had been breathing too much carbon monoxide, their cheeks sunken, their eyes blisters of light. Sean used to fancy himself Burroughsian. He had read *Naked Lunch* soaked in the sun of his backyard when he was a teenager. "That's where I want to live," he thought of its farcical, druggy, politically pointed landscape.

Richard told him facts about Willie: a writer, he was actually at Columbia at the same time as Sean. Sean palpitated to some quality about Willie, but then he was distracted by a fox-faced waif who wanted to talk about what sign he was.

Cut. Hours denied. Sean squeezed in with all the other young men as the hour approached four. He looked over towards a shelf for drinks along the opposite wall. The jukebox was humming like a spaceship behind him. There was Willie looking his way. So alertly. His hair cut short, Kraftwerk- or the Shirts–style: that is, like a member of an art band. He wore a black polo shirt, black jeans, his blue-silver sneakers emblazoned with a gray "N" on the sides. He was bantamweight, two or three inches shorter than Sean, wiry, lively, shaken free somehow of the sameness to his left and right.

Sean didn't feel as if he had approached Willie, or as if Willie had approached him. But in a few minutes, by shifting with the tide of boys in a phosphorescence of party lights, they were standing next to each other, talking.

"What'd you do tonight?"

"Went to Taste of Tokyo with Richard. Ate sushi."

They were talking about nearly nothing. Sean noticed three different looks from Willie. In one, he tilted his head to the side. There his bones were as fine as a greyhound's, his features geisha-simple, his eyebrows and lips feminine. In the second, he shattered all this Oriental-teacup perfection in a raucous, giggling explosion. He looked to Sean like some of the more drunken, happier photographs of Frank O'Hara. Then he'd look straight on, becoming an all-American high-school boy, solid, burning with the will to be President, or a great American novelist, or Albert Schweitzer. A pro, Sean cataloged all his expressions quickly and fully.

"What's your name again?"

"Sean Devlin."

Sean waited a beat for a reaction. There was none. He felt relieved, somewhat, but also pinched that he wasn't quite as excessively famous as he'd imagined during his flight from recognition, when he was trying so hard to smudge the features off his own face. And anyway, why hadn't Richard told him?

"I'm working as an usher at the Met. You wanna see the Cuban folk dance troupe next week?"

"Not really. I don't think I could dig socialist flamenco."

"I'm going to Miami to visit my parents the next day. So I'll give you a call when I get back."

Sean flinched. He'd really only declined so that he could use the phrase "socialist flamenco" to prove his edge, his wit. And because he didn't care about Cuban dance. But obviously he'd been flashed and hadn't flashed back. No sooner had the lit match been blown out inadvertently by the unexpected breeze of Sean's showing off than Willie's friends were upon him. Let's go here. Let's go there. He could practically smell the hash, the lure.

"I'll give you my number."

Sean gave him his. He gave Sean his.

When Sean looked down at the phone number, he smiled. He recognized the skulduggery of a kin. Willie had written out his name and number in the squiggly script of a horror movie on the back of a chopsticks wrapper from Taste of Tokyo.

"Damn," Sean said out loud, drunk, and feeling something like love.

•　•　•

Eventually Willie called. Sean had tried his number a few times, but no answer. Weeks went by. Then, *brrrrrng*.

"Do you want to hear my friend Brent's band?"

Seeing a band was much more along the lines of a romantic date to him than a flash of feathers in Cuban, sitting alone, while his love interest was forced to march by in a red suit like those worn by the monkey soldiers in *The Wizard of Oz*.

"You want to come by here first?" Sean asked.

The evening of the date was a Friday. Sean responded to the crackle in the intercom dancingly. Dressed in fashionably beat black, he tapped his way down the broken spine of wood stairs in his loft building. He was thinking that even though, at twenty-four, Willie was two years younger, he'd been making most of the moves so far. He was remembering an article he'd read in a women's magazine about regaining your virginity. He opened the door.

Willie wasn't fashionably dressed in black at all. He was actually looking strongly all-American. The tan he'd collected in Miami visiting his parents was as dark brown as the brown paints in the Paint-by-Number kits Sean used so exhaustively as a kid: the color of the tree trunk, the color of the pony in the field. He knew Willie was Jewish-American. But now he looked more Semitic—desert Egyptian, Israeli soldier—except for the gray Exeter T-shirt that showed a light bulge of muscles.

"I was just at Big Gym. Can I take a shower?"

Sean was amused. Willie's hair had grown in the month as well. It was curly black, very curly black. They walked upstairs. Sean's heart was pumping as quickly as if he'd just smoked a bunch of menthol cigarettes. He immediately handed Willie a cheap white towel stitched with the blue letters YMCA. Willie found his way to the severe shower, looking at everything while pretending not to be looking at anything. But his brown eyes had a laser quality so strong they appeared to be black. He'd certainly caught sight of last night's opened can of tuna lying on the counter.

When Willie stepped out of the shower he wore nothing but the towel. There he stood, wet and stalled on the linoleum floor of the kitchen. Sean only stared. He felt Willie was showing him his wet chestnut skin and the pencil smudge of hair in the armpits just as women in Muslim countries supposedly presented them-selves to be inspected to secure a transaction of dowry and prop-erty. He shyly dropped a spatula as Willie hurried by.

"It's hysterical," Willie was saying of the Big Gym. "Someone's sweat socks were stolen in the locker room, obviously by a queen with a twitch for nasal odors. An odor eater! And then this butch number was trying to act as if it were a violation of his rights. All in this broken-down bordello."

They giggled. Sometimes in the pandemonium of both their giggles, they'd lock into the same frequency, just for a second, and then it would be gone. But those interstices were the spots where love's arrows got through.

Oddly and uncharacteristically, Sean—who lived by cans of soup and eating take-out Chinese—decided he'd cook a supper for Willie before the rock show. He'd bought a bulge of raw, red meat at a French butcher shop on Greenwich Avenue: all white tiles, white aprons, authentic pinched manners. He was making a bloody steak tartare because it was a flourish and easy. He cracked into its belly a yellow yolk, then scattered capers as freely as pep-per. He handed the plate to Willie, who was sitting wedged on the couch behind the glass coffee table on which Sean used to cut his coke.

Willie rested his plate delicately, suspiciously, on the smudged glass.

"What's this?" he asked.

"Steak tartare."

"American steak tartare?" He'd lived in Paris after Columbia, working at a small restaurant named Petit Robert near Place de Clichy for his francs for rent until he developed hepatitis from mussels. "Do you mind if I cook mine?"

Willie was already moving in his wily manner before Sean could answer. He was in the kitchen raising a magic cloud of steam from the cooking meat. When he returned, his pink Russell Wright plate had become the surround for an oversized hamburger without a bun. He'd even discovered a bottle of ketchup in the refrigerator.

Sean felt a wheeze of embarrassment. He was used to being the tighter one in most exchanges. Suddenly he felt sloppy.

"I'm just afraid of microscopic bacteria in raw meat," Willie explained summarily, with some of the comic paranoia of Woody Allen.

"My uncle was Moe, one of the Three Stooges," he added as a different kind of explanation. "He lives in L.A." Sean tried to see the famous Stooge in Willie's fine features but couldn't.

Soon they were off to Eighth Street, where Brent was playing with his band, the Zippers. Past the Eighth Street Playhouse, where it was always Halloween at midnight on weekends, when crowds gathered for the showings of The Rocky Horror Picture Show. After passing through a dingy red curtain, they walked down steep black linoleum stairs to a candlelit table near the front. Willie's face was a stone tablet of irony. Sean tried to read it. He kept looking sideways during the set. He was definitely enamored.

Brent's band was refreshing in its mimicries. Quotation marks might as well have been one of their instruments. But although the references of the round drum, the black leather jackets, the slick hair, the deriding beat were plain, the edges of a lark were lost in the self-absorbed pool of Brent's expression. Sean could see from the way he cricked his swept blond hair back from the bony clarity of his face that he was enamored with the possibility of seeing himself in the mirror of watery Fame. Sean even felt jealous for an uncomfortable five minutes afterwards when they talked with Brent at the edge of the stage. Willie was playing him more adroitly than Brent had played his own guitar.

"You were as coy as Jim Morrison," Willie was overcomplimenting Brent. But, thankfully, as soon as he'd dropped his bouquet, he was finished. Sean knew that he did exactly the same routine himself, the same manipulating of the affections of self-absorbed heartaches.

"Teasing the actors?" he asked Willie, to show that he had flagged the exchange.

The clock tower of the Jefferson Library burned against the purple-blue sky this first weekend in July, 1978. The time, 10:15, was announced in the moon face of the clock rising from the building's gingerbread brick organza.

"You wanna go to my house?"

"Sure," Sean answered.

•   •   •

Willie's "house" was a loft on Prince Street off the Bowery, not so far from Sean's. And not so different. The block was dark, its darkness even more congealed than his. The buildings directly across the street were burned husks. "The landlords burn them to collect the insurance," Willie explained. "Then the bums move in."

Willie lived on the second floor of the building. More convenient, Sean thought. Willie's was one vast room that stretched into a dark background too undifferentiated to see at first. Tall front windows in green frames looked across to the bombed destruction.

"It's like photographs of German cities after World War II," Sean offered. "Like Dresden."

"That's my neighborhood you're knocking."

The front third of the loft was lit by a clip-on metal light. Instead of a black statue of Mephistopheles, Willie had rested a white reproduction of Apollo Belvedere on a white plaster Greek column. His red IBM Selectric typewriter, the same model as in *A Clockwork Orange,* was set on a gray metal typing table with adjustable flaps. A sleek German stereo occupied a shelf, and tall speakers glared down facelessly from four corners.

Sean lifted a needle sensitively, then placed it on a swirling record before he said much, before he made polite gestures. The record was *Darkness on the Edge of Town,* Bruce Springsteen's latest. Sean hadn't paid attention to Springsteen. He studied the face tinted bruised red in the V-necked T-shirt on the album cover. He thought he could see something of Willie in Springsteen's ambivalent, hip demeanor. Sean didn't particularly thrill to the loud saxophone, drums, and overly dynamic renditions at first. He noticed the titles were printed on the jacket in pica: "Badlands," "Candy's Room," "Racing in the Street." He had been lost so long in the artforms of downtown and uptown that he'd escaped any feeling for New Jersey high-school sensibilities. But Willie's enthusiasms were infectious to him. They veered more towards what Sean had identified as "straight-boy"—like the radicals he and Arnie were attracted to at Columbia—but with some drag and swish thrown in. Their two-year age difference meant that Willie was already invested in another wave, perhaps.

"I love Bruce," Willie went on absorbingly. "My friend Terrence from Great Neck ran into him on Eighth Street the other day. He followed him to tell him how much he loved 'Adam Raised a

Cain.' Bruce invited him to have a coffee with him. It was the biggest day of his life. I saw him play the Academy of Music. . . . Do you want a vodka?"

"Yeeeeees," Sean enthused.

Willie lit a ceiling light by pulling on a chain. A second third of the loft was exposed, a kitchen with a gray Formica table in the center, full of scattered rusted forks. The vodka was Gordon's, with an orange top. Willie poured the featureless liquid over ice cubes to hand to Sean, then returned to the front to sit on a red rubbery couch next to a white rotary phone. Sean sat in a tall proctor's armchair that felt to him as if it had been lifted out of a novel about an English boarding school.

"That was my grandmother's," Willie giggled, resting his legs on a low wooden coffee table. "She was crazy. I used to go visit her every Friday night, Shabbat. So I'm always afeared I'll go crazy too."

Sean imagined that he could see lanterns of madness lit in Willie's eyes. But he could just as easily not see destiny in that configuration. And of course Willie was too young to support any tragic interpolations for very long.

"I'll show you the outside."

They tromped through the last third of the loft, where Willie's huge double bed filled most of the available space. Its headboard was a bookshelf reaching to the ceiling filled with all his books from Exeter Academy, where he went to high school, and Columbia. Sean recognized in a glimmer the silver glint of the volumes of Greek dramatists. Willie worked to unhinge a shutter securely shut against an obvious threat of robbery. Released, he and Sean clambered onto a back roof, vast, yet backed against a torched X ray of an abandoned building. All over the roof stood skeletons of plants in terra-cotta globes.

"All plants die under my tutelage," Willie whispered. "My mother gave me these. But I forgot to water them."

"This is the Cemetery of the Botanically Damned."

They stood under the July sky carefully watching the stars, testing each other's skills in identifying constellations. Up from a low wall came the ink-stained face of a bum. He possessed the jowls and voice of a character actor assigned uneducated-uncle parts, or one whose face was splattered in the fiery mud of a volcano or a mud slide. "Willie!" he yelled out.

"Jimmy," Willie answered comfortably, familiarly.

"You're an ace. You told the Italians to leave our building alone, didn't you? Here's a gift."

The bum was gone, leaving behind a half a bottle of Gordon's vodka. He even knew Willie's brand.

"My landlords," Willie explained. "They call off their Dobermans for some reason when I walk in their place around the corner, where they sell ovens and restaurant appliances. They love me. I get them tenants. But I talked them into letting the bums squat in the those monstrosities across the street without hassling them."

Sean was impressed. He had seen the powers of Willie's charm in his oblation from Jimmy. He had seen as well old-style do-gooding politics. Willie could have gone into politics and succeeded. But he gave it all up, at least on the surface, to be a writer.

This was the finest date Sean had ever been on. Of course he could count the number of times he'd formally been on a date.

They examined their way in the dark towards the front, where the Springsteen record was spinning soundlessly, its needle having withdrawn automatically to its perch, and resumed their slouches in the same couch and chair.

"My father always wanted me to be a lawyer. They're not thrilled with my being a writer."

"My parents never wanted me to be a pornographer, either."

"But film is magical, because it's a universal language. It's definitely the art form of this century. Writing is limited by dialects. Movies are a bigger language."

"Maybe you should write screenplays. For me."

A little round gold Tiffany travel clock was producing a light dust of ticking while they talked. They were both smoking a lot to keep their heads stoked.

"What was your first sexual experience?" Willie asked.

"I was at a dinner party—gay, of course—where everyone went around and told theirs."

"Straights talk about that stuff too."

"I know."

"So what was it?"

"I was thirteen, my friend was twelve. He was like my first boyfriend. I slipped a pineapple from a can over his thing, sprayed whipped cream on, and lapped the whole concoction as if it were an ice-cream sundae."

"Wow. I'm impressed. Will you do that to me?"

They giggled.

"What was yours?"

"Terrence, the one who ran into the Boss. Anyway . . . we used to play hypnotism. I'd hypnotize him and he'd do things with me. It was as corny as a watch on a chain. And he's straight."

Sean felt exposed by the lightness of Willie's joking about hypnotism. He hadn't let on about his own explorations in this area. But certainly the word "hypnotism" threw him down into a dark hole, and to cut the spell, he picked up a *New York Times* from a side table.

"They have the most beautiful photographs in the *Times*. Each one is filled with static."

As easily as if they were turning the gray paper's oversized pages, Sean and Willie veered into a slightly different conversation.

"I don't care if there's a nuclear war and the world blows up. It'll just be a technical malfunction. A blown circuit," Willie said.

"How can you say that? Nuclear expolosions destroy souls."

"What's so special about human beings?"

"I think it's all to a purpose. I think the bomb has made us classless. Or is beginning to."

"When it's my time to die, I'll just see it as a technical problem."

"If I had any say in it, I'd fight to save your life even if you didn't want me to."

Sean and Willie were already developing subtle rhythms of syncopation and predictable counterpoints that soon became comfortably familiar between them. Sean always remembered Willie's glib toss about the meaninglessness of life. He held on to it. Willie always held on to what he would describe as Sean's obliviousness, his unwillingness to leave. When Willie later would tell the story of that night, he'd exaggerate to the point of a stark lie that he had merely been a polite host and that Sean pushed his stay so long, debated so ardently, that he couldn't catch any hints about the lateness of the hour until the full sun was bearing down hotly through the row of drapeless front windows.

"D'you wanna sleep over?"

They did finally go to bed. Sean felt a numbness in his hands and feet from the amount of vodka he'd drunk. But the fancifulness of harems and Israeli soldiers and Arab emirates swilled in his brain enough to wash everything with orientalism. With Willie's overly alert eyes shut for a while, Sean was able to concentrate on the tangy taste of his dark skin, the sharp, soft smell that rose from the pucker of his asshole, the soldierly bravery of his cock, which didn't go down. Sean was thinking "perfume" when he licked the armpits, when he licked the bottoms of his feet. He was pretending he was a servant boy of a pasha in the Far East. In an accidental crisis they both shot their loads. And then the true intimacy of shared slumber set in, more powerful than all the athletics of their coming.

Sean roused himself early, sitting for a few quiet minutes in the severely functional, small bathroom off the bedroom, reading from Willie's weighty tome of D. H. Lawrence's collected poems. He was reading "Snake": "A snake came to my water-trough / On a hot, hot day, and I in pajamas for the heat, / To drink there." Then he heard phones ringing; then he heard shuffling. Willie stuck in his head, his hairs stuck together by a glue of sweat.

"I forgot," he said, slapping his palm exaggeratedly against his cheek. "I'm having a July Fourth barbecue for some friends. Even though today's July second. My friend Dale's here to help me."

Sean tried to adjust, felt nervous, wanted to hang back, then finally left the bathroom to meet Dale.

Tall, thin, sallow, and unctuous, a bit like a servant, like an East Village Uriah Heep, Dale was carrying a few brown paper bags filled with hot-dog rolls, wieners, potato chips, a Brobding-nagian ketchup, sweet gherkin pickles, more potato chips, white plastic forks and spoons, paper cups, bottles of brown and white sodas. Sean recognized Dale from the Mineshaft. He'd never met him. But he'd watched as he'd licked the behind of a hairy punk-rock singer who'd gone to Columbia too, down on his knees in an amber bog of pee in the bathtub room, his partner talking non-chalantly and loudly to all his buddies. The game was a version of I Don't Exist, I'm Nothing But a Hound Dog, I'm Your Shadow that Sean knew well. Sean and Dale checked each other out in the kitchen knowingly, sniffingly, like shy dogs.

"We're actually working together on a film script," Willie explained while running water to rinse bulbous, pale-red New Jersey beefsteak tomatoes. "Sean's a filmmaker," he explained in the other direction.

"I know."

"It's called *Gang*, about Chinese gangs in Chinatown."

"Mmmmmmm."

Soon the shutters were thrown open. Willie was cooking hot dogs on an open grill. A bunch of friends, all men that afternoon, were sitting around a redwood picnic table, popping cans of Budweiser. One was Darryl, a black writer who'd been at Columbia, too. Though he looked endearingly streetwise in his purposely appointed anonymous coat and hat, he spoke admiringly of Virginia Woolf and imagined many of her affectations. Darryl emanated a true serious-mindedness that allowed many people to believe in him. He had been a roommate of Willie's at Columbia. He was Sean's and Willie's first mutual friend. Willie's boss at the Met, Peter Perstroichja, was there as well. He brought with him some vinegary beet juice he insisted everyone try. Gray-haired, hugging everyone, Perstroichja talked animatedly with an Eastern European accent about opera divas, of whom Sean knew nothing, and about curious crosswords of friendships with immigrant boys in which support and promises were exchanged for delight and hopeful gropes.

Dale murmured quietly to Sean, always with mischievously happy eyes that belied his robotic tone.

"Who have you been seeing?" Sean asked.

"Tava von Will."

"Really? He broke the skin of my butt in the trucks one night around the corner from the Spike. Is he still Hitler's right-hand man in America?"

"You know how he likes to crucify himself? He has a long rap about Christ's blondness. I never saw before how the Nazi movement was a group believing they were victims."

"Did he put you through your paces? Did he choke you until you experienced a flicker of unconsciousness?"

Dale allowed the two conniving yellow candles in the saucers of his eyes to answer.

A few others Sean met were filling in words and phrases. None of them had been at the table at the Ninth Circle a few weeks earlier. Jimmy showed up with yet another vase of distilled booze. He yelled out his remarks. Sean was beginning to notice how Willie attracted people around him—oddly enough, because he wasn't particularly friendly, outgoing, or engaging. Yet he was animated and had an ear for listening that drew them.

"You're much better for him than Rickie," Darryl said forwardly. Darryl's controlled expressions, as he sucked on a menthol, allowed him to get away with many such daring, catty jabs.

The party loosened up towards dusk. The promise of Christopher Street blocked off and fireworks set to turn the dimming sky into a facsimile of Studio 54 beckoned. As they scampered down the stairs, out onto the street, heading west, Sean seized a chance to talk with Willie for the first time that day.

"Who was Rickie, anyway?"

"He was a straight boy who lived with me. I was in love with him. It was bad this whole last winter. He had a girlfriend. I'd spy on them. I followed them to Phebe's and sat at a nearby table as if I were in disguise, but Rickie of course knew just who I was. We had sex. But he wouldn't love me. So I had to go on Thorazine. Which was wunderbar. It was like looking at everything from so far away, with no emotion, just as clearly as if I were watching somebody else's tiny video of a life. I'm still getting over Rickie's pale white skin."

"Someday I'll tell you what *I'm* getting over."

"I know most of it by now."

Sean, realizing that Willie had been hearing stories about him, felt as if he wanted to fire a musket at someone, or into his own foot. Then he relaxed again, smelling the colored air as they walked by a cemetery of ancient, gray, porous headstones on Prince Street he remembered from *Mean Streets*.

Christopher Street was a fair, a gay carnival overlapping with the July Fourth weekend. All its blocks were filled. Camille O'Grady was singing at a corner on a wooden stage that resembled the platform in Puritan villages where social criminals were displayed in pillories. Her mike was about as powerful as a transistor radio. She spent much of her set expostulating about herself. Sean stopped to listen for a few minutes.

"The first band I played in was at Saint Mark's Church and Folk City," she was hollering. "We were prepunk. Because we wore leather jackets they billed us as a fifties revival group. I'm not punk. Punk is done by kids. I try to take a point of view of someone who knows something instead of all that posturing kind of shit. I played at the Bottom Line and also at the Mineshaft."

The dregs of the party continued on their their way down Christopher Street towards the fireworks. R.J. was there. Sean introduced him to Willie. Those two caught on almost at once to each other's personalities. And then the booming began along the river, fired by barges, echoes of the Bicentennial two years before. A desire to restage that anniversary went on for a few more years, then died down.

"It reminds me of Bloomingdale's, Fiorucci's, and a tourist riverboat up the Mississippi," Sean tried to say, garbling some of his words. He was handicapped by the afternoon's cans of Budweiser.

• • •

By August, Sean and Willie were serious enough about keeping alive the delight of the flame they'd created that they decided to take a vacation together on Fire Island. Not the gay part, Fire Island Pines or Cherry Grove, but in a shack on something called Skunk Hollow, a condemned strip meant to be converted soon into a state park. Willie had been tipped off about a cheap cottage that was available.

They rode on the unprotected upper deck of the ferry to Davis Park, with families lugging striped tents, dizzying beach balls as surreal as gum balls, and styrofoam coolers. They didn't feel themselves part of the general familial gaiety. Because their shack was seven miles up the beach from the Pines, the location of the nearest supermarket, Sean and Willie lugged many days' supplies in an old green army duffel bag and an assortment of plastic bags from the Red Apple supermarket on Second Avenue.

"I wonder if we took the wrong fork in the road." Willie was referring to the dozens of well-oiled gay men who'd transferred from the old boxcar LIRR train at Sayville to a ferry to the Pines. They seemed bound for a sleeker destination.

"I prefer exile," Sean said grandly, seduced by the pinpricks of salty air sticking his squinting face.

They carried, and dragged, their bulging packs like two characters in a fable three miles along the beach to Skunk Hollow. Sean at once weakly and whiningly collapsed, using the forest-green army bag as a boulder to rest his head. Willie had to circle back to retrieve him.

"Come on," he was saying, barely heard above the wide surf.

"How can I? I feel as if I'm frying in a skillet."

Skunk Hollow was much like its name, and like the reverse of its name. Their home for a few days was perched on top of a hill, a close cousin of the shifting dunes all around. A hillbilly hand pump on the porch was their only source of water. A constant smell of bad eggs filled the kitchen, either from gas or nearby sewage. Yet the spare structure, with one main kitchen/living room, and a bedroom to the side, was a Shaker temple of simplicity. Windows on both sides framed views of the quiet, rolling bay in one direction and the moodier, violent ocean in the other.

For a day or two they stayed within the circle of ocean, sky, and land drawn around their shack. They counted vermilion jellyfish on their tan, empty beach. Took showers by emptying buckets of water onto each other, recording everything in a purplish tint on Polaroids that whirred onto the rickety porch like baseball cards being quickly traded. Their only neighbor was an old hippie nudist who sat leering down on them occasionally from the distressed, shingled roof of his own condemned shack nearby. They pretended he was the spirit of Gay Love come to endorse them. At night they drank the Astor Place red wine they'd brought, and cooked campfire basics: hot dogs and beans, Spam. Willie had been an Eagle Scout.

"And you were on your high-school wrestling team," Sean said in the middle of a dinner lit by broken refractions from a few kerosene lamps. "Your résumé is impeccable."

"One night I went to Cowboys and spotted my old high-school wrestling coach."

To break the mellow spell of heat and indolence they decided on the third day to hike to the Pines for tea dance, a disco held outdoors every evening towards sundown. They set out around two and didn't arrive until five. As they stepped onto the perfectly intersecting walkways, past houses as arranged as suburban mansions on other parts of Long Island, with the music of Donna Summer enveloping them in a familiar enchantment, Sean and Willie immediately felt out of place. Creeping towards the harbor, where yachts docked conspicuously, then finding a patio table for themselves at a drinks-dance plaza made of pinewood and filled with flushed partiers, they were forced to see themselves as the disastrously mosquito-bitten Robinson Crusoes they were.

"What do you want to drink?"

"Piña colada."

"It might taste like shampoo."

"The smell of coconut here is enough to knock out a cheetah."

But the slick accretion of chic compelled them to stay. A photographer Sean recognized was dressed in black Batman leotards, his face masked with an angle of a black nose, white circles painted under his eyes. With him was a thin young Filipino, dressed identically in red, who fetched their drinks and played his Robin. Gerard Falconetti, whom Sean also recognized, was blaring French in too many directions at once. A French-Italian model wore green silk trunks like a boxer's and a T-shirt cut like a shift. He was trying to find his balance disembarking from a speedboat shaped like the snout of a shark, but he never did. Sean detected the teeniest Nazi pin on the faded blue police shirt of a man he knew to be a Jewish dress designer. But mostly the porch remained a wash of happily dancing hysterics who were too high to hone a personal message. If "If I Can't Have You" had been sung live, Yvonne Elliman's voice would have been stripped irreparably by the time everyone skulked back into the shadows cast by the roughage of trees along the walks, fiery torches convincing some of the renters their bungalows were Roman. Sean and Willie left just as the walkways were crowded with shoppers carrying their dinners packed in brown paper bags from the one exorbitant market. When the Batman photographer walked by, a silver ID bracelet dangling on his wrist, he spat on the ground as if he were directing a comment at Sean.

The idea for "day trippers" was to find a house for a steak dinner, take a nap, dare drugs as shocking to the nasal passages as cold, snorted snow, then spend the rest of the night in the Meat Rack or the dance hall, winding up washed on the beach in the morning in the sun like paralyzed starfish.

"Get me home," Sean said.

"We'll never get home before dark."

Willie was correct. They walked for miles, and hours, along a beach that grew entirely black except for the light of the half-

moon and the little communities lit up over the dunes to their left every half-hour or so. Both defined themselves as separate from the Pines, which was more in fashion that year than any other year. They were able to be so happily exiled because of the luck of meeting each other. Their friendship was beginning to allow them to stray. Of course, both had. But those were the predictable strays of eccentric second-guessing and next-stepping. Now they were going to initiate each other into the secrecy of quiet time, of lying around like dogs, of hump and snore.

When Sean and Willie arrived back that night they scattered a herd of deer at their windowsills; snakes that slithered fast, leaving behind trails found the next morning; and badgers and raccoons. To recover from their trek to the Pines, they sat around a lemon mosquito candle on the back porch, smoking cigarettes and watching the many shooting stars. This last week in August was always shooting-stars season.

"You know what my grandmother always said—'I hate, I feel good.'"

"The crazy one."

"Yes. But my other grandmother in Florida has slept with my grandfather every night for sixty years. They're so cute together."

"I read this interview in the *Advocate* with these two old geezers who'd lived together fifty years. They said that sleeping together was the most important part. That your hearts started to beat in sync."

"I thought you'd just been reading the pink pages."

Sean laid his hand on the back of Willie's. "What nice paws you have, Willie."

"You're a nice beast."

"Dove."

That night their lovemaking was dirty. Sean loved the taste of asparagus in Willie's cum. He loved nestling in his behind, as plush as a mossy path in a forest. The next morning they were still tumbling as sunrise transformed their pulled white window shade into a perfect rectangle of flat colorlessness.

But the change became apparent the following morning, near noon, when Sean was napping on a hammock. He dreamed that he and Willie were standing in a log cabin just being built, its beams a ribcage. Willie was hanging up his wet clothes to dry. But he wasn't hanging up Sean's. Sean was worrying over this over- sight, this self-absorption by the Willie in the dream, when he was awakened by Willie. This time he saw a new look in Willie's brown eyes. There was love in those eyes, a sort of adoration. And it was directed at him. Sean had never seen, or allowed himself to see, such sentiment directed at him before. He was the one with the gaze. He had to be the adoring one, the one in lapsed control. But of course when he allowed Willie the weakness of his love he felt a door open in himself. He was suddenly in a new room, and there was never any going back.

They didn't talk. Neither was corny. Instead they climbed to a crest of the dune behind their rental until they arrived at a bal- anced bump of sand where they could see both sea and bay. A fil- lip of wind kept erasing their sense of where they were just as quickly as the noon sunlight was producing one perfectly etched impression after another. This was a big, epic split second. The rest of the two days was just its mild erasure.

• • •

The next week, the first in September, Willie visited his parents in a guarded community on a lake in Miami. He'd slipped into this habit of regular recoveries there: from hepatitis, from colds and flus, from the cracks of his unrequited love affair with Rickie. He was also carrying a valentine for a kid, Jimmy Brown, who'd been in the Navy and was now working his way through Miami as a

bartender at gay bars. South Miami Beach was the territory of
Willie's grandparents and their friends, either in their own apartments or in the many nursing homes where they rocked on front
porches. The libidinal Miami that Willie loved was reserved for
Cubans. With his grandfather, he traveled to their dog fights. With
the bartender, to cha-cha parlors where false Rositas were picked
up by false Romeos. He loved a Mr. Miami Contest he happened
to catch at a fake western bar.

Sean soon received his first note from Willie, a writer, it
turned out, with a crisp bite and a satirical eye:

> Dear Sean,
> The lake is very still tonight, the red lights across the way
> are not disturbed by ripples. The crickets are no more
> intense than those on Fire Island, but their rhythms are
> perhaps a bit more complicated. The view as I look out
> towards the lake is the same as from our porch. Cas-
> siopeia in the same position. I suppose this is why I am
> thinking of you tonight, although I've thought of you
> without the aid of the stars.

A few days later he received his second:

> Dear Sean,
> The other night my parents took me to a cheap Italian
> restaurant. They have this annoying habit of trying out
> cheap restaurants which they've read about somewhere
> on their children. This was one of the better ones, but the
> clientele and dinner conversations ruined my appetite.
> The people around were all the kind who haven't had a
> thought worth mentioning in weeks, months, and there-
> fore remain silent at restaurants. Preferring, along with

their companions, the conversations of those around them. It was in this atmosphere that my parents decided to embark on a discussion of my mental state, complete with a heart-rending speech by my mother on the subject of my happiness; my ability to lead a "normal" life with a "woman"; to choose my own lifestyle, not influenced by "others" (read "deviants"). She kept referring, with a complete lack of mystery or possibility for double meaning, looking me straight in the eye with gravest most motherly concern in her voice and expression, to my "big problem." A problem which she claims I had mentioned many years ago after talking with my rabbi (the one who accused me of being a queer), and which was so big, I had claimed, I couldn't discuss it with them at such an age. She also asked me whether I was still depressed about the bad love affair I'd had with "this person last winter" (lack of gender can mean only one thing—or am I just nervous?). Anyway, Sean, this was a most uncomfortable scungilli dinner for your humble narrator. I grinned a lot (a mother can see right through a nervous grin), and promised to see a psychotherapist twice a week for the rest of my unnatural life. I realized this script did not include "son admits to being queer in Italian restaurant," and therefore did not respond to her less than subtle accusations. The tyranny of the maternal innuendo!

And then as many days later, the third:

Sean,
I miss you. I didn't miss you too much until I saw young Jimmy Brown. After I was with him for a while I began to miss you very much. No, I did not have sex with him. Yes,

this was because I was thinking more of you than I was of him. No, this does not imply that you have any responsibility, reciprocal or otherwise. This is purely a personal choice, and had to do with this particular occasion. Yes, I do think of you every time I look at the ocean horizon (a certain two-toned part of your face). Yes, I think of you when I look at myself in the mirror after a shower, and when I stretch out on the couch late at night with my shirt off, at my reflections in the glass wall. Surprisingly, I can't remember a dream about you; not surprisingly, you are my prime j/o phantasm. On tonight's TV News they asked all these teenagers if they had fallen in love over the summer. They all said yes, but that they'd all broken up now that school was starting. Touching. I hopé I can be open enough to be vulnerable to you. I hope I still feel this way when the irresponsible summer haze is blown away by the reality of an autumn breeze. I hope you like me despite that last horrible line. Clearly this letter is petering out, and I am succumbing to my subconscious's desire to take over completely. And so, to sleep. I will see you in a week.

Love,
Willie

The day Willie was set to return, Sean—feeling prodded and pressured by the love notes and unable to film a reel to leave tucked in a projector on Willie's kitchen table—wrote his own prose-poem note. He ran over to Willie's loft, four or five long Bowery blocks from his. Willie had given him the key to take in the mail, which he did for the first time. Junk mail.

Getting ready to deposit his own poem on the Formica kitchen table, he found a poem left behind that threw him temporarily from his fast course. The poem had obviously been written by Willie after Fire Island. But its lines zigzagged complexly through Sean's memory of Willie's loving gaze, and of his heavy-breathing notes from Miami.

These were the nearly invidious stanzas, typed in blue ribbon on graph paper:

Sean,
you numb me.
you make me forget Rickie.
But as soon as I am alone,
I feel Rickie's white skin.

The air conditioner cools three square feet of
this twenty square feet room. When I'm next to
it, I am relieved. As soon as I step away . . . well . . .
you know what I'm going to say.
I think of the loft we are going to move into.
Strictly in my imagination you understand, I've
never discussed it with you; but I think of the
rooms, bedroom, workroom, set off, sound proofed
with separate entrances. Rooms for being alone at night.
Rooms for exorcising sarcophagi, rooms to protect us from
each other.

The sun on Fire Island spreads itself evenly
over my body.
Today you are the sun and tomorrow the smell of sex
will be your calling card.
I know your eyes are not unlike the horizons, and you
interact with the environment in such a way that both
seem somehow improved by the other's presence.

*The first day we noticed mysteries. The second day the
first were solved, new mysteries developed. Einstein
ended the debate between Ptolemy and Copernicus
by announcing that both were correct, it only depends
on the coordinate system.*

*I don't think I'd ever return to Rickie, if he should return
to me. But I know I'll never feel the same passion.
At certain spaced moments of passion, you erase his memory.
At others, you emphasize his absence.
A terrible line, a terrible truth.*

Sean did feel a cry in his chest. Like a tragic figure in an operatic jealousy, he had discovered a slip in the procedures. Should he tell? Should he not tell? Should be rip the poem to shreds and scatter it over Willie's royal bed? Certainly not. Sean knew the intricacies of his own heart. Sean forgave Willie his feelings on the spot. Indeed he felt freed by them, as they were as incorrect as so many of his own towards or away from Willie. He sensed the possibility here for an alliance of true kin. He might not have to strain to sing a romantic medley whose highs and lows felt impossible to him now. He left the poem blown aside, as he'd found it, on the counter by the stove beneath a lizard-green bottle of leftover pickles from the barbecue. Then he placed his own missive of blue ink (handwritten) on pink three-holed paper on the blank slate of the fifties-style kitchen table:

Dear Willie:
I just had an attack of Hello! Last night when I talked to you on the phone I was still in a cautious state, not getting my hopes up, in case you might not be back until Monday. Since last night have let myself get all excited again. There's nothing I'd rather do than be here now in 3-D and

sleep holographic sleep avec toi. Tomorrow I will see you. You will be so glad to see me. (?) It was a relaxing week but now I am starting to burn down again w/familiar fire. My running over here to leave this note is probably the kind of thing to make you look at me—after all a 26 yr. old man—and say "You're crazy." Well, yes and no. But these kind of feelings can only go like arrow to tree trunk (O hot cock!) the way when I'm feeling good I go straight in my mind to you (O hot cock!). This is a romantic note. Truth wears lipstick; carries K-Y in hip pocket of Levi's 501 button-down jeans with white Fruit of Loom Woolworth's / Kresge's underwear. There is no place I'd rather be now than here—welcome back to NYC, Willie.

XXX,
Sean

. . .

One day in late September, while leafing through the pink pages of the *Advocate,* Sean felt a familiar clutch. The ocular tease that did it to him was a blurry gray photo of a young man with no shirt, boxing gloves, Brillo hair, a Rocky Marciano face, sparring with the camera. ("Who was holding it?" Sean thought jealously, instantly obsessed by the white-trash macho.) The caption beneath the picture, with phone number: "Rocky."

Until that moment Sean had been faithful in his feelings for Willie. The two had been walking or cabbing the long blocks between their lofts several nights a week. Sean had also been beginning falteringly to jump-start his filmmaking. He was inspired by Willie's writing of an obsessive novel about his love for Rickie, his tracking of Rickie and his girlfriend. It was a detective-style novel transposed to the East Village and to a filled police blotter of romantic crimes. Sean was bringing home tulips, orchids, poppies, roses, irises, and calla lilies from a flower shop at Sixth Avenue and Houston to film. Not certain where to go from there, he hung the streamers of inconclusive footage like underwear next to his editing machine.

Sean didn't want to pay the hustler the sixty dollars he charged. That was too simple, too old. So he thought of a new ploy. For Sean, anyway, the charge wasn't doing the nasty, but rather just being in the hustler's den, taking in the alien's life on the surface of his hungry, ever needy eyes. So he dialed.

"Is this Rocky?"

"Yup," answered the low voice, like the unreal voices of TV cowboys Sean grew up desiring. He loved the garbled tone, as if Rocky were rolling around pebbles in his unruly mouth.

"I was wondering if you could use a houseboy to clean your place, wash your dirty socks, do laundry."

"Hey, Henry Boy. Pick up!" shouted Rocky.

"What's shaking?" said the new voice, thick with American regionalism and blue-collar status.

Sean had always been less impressed by the class warfare of Marxism than by the class lust he saw so often. So much of attraction was a white flag of peace. It was the motor of *Lady Chatterley's Lover* or, for gays, *Maurice*. Sean, this afternoon, wanted a stable boy, a boxer. And when that desire was at rest, he wanted to return to Willie, fellow artist and middle-class co-conspirator.

"What's your name, boy?"

"Doug," Sean lied.

"Our boy Doug wants to be our houseboy and do our laundry and shit," said Rocky.

"Forget it."

"Why?"

Henry Boy had already hung up. He didn't explain his reservations. But Rocky was intrigued.

"We're just two lazy masters hangin' out here. Too lazy to do shit. We need a slave boy like you to clean our belongings."

"You want me to come over?" Sean provided.

After a few more minutes of gosh-darn talking—an aphrodisiac poured into Sean's ears—he copped an address for Rocky and Henry Boy on West Twenty-ninth Street between Eighth and Ninth Avenues, a location Sean didn't know well. He gained his bearings by going first to the General Post Office on Eighth and Thirty-first, a Washington, D.C., monument of pillars and endless stairs in the middle of Manhattan, then just bore left until he arrived at a green picket fence. The block was made up of formerly handsome town houses in subtle shades of red brick that had seen better days. He walked down a few cracked steps to a green screen door. The outside decor was like that of Dorothy's Kansas. What lay inside was quite different.

Rocky half-opened the screen door, then allowed its weight to fall on Sean to open the rest of the way to let himself in. He was, of course, preoccupied with the phone, so Sean's eyes were free to rove.

Sean saw that Rocky was more ravaged than his picture let on. He did have all the attractive geology of powerful chin and cheek muscles; his hair was an unkempt curly brown; hair grew all over his body, at least as much as was left uncovered by green army khakis, white T-shirt, and dirty white basketball sneakers. But he had a cough, probably from all the Marlboros whose butts were stashed in full ashtrays. His knuckles were bruised. There was something punchy about his entire appearance. That part of his boxer promo was accurate.

"Yeah, I'm an Italian stud," he was reciting, bored, into the mouthpiece. "Recently divorced. Twenty-eight. Six feet. One-eighty. GQ face. Colt body. It's sixty at my place. A hundred at yours, plus the cab."

He hung up, the deal obviously queered.

Sean thrilled just as much to his surroundings as to Rocky, if not more. The room was a shambles, a heap of underwear, shiny dildos, bulging suitcases, gym bags, broken chairs, Salvation Army couches. The windows were dusted over with spider webs, like garage windows in Sean's hometown.

Out from the side, as if onto a stage, walked Henry Boy, who turned out to be remarkable: blond hair seemingly spun from Rapunzel's stash; skin as taut and lucent as a tadpole's; eyes so blue they were gray. In red trunks, gray Y shirt, sneakers exactly like Rocky's, he sparred with Sean without saying a word. With him was an obvious john, the very archetype of a john, middle-aged, fat, dressed only in skimpy white briefs that hung down from his navel in a limp frown. All jowly and pink, he was led by Henry Boy into a backroom. Sean loved that everyone was pushing the cartoonish limits of their own lives, daring to become pure caricatures in pursuit of some dream, or coin.

"What d'you like?"

"Feet," Sean piped up.

Back on the phone, sitting on the ratty couch, a few barbells tossed to his side, Rocky stretched out his feet for Sean to explore. He did, feeling the rubber of the sneakers as if they were made of skin, inhaling the stained burlap of gray athletic socks, and finally the encrusted, pulpy feet. Rocky then pulled him up towards his zipper, where Sean tasted rutabaga. He felt pacified as it grew in his mouth and down the bends of his receptive throat. Rocky quickly withdrew himself again. He was obviously in rhythm with a drug, speed or cocaine. Sean knew the temperamental percussiveness well.

"There are dirty dishes in the sink. You do dishes?"

"I even do windows."

"Take off your clothes."

Sean did. The sensation was minimal, chilly, Septemberish. He watched pink leaves fall from trees he couldn't identify through a window behind the sink. The dishes, mostly plastic, were palettes of dried ketchup, rigid pasta, smeared tips of broccoli. He delighted in the yellow Joy dishwashing liquid but was truly repulsed by the swamp of the kitchen sink. He began plotting his exit.

"You know how to fight, street-fight, defend yourself?"

"No," Sean admitted, coming back to stand in the living room. He was still enamored of Rocky. He wanted to take care of him, and to be protected in turn by him. Hustling, after all, was only incidentally about procuring and satisfying, about juices and groans. Much was involved in the completion of emotional transactions, equations of subtle import.

"Henry Boy, Doug here doesn't know how to fight. Show him."

Henry Boy finally responded. His john left standing like a snowman coming apart in particles in the shady bedroom doorway, he conceded to teach Doug to fight. He'd actually responded to the unequal footing. You know how to do this? you know how to do that? he was asking as he swatted Sean with different strokes to face, chest, balls, stomach. Sean felt as if he were fighting off mosquitoes.

"Lay off, Henry Boy. . . . He gets a little carried away sometimes," Rocky apologized.

So Henry Boy receded into the black rectangle with his silent, pudgy victim. Finally off the phone, Rocky drew Sean towards a green duffel bag.

"You got money for a deposit?"

"What kind of deposit?"

"Well, I'm giving you all my clothes to wash at the Laundromat down the street. I have to trust you to come back with the goods. What do you have on you? It's a deposit."

Sean found two crumpled twenties in his front pocket. He hadn't brought his wallet, fearing pickpocketry. Rocky swiped the two bills casually, promising an exchange for his cleaned and folded sheets and underwear.

"Next time I'll give you better stuff. I'm from Washington, D.C. A lot of hustlers stay here from around the nation. If you're good, I'll hook you up with them and you can do theirs too."

Sean was happy to agree. Washington, D.C., meant taboo to him after his recent danger. A taste for life, or antilife, was obviously returning. He bore the knapsack, similar to that in which he and Willie had packed their gear for Skunk Hollow, down Eighth Avenue to the Laundromat. His domestic skills weren't quite as developed as he'd let on. He never did his own laundry. He left all those decisions about bleaching and separating and folding to the Korean ladies who stood so sprucely, so soaped, behind the counter next to the weighing scale at the laundry on the Bowery. Now he was forced to ask for advice. Another Korean woman, quite similar in her perfectionism to the ones at his local Laundromat, instructed him in buying a packet of soap. Sean did love handling the socks and underwear. He was less fulfilled by all those sheets Rocky had stuffed in. A Harley-Davidson biker's towel he found especially appealing.

He slouched in a fluorescent orange plastic chair on four metal legs waiting for the spin to run its cycle. On the windowsill he found a copy of Rimbaud's *Drunken Boat*, Annie's favorite, perhaps left by a student. He'd been reading poetry a lot in the past few months. He lazily read a few lines:

> *True I have wept too much! Dawns are heartbreaking;*
> *Cruel all moons and bitter the suns.*
> *Drunk with love's acrid torpors,*
> *O let my keel burst! Let me go to the sea!*

He let the book drop and watched people distorted into shadows by the thick plate-glass window separating him from them. He enjoyed the mindlessness of his chores as a houseboy. He didn't need them punctuated too finely by literature, no matter how decadent and swooning.

Back in the basement apartment an hour later, his mission completed and the sack filled with folded sheets, Sean found that Rocky had left in a dash. "On a job," Henry Boy explained flatly.

"But I gave him a forty-dollar deposit. D'you have it?"

"Nope. You can wait if you want."

"I don't have long."

"Do this, then."

Henry Boy guided Sean into the bathroom and revealed to him in all its funkiness their white porcelain tub on bronze griffin's feet, a convex collector of hair and nails and smears of a black gouache of human dirt. Sean balked, drawing back as if from a much larger discovery. Henry Boy, dressed now only in a cranberry towel that fell beneath his knees, seemed insulted. Sean finally allowed himself to look at him, the embodiment of all those cliches about statues. But Henry Boy was off into the main room, where, tucked in the antennae of a TV that was broadcasting a Merv Griffin talk show, he suddenly found the two bills. At first Sean was relieved, then not. He could tell that Henry Boy was pretending as he diffidently handed over the bills. So he must have known all along. He must have wanted Sean's company.

To try to salvage that missed glimpse of Henry Boy, he reached down towards the bulge under the cranberry drape. But Henry Boy slapped his hand aside, furious, imperious, uninterested. He showed him to the door. Enduring the exile and the nudge out the door by the beautiful glimpse of an elbow, Sean made his way back up the stairs, slowly, feeling very alone.

Eighth Avenue was an upbeat symphony of everyone return-ing from work at five o'clock on a seasonable day with yellow light filtering through maple leaves, all sorts of leaves falling rockingly down onto the streets, some only making it as far as a shoulder, or a clutch of big hair.

As he headed aimlessly downtown, Sean suddenly remem-bered his life. He remembered Willie. What had happened? He could understand how someone might commit a crime of passion and then wonder what they had done. He'd enjoyed temporary insanity. He used to live for temporary insanity. So he didn't pres-sure himself to explain himself to himself that afternoon, or for many afternoons to come. His history was a series of moments, a voyage out. Period. But then that period could be followed by an ellipsis.

It's as if sex is an envelope, Sean was thinking as he hurried towards the Village in the bronze scallop shell of New York autumnal color and light. It's passed on as a mystery to be carried, burning hot, in the palm. But never opened. And then passed on again.

•   •   •

At about three in the morning of New Year's Day, 1979, Sean and Willie stood in the vague light of a traffic triangle at Fourteenth Street and Tenth Avenue waiting to be allowed into the Anvil. They were near the spot where a young twenty-three-year-old dancer from Les Mouches had been stabbed to death with a chef's knife in September.

Across Tenth Avenue brooded Sterling Provisions Corpora-tion, a meat-packing plant. Sean imagined he could smell the pot-ted meat, even though this was a holiday. Zenith Auto Leasing Corporation announced itself by a large sign from a large, open lot opposite. At the Gulf station across the street, a grease monkey was fueling a trunk with gas. The door of the Anvil was worse than Studio's to Sean, because all ploys of caste, like the signed cards from attorney Roy Cohn that could get anyone into Studio anytime, no matter how crowded, were negligible at the Anvil. Dispossession ruled.

"Did you ever?"

"Never."

Sean and Willie had already graduated to a language of understood gaps that made sense only to them. Meaning that the fall and winter had gone well. On Christmas Eve they'd hurried to Macy's an hour before closing, bought a black-and-white TV for Sean's loft, on which they'd watched *Miracle on 34th Street*. For New Year's Eve, they steamed live lobsters from Chinatown, making much of the lobsters' slow suffocation in Willie's bathtub and of their final Balinese dances of death when their claws were released from red rubber bands. The execution in a screech of white steam sent both killers into a decrepit guilt for about five minutes. But all was washed back by cheap yellow champagne.

Soon they were allowed inside. The mood was Transylvanian mixed with Wagnerian mixed with Village People. Sean had certainly been shoehorned into enough crowded bars over the past seven years to be nonplussed by all the pressing and shouldering, the displacement of boulders by rocks, and rocks by falling streams of unified whim. He tabulated the usual synesthesia quickly: the stage filled with the shaved heads of black men with arms up their rears, the spangled curtains of fleshy dancers parting, the calisthenics of those powwowing their feet on the curvature of the wooden bars, the projectors running strings of funky pictures through their illuminating teeth. Black balloons tumbled from pirate's nets. Shouts were muffled by groans. For a moment in the toilet Sean's nose was pressed up towards a crack in a window for a sniff of fresh air while someone was probing his behind with a finger or a hand. Then he returned to Willie.

"I used to come here when I was a pup," Sean said.

"This song was young when we were."

"Don't waste one word, one breath."

There she was. Annie. She was the one handing out her dictums so freely, so frivolously. She had always been frivolous with moral truths. Why was she in town? Sean was hugging her in what was by now a hallucinogenic shuffling of everything. Edgar was with her. Soon enough Arnie walked up too. And R.J., all teeth and chatter. Robert Mapplethorpe, whom Sean would become friendly with in the next year, was reintroduced to him in a hanky dance of primary colors: black, blue, red, white.

In that cluster of human slides Sean felt a pop of happenstance. Certainly seeing Annie registered high on a scale of seeing and recognition that evening. He was exultant, confused, embarrassed, happy, sad. He felt funny introducing Willie to Annie, so he didn't. Yet nothing could be more tender between Sean and Annie than a quick, smart shuffle of recognition. Then all was cleared just as suddenly again.

None of Willie's many friends seemed to be frequenting the Anvil, at least not on that pivotal day-for-night.

"I love you."

"I love you too."

Sean and Willie were being squeezed off to the side by the crowds.

That was when Sean felt something. It was a wringing, as if his heart were a humid towel being emptied of heavy plutonium moisture. This was a good feeling, this feeling of condensed rather than scattered loving, but new, uncomfortable. He'd been so used to the pinball game of the last few years played along an axis of dick and brain. He was aching for Willie as much in his hands as in his chest.

Soon someone walked over whom Sean recognized from Big Gym, where he'd started going with Willie. He was tall. Sean had been impressed by seeing a picture of him in *Drummer* wearing a torn jockstrap that looked like a hairnet. He liked to haunt the locker room inviting adoration. Sean couldn't help thinking him best cast in a gay version of *American Gothic,* with a pitchfork picking at his nipples. He was that kind of gangly, drawling faux farmhand. He introduced Sean to a friend whose name Sean couldn't quite catch, something like Wotan Douglas, a flight attendant from Quebec.

"It's a good night for a Wotan," Willie joked, referring to the Wagnernian music fulminating more and more encompassingly all around them, hovering about the stage as violet-purple smoke bombs exploded. Its tasteful romanticism was being allowed to layer itself more thickly over the club than would be possible on any other night of the year.

"Not 'Wotan,' 'Gaetan,' " the well-nippled model corrected.

Sean took a moment to look at Wotan / Gaetan. He was the kind of gay boy whom everyone seemed to find attractive except him. The Flamingo was filled with choruses of him. Sean preferred the fierce independence of Willie's looks. Gaetan's sandy hair raked boyishly over his narrow forehead. His T-shirt was already appropriately ripped, pointing to blond hairs on a smooth rampart of chest. He was stoking his nose with a bottle of poppers. The elixir ground what sounded to Sean a French accent, obviously Quebecois, into a pulverized midwestern that mismatched his friend's. The friend was pleased, smacking, at the rarefied company he was suddenly keeping in this flight attendant, this devotee of air.

"Pleased to meet you," Sean said with a falsely polite tone Willie revealed later he instantly knew to be a register of judgment and boredom.

Willie interjected himself, as he was only too eager to do. He began commenting on the orchestral music accompanying the climb of the snake, a zoological dildo of the natural world, into the behind of a buzzing Negro dancer: all nineteenth-century imprimaturs of decadence. The music was the prelude to *Das Rheingold*. Willie's became a talk Sean would always throw up before him in the next years, along with the tales of their first night, and Skunk Hollow. It was a talk that was the beanstalk grown from his usher's job at the Met.

The music was a gorgeous rising and falling of hunting horns and hills of violins. Sean was so used to the Bee Gees that he could barely recognize the orchestral strings audaciously being introduced into the saloon of the Anvil under the veiled excuse of a holiday specialty. The effect of the Rhinemaidens' voices was to raise the decadence of the club to pre–World War II Berlin standards.

"It's very gay, the whole *Ring* cycle," Willie was shouting as they moved farther back into a scrim of black cardboard. "At the end of the opera there's a rainbow. It's interesting that it's a rainbow. It's like the germinal epoch of the homosexuals of the nineteenth century—Oscar Wilde, or Rimbaud and Verlaine."

Sean didn't know opera very well, though he appreciated from the soundtrack that harps could serve as butterflies' wings on which reedy clarinets benefited from a free ride. He loved the voices of the Rhinemaidens. They tickled his chest more homeopathically than amyl nitrite, but to similar effect.

"I used to wonder what those old queens saw in opera," Sean was admitting. "But you're helping me to put on their ears and eyes. I know you well enough to know you're snowing me, too. But so what?"

Willie was sinuous from all the attention. It was as if his ideas were a music, an aria, a solo. He was alone on the stage of all this, no matter who was around. At least for Sean. For both of them, the way to their hearts was through their heads. This was Sean's current recipe for love. And beyond recipes, he just liked how he felt with Willie. He liked that they both knew that at the Anvil that night they were viewing some snippet of history.

"*Die Walküre* is about passionate love and incest," Willie continued, glad, he claimed, just to be able to communicate, glad to be rid of trying to talk to his parents—he'd been on the phone with them in a crisis mode ever since their September dinner at the Italian restaurant. He said he was coming to accept himself as the warm egg laid under their natural rump, and not expect much more. It was his New Year's resolution.

"The French horns . . . the French horns!" Sean was exulting, almost in tears.

"Have another schnapps," Willie said hopefully, glad for the ecstasy. He was a romantic about ecstasy.

"Then what happens?"

"Siegfried falls in love with his aunt," Willie said, as if the drama of meaning were self-evident. When it wasn't, he plowed on anyway. "It's 'the love that dares not speak its name.' *Siegfried* is about the education of the hero. At the end of the opera, Brünnhilde is lying asleep. He wakes her up. There's a thirty-minute passionate duet. It's passionate love. That's the gay movement, the GAA, Stonewall, the Firehouse. It's the education of the hero. And then you end up with this great, passionate love. Everyone's young, handsome, beautiful, and at the end you find your sleeping princess, or prince, and wake them up."

In a lapse, while the motif onstage was being cranked along from fist fucking to a simpler scene of involuntary ejaculation by a pimply hanging teenage boy, the music had descended by indeterminate chromaticism, as if someone were walking down the stairway of the keyboard along the black keys rather than the white, to a less delightfully aortic expansion, or heartbeat.

"What's this?" Sean asked, let down by the ambiguity, the sheer down-ness. "What's this?"

"*Götterdämmerung,*" Willie shrugged, not particularly listening any longer. "It's the Twilight of the Gods, where death and destruction reign. The Rhine overflows."

"How does that fit into your grand scheme?" Sean challenged, humorously but not without intent.

Willie didn't seem set to respond. Then he remembered the hook that allowed him to be engaged again.

"This is Martha Mödl singing!"

When he registered Sean's uninformed face, he tried to fill in.

"She's a German soprano."

"Peter Perstroichja?"

"Exactly," said an impressed Willie. "He gave me this very record. The inscription he twisted her arm to write says, 'To Willie. Keep on loving Wagner and we'll remain good friends. Love, Mödl.' "

The soundtrack had begun to alleviate itself from all the stressful thunderstorms at last. Sean was used to not knowing where he was. But he wanted a kiss to find his way home. So he dove into Willie's mouth as if it were an absolute. There he did find: kindness, knowledge, love, sarcasm, doubt, happiness, incredible idealism. He loved him. That was a truth, a truth he could have sworn to under the intoxication of vodka martinis. The tunnel of their kiss was its own brief exploration of the *Ring* cycle.

Out the corner of his eye, Sean shot a look sideways towards the crowd, animated by the natural anesthetic of operatic decadence. Gaetan was crowding his view with blond hairs plastered over his forehead in a Caligulan pattern of golden ivy. The music had turned into an unemotional freak show.

Sean felt a chill.

PERMISSIONS ACKNOWLEDGMENTS

GRATEFUL ACKNOWLEDGMENT IS MADE TO THE
FOLLOWING FOR PERMISSION TO REPRINT PREVIOUSLY
PUBLISHED MATERIAL:

NEW DIRECTIONS PUBLISHING CORPORATION: EXCERPT FROM
"THE DRUNKEN BOAT" BY ARTHUR RIMBAUD FROM *A SEASON
IN HELL & THE DRUNKEN BOAT* BY ARTHUR RIMBAUD,
TRANSLATED BY LOUISE VARESE, COPYRIGHT © 1961 BY NEW
DIRECTIONS PUBLISHING CORP. REPRINTED BY PERMISSION OF
NEW DIRECTIONS PUBLISHING CORPORATION.
VIKING PENGUIN: EXCERPT FROM "SNAKE" BY D. H.
LAWRENCE FROM *THE COMPLETE POEMS OF D. H. LAWRENCE* BY
D. H. LAWRENCE, EDITED BY V. DE SOLA PINTO AND F. W.
ROBERTS, COPYRIGHT © 1964, 1971 BY ANGELO RAVAGLI AND
C. M. WEEKLEY, EXECUTORS OF THE ESTATE OF FRIEDA
LAWRENCE RAVAGLI. REPRINTED BY PERMISSION OF VIKING
PENGUIN, A DIVISION OF PENGUIN BOOKS USA INC.

A NOTE ON THE TYPE

THE TEXT OF THIS BOOK WAS SET IN BERKELEY OLDSTYLE, A
TYPEFACE DESIGNED BY TONY STAN BASED ON A FACE ORIGI-
NALLY DEVELOPED BY FREDERICK GOUDY IN 1938 FOR THE
UNIVERSITY OF CALIFORNIA PRESS AT BERKELEY.
COMPOSED BY NORTH MARKET STREET GRAPHICS,
LANCASTER, PENNSYLVANIA
PRINTED AND BOUND BY R. R. DONNELLEY & SONS,
HARRISONBURG, VIRGINIA
DESIGNED BY IRIS WEINSTEIN